WILD CARDS RULE!

BLOAT—the teenage governor of the Rox. Cursed with a huge, disgusting body and vast mental abilities, he tried to mix power with compassion.

DR. TACHYON—Former champion of the Jokers. Tachyon had unjustly fallen from their good graces and was abandoned in his greatest hour of need.

BLAISE—Blaise Andrieux was a psi lord like his grandfather—the thought of whom consumed him with unthinking hatred. Blaise was violent and perverted in ways Dr. Tachyon could only guess at.

SHAD—Black Shadow, Wall Walker, Neil Langford ...he'd been playing all these parts for so long he'd lost track of who he really was.

CHALKTALK—A tortured, mute girl with the ability to jump into alternate realities...and a being with amazing appetites.

CAPTAIN TRIPS—He'd been a member of the counterculture most of his adult life. Now that he was at last genuinely, authentically underground, it scared the hell out of him.

JOKERTOWN SHUFFLE

A Wild Cards Mosaic Novel

Edited by
George R. R. Martin

Assistant Editor
Melinda M. Snodgrass

Written by
Stephen Leigh
John J. Miller
Melinda M. Snodgrass
Walter Jon Williams
Lewis Shiner
Walton Simons
Victor Milán

BANTAM BOOKS
NEW YORK • TORONTO • LONDON • SYDNEY • AUCKLAND

JOKERTOWN SHUFFLE

A Bantam Spectra Book / September 1991

ISBN 0-553-29174-2

Published simultaneously in the United States and Canada

PRINTED IN THE UNITED STATES OF AMERICA

RAD   0 9 8 7 6 5 4 3 2 1

once again to Parris,
wild card widow and all-around ace,
for putting up with us all these years

JOKERTOWN SHUFFLE

The Temptation of Hieronymus Bloat

by
Stephen Leigh

I

I don't know why I'm starting this or what I'm going to do with it or just who it is I'm talking to. I guess . . . I guess the reason is that I want someone to remember what happened here when it's over. Lately I've been thinking that the Rox won't last long.

It can't; THEY won't let it.

Do I need to explain who "THEY" is? I didn't think so. I can tell you this, man—whoever *you* are—if you need to ask, then you ain't a joker, are you?

There's one question to answer, I suppose. No one ever really asks me directly, but I always hear it, like a little tinkling chime in the clamor of thoughts. I hear it whenever someone looks at me or even thinks about me: *What's it like to be so fucking gross? What's it like to be a head and shoulders sitting like a wart on a body that takes up an acre of ground and feeds on sewage?*

What's it like? God . . .

Okay. Let me try.

Find a room. A huge, empty space. Don't make it too goddamn comfortable—be certain that the floor's cracked and damp, the air's too cold or too hot, the overall atmosphere's tottering on the edge of gloom.

1

Then find a chair. A hard and unyielding and splintery one that makes you want to get up and walk around after sitting in it for even a few minutes. Bolt it to the floor in the middle of your room.

Get five hundred television sets. Bank them all around the chair, a Great Wall of blank screens. Now wire each of the sets to a different channel, turn up the sound, and switch on every one of the mothers.

Sit buck naked in your splintery chair in the middle of that ugly room before all the televisions. Have someone chain you to that nasty chair, and then stack a couple hundred lead ingots in your lap. Make sure the binding's tight so you can't move, can't scratch yourself, can't hold your hands up to your ears to blot out that terrible din, so you're utterly dependent on others to feed you or clean you or talk to you.

Hey, *now* you're beginning to feel like Bloat. Now you have some idea of what it's like.

I hear you. (I always hear you.) *C'mon,* you're saying. *You have the ability to read minds. Ain't that a gift, a little kiss from the wild card deck?*

Okay, I can read your mind. I have Bloat's Wall, which keeps the nats and aces away from the Rox unless they really *want* to be here. I have my own army of jokers who protect me and care for me.

I make the Rox possible. I'm the governor. I have power. There's no Rox without me. Bliss, right?

Yeah? Well, that's bullshit. Crap. A load of bloatblack.

You think I really *rule* this place? You gotta be kidding. Look, I used to play D&D. Most of the time, I ran a character who controlled a little kingdom in the scenario our Dungeon Master had dreamed up. Y'know what? That fantasy's about as real as the "kingdom" I have here.

You can't hear what they're thinking when they talk to me: Prime, Blaise, Molly, K.C., the other jumpers. Even the jokers, even the ones the wild card cursed. "God, I'm glad I'm not like *him*" or "I don't care how much he knows or what kind of powers he has, he's just a fuckin' *kid....*"

I know. I know what they think of me. I know what they think of the Rox too. My Rox is a convenient refuge, but if Ellis Island sank into New York Bay tomorrow, they'd find another place. The jumpers would melt into the city's back alleys; the jokers ... the jokers would do what jokers have always done: Shrug their shoulders—if they got 'em—and head for Jokertown.

So just what am I going to do? Threaten to take my basketball and go home, huh? You think *I'm* likely to go anywhere at all? Man, I was lucky I managed to get here three years ago when I was only the size of a school bus. Now...hell, the blue whale's no longer the world's biggest mammal. I'm bigger than a whole *pod* of fucking whales.

What's it like?

You can't visualize Bloat. You can't empathize with me. It's not possible.

Every goddamn joker's hell is individual and private. So just leave it that way.

I hate being judge and jury. I even know why.

My parents were weak-willed. Hey, sure...most kids blame it on their folks.

But why not? Mine were spineless, *accommodating* people who let the neighbors, store clerks, and anyone in a position of authority push them around. They were two *nice* people who would gladly change their opinions and back down at any hint of opposition. They were two *charming* people, really, who let the neighborhood scum intimidate and harass their son, the high school poet; their son, the "oh, what a talented *artist*"; their son, the-one-with-his-head-in-the-comic-books.

They kept telling me (when I came home with bloody noses and black eyes and torn clothes): "Well, if they're bothering you, why didn't you just walk away? Maybe it's something *you're* doing. Concentrate on your drawing or your writing or your schoolwork, Teddy. Play that strange fantasy dice game of yours or read a comic book. When you grow up a little, they'll stop."

They were two *compassionate* people who, when Ted slammed into puberty by turning into a slug the size of a subway car, didn't just abandon me. No. First they called the Jokertown Clinic, and *then* they disappeared.

Gone. Vanished.

Well, Mom and Dad, Teddy sure as hell grew up, didn't he? I wish I were less your son now, because just getting big didn't help and I'm still carrying all your emotional baggage with me.

So how do I do what I want to do? How do you find a

way to mix power with a little compassion? How do you make the other players on the stage of the Rox see that they're too damn shortsighted and selfish? How do you stay an idealist in a world of greedy pragmatists?

They brought in a case for me to judge today. "The gov's court," they call it, mockingly. Still, they bring in these cases because I insist on it. Okay, let's be honest—the usual "justice" on the Rox is violent and final. Actually, they come only when the antagonists aren't already dead or maimed.

I knew who was guilty before they dragged either one of them in front of me. I always do.

Blaise escorted them, but Kelly was with the group— Kelly whom I find so achingly attractive, who is still so innocent in her way. I like to watch her; I like to fantasize about how it might be if I were normal or if I were one of them. I could read vague, contradictory feelings as Kelly approached. Darker, more violent thoughts eddied from Blaise and K. C. Strange, another one of the jumpers, while fright mingled with relief from Slimeball, the joker they were hauling toward the Administration Building.

I told everyone around me that company was coming, and chuckled. My joker guards came to attention around the lobby. Kafka came scuttling in from his workroom, his mind still snared in the maze of blueprints he'd been studying. Around me, jokers turned to watch: the ever-loyal Peanut, Mothmouth, Video, Shroud, Chickenhawk, Elmo, Andiron—a dozen others around the floor or looking over the lobby's high balcony.

Eddies in the currents of thoughts. I could feel the rest of the Rox too: File, lost in rapture–ecstasy in some hovel in the north end of the island; Charon, heading out from the Rox toward the siren call of some joker in New York. My guards had tightened their grips on their weapons.

Blaise's little group entered the lobby noisily, throwing a blast of cold air into the building. Slimeball was being dragged by main force between K.C. and Kelly. Blaise was shouting before they were even halfway to me, ranting.

Kafka cleared his throat. His carapace rattled like a pair of cheap castanets. At the same time, Shroud slammed the bolt home on his .22 Remington single-shot rifle. I caught amusement from Blaise (*fucking popgun*). Blaise isn't the psi lord his grandfather is; his mindshields leak, dribbling thoughts like an incontinent child.

Kafka began scolding Blaise. "Show a little decorum, please." Like a parent lecturing his son—it went over about that well too. "We've discussed this before. The governor deserves your respect. That's as much a part of your rent as anything else."

Blaise glared at Kafka. I caught an image of a roach being squashed beneath a huge foot. *Little fucking insect*. I laughed again. Then the thought drifted away as he looked up at me. *He titters like a goddamn schoolgirl. So fucking gross. The smell's worse than usual.*

Almost in response, a rippling went through me, along with a sense of release and relief. I could feel the thick sludge of bloatblack rolling down my sides. There was a sound: soft, squelching, nasty, like thick mud being squashed between two hands.

"Governor," Blaise said then, and he gave the title a big mocking lilt. I ignored him, paying more attention to Kelly than Blaise; she was trying, unsuccessfully, to ignore my continuing defecation. Kelly's hands went to her hips—a pose of defiance and arrogance that was totally at odds with her thoughts. *Poor ugly big thing . . .*

I smiled at her, a waif in torn jeans, her tits rounding under the *Free Snotman* T-shirt, her eyes huge and the color of the deep sea under her soft hair. "Governor," she said, echoing Blaise, but her voice was soft and pleasant, and she smiled back at me.

A prom princess in rags. I found her much more attractive than, say, K.C. Kelly wasn't a jumper, not yet. Prime hadn't *initiated* her—but then, Prime wasn't into much except blond young boys in recent months, not since the Oddity killed David. Kelly was one of the hangers-on, one of the jumper wannabees, a runaway teenager from the city. There's a lot more of them than actual jumpers. Given Prime's obsession with David look-alikes, Kelly and most of them would stay wannabees too.

I like to watch her. I stare when she walks by my building, and I dream about Kelly, sometimes . . .

But Blaise glared at her now, and she went sullenly quiet. "If I may beg an audience with Your Fucking Excellence," Blaise began.

Such defiance: a symptom of my difficulties. I had to laugh again, even though the whole problem is that none of them take *anything* seriously. They *play* at creating a new

society; I can't get them to understand how important all this
is.

Kafka rattled in outrage. I felt my joker guards' minds
become suddenly more focused and intent. For a moment, I
toyed with the idea of just sending Blaise, Kelly, and K.C.
away. The laughter had come, but I wasn't amused. Not
really.

I could hear most of Blaise's thoughts. I knew that—like
Kelly and K.C. too—at least part of Blaise's insolence was
show, put on from simple peer pressure. He didn't want to be
weak in front of the others. No, not Blaise. In fact, he didn't
want to be here at all.

"I'm listening, Blaise. I always listen when a joker's in
trouble. And Slimeball's certainly a joker, isn't he?" I finished, and *tittered*, as he'd call it. I paused, looking right at
K.C. "I'm *always* listening. Always. Even though some
people are thinking I sound like some stupid fucking two-
year-old when I laugh."

K.C.'s face reddened—I'd quoted her thoughts, you see.
For a moment I felt a little ashamed of myself. No matter
how many times I demonstrate my ability, I always get that
reaction. People aren't used to having their precious private
thoughts stolen. They don't feel anything, they don't see me
doing anything unusual, so they forget.

Kelly's thoughts, at least, are usually kind.

Blaise was pissed. "Well, I stopped K.C. here from
offing your precious joker. I should have gone ahead and offed
the mother, though. This is the second time Slimeball's been
in our food stores."

I knew that. I'd long ago caught the thoughts from
Slimeball and K.C.

"K.C. and Kelly caught him, and the little fucker sliced
at them with a knife. What you gonna do about it?"

I knew what Blaise wanted me to do. The image was
very clear. His justice is very black and white. Simple.

I glanced at Slimeball. He'd been radiating wordless
chattering fear since the incident, all shot through with
unresolved hatred toward Blaise. His salamanderlike skin was
gleaming with sticky oil, the flat pads on the ends of his
fingers crushed into his palms. His bulbous eyes, vertically
slit and golden, were momentarily lost under thick translucent lids as he blinked. His mouth opened; a forked snake's

tongue wriggled out briefly from between snaggled incisors, and then retreated.

"You lied to me," I said to Slimeball. "That's very, very bad." I *tsked* and shook my head. "You promised you'd leave the food alone. I ordered you to stay away, and I warned you about bothering them again. Remember? We're all one big happy family on the Rox."

K.C. guffawed at that, but no one else laughed.

"What happened, Slimeball?"

That's a mind reader's trick: just ask a direct question. It jars them away from the stream-of-consciousness images and forces them to focus. I hardly listened to Slimeball's words; I was watching his mind. I could sense his hunger all the while he was talking. The words didn't matter—he'd gotten hungry, a common enough thing on the Rox. A simple thing. He'd thought he could get away with stealing from the jumpers.

He'd been wrong. That's all.

Blaise broke in then. "Bloat, I want the problem taken care of. Permanently. You do it, or I will," he said. "Make the fucker an example to everyone else."

He stared at me. *I'll kill him*, Blaise told me then in his mind, deliberately and consciously pushing the words forward. Like he thought I might be hard of hearing in my mind. *You make sure Slimeball gets fed to the sewerage system, or I'll do it myself. Either way, you eventually eat the mother. Your choice*—"Governor."

"I don't kill jokers," I answered him aloud.

He snorted at that. "The whole goddamn *world* kills jokers. What makes you so special?"

I could've told him. I could've told him how it's a curse to always *know*. Hey, I know everything. I know that the jumpers have stolen more food from the jokers than the reverse. I know that hunger's a problem for both sides here on the Rox. I know that Slimeball has about as much intelligence and moral sense as a six-year-old, and while he was genuinely sorry now, he'd forget all this and probably do it again.

It's easier not to know. But I always know the truth. I know *all* the facts.

It's hard to hurt someone whose most intimate thoughts you've experienced. It's hard when you know that their pain is going to be broadcast back to you and *you'll* have to listen to it. It's hard when you see that there's never—NEVER—just black and white.

  Wrong or right.

  Evil or good.

  Not for me, certainly. There are things I've done . . . Just by being here and creating the Rox, I'm responsible for a lot of deaths. My Wall isn't kind, and Charon doesn't stop for passengers who change their minds. Kafka tells me that the waters of the bay under the Wall are full of skeletons. *My* victims, directly. There's a lot of the violence in New York done by people who live here. People I protect.

  I tell myself that's only justice.

  I stared down at Slimeball over the slope of my body. Filling your belly shouldn't be a capital offense, no matter what the circumstances.

  "What're you gonna do, Governor?" Blaise is as impatient as Kelly is lovely. Glitteringly dangerous. As close to amoral as any mind I'd ever experienced. He wanted me to kill over a few damn Twinkies.

  Hell, I didn't know what I was going to do. Nothing felt good—there wasn't any right or wrong here. When you know all the facts, that's what you always find out. Every decision is unfair. Yet if I just shrugged this off, I'd undermine any progress I've made in that last several months toward actually *being* the governor. But I don't kill jokers either, and if I came down on the jumpers, I could lose their support— they're as essential to the Rox as I am.

  Look, it was all fucking fun and games at first. Big kid Bloat takes the Rox and keeps the bad ol' nats away. But it kept getting more serious. It stopped being some comic-book plot and started being real. The thoughts kept coming louder and louder, and I couldn't shut them out anymore, and suddenly nothing was quite so funny. David died under the Oddity's hands, everyone started grabbing for control of things instead of cooperating, and the conditions for jokers in the world outside just kept going into the fucking toilet.

  Blaise wouldn't let me think. "Bloat? Hey, Bloat!"

  I glowered down at them all, angry now. "Slimeball's at fault," I barked at them finally. "I warned him about the food. But I'm not going to kill him for that, Blaise. Slimeball, you're one of the bloatblackers now. You'll haul my shit until I'm sure that you'll stay away from the jumpers. If you're found in their part of the Rox again, they have my permission to do whatever the hell they please with you. Understood?"

Relief was coiled around disgust in Slimeball. K.C. shrugged her shoulders. Kelly looked at me with her small smile.

Blaise scowled. "I *will* kill him if I see his oily face again," Blaise proclaimed loudly. "I don't need your *permission* for that, Bloat."

"Blaise," Kelly began placatingly. "The governor's—"

Blaise rounded on her, his fist raised. I could feel the violence in his mind leaking out like molten lava.

"Stop!" I shouted, and the fury in my voice caused gunbolts to click back. Blaise radiated a sudden fear. I could feel the heat on my face as I continued to shout. "You damn well do need permission. I *am* the Rox. Me. Without my Wall, the nats'll be swarming on this place like maggots on roadkill. They'll bury you here. I hear your thoughts. You think I'm weak. 'Bloat doesn't kill, he can be pushed around.' I hear you."

I looked at the jokers watching the confrontation. I listened to their thoughts. They were as violent as the jumpers. I knew I had to end this now or someone would do something really stupid.

"Kafka," I said. "Blaise needs to bow to me before he leaves. I want to hear him thank me for taking the time to judge this case." I paused. "And if he won't do it, blow him away."

Blaise was confused. His mouth gaped. He thought for a minute of mind-controlling my jokers, but there were a lot of us around, and he suddenly wasn't sure he could handle us all. He sputtered. "You're bluffing. You ain't gonna do that. That ain't your way." It was just mind static.

I giggled at him. "Try me. Go ahead. Hey, if you die here, the only thing that's going to happen is that K.C. or someone else will take over for the jumpers. Why, I'll bet K.C. might even be happy to have the competition thinned out." K.C. gave me a dangerous look; I ignored it. "You'd be no loss to me at all, Blaise. None at all."

Blaise hesitated, his thoughts all jumbled. I really wasn't sure what he'd do. My jokers waited, patient and a little too eager. I think it was their faces that decided him more than anything else.

He took a step back toward me and ducked his head stiffly.

I giggled. "You do that very nicely. And what else?"

Scowl. Frown. Pucker. "Thank you." The words were almost understandable. Inside, he was fuming: *Fuck you, you bastard.*

"I'm not really into boys," I told him. "Not like Prime. Now if you were as good-looking as Kelly . . ."

Blaise's face colored nicely; so did Kelly's. Blaise spun angrily on his toes and stamped away to the laughter of the joker onlookers. K.C. followed with a last look back at me; Kelly gave me a long stare (*poor thing*) and went after them.

Slimeball was laughing, too, until Peanut took him by the arm and pointed him toward the mounds of bloatblack. "Start shoveling," Peanut said.

And then we all laughed at Slimeball.

Jokers are allowed to laugh at jokers.

Kafka looked up at me. *Children. You all argue like such children.* The insectlike man sighed. He told me something that sounded like wisdom. Maybe it was.

"Bluffing is a very dangerous game," he said. "Especially with Blaise."

I would remember those words, later.

And Hope to Die
by
John J. Miller

*But down these mean streets a man must go who is
not himself mean, Who is neither tarnished or
afraid....*

—RAYMOND CHANDLER

1.

Brennan woke suddenly, though the night was quiet and
Jennifer was sleeping undisturbed beside him. He wondered
what had woken him. Then he caught again a faint whiff of
grease and gun oil, and sat up as the night was split by
thunder and fire.

He pushed Jennifer off the right side of their futon and
rolled to the left as a bullet seared his side and another
ripped through his upper thigh. He gritted his teeth, ignoring the agony that lanced through his leg as he dove naked
through the darkness. His first thought was to draw the fire
away from Jennifer. His second was to get the bastard who
was doing the shooting.

There was a problem with that. Brennan no longer kept
weapons in the house. They were all locked away in the
backyard shed as a repudiation of the life he'd once lived. He
regretted this decision as a stream of bullets tracked him
while he hurtled through the bedroom door into the interior
of the house. There was the sound of smashing glass, and a

stabbing winter wind struck Brennan as the assassin crashed through the bedroom window and followed him.

Brennan headed for the kitchen, stopped, and reversed his field as he heard a second hit man breaking down the front door. He turned for the door that led to the backyard. His only hope, he suddenly realized, was to get outside where he could use his hunting skills to neutralize the numerical superiority of his heavily armed opponents.

Brennan flung himself through the back door, dodging left and rolling on the ground. Another assassin was waiting for him, but Brennan went through the door too quickly for the killer to draw an accurate aim.

Brennan gritted his teeth against the pain lancing through his leg as he sprinted across his meticulously raked sand garden, ruining the serenity of the gravel-sculpted waves with footprints and bloodspatters. The assassin was too slow to track him, and a fusillade of shots ripped into the ground at Brennan's heels as he dove into the thick brush surrounding his isolated country home.

The cold night air frosted Brennan's breath as he stood naked on the frigid ground. His bare feet burned in the snow, and his thigh throbbed as it dripped blood, but he scarcely felt the pain as he crouched low in the snow-laden bushes.

A second black-garbed figure joined the one who'd been lying in ambush in the backyard. They conversed in low unintelligible voices, and one of them gestured toward the forest in Brennan's general direction. Neither seemed eager to go into the darkness.

Brennan grimaced, forcing his mind into dispassionate rationality. His biggest problem was time. His assailants could afford to wait him out. He was crouched naked in a frigid winter night that was already sapping all the warmth from his bones. He had to get to the shed behind the greenhouse before he became an immobile hunk of frozen meat.

Just as Brennan convinced himself to move, the assassins were joined by a third figure, who thumbed on a powerful flashlight and aimed it into the woods just to Brennan's left. Brennan's hopes sank even lower. Now it would be almost impossible to get away. The hit men could jacklight him and shoot him down the moment he moved. But if he stayed put, he'd freeze and save them the effort of pulling the triggers.

He scrabbled through the snow with fingers stiffened by

the cold and found a fist-size rock that was slick with ice. It was a poor excuse for a weapon, but it would have to do. He shifted silently as the beam from the flashlight swept closer. He stood to throw the rock; then suddenly something fell from the loft window overlooking the backyard.

A tiny figure, no more than ten inches high, landed on the shoulders of one of the assassins with a thin high-pitched scream. There was the gleam of metal flashing in the light of a slivered moon, and the figure screamed again and stuck what looked like a fork into the back of the assassin's neck. The hit man yelled in pain mixed with fear and swatted at the creature. It fell to the cold ground in a pitiful little heap and lay unmoving.

Brennan's heart fell as he realized that it was Pumpkinhead, one of the manikins he'd rescued from the tunnels under the Crystal Palace. There were about thirty of them, children of a strange joker they'd called Mother. They'd been Chrysalis's eyes and ears through the city, but with Chrysalis dead and the Palace destroyed, Brennan had brought them to the country to live with him and Jennifer.

And now they were supplying the diversion Brennan had prayed for. They leapt screaming from the loft window, falling upon the assassins like living rain. They were armed with whatever feeble weapons they could find about the house—forks, kitchen knives, even sharpened pencils. They outnumbered the assassins ten to one, but they were all small and weak. Brennan watched with horror as the killers got over their initial surprise and swatted them down like kittens.

Curly Joe was the first to follow Pumpkinhead out of the loft window, and quickly into oblivion. He'd missed his intended target, who stomped him into the ground with bone-crunching force, quickly silencing his thin reedy cries. Kitty Kat managed to sink a kitchen knife into her target's ankle before she was smashed by his flashlight. Lizardo jabbed his foe in the shoulder with a pencil but was too weak to do much more than break the hit man's skin before the thug broke his scaly neck.

Brennan clamped down on his anger and pity and moved as quickly as he could, ignoring the pain running through his injured leg, ignoring the stones, sticks, and sharp slivers of ice that tore at his bare feet.

He flitted through the snow-shrouded trees like a ghost, circling around the A-frame and the greenhouse beyond. He stopped at the shed behind the greenhouse and cursed. He'd forgotten the key. He drew himself back to try to batter down the door, but a small hissing voice stopped him before he could strike.

"Boss! Boss, the key!"

It was Brutus, a foot-tall manikin with leathery skin that sagged in puffy pouches about his gray, hairless face. Brutus had settled into the role of the tribe's chief. He was more intelligent than most of the homunculi, but even he was no brighter than a smart child. At the moment, however, he seemed to have assessed the situation with remarkable accuracy. He tossed the key to the shed's padlock to Brennan, who caught it with cold clumsy fingers and tried to fit it into the lock.

Brennan fumbled a few times before the key finally clicked into place. He threw open the door and took down the bow that hung in a bracket nearby, quickly stringing it with the line dangling from one of its tips. It was only a hardwood recurve with a sixty-pound pull, but it was powerful enough. He grabbed the quiver that hung from the bracket and stepped back into the night.

Brennan no longer felt naked or cold. His anger spread from his gut outward, warming him as he ran over the snow back to the house, Brutus following on his heels.

The scene in the backyard was worse than Brennan had imagined. Tiny broken bodies violated the calm serenity of his Zen garden. Crushed and pulped, the manikins had fought fiercely and hopelessly against giants who could kill them with a single blow.

Brennan cried out in sorrow and rage, freezing one of the assassins in the act of squashing Bigfoot with the butt of his assault rifle. As the hit man looked around with his rifle lifted, Brennan sank down to one knee, drew shaft to ear, and loosed. The razor-tipped hunting arrow cut silently through the night and struck the assassin high on his chest. He fell backward, slamming against the wall of the A-frame, then crumpled forward and dropped his weapon.

An eerie cry of triumph rose from the living homunculi as Brennan drew a second shaft, shifted aim, and fired before the other hit men could react. He gut-shot his second target, who was swarmed by the remaining manikins. The killer screamed wordlessly and tried desperately, futilely, to crawl away.

The third assassin clicked off the flashlight he'd been using as a club, turned, and ran back into the house. Brennan fired and saw his shaft strike home, but the assassin kept moving.

Brennan nocked another arrow to his string and stood, listening. The assassin being pummeled by the manikins had finally stopped screaming. The first one Brennan had shot was dead.

"See to your people," Brennan told Brutus, then limped over to the back door. He stood listening for a moment but could hear nothing move inside. He couldn't wait long, even if the assassin was lying in ambush. He had to go in.

He scooped up the assault rifle dropped by the first assassin, then went through the doorway low and fast. The house was still dark, still quiet. From the front Brennan could hear the sound of a receding car engine.

He flicked on the bedroom light. The room was a shambles. The window had been shattered, and glass lay all over the floor. Bullets had stitched the walls, smashing the framed Hokusai and Yoshitosi woodblocks hanging over the futon where Jennifer lay quiet and still as death, awash in a sea of blood.

Kien liked his new body. It was young, had two functioning hands, and best of all had ace capabilities that he'd quickly gotten use to. He could see how Philip Cunningham had enjoyed being Fadeout. But there was one problem with the body. It was not of his race. Kien wondered if that was the cause of the dreams he'd been having lately.

His father had been visiting him, speaking softly of the good old days back in Vietnam when Kien had worked in the family's small store. He had always been a dutiful son, though the stifling life of a storekeeper in a small village had bored him unmercifully. But he had stayed on until his father had been murdered by the French in the last days of the Vietnamese rebellion against their European masters. Then, and only then, had Kien moved on to the city and joined the army of the fledgling Republic of Vietnam. Of course, he had had to change some things to blend in. There was no way he was going to have a successful military career with an ethnic Chinese name among the extremely prejudiced Vietnamese.

"Once again you have abandoned us," Old Dad told him, waving the cane that he often used to emphasize his arguments. "First you turned your back on your family when you pretended to be Vietnamese and took the name Kien Phuc. And now you go even further. You've become a white man."

It was difficult to argue with a dream, but Kien tried. "No, Father," he explained patiently, "I have abandoned no one. This is all part of my plan, a misdirection to finish off my enemies."

The spectre snorted, unconvinced. "You always were a tricky one, boy, I'll give you that."

"Tonight," Kien said, "Captain Brennan dies. And his bitch who'd taken half my hand." He smiled at his father. "That will be the second woman of his I've killed. Too bad he won't live to realize that."

"And after this Brennan?"

"After Brennan, then Tachyon. He knows too much, and he could easily discover my newest secret, that I still live in the body of Philip Cunningham. Tachyon has to die."

"When?" his father asked.

"Soon. Today. When the Egrets return with the heads of Brennan and his bitch."

Old Dad frowned. "It sounds like you're planning on keeping that body," he said.

Kien shook his new head. "Only until my enemies are dead."

"Have you ever run out of enemies, my son?"

Kien smiled.

2.

Brutus climbed up the back of the car seat and dropped down onto the van's passenger side. "Miss Jennifer has stopped bleeding, but she looks funny."

"Funny?" Brennan asked, not daring to stop even for a moment to check on Jennifer's condition.

"She's getting clear, like she's fading," the manikin said.

Brennan gritted his teeth, concentrating on his driving, afraid to give full vent to his feelings. Since entering the city limits, he'd kept the van at the speed limit. He couldn't afford to be stopped by a traffic cop, not with Jennifer's life hanging so tenuously that any delay might be fatal.

He'd driven like a madman down Route 17 before reaching the city. The old road was narrower and more twisting than the Thruway but was also darker, had less traffic, and was rarely patrolled by the state troopers. And rocketing along the road like a meteor on wheels, he needed a quiet, unpoliced road.

He fought to keep his attention on driving. His mind kept wandering back nearly sixteen years to a situation that was achingly similar to this one.

It was back in Nam. Brennan and his men had captured documents that contained enough evidence to connect General Kien solidly with all his various criminal activities, from prostitution to drug running to consorting with the North Vietnamese. But they never reached base with the evidence. Brennan and his men were ambushed while waiting for their pickup. It had all been a setup by Kien. In fact, the general personally put a bullet through the head of Sergeant Gulgowski and taken the briefcase with the incriminating documents. Brennan, momentarily paralyzed by a bullet-creased forehead, was lying in the jungle surrounding the landing zone. He'd witnessed the slaughter of all his men but had been unable to do anything about it.

It had taken Brennan nearly a week to walk out of the jungle. Once he reached base, exhausted and more than a little delirious from wounds, infection, and fever, he made the mistake of denouncing Kien to his commanding officer. For his trouble Brennan was nearly thrown in the stockade. Somehow he managed to control himself, and rather than a court-martial he was let off with a warning to leave General Kien alone.

That night he'd returned to Ann-Marie, his French-Vietnamese wife. She'd thought he was dead. Pregnant with their first child, she cried in his arms with relief; then they made love, careful of their son swelling her usually lithe form. As they slept, Kien's assassins crept into their bedroom to silence Brennan permanently. They missed their prime target, but Ann-Marie had died in her husband's arms, and their son had died with her.

"There's the entrance," Brutus said, yanking Brennan back into the present.

He pulled into the curb before the Blythe van Rensselaer Memorial Clinic, threw the door open, and limped around the front of the van before the sound of screeching brakes had died on the still night air. A fine snow fell like a freezing mist,

the tiny flakes clinging momentarily to Brennan's face before
melting in his body warmth.

He went through the double glass doors that *whooshed*
open automatically as he approached and looked around the
lobby. It was deserted except for an old joker who seemed to
be sleeping in one of the uncomfortable-looking plastic chairs
and a tired-looking nurse who was scanning a sheaf of papers
behind the registration counter. He went up to her.

"Is Tachyon in? There's an emergency—"

The nurse sighed and looked at Brennan with weary eyes
old beyond her years. He wondered briefly how many people
had said these very words to her, how many desperate
life-and-death situations she'd had to deal with.

"Dr. Tachyon is busy now. Dr. Havero is on call."

"I need Tachyon's expertise—" Brennan began, then
stopped.

From somewhere came the faint whiff of salt and fish and
briny water. From somewhere came the unmistakable tang of
the sea.

Brennan whirled around. A cluster of vending machines
was set off in the corner of the receiving area, offering soft
drinks, soda, and candy. Standing before one of them was a
huge figure in priestly robes, humming softly to himself as he
made his selection.

"Father Squid!" Brennan cried.

The priest turned his head toward the reception desk,
the nictitating membranes covering his eyes blinking rapidly
in surprise. "Daniel?"

Father Squid was a stout joker, huge in his priestly
cassock. A few inches taller than Brennan, he weighed about
a hundred pounds more. He looked solid, not blubbery, with
broad shoulders, a thick chest, and a comfortably padded
stomach. His hands were large, with long, sinuous-looking
fingers and lines of vestigial suckers on their palms. He had a
fall of tentacles instead of a nose, and he always smelled
faintly, not unpleasantly, of the sea.

He was Brennan's friend and confidant. They'd known
each other since Nam, where the priest had been a sergeant
in the Joker Brigade and Brennan a recondo captain. "What's
the matter?" he asked.

"Jennifer's been shot," Brennan said tersely, "and she's
fading. I need Tachyon."

Father Squid moved quickly for a man his size. He rolled

up to the desk with a smooth, fluid gait and said to the nurse, "Call Tachyon, now."

She looked from the priest, a well-known figure about Jokertown, to the mysterious stranger who'd just come barging in. "He's resting," she protested. "Dr. Havero—"

"Get Tachyon!" Father Squid barked in the voice he'd used to chivvy know-nothing joker kids when they hit the jungle for the first time, and the nurse jumped and reached for the phone. The priest turned to Brennan. "Bring Jennifer in. I'll get a gurney."

Brennan nodded and limped back to the van.

"What's up, boss?" Brutus piped.

"We're going in," Brennan said shortly. He gathered together the blanket wrapped about Jennifer and carefully lifted her from the van. She felt no heavier than a child in Brennan's arms. She was fading away, unconsciously using her ace power to turn insubstantial to the world.

"Put her here," Father Squid said, suddenly materializing behind him with a gurney. Brennan laid her down carefully. Brutus leapt onto the cart and clung to her blanket as Brennan and Father Squid wheeled her into the clinic's receiving area.

Tachyon was standing at the desk, knuckling sleep from his lilac eyes. The diminutive alien was still wearing a wrinkled white lab coat that looked like it'd been slept in. "What's this all about? I told you—" He turned toward the doors when they *whooshed* open. He stared for a moment, frowning, then his eyes went wide in astonishment. "Daniel!"

He took a quick step forward, arms wide as if to embrace Brennan, then stopped short as he saw the look on Brennan's face and remembered the circumstances of their last parting. "It's . . . good to see you," he finished somewhat lamely.

Brennan only nodded. The two men had been through a lot together, from battling the Swarm to fighting Kien and the Shadow Fists, but Brennan still found himself unable to forget what had happened the last time they'd seen each other.

It had been over a year ago. Brennan and Jennifer had tracked down Chrysalis's murderer, Hiram Worchester, to a hotel in Atlanta. Tachyon, who had also been on the scene, made a fine little speech about how things should be handled in strict accordance with the law. Tachyon, of course, got his way since he backed up his speech by mind-controlling

Brennan. Worchester had later turned himself in to the police and copped a plea bargain that kept him out of prison. Chrysalis was dead, and Worchester had a suspended sentence. True, equitable justice.

Still, Brennan couldn't let himself brood on the past. He had another life to worry about now. Jennifer's.

For the first time, Tachyon looked down from Brennan to the gurney. "What happened?" he asked.

"Three men hit our home this morning," Brennan said shortly.

Tachyon leaned over and peeled the layers of blankets away from Jennifer. She was translucently pale, the only color about her the crimson-soaked bandage that Brennan had wrapped around her forehead.

As the ace known as Wraith, Jennifer Maloy could turn insubstantial to the physical world. She could walk through walls, sink through floors, and pass through locked doors as quietly as a ghost. But now, wounded and unconscious, her mind adrift in the uncharted depths of a black coma, there was nothing to anchor her body to the physical world. She would fade until nothing was left.

Tachyon looked up at Brennan. "We'll take her to a security room on the top floor," Tachyon said in a low voice. "I'll examine her thoroughly there."

They went down the corridor, up an elevator to the top floor, then down another corridor that was dark and obviously rarely used. The room they took Jennifer to had a steel-reinforced door and thick wire mesh on the windows. Once inside, Brennan carefully lifted her onto the bed and watched anxiously as Tachyon examined her.

"Will she be all right?" Brennan finally asked after Tachyon straightened up, a distant, worried expression on his face.

"Her wounds," Tachyon said, "are not life-threatening. You did a good job of field-dressing them, and I can carry on from there. She should be in no danger from them."

Brennan detected a hesitancy in Tachyon's voice. "She *will* be all right?"

Tachyon's eyes, as he looked straight at Brennan, were uncertain. "There is something else . . . wrong. Terribly wrong. I could not touch her mind."

Brennan stared at the alien physician. "She's dead?" he asked in a low, dangerous voice. Father Squid put a steadying hand on Brennan's right forearm as Brutus moaned softly from the head of the bed.

Tachyon shook his head. "Look at her, man. She still breathes. The blood still rushes through her veins. Her pulse is steady. Faint, but steady."

Tachyon seemed to be speaking in riddles, but the years Brennan had spent in a Zen monastery made him used to that. Tachyon was making a *koan*, a Zen riddle designed to teach a subtle lesson about the nature of life.

Brennan's mind seized on that familiarity of form like a life raft tossing about on the ocean of emotion raised by the possibility of Jennifer's death. "When is life like death, and death like life?" he said so softly that Tachyon and Father Squid could barely hear him. He looked from the priest to the doctor. "When the mind is gone," he finished.

Tachyon nodded. "That's correct. The strange thing is, I can detect no organic reason for her. . . emptiness."

"Was she attacked on the mental plane?" Father Squid asked.

Tachyon shook his head. "I could detect no damage to indicate forcible entry and removal of her mind. It's almost as if it'd been lost . . . somehow. . ."

"Can you find it again?" Brennan asked.

Tachyon looked at Brennan, uncertainty in his eyes. "I wouldn't even know where to begin," he said simply.

Brennan groaned and grabbed the bed's headboard with enough force to crush a section of its tubular piping.

"There's Trace," Father Squid said.

"Trace?" Tachyon snorted and shook his head. "That charlatan!"

Brennan looked at Father Squid. "What are you talking about?"

"A mysterious ace who calls herself Trace. No one seems to know much about her, but she has strange mental capabilities. She can find nearly anything that's been lost by 'looking' back on its pathway of existence."

"Can she find lost minds?" Brennan asked.

"I doubt it," Tachyon said firmly.

Father Squid shook his head. "I don't know," the priest said. "She has other rather odd powers. Or claims to."

"Get her," Brennan said. "Get anyone who can help."

"I'll try," Father Squid said doubtfully.

"If you can't bring her here," Brennan said forcefully, "I will."

The priest shook his head. "No amount of coercion would ever work on Trace. If she wants to help you, fine. If not, nothing on earth will ever make her change her mind. And she is the wrong person to anger."

"So am I," Brennan said.

"Don't make a hard situation more difficult," Father Squid pleaded.

"Okay." Brennan took deep breaths to calm himself. "Go make the call, or whatever it takes to get this Trace here. Tell her I'll do anything I can, anything she wants, if she'll only help."

Father Squid, eyes closed, nodded. "I already have," he said.

Latham chivvied the last bit of eggs Benedict onto his fork with the last half of the last muffin on the plate sitting on Kien's desk. "Bloat is getting to be something of a problem," he told Kien.

Kien poured himself another glass of fresh-squeezed orange juice from the decanter on his silver serving tray and washed down his caviar-covered muffin. He loved freshly-squeezed orange juice almost as much as he loved wielding authority. Almost. Combining the two into a power breakfast was the perfect way to start the day. "Can we do without him?" he asked his lieutenant.

Latham considered the question as he chewed and swallowed, and finally shook his head. "Not yet. Perhaps soon." He fastidiously wiped his lips with his linen napkin. "I created another three jumpers last week. Soon we'll have a force big enough to deal with all the grotesque jokers Bloat has accumulated on the Rox."

"Three?" Kien repeated, impressed. Latham had gone without sex, as far as Kien knew, for the first twenty years he'd known the man. Now that his ace had turned, the heretofore abstemious lawyer was acting like a damn rabbit. Still, it was all to Kien's benefit in the long run. Latham created the jumpers, and Kien controlled them through his loyal lieutenant. Soon they'd be potent enough to add as a third main branch to the tree of the Shadow Fists: Immaculate Egrets, Werewolves, and jumpers.

Kien, in fact, had already availed himself of their services, obtaining through them this fine ace body that had once belonged to one of his less-loyal lieutenants.

The jangle of the telephone sitting on the edge of his desk cut through Kien's reverie. "Yes," he said quietly into the receiver as Latham looked on curiously.

"It's Lao."

Lao was the head of the assassin team he'd sent after Brennan and that bitch of his. Kien didn't like Lao's tone of voice.

"Yes." Kien's reply was sharper this time, and Lao hesitated.

"We—we ran into some unexpected difficulties," he finally said.

"Is he dead?" Kien asked in a hard voice.

"The woman is . . . I think . . ."

"You 'think,'" Kien ground out. He growled deep in his throat, his fury robbing him of the ability to articulate. He waited for the blaze of emotion to fade so he could speak clearly again. "All right. You and the others come in. I shall give you a chance to redeem yourselves."

There was another long silence, and then Lao said, "The others are dead."

Kien swallowed his fury. "All right. I will give *you* another chance. Do not fail me again."

He didn't hear Lao's voluble reassurances as he hung up the phone. Good help, Kien reflected, was so hard to find these days. Wyrm was dead, Blaise—well, there was a possibility, but it was difficult to control the little bastard. The Whisperer—impossible to reach on short notice. Warlock and the Werewolves . . . another possibility, but Kien had secrets, many secrets, that he didn't want exposed. Latham, though, already knew most of them.

"I might," Kien said, struck by sudden inspiration, "have need of your jumpers again. Round up three or four that you can trust."

Latham nodded slowly. "All right. Three or four trustworthy, disposable jumpers."

"'Disposable,'" Kien repeated. "Good point."

They could get rid of them after the job and keep Kien's newest secrets even more closely held. Latham stood, folded his napkin down neatly on his breakfast tray, nodded, and left the room. Kien scarcely realized that he was gone. He was wondering what it would feel like to wear, like a newly purchased coat, the body of his longtime enemy.

3.

Brutus jumped down from Brennan's shoulder to the head of Jennifer's bed. He laid a tiny hand on her forehead and shivered. "She's cold, boss, real cold."

Brennan could only nod. The wait was excruciating. Tachyon had dealt with Jennifer's wounds as best he could, then had to leave on clinic business, leaving Brennan, Brutus, and Father Squid to their bedside vigil. It didn't help that Father Squid could offer no suggestion as to how long they'd have to wait for Trace or whether she would even show up.

"Not much is known about her," Father Squid explained, "other than the fact that she possesses mental abilities of the highest order. Some say she's a hideous joker, others that she's a beautiful ace. No one can say for sure because everyone who looks at her sees something different."

Brennan frowned. "How can that be?"

Father Squid shrugged massive shoulders. "It is apparently her will to vary her image with each beholder. No one can say why that is. Some claim that she's mad."

"Not very flattering," said a voice behind Brennan, "to say about someone you need help from."

Brennan started, hand reaching for the Browning High Power holstered in the small of his back. He had heard no one enter the hospital room, and with nerves stretched by worry verging on desperation, he acted without thinking. But even as he drew his gun, he lowered it.

Facing him, standing straight and unhurt, was Jennifer Maloy. He had to glance down at the real Jennifer lying comatose on the bed to make himself believe that the image before him was some kind of simulacrum. He glanced at Father Squid. He, too, seemed taken by some sort of vision.

"Holll-eeee," Brutus said. He jumped from the top of the bed's headboard and landed lightly on Brennan's shoulder. He clung on by winding a small fist in a lock of Brennan's hair and then said in a low voice that only Brennan could hear. "It's Chrysalis, boss. In the flesh. And bones. But it can't be. She's dead."

"Guns won't help, either," the Jennifer simulacrum said. Brennan realized that the newcomer wasn't speaking with Jennifer's voice. "I could," she said, "if it's that important."

And she was.

"Thank you for coming," Father Squid said.

Trace dropped into the uncomfortable hospital chair placed next to Jennifer's bed. "Nothing else to do," she said. "Thought I'd drop by and see what you wanted."

"How'd you get through the clinic's security?" Brennan asked.

She shrugged. "It wasn't hard."

"Can you help us?" Father Squid asked.

She looked at the priest, then Brennan. Brennan's eyes locked with hers, and he felt a shiver run down his spine, as if she were holding his naked brain in her hands. Her eyes shone like cateyes in the dark, and then they were Jennifer's again, and she smiled a bright Jennifer smile. "I see," she said. "I suppose I could take a look around. But what's in it for me?"

"Anything," Brennan said. "Anything you want."

She looked at him with Jennifer's face in a way that tore the heart from him. "*Anything*?" Trace repeated, giving the word a light, provocative lilt that made Brennan clench his teeth.

"Anything that I can give," he said. "If you're as powerful as you claim to be, you should realize the extent—and sincerity—of my offer."

She shrugged. "Just wanted to hear you say it in words. Words make things seem more real to you people."

"But not to you?" Brennan asked.

"Words have their place. But I can see beneath their surface, down to their real meanings." She frowned momentarily. "Your words are real enough. You mean what you say."

Abruptly, Trace sat forward, turning her attention from Brennan and focusing on Jennifer. There was a long uncomfortable silence, then Trace sat back in the chair again, nodding. She looked at Brennan. "You're right. She's gone. She must be lost, wandering somewhere. The body won't last much longer without the mind."

"Can you help?" the priest said.

"I suppose."

"Will you?"

"Oh, I guess."

Brennan realized that he was holding his breath and released it in a long sigh.

"In exchange for what?" Father Squid asked.

"Oh—" she waved it away—"we'll talk about that later."
She turned her gaze on Brennan. "Go away now. Your brain is
emitting too much static. I can't concentrate."

"All right." Brennan nodded at Father Squid who followed
him and Brutus out of the room into the corridor beyond.

"You should have decided upon a settlement back then,"
Father Squid told him. "Trace has been known to exact a
heavy price for her services."

"I got that idea," Brennan said, "but the important thing
is that she find Jennifer's consciousness and bring it back to
her body. I can settle with her later."

"I hope it will be that easy," Father Squid said as
Brennan picked up Brutus and unzippered his leather jacket.
Brutus snuggled down inside it and reclosed the zipper until
only his head was showing.

"Easy or not," Brennan said, "if she brings Jennifer
back, we'll settle fairly. Now tell me what you know about
Kien's death."

"You suspect him?"

"Always."

Father Squid nodded ponderously. "I don't know much
of anything beyond that which was in the papers. It was a
heart attack, apparently, sudden and unexpected. Wait a
minute," he said, his long, slender fingers waving in sudden
excitement. "There was something else. I remember talking
with Cosmo Cosgrove—you know, from the mortuary."

Brennan nodded. The Cosgrove brothers were Jokertown's
preeminent morticians.

"Now," Father Squid continued, "the Cosgrove Mortuary did not handle the affair, but, well, apparently morticians
talk among themselves, and Cosmo told me that Kien's
mortician mentioned that there was something irregular about
the body."

"'Irregular'?" Brennan asked. "Like what?"

Father Squid shrugged. "He knew no details. Just that
there was something odd about the corpse."

"I'll bet," Brennan muttered. "Is Fadeout the head of
the Shadow Fists now?"

The priest nodded. "As far as I can tell. The Fists have
kept a very low profile in recent months. As profitable—and
cold-blooded—as ever, of course, but the Shadow Fist Society
has been avoiding rather than seeking headlines recently."

Brennan nodded. "That sounds like Fadeout, all right.

He'd try to operate as circumspectly as possible. He'd consider it a good business practice." He looked into the priest's eyes. "Thanks, Bob," he said.

"For what?"

"For being here when I needed help."

"What else is a priest for? I still have high hopes for your soul, Daniel."

"At least someone does. Keep an eye on Jennifer for me."

Father Squid nodded and went back into the room. Brennan and Brutus went down the corridor, took the elevator back to the first floor, and went out into the night.

Brutus, huddled under Brennan's leather jacket, shivered. "I'm cold, boss."

"Don't worry," Brennan said. It had started to snow again, and the wind was blowing hard. Brennan turned his face into the driving snow as he headed toward his van. "I'm sure things are going to warm up very soon now."

"Shit," Brutus said, and huddled down even more.

Kien looked up from his desk when Rick and Mick entered the office. The joker brothers were Siamese twins, of a sort. They had one pair of legs and one trunk, though their body bifurcated halfway through the rib cage, giving them two chests and two sets of arms and shoulders. Though they were impressive physical specimens, Kien sometimes thought that they didn't have half a brain between them.

"Guy here to see you," Rick said.

Mick looked at his brother with a hurt expression. "*I* was going to tell Fadeout that. *I* spoke to the guy, after all."

"You spoke to him, but it was *my* idea to see the boss first before letting him in."

"Your idea? I—"

"Please," Kien said, holding up a hand. It was times like this that he missed Wyrm. "Does the gentleman have a name?"

They both thought about it, said "Cowboy" simultaneously, then glared at each other.

Kien stiffened. That was the name Daniel Brennan used when he'd gone undercover and joined the Shadow Fists in an attempt to bring them down from within. His ploy failed because he blew his cover to save Tachyon's life, but he managed to do a fair bit of damage to the Fists before giving himself away.

Kien knew that Brennan and Cunningham had been chummy. Now, he thought, he'd discover exactly how chummy.

"Show him in," Kien told his joker bodyguards.

He made himself sit calmly when his longtime enemy entered the room. Brennan was wearing a mask, a simple black hood, that he took off after Rick and Mick had left the room, shutting the door behind them. He looked fit and tanned despite the winter season. He hadn't gained a pound since Vietnam, though his face had more lines in it and his hair was flecked with grey.

He looked around the room curiously, then at Kien. His eyes were as flat and hard as Kien remembered them, though they had an even greater bleakness, as if a major new worry was gnawing at him. His bitch, Kien noticed, wasn't with him. Maybe the hit hadn't been a total washout after all.

"Don't you think taking the man's office when you took over his organization was a bit much?" Brennan asked suddenly.

Kien shrugged and smiled. This was his hidden hole card, the ace up his sleeve. Brennan thought he was Fadeout. That was all the advantage Kien needed to finally crush his long-time foe. "Why not? It's a nice place and the lease suddenly became open. Besides, I felt that it would help provide for a smoother transition of power."

Brennan nodded, as if he bought the explanation, then sat down without being invited. Annoyed, Kien opened his mouth to say something, then suddenly closed it. Cunningham apparently tolerated such behavior.

"Back in town for a visit?" Kien asked in as casual a voice as possible.

Brennan nodded. "Someone hit my house this morning."

Kien put a shocked look on his face. "Any idea who?"

"I would guess Kien," Brennan said steadily, "if he wasn't dead."

Kien nodded. "Good guess, but he's dead. I saw his body myself."

"You sure?"

"I'm sure."

"I've heard," Brennan said, "that there was something a bit odd about the corpse. Something that usually doesn't happen to heart-attack victims."

Kien shifted uncomfortably in his chair. "Ah, the severed head, you mean," he guessed.

Brennan nodded silently.

"Well," Kien said, suddenly inspired to mix truth and lies in equal proportions, "there was a lot of information locked up in his brain."

"Deadhead?" Brennan asked.

Kien tried to look defensive. "There was a lot I needed to know."

Brennan let out a deep breath. "I guess I can believe that."

Deadhead was an insane ace with the capability of accessing people's memories by eating their brains. When Kien had set the trap to catch the disloyal Philip Cunningham, he used his own corpse as bait, having been jumped into the body of Leslie Christian. He then had his head removed from his own body so Cunningham couldn't feed the brain to Deadhead and uncover his plot.

"If Kien didn't send the killers, then who did?" Brennan asked, half to himself.

"Well, Captain, you've made a few enemies along the way." Kien paused as if deep in thought. "And I can't pretend to have total control over the Shadow Fists, particularly the Egrets. Maybe elements loyal to Kien's memory finally tracked you down and tried to eliminate you."

"Maybe," Brennan said tightly.

"And you know," said Kien, as if struck by sudden inspiration, "maybe these same elements will be going after Tachyon as well. Maybe someone should warn him."

"Maybe," Brennan said thoughtfully. "I'll mention it to Tachyon when I go back to the clinic to check on Jennifer."

"So you've seen Tachyon already?" Kien asked.

Brennan nodded abstractedly. "I took Jennifer to the clinic. She was wounded during the hit."

"Not too seriously, I hope," Kien said as he stifled his glee.

Brennan stood. "No, not too seriously."

Kien rose to walk him to the door. "I'm sure she'll pull through. And if you need anything, just call."

Brennan slipped the hood back on and stared at him with his hard unblinking gaze. "All right," he said, and left the office, going by Rick and Mick who were arguing because Rick couldn't concentrate on his comic book while Mick had the television on.

Kien watched him go, a smile of sudden unexpected glee

on his face. He had managed to maneuver all of his targets into the same basket. Now he could strike once and get rid of them all.

4.

"What's up, boss?" Brutus asked when Brennan returned to the van.

Brennan glanced down at the homunculus, who was huddled against the cold in one of Brennan's old work shirts that he'd dragged up from the back. "I don't know," Brennan said. "But I don't believe that things are as they seem. As is usual in this town."

He started the van and pulled away from the curb.

"Where're we headed?" Brutus asked.

Brennan glanced at him as he drove into an alley that bordered Kien's apartment building. "I'm going back to the clinic," Brennan said, "but you're staying behind to keep an eye on things here."

Brutus stretched, peering over the edge of the dashboard. "It looks cold out there," he said.

"All the more reason to find a way inside as soon as you can."

"Right."

Brennan pulled up next to a pile of overflowing garbage cans and opened the van's passenger door.

"So what am I supposed to be watching?" Brutus asked.

"Cunningham."

"Why?"

Brennan shook his head. "I'm not sure. Cunningham seemed...odd. Not normal. I can't really put my finger on it, but things aren't right. He called me 'Captain.' He's never called me that before. There's no way he could even know I'd been a captain in the army...unless..." Brennan shook his head again.

Brutus grunted and jumped down from the van. The sun had risen, but the sky was dark with clouds and the promise of snow. A cold wind cut through the alley as Brutus scurried behind a pile of garbage, mumbling to himself. Brennan leaned out of the van's passenger door as Brutus disappeared in the trash.

"And Brutus."

The manikin poked his head from around a grease-stained brown-paper bag. "Yeah?"

"Be careful."

The homunculus smiled. "You too, boss," he said, then vanished into the garbage.

Brennan pulled the door shut and drove off, telling himself not to worry. Brutus had been one of the Chrysalis's best spies. He knew how to take care of himself.

Chrysalis. His thoughts turned to her for the first time in quite a while. They were linked inextricably with the events that had occurred the last time he'd seen Tachyon, when he confronted the doctor, Jay Ackroyd, the P.I., and Hiram Worchester, Chrysalis's murderer.

Ackroyd had been incensed with Brennan. For a man neck-deep in a sordid and violent business, he had a more than somewhat unrealistic view about violence. But Brennan didn't hold that against him. He never held a man's ideals against him.

But Tachyon. Tachyon had missed an important point with his speech about slavish obedience to the letter of the law. Laws are only words written on paper, words that change on society's whim and are interpreted differently daily by politicians, lawyers, judges, and policemen. Anyone who believes that all laws should always be obeyed would have made a fine slave catcher. Anyone who believes that all laws are applied equally, despite race, religion, or economic status, is a fool.

The only thing a man can do is decide for himself what is right or wrong and what must be done to combat the wrong. And then he must face the consequences of his decision, no matter what they are.

Brennan pulled up before the Jokertown Clinic, killed the engine, and got out of the van. He walked through the sliding glass doors that led into the receiving area and entered chaos.

A half-hysterical woman was shouting to a harried-looking nurse that no, dammit, her baby was always that sort of suffocated purplish color, but still, *her gills just weren't working right*, while another white-uniformed nurse was explaining to an excessively furry man that Blue Cross usually didn't consider electrolysis a necessary medical procedure, no matter how badly he wanted a career in the food-service industry. Another joker—female and quite attractive if you discounted the mottled, flaking condition of her skin—was sitting reading an eight-month-old copy of *National Geographic* while her toddlers slithered after each other in and out of the chairs, circling around a gaunt, hollow-eyed old joker who was coughing continually and spitting up unhealthy-looking gobs of something into a styrofoam cup clutched firmly in his chelate forepaws.

Someone behind Brennan muttered, "Excuse me," in a harried voice, and swept by. It was Tachyon. He was accompanied by a woman who was attractive in a gaunt, hard-edged sort of way, despite the eye patch and the jagged scar that ran down her right cheek. She moved in a graceful economical manner that suggested she knew how to handle herself in almost any situation. That was rather a necessity for anyone who spent a lot of time around the doctor.

"Tachyon."

He turned with a put-upon sigh that caught in his throat as he recognized Brennan and he frowned at the expression on Brennan's face. "What is it? Is Jennifer—"

"We have to talk," Brennan said, glancing at the woman. "Somewhere in private."

She looked curiously from Tachyon to Brennan and back again to the alien. Tachyon gestured at her vaguely with his small delicate-looking hands. "Daniel, this is Cody Havero, Dr. Cody Havero. Cody, this is, uh, a friend of mine..."

As usual, Tachyon's mouth had worked faster than his brain, mentioning Brennan's real first name. Brennan, exposed last year as the mysterious bow-and-arrow vigilante known as Yeoman, preferred to keep such information private.

"Daniel Archer," Brennan supplied.

Tachyon nodded, and Havero offered her hand.

"What is it? Is Jennifer all right?" Tachyon repeated.

Brennan shook his head as he released Havero's hand. "I haven't had a chance to check on her yet. There's something else we have to discuss. Immediately."

Havero glanced again from Tachyon to Brennan. "I can take a hint," she said. "I have to go over some patient histories with Nurse Follet at the front desk. We can finish our discussion after you two are done."

"Right," Tachyon said. "Thank you, Cody." He glanced around the reception area. "Come," he said to Brennan, taking his arm. "The coffee machine seems to be deserted. We can talk while I get some caffeine into my system. It looks like it's going to be one of those days."

Mother and gilled baby rushed past them with a sympathetic nurse, and the squealing joker children played tag around them as they walked by, but the area around the vending machine was deserted. Tachyon put eighty cents into the coffee machine and got a small paper cup full of a black, strong-smelling liquid.

"Can I get one for you?" Tachyon asked Brennan, but Brennan shook his head. "That's right," Tachyon said. "You take tea. I can have some brought from my office—"

Brennan shook his head again. "Let's get down to it, Doctor."

Tachyon looked at him, hurt in his lilac eyes. "We used to be friends, Daniel. We fought the Swarm together! We—"

"We fought many battles together, Doctor," Brennan said stiffly. "That didn't keep you from walking into my mind and taking it when you saw fit."

"I had to do that! You were going to kill Hiram, and Jay wanted you sent to jail! Burning Sky! What was I supposed to do?"

"There are no easy answers," Brennan said. "Neither of us follows the herd. Both of us do what we have to do. Both of us have to live with the consequences of our actions."

"We were friends," Tachyon whispered.

"Once," Brennan said.

There was a moment's silence, and Tachyon looked down into his coffee cup. He took a sip and grimaced. "Now it's cold," he said. "Well. What did you want to see me about?"

"I think that Kien may have been behind the attack," Brennan said.

Tachyon stared at him. "Nonsense," he snorted. "Kien is dead."

Brennan shook his head. "Maybe. But maybe he's reaching out from the grave. Maybe he gave his underlings orders to kill all his enemies when he died."

Tachyon frowned, considering it. "Why would they wait over a year to strike?"

Brennan shrugged. "I don't know. But remember. You were on Kien's hit list too."

"I was, wasn't I." Tachyon sighed. "Yet another complication in an already too-complicated life." He looked at Brennan and was about to add something more, but a shout from the reception desk made them both turn and stare.

"Tachyon!" Havero called out suddenly. "Alert the staff, stat! Something's—"

Even as Havero spoke, there was a commotion at the door. An ambulance, lights flashing, sirens wailing, roared up and braked to a sudden halt. Havero reached over the counter, punched a button on the hospital intercom, and was reeling off orders as the ambulance attendants leapt out of the vehicle. One ran around to the rear of the ambulance; the other approached the clinic's double glass doors, which *whooshed* open as he neared.

"Gang fight," the driver cried. "Killer Geeks and Demon Princes. We've got a load, and there's more on the way."

Tachyon cut across the reception area, Brennan on his heels. The driver headed back to help the attendant open the vehicle's back door. They slid a blanket-covered gurney from the ambulance, and Havero, standing in front of the reception counter, screamed, "Everyone get down!"

Brennan and Tachyon reacted with the reflexes of seasoned combat veterans. They hit the polished linoleum floor as the figure on the ambulance gurney sat up, threw his blanket off, and emptied a clip from an Uzi into the reception area at full automatic.

Brennan rolled as he hit the floor. In a frozen second he saw the bullets whine through the reception area like a swarm of angry bees. The old man spitting into the cup was stitched across the chest. He hunched forward and slid off the chair, surprise and pain on his face as his expression froze and his eyes glazed.

The woman reading the *National Geographic* was unharmed until she saw her children cut down as they stood rooted in terror in the center of the room. She leaped to her feet, an endless hysterical scream ripping out of her throat.

The furry guy was lucky, too, but Cody Havero's luck was miraculous. The gunman seemed drawn by her scream and half instinctively swept his weapon in her direction. But she leaned backward, doing a strange sort of limbo, and Brennan saw out of the corner of his eye that most of the burst punched through the counter above her.

By then, he had reached the Browning holstered in the small of his back. Stomach pressed tight to the floor, he drew and aimed with one fluid motion, almost forgetting that he had a gun, replaying in his brain the instant coordination of muscle and mind that was his when firing a bow. He held the pistol out before him, both arms extended, hands clasped loosely, muscles relaxed, eyes almost closed. He squeezed off a single shot, and the man sitting on the stretcher bucked backward. Brennan's mind trapped the moment like an insect encased in amber. He played it back as the man fell and saw a round black hole punched in the middle of the assassin's forehead.

"Christ!" one of the ambulance attendants swore, and fumbled for something buttoned up under his coat.

Brennan now knew that he had plenty of time, and he knew that they needed some questions answered. He shot both attendants in their kneecaps.

Tachyon was on his feet before they hit the floor. The hideous screaming of the joker mother suddenly ended, and she slumped into the pool of her children's blood. Brennan glanced at Tachyon.

"Told her to sleep," the little alien said shortly. He stood, fury clenching his delicate face into a hard, angry fist. "Ancestors! In my clinic. *My* clinic!"

"Better see to Dr. Havero," Brennan said. "I think she took a round."

Havero straightened as Tachyon ran toward her and waved him off. "Two rounds," she managed to say. "Just flesh wounds. I'm all right."

Tachyon changed direction in midstride, heading for the leaking bodies of the joker children. Brennan didn't bother. He could still see the snapshots his mind had taken of the bullets ripping their bodies, and he knew there was no hope. He went to Havero. She had two flesh wounds, upper arm and calf. The bullets had missed all bones and major blood vessels.

"How'd you do it?" Brennan asked her as Tachyon moved helplessly from corpse to corpse.

She shifted her weight and grimaced. "The old Havero luck," she said.

Brennan nodded. I should be so lucky, he thought.

The reception room was suddenly the focal point of an explosion of activity. Brennan knew that he had little time to waste. Someone had assuredly called the police, and he couldn't be here when they arrived. Also, maybe this was just a diversion. Maybe the real attack had gone through a side entrance and up a freight elevator to a supposedly secure room on the clinic's upper floor.

He walked calmly toward the two hit men still writhing on the floor. Neither looked very happy, but then, neither did Brennan.

"Talk," he said to the one who had been the spokesman.

"I don't know, I don't know nothing, man."

"How about a busted elbow to go with your blown knee?" Brennan asked, aiming the Browning.

"No, man, I swear, I swear to Christ!"

Brennan aimed his pistol. The hit man shrieked and blubbered, but his cries didn't stop Brennan. Tachyon did.

"He's telling the truth," Tachyon said. The alien sounded bone-weary but not especially surprised at the violence that entangled him. "They're freelance muscle, hired by the man on the gurney whom you shot. And he's not going to talk anymore."

Brennan nodded and holstered his gun. "Yes he is, in a way," Brennan said. He hunkered over the body and tore off its shirt, pointing to the bulky bandage high on the left shoulder blade. "I hit the only survivor of the attack on my country place right about there. This was his second try." He stood, reached into his back pocket, and took out an ace of spades. He scaled it at the body, and it stuck, face up, to the blood running from the dead man's forehead. "Something for your friends from the law to think about when they finally get here from the doughnut shop," he said, and turned away.

"Wait a minute," Tachyon said. "Where are you going?"

Brennan glanced overhead. "To check on things."

Tachyon nodded. "I understand. Be careful."

Brennan nodded. Avoiding the lumbering elevator, he took the stairs up to the clinic's top floor. The corridor was dark and quiet. He went down it like a skulking cat, and when he flung open the door to Jennifer's room, a startled Father Squid whirled to stare at him.

"What was all that commotion down below?" the priest asked.

"Another hit," Brennan said briefly, holstering his Browning.

"Everyone all right?"

Brennan shook his head. "I think they need you down there, Father."

The priest crossed himself and dashed out of the room.

Trace was sitting in a chair by Jennifer's bed, looking like a statue of the wounded woman. Jennifer herself had faded to the point of translucence. She looked like a serene, beautiful corpse.

Brennan winced. This couldn't be doing her any good. He started to say something, but Trace looked up and rubbed tiredly at her eyes with the heels of her hands.

She looked at Brennan. "I found her," she said wearily. "She's lost, afraid and wandering. She wouldn't come back with me."

"You have to bring her back," Brennan said.

Trace shrugged. "I can't. She doesn't trust me." She looked at Brennan speculatively. "But maybe you can. If you have the guts."

Brennan started to answer her, but she held up her hand. "Don't be so quick to commit yourself," she said. "I know you're tough and brave and all that, but physical bravery has little to do with this." She pursed her lips and looked at Brennan seriously. "Your Jennifer was in a deep dream state when you were attacked. Instead of snapping back into her body, her mind somehow shunted itself off into another plane—another dimension. I suspect that this has something to do with the nature of her ace powers, that when she turns immaterial, she somehow shifts through adjacent dimensions."

"And this time," Brennan said, "only her mind shifted. Her body stayed behind, and she can't find her way back to it."

"Correct," said Trace.

"What's this other dimension like?" Brennan asked.

"Now it's just a gray void, but that's because Jennifer's conscious mind is dormant. Once a waking mind enters it, it'll become the living manifestation of the archetypes that govern that mind."

Brennan frowned. "I see. I think. But what's so dangerous about that?"

"If you enter this dimension, it'll become populated by the driving images, by the symbolic figures that stalk your subconscious. Do you dare face them?"

Brennan hesitated. He had no great desire to examine closely the hidden secrets of his mind. But it seemed he had no choice. He nodded.

Trace smiled, but there was little humor in it. "All right," she said. "I guess we'll get to see how brave you really are."

*   *   *

Kien got up, walked to his office door, and closed it, shutting out the annoying *beep-boop-bap* coming from the antechamber where Rick and Mick were playing Donkey Kong on the Atari.

It baffled Kien why anybody would waste his time like that, but he allowed lesser men their *divertimenti*. He had his own plans to occupy his mind. He should be hearing from Lao about the hit on the clinic at any time now. If Brennan and that arrogant little space bastard were dead, fine. But Kien had the feeling that it wouldn't be that easy, that he would need a more subtle web to ensare them. Then, spiderlike, he could suck out their juices and cast aside their desiccated corpses like yesterday's garbage.

Yes, he told himself as he sat back in his chair, feet on his desk and fingers interlaced behind his head, nice image. I like it. I am a spider, a great, powerful emperor spider who sits in the center of his web, patient and cunning, reading the vibrations made by lesser men as they scurry like trembling flies from strand to strand. I pick those to reward and those to use and discard. I've come a long way since Vietnam and the store that was my father's.

His father, Kien realized, had frequently been on his mind lately. It wasn't like him to be obsessive about the past. Thinking about the past did no good. It couldn't change things. It did no good to brood about the old man's death, the way Kien had found him lying slaughtered on the dirt floor of their store. Kien had never had much as a child. He endured poor food and patched clothing, and was jeered at by the other children in the village as much for his pauperish appearance as for being Chinese. But the French bastards who murdered his father took what little money the old man had accumulated, dug the strongbox right out of the secret place where Old Dad had kept it hidden. They left nothing for Kien. That was why he had to change his name and go to the city. He didn't desert his family. He did what he could for them—

There was a sound, a knock on his door, and Kien started. "Come in," he said.

It was Rick and Mick. "Just got word from your informant on the police force," Rick said.

"He kept an eye out like you told him," Mick added, "and went to the scene when the call came that something was going down at the Jokertown Clinic."

"And?" Kien prompted.

Rick and Mick looked at each other, and Kien realized that neither wanted to be the bearer of bad tidings. They nudged each other a couple of times, and Rick finally came out with it. "Lao's dead. Shot once through the forehead. There was an ace of spades on his body."

Kien clenched his teeth. "And Brennan and Tachyon?"

Rick and Mick shook their heads. "Don't think they were hurt. Lao got some joker kids, a joker geezer. He also wounded one of the doctors. Tachyon's still at the clinic, but from what the witnesses said, this Brennan guy just disappeared. He kneecapped the guys Lao hired to help him and left them behind for the cops."

"But they don't know nothin'," Mick was quick to add. "They're not Fists. They're not connected to you."

They seemed to expect some kind of explosion, but Kien just nodded. "I'd planned for this possibility," he said. "If you want something done right," he mused aloud, "you have to do it yourself."

He stood, clasped his hands behind his back, and started to pace around the room. "Tachyon's no problem," he muttered. "I can deal with the little fool anytime I want to. It's Brennan I have to track down as soon as possible." He fixed Rick and Mick with a stare. "Where would he go after the attack?"

Rick and Mick looked at each other, looked back at Kien, and shrugged.

"He would be worried about his bitch. Yes. His sentimentality would get the best of him, and he'd head right for her side to make sure that she was all right." He stopped, stared at a three-tiered glass stand that held part of his fabulous collection of ancient and rare Chinese ceramics. "He said that she was at the clinic, but they wouldn't just put her in an open ward. She'd be somewhere that they thought was safe." He paced back to his desk. "Where, precisely, would that be?"

Someone behind him sneezed.

"Bless you," Kien said reflexively.

"I didn't sneeze, boss," Rick said.

"Neither did I," Mick added.

Kien whirled around. "Then who did?"

"I think it came from there," Rick said, pointing at the vase on the middle tier of the glass stand.

It was a green-glazed vase with a black background dating from the Yung Cheng period. Very old and extremely rare in color and form, it was one of the cornerstones of Kien's art collection. He frowned, stood, and went back to the glass stand. He peered into the vase.

Inside was a manikin, a wrinkled, leathery-looking homunculus whose skin seemed about five sizes too large for his body. He had both hands clamped over his nose and mouth, and tried to stifle another sneeze. It came out with a tiny *blatting* noise. He wiped his nose on his arm and stared back up at the huge face looking down at him.

"Oh, shit," he said.

5.

The city was afire, though it did not burn.

Brennan had never felt such heat. The air shimmered with it. It rose off the pavement in waves, licking his face like the fetid tongue of a great panting beast. It crawled over his body, sending tendrils of sweat trickling down his back and legs. If he had been of a religious bent, he'd suspect that this was hell. He remembered the motto commonly found embroidered on jackets favored by combat vets in Nam: *I'm going to heaven when I die 'cause I've already spent my time in hell*.

Maybe this wasn't hell, but it was the city of Brennan's worst nightmares. He moved on down the alley, stepping over the bubbles of asphalt oozing through the cracks in the pavement. The buildings surrounding him were decaying, the streets buckling and choked with uncollected trash. It was a ghost town. No one but Brennan walked the garbage-infested streets.

He emerged from the alley and looked up at the rusted and bent sign hanging overhead from the streetlamp: *Henry Street*. The Crystal Palace, then, should be ...

Brennan looked down the street, and there it was. The Palace still stood in this place. And if the Palace still stood ... Brennan found himself drawn down the street like a sailor pulled helplessly to siren-infested rocks.

The door to the Palace was unlocked. Inside it was dark and cool. Brennan felt a shiver go through him as the sweat running down his face and body suddenly evaporated, leaving him cold and clammy.

Maybe it was the coolness of the Palace's interior that

caused the shiver. Maybe it was the sight of her sitting in her customary table in her customary high-backed chair, barely visible in the dark, her customary glass of amaretto sitting by her hand.

"Chrysalis," Brennan whispered.

She looked at him, the expression on her fleshless face as unreadable as ever. Chrysalis was a woman of blood and bone, her skin and flesh invisible, her muscles mostly so. Some found her hideous. Brennan had been fascinated by her.

"Is it really you?" he asked.

"Who else would be sitting in this place, in this body, drinking amaretto from a crystal glass?" the spectre asked.

Brennan shook his head. She hadn't really answered his question. Perhaps the rules governing this skewed dimension didn't allow her to. Or perhaps she was forbidden to speak clearly by the rules that governed his skewed subconscious.

"You knew everything that happened in Jokertown," Brennan said. "What about in this place?"

"I know you," she replied. "I know something of that which goes on in your mind."

"Can you help me?" he asked. "Can you help me find Jennifer?"

If the spectre was upset by his mention of her rival, she didn't show it. "Look in the center of things," she told him. "You will find that which is most precious to you in the arms of your greatest enemy. But be careful. You are not alone in this world."

"Is this place," he asked her, "real?"

"It seems real enough to me," she replied.

"Me too," Brennan said in a small voice. He hesitated. He wanted to touch her, but somehow he didn't think that was a very good idea. He was afraid that she would dissipate like smoke. Worse, he was afraid that she would feel warm and alive, like solid flesh. "I have to go," he finally said.

Chrysalis nodded. "Another quest," she said as Brennan backed out of the room. "Be careful, my archer. Be very, very careful."

It seemed to Brennan that she looked sad, but there was nothing he could do to cure her sadness. He just took a piece of it with him as he left the Palace for the last time.

Outside, the sun was so bright that he had to blink against its glare. It hadn't gotten any cooler, either, and he broke out in an instant sweat as he stood outside the Palace considering his next move.

If he was to take Chrysalis's advice, he should look for the "center of things." That, unfortunately, was a rather nebulous description. He started up the street, thinking about it, and then he noticed that another part of Chrysalis's prophecy had come true.

He wasn't alone.

There were people on the street. Most were wearing the blue satin jackets of the Immaculate Egret gang, or the face masks of the Werewolves. They stood singly or in small groups, in front of, behind, and all around him.

Brennan reached for the Browning holstered in the snug of his back but came away empty. His gun, it seemed, hadn't been translated to this place with him. Then he suddenly realized that it might not matter whether he had his gun.

All the men surrounding him were already dead.

All were bloody. All had open wounds. Most had arrows sticking in chests, throats, backs, or eyes. Their faces, as Brennan watched them approach, were mostly familiar, and he realized that these were the men he had killed since coming back to the city.

There were a lot of them.

Brennan was momentarily frozen, unable to decide upon a plan of action as the dead men approached. There was a sudden movement, a sudden flicker of motion that Brennan caught out of the corner of his eye. He whirled to face it head-on and saw a ghastly-grinning man with a horribly tattooed face standing within arm's length of him.

It was Scar, the teleporting ace and gang leader who Brennan had killed when he'd first come to the city. Scar's face was tattooed with the scarlet and black whorls that were the mark of the Cannibal Headhunters. He was a sadistic ace who took vast delight in utilizing his power to help him slowly slice up his victims with a straight razor. "I'm back, asshole," he said in a ghastly whisper through the throat that Brennan had crushed with a bowstring. "And this time I've got help." He gestured at the company of dead men slowly surrounding them in the brutal heat.

"You'll need it," Brennan said with a confidence he didn't totally feel. "I already killed you once."

Scar hissed in rage, disappeared, and reappeared right in Brennan's face. He slashed out with his straight razor. Brennan ducked and half blocked the blow, but not before the razor cut across his chest, slicing his sweat-soaked T-shirt and scoring the flesh underneath. Scar disappeared, then flicked back into existence half a dozen feet from Brennan.

"Time to play," the sadistic ace said.

Brennan felt blood mingle with the sweat running down his chest, and he suddenly realized that he could die in this place. He looked around quickly, spotted a narrow gap between two dead Egrets who were closing in on him, and sprinted for it. Brennan stiff-armed the Egret who moved to intercept him and pushed his way through.

"Run, you bastard, run!" Scar screamed with crazed delight. "You'll never get away, never! You're meat—dead, rotting meat!"

Brennan ran, the dead men on his trail, Scar watching and laughing horrible constricted laughter.

Rick and Mick held up the pickle jar and looked at it intently. Brutus stared back at them, his face forlornly pressed up against the glass, bruised and swollen. Blood trickled from his nose, and he tried, unsuccessfully, to cradle his broken right arm as Rick shook the jar and watched the joker bounce around.

"Why are we bringing the little geek with us?" he asked Kien.

Kien glanced down at him as he drove carefully through the flurry of fat damp snowflakes. "Ultimately, as a receptacle for Captain Brennan's soul. After we've captured them, I've decided to have our jumper allies transfer me to his body for a while and him to that thing."

"Cool," Rick said. He gave the bottle another shake.

"Better take the lid off and give the geek a little air," Mick said. "He's starting to turn blue."

Kien chuckled indulgently, then turned his attention back to the street. Kien didn't like driving, and he liked driving in snowstorms even less, but he wanted privacy on this trip. Once it was over, he would have another body, another identity, one that no one would survive to know about. Not the jumpers who would effect the transference. Not even Rick and Mick. He glanced at the monsters torturing the helpless little joker. They were getting almost as much fun from that as they had when they manhandled the joker until it told where Jennifer was being kept in the clinic.

They had their crude uses, but Kien knew he wouldn't miss them. It was time to invest in a better grade of help.

Kien pulled into the clinic's parking lot, next to the van that had ARCHER LANDSCAPING AND GARDENING painted on its side. It had taken months of detective work to track down Brennan and his bitch, but nothing was beyond Kien's power. Nothing.

"All right. Wait here until I send for you, then bring your friend," Kien said, gesturing at the pickle jar.

Rick held it up, giving it another shake as Kien slipped out of the car. Kien would miss the thrill of being an ace when he gave up this body. He faded down to his eyes—it had taken a little practice to realize that when he faded out totally, he was also totally blind—and moved through the falling snow like an animated silhouette. He made his way to an unlocked service entrance at the back of the clinic and silently slipped inside. He paused for a moment, orienting himself, then went to the room on the top floor the pathetic joker had told him about.

It was easy to fade to nothing whenever he saw an approaching nurse or orderly, easy to fade his eyes back in when he heard them walk by. No one saw him. The door to the room was shut. Kien looked through the small window set high on the security door and saw Brennan's bitch lying in the bed, her forehead bandaged. The big joker priest, Father Squid, was standing next to the bed. Someone was sitting in a chair next to the priest, but the priest was in the way, and Kien couldn't identify him. Or her.

Everyone was intent on Brennan's bitch. Kien drew the gun he carried in his coat pocket and pushed open the door. "Be quiet," he said in his most commanding voice, "and I'll let you live awhile."

The priest turned and stared. Kien let his gun fade in until everyone could see it. "Don't be stupid," Kien said, and the priest held his ground, an unreadable expression on his ugly joker face. "Stand back, slowly. And remember, I'm not afraid to shoot."

"Listen to him," the joker priest said. "It's Fadeout, of the Shadow Fists. He means what he says."

"You're right," Kien said, laughing aloud, "but also wrong. Very, very wrong."

There seemed to be no reason to remain invisible any

longer. Kien faded in as the priest stepped back from the bed, and the person sitting in the chair looked up at him.

Kien stared. It was a small Asian man, white-haired, wrinkle-faced, with a long, sparse chin beard. He was dressed in shabby, patched clothes. It was his father.

Kien's gun shook as he pointed it at him.

"Such a son," his father said in the familiar hated tone of voice.

The old man shook his head sadly, and Kien started to lower the gun. It's a trick, he suddenly thought. It's got to be a trick. He raised the gun again, trembling fingers almost pulling the trigger unwillingly.

"Who are you?" Kien asked.

The image of his father shook his head again, sadly. "It is an evil child who doesn't recognize his own father, Hsiang Yu," the apparition said.

"What do you want from me?" Kien shouted, unnerved at the spectre's use of his real name.

His father shook his head. "Only the respect due me. For that," he continued, "I will give you a gift. Your greatest, fondest desire."

"What's that?" Kien asked in a shaken voice.

"Do you want the head of Daniel Brennan?" his father purred.

Kien's eyes grew wide. "You know I do."

"Then you shall have it," Kien's father told him. "If," he added in the voice of a devil, "you are man enough to take it."

His father pointed to the other side of the bed. Kien carefully leaned forward, looking over the bed, and saw Brennan lying asleep on the floor.

Kien smiled wolfishly. "This is a great gift, oh Father," he said, and pointed his gun at Brennan.

His father shook his head. "You were always one for taking the easy way, my son," he said.

Kien glanced at him, but before he could say anything, there was a sudden, terrifying wrenching. Kien felt his mind whirling into a mad vortex. He closed his eyes, but it wouldn't stop. He tried to vomit, but he couldn't. He swallowed hot bile, and when he opened his eyes again, he lurched forward to steady himself against the great teakwood desk that stood in the office of his apartment that overlooked Central Park.

He took a deep breath, fighting the nausea still rumbling through his stomach, and looked around. It was his office, all right. Everything looked normal. All his art treasures were in their places, all his expensive furniture polished and unmarred, even the surface of his teakwood desk, which had been horribly damaged during his faked death when that idiot Blaise had pinned his watchdog joker to its surface with a letter opener.

He ran his hand pensively across the desktop that was so highly polished that he could see himself in it. He leaned forward for a closer look, mumbling to himself as he realized that he was back in his old body. He was Kien again. He looked at his right hand and wrung it with his left, and then laughed a short relieved laugh. At least he had two whole hands. He looked away, startled when the door to his office opened.

Wyrm stood in the doorway. But that couldn't be. Wyrm was dead. He looked dead, Kien suddenly realized—and pissed.

"I wasss your loyal sssservant," the scaleless reptiloid joker hissed, "and I died becaussse of your ssschemes."

"It wasn't my fault," Kien protested. He still half refused to believe that Wyrm was standing before him, but the evidence was hard to ignore. It looked like Wyrm, talked like Wyrm, and even had a big ugly wound in its throat where Fadeout had stuck it with the same letter opener that had killed the watchdog joker. "Fadeout killed you," Kien added.

Wyrm approached, still looking angry, and Kien drew back behind his desk. Wyrm was inhumanly strong, and his bite was highly poisonous. Kien knew that he was no match for the joker.

"I died," Wyrm hissed furiously, "becaussse you wouldn't give me the loyalty I alwayssss gave you." He loomed over Kien like an avatar of death, and the general cringed. Kien pictured Wyrm's great gaping maw crunching down ruthlessly on his throat.

"Don't," he managed to get out. "Don't," he repeated, shielding his face with his arms.

Wyrm drew back with a sneer. "You're not to meet your desstiny at my handsss," he said, clenching and unclenching powerful fists. "But out there." The joker pointed out the window facing Central Park.

Kien came around from behind his desk cautiously and

peered out. Central Park was gone. In its place was a dense, thick jungle.

Just like home, Kien thought. Just like Vietnam.

6.

Brennan ran, pursued by dead men and Scar's maniacal laughter.

Scar was toying with him, Brennan realized. The teleporting ace could have forced a face-off, but apparently wanted to make Brennan suffer before finishing him off. He flickered just in front of or just behind Brennan, slashing ferociously with his razor. Sometimes Brennan dodged or blocked, sometimes he didn't. His shirt was soon in tatters, and he was leaving a splattered trail of blood for the pursuing dead men to follow.

Even without Scar, there were too many corpses to handle. He needed help, and he needed weapons, preferably both. But the run-down streets were deserted, the decaying buildings dark and empty.

Brennan was in excellent physical condition, but his pursuers didn't tire. He knew he couldn't keep running and running. He'd eventually fall exhausted, and then his foes could deal with him at their leisure. Somehow he had to shake the pursuit, which seemed unlikely, or at least break up the pack and deal with it in small groups.

A familiar building caught his eye as he surged up the street, gasping in the killing heat, throat dry, heart starting to pound. It was the Famous Bowery Wild Card Dime Museum. Inside it would be cool, and dark, with plenty of hiding places.

He pounded up the stairs, twenty yards ahead of his nearest pursuer, and slammed hard against the front door. It swung wide open, and the cool, dark interior of the museum beckoned him. He dashed inside and put his back against the wall, catching his breath before moving into the interior.

He looked around at the familiar exhibits, the wall of monstrous joker babies floating in jars, the diorama of the Four Aces, Earth verses the Swarm, Kien's assassins attacking him and Ann-Marie. Brennan stopped and stared. There was, of course, no such exhibit in the real Famous Bowery Wild Card Dime Museum, but then, this wasn't the real Famous

Bowery Wild Card Dime Museum. This version of it had been conjured from the depths of Brennan's mind and was filled with the archetypes and images that had shaped his psyche over the years.

He wandered on to the next exhibit. It was the Fall of Saigon recreated in all its casual brutality. Brennan was in the foreground ripping off his captain's bars and walking away from it. There was a scene of him fighting some forgotten battle in some forgotten Asian country during his mercenary years and one of him practicing Zen archery in the temple with his *roshi* Ishida looking on. There was Brennan after his return to the States in Minh's restaurant, but too late to do anything besides avenge his comrade's death at the hands of the Immaculate Egrets. There was Brennan meeting Chrysalis, Brennan fighting the Swarm, Brennan and Jennifer.

He wandered on in a daze. The last exhibit took him full circle in time and history, and he found himself looking at a diorama that was similar, so similar, to the first one he'd seen. Kien's assassins were breaking into his house, but it was Jennifer, not Ann-Marie, lying covered in blood.

Am I doomed, Brennan wondered, to repeat the cycle of death time and time again despite my best intentions? Are destruction and violence always to follow me like vicious pet dogs that I can never tame? He reached out a hand toward the wax figure of Jennifer in the last diorama, and a sound made him stop, turn, and look.

Scar stood at the head of the pack of dead men, grinning like an idiot.

"You think you're so smart," Scar said, mockingly. "We knew this was the first place you'd go." He looked over and pointed at a diorama that Brennan hadn't noticed before. "Wanna see the future, asshole? Look over there."

It was a scene of Brennan lying bloody and torn, Scar crouched on his chest, holding a dripping straight razor in one hand and Brennan's heart in the other.

Brennan turned to face the sadistic ace, and the myriad pairs of shining, unblinking eyes of all the men Brennan had killed since coming back to the city. There was nowhere to run, no place to go. "Let's see," he said, "if dead men can die twice."

Scar grinned, lifted his razor, and flickered out of sight. He popped into existence three feet to Brennan's right. Brennan moved to block him, but something interceded.

Something that appeared from the shadows at Brennan's back quick as a cat, and struck Scar with a wooden staff. Scar took the blow on his throat and staggered back, wide-eyed and gaping like a suffocating fish. He dropped his razor, went down on his knees, and like Brennan, stared at the newcomer.

It was a man, a young man in his midteens. He was shorter than Brennan, slimly built but lithely muscled. He wore black pants and black slippers, and handled a *bo* staff with the ease of an expert martial artist.

Scar looked from the newcomer to Brennan, hate glinting in his crazed eyes. He sighed, as if with a final expulsion of breath, "Not again . . ." and collapsed on the floor, his hands clutching his severely crushed throat.

A murmur rose from the ranks of the dead men as the newcomer spoke. "You know who I am," he said in a soft youthful voice. "You know that I stand with this man. As do," he said, gesturing with his staff, "these others."

The dead men looked around the dark chamber, as did Brennan. His lips worked, but he was too stunned to speak. There was his old comrade the Tiger Scout Minh, with his daughter Mai, who had sacrificed herself so that the earth would be free of the Swarm. There was Sergeant Gulgowski and his squad from Nam. There was Chrysalis with a swarm of manikins at her feet.

The dead men still outnumbered them, but punks and bullies that they were, they no longer seemed to have guts for a fight. Brennan watched in astonishment as they drifted back slowly through the darkness until all were gone. And when he looked around, all his old friends and allies had also disappeared, all except the youth who stood before him.

"Who are you?" Brennan asked quietly.

His young ally said nothing but turned slowly to face Brennan for the first time. Brennan stared into his face and thought, My God, he's got Ann-Marie's eyes. He smiled, and he had Ann-Marie's smile too.

"Are you real?" Brennan whispered.

"As real as I would have been if things had worked out differently." He leaned on his staff, still smiling. "Come," he said, "it's time to go to the center of things. Everyone is waiting."

Brennan nodded. There was much he wanted to ask the boy, but he stopped himself. Somehow, he thought, it was better not to question some things. Some things it was better simply to accept.

The two left the Dime Museum in companionable silence. In the company of the boy the city no longer seemed so deathly hot, so terribly decayed. Brennan noted signs of life as green plants thrust through the cracks in the sidewalk, and a cool breeze blew through the concrete canyons.

The walk seemed to last a long time, but Brennan didn't mind. The farther they went, the more calm he felt. They were headed, he realized, toward Central Park. Of course. The "center of things."

Only this was not the Central Park that Brennan knew. It was a jungle that seemed to have been lifted out of Southeast Asia and transplanted into Brennan's dream Manhattan. Brennan and the boy stopped at the edge of the jungle.

"You have to proceed alone," the boy told him.

Brennan nodded. "Thank you," he said, "for your help and your companionship. Will I ever see you again?"

The boy shrugged. "Many things are possible."

Brennan nodded again. He opened his arms. The boy came to him, and they hugged fiercely. Brennan kissed the top of his head, and then they parted. The boy smiled and, twirling his staff, disappeared into the heat waves rising up from the streets of the smoldering city. Brennan watched him until he was gone, then plunged into the jungle.

Kien hated the jungle. He'd always hated the jungle. He was an urbanite at heart. He liked air-conditioning, ice cubes in his drinks, and buildings with real floors and walls, all of which were rather lacking in the jungle.

But Wyrm had told him that his destiny was here, and he wasn't about to argue with the dead joker. He hit upon a strangely familiar path as soon as he reached the jungle. He half knew where it would take him as soon as he found it, so it was no real surprise that he came upon the village where he'd spent his childhood. It was strange, but Kien was beyond surprise by now. He accepted it as he accepted all the strangeness of this place, but he approached the village with all the caution that he could muster because he still had the feeling that death could be found here much as it could be found in the real world.

The village seemed deserted. He headed straight for the

dirt-floored store that was his father's, where he'd spent so
many hated hours when he was a child.

His father, Kien thought, had been such a hypocrite,
always crying and moaning about how poor they were. He
would scarcely put decent food on the table, let alone buy
decent clothes for his children. It was bad enough growing up
ethnic Chinese among the damned Vietnamese. It was worse
to wear ragged and patched clothes that made him the
laughingstock of the village school. And it wasn't, Kien
remembered as he approached the store's entrance, that they
didn't have the money. No. Kien's father, besides being a
shrewd businessman in his dealings with the village, was also
a blackmarketeer. He sold weapons, munitions, and medicine
to the insurgents fighting the French, and everything he sold,
he sold dear.

Kien walked into the dark interior of the store. Old Dad
had plenty of money. In fact, Kien knew where the miser hid
it, buried beneath a pile of cheap straw mats in a cache dug
into the store's dirt floor. Right *there*.

As Kien looked at the spot in the floor, he was seized
with the same compulsion that had once gripped him over
thirty-five years ago. He took a sharp-pointed mattock down
from those hanging from hooks on the wall and roughly
pushed the pile of cheap mats away. He started to dig in a
frenzy, cutting quickly through the cool, slightly moist soil
in a spate of wild hoeing. Within moments he had dug a hole
over two feet deep, and the blade of the mattock hit something that clanged with a metallic *chink*. He dropped the
mattock, grubbed with his hands in the dirt, and pulled out a
metallic strongbox that felt heavy with the weight of untold
riches.

"You!" a voice squeaked in rage.

Kien looked wildly over his shoulder. It was Old Dad.

"What are you doing there? What are you doing with my
box?"

"I—" Kien began, confused by the blurring of memories
and events unfolding before him.

"My son, a thief," the old man said haughtily. He raised
the cane that he always carried and struck Kien sharply on
the shoulder. Kien ducked his head like a turtle retreating
into his shell and took the blow as he always did.

Old Dad struck him again and again, and something
snapped in Kien. He wailed in anger and pain, reached out

and grabbed the object nearest to him, and struck out wildly at his father. He felt the shock of contact run up his arms, and his father stopped beating him. He opened his eyes and saw the truth that he had hidden with a thousand elaborate lies. He saw the mattock blade embedded in the center of his father's forehead. Old Dad looked at him with astonished, already glazed eyes.

He was dead. Kien had killed him. There was only one thing to do now. He had to run. He needed money. He reached gingerly over his father's cooling corpse and lifted the key the old man wore on a thong around his neck. He put the key into his pocket and tucked the strongbox under his arm. It was heavy, heavy enough to buy him a new life and a new identity in Saigon. He could finally get out of the jungle.

He rushed out of the store and came face-to-face with Daniel Brennan. The two stared at each other like the old enemies they were.

"What are you doing here?" Kien ground out.

"Looking for something you took from me," Brennan said. His eyes went from Kien's face to the box, and he remembered what Chrysalis had told him when he'd first come to the strange place.

Kien, too, looked at the box. "This is mine," he said. "I took it to buy myself a new life."

Brennan shook his head. "It is the means of my new life," he said, advancing.

Kien looked wildly around, but there was nowhere to go. He tried to dodge past Brennan, but Brennan was too fast for him. They grappled for the box, and it fell to the ground and burst like a ripe watermelon. Golden light shone out of the box so powerfully that it nearly blinded both men.

They shielded their eyes and stared as a tall slim figure stepped out of the light. It was Jennifer Maloy, naked and beautiful and alive.

She looked around dazedly, then saw Brennan. They met and embraced while Kien crawled to the shattered remnants of the strongbox, moaning like a lost child. Brennan hugged and kissed Jennifer, wanting never to let her go, but he finally had to release her to take a breath.

"I was so lost and afraid," she said. "I couldn't find my way back to you."

Brennan smoothed her hair and smiled. "It's over now," he said. "Let's go home."

Jennifer looked around in bewilderment and finally focused on Kien, who was staring like a broken man at the smashed and empty strongbox. "What about him?" she asked.

Brennan felt totally serene. It surprised him. All of the hate and anger had been burned away, perhaps by the joy of finding Jennifer again. He wondered for a moment if somehow, some impossible way, he'd achieved enlightenment, the ultimate Zen goal of a totally self-realized man, then rejected that notion as farfetched. He was hardly worthy of such a state.

"I don't know," he said. "Maybe we should just leave him."

Kien looked up for the first time. "Leave me? Here?"

Brennan looked at him with cold eyes. "Why not?"

Kien jumped up and hurled himself at Brennan. Brennan met his furious attack calmly, serenely, simply pushing him aside, and Kien fell panting to the ground.

Brennan looked around. "This doesn't look like too bad a place to me," he said. "Probably better than you deserve."

"The jungle?" Kien cried, looking around wildly. "You don't know what I've done to escape this place! Don't leave me here!"

The desperation on Kien's face was almost enough to incline Brennan to pity. Almost. But there was little he could do about it anyway. He and Jennifer started to fade—or this strange little universe, this simulacrum built from the mortar and bricks of Brennan's memories and psyche, started to fade. They were never sure which.

But they heard Kien scream, "Don't leave me here forever," and it echoed over and over again as a reedy voice crying, "ever . . . ever . . . ever . . ." like a condemned man questioning an unendurable sentence.

Then there was silence.

7.

Brennan opened his eyes, rubbed them vigorously, then stood and leaned anxiously over Jennifer. Her eyes fluttered, then opened, and she smiled. Brennan didn't know whether to laugh or cry. He leaned over and hugged her fiercely.

He turned and looked at the rest of the room for the first time.

Father Squid was staring at them with wide-open eyes.

Kien's body—Fadeout's body—was lying slack-mouthed and drooling on the floor. The door to the room suddenly swung open, and there was Rick and Mick, carrying a large jar tucked under Rick's right arm.

"Okay, boss," Rick said. "Here we are." They stopped, looked around, looked at each other, and said, "Oh-oh" in unison.

"We've been tricked," Mick added. "Something's wrong with the boss."

"Let's get out of here," said Rick. They dropped the glass jar as they ran from the room, and it shattered.

Brennan made a move to follow them, then stopped as he saw Brutus among the remains of the glass jar. The homunculus was bloody and torn. Brennan rushed over to him and kneeled. He reached out a hand but didn't dare touch him. He knew there was nothing he could do to mend the damage his comrade had sustained.

Brutus looked up at him, barely able to see through swollen, bruised eyes. "Sorry I told where you were, boss, but I guess it worked out."

"It did," Brennan said quietly.

"Did we get Jennifer back?"

Brennan glanced to his side to see Jennifer kneeling down next to him.

"You did, Brutus," she said.

"Good." His tiny body was wracked by a spasm of coughing, and he leaned back among the shards of glass. "This is damned uncomfortable," he said, and closed his eyes.

Brennan sighed and leaned back on his heels. Jennifer gripped his forearm and laid her head against his shoulder as Father Squid crossed himself and quickly whispered the prayer for the dead.

"You did very well out there," a voice said. Brennan looked up to see Trace standing over him and Jennifer. "Satisfied?"

Brennan looked at her before answering. She was a young woman—slim, dark-eyed, with high cheekbones and Indian eyes. He didn't know who she was for a moment, then he remembered. She was his mother, who had died when Brennan was very young. He didn't remember much about her, only gentle hands and soft songs sung in Spanish and Mescalero Apache.

Brennan felt he couldn't be ungrateful. He had, after all, gotten Jennifer back. But he looked down at Brutus's shattered body and knew there was still immense suffering and injustice in the world, and no matter what he did, he couldn't stop it all.

Trace shook her head. "You are very hard to please," she said, not ungently.

"I guess I am," Brennan admitted. "Did you trick the joker into bringing Brutus back to us?"

"It was easy," Trace said. "Everything I do should be so easy."

"How much was *you* in that place," Brennan asked, "and how much was real?"

"Haven't you learned your lesson about the reality of reality yet?" Trace asked.

"I don't know," Brennan said. "I just wish it weren't so hard."

"It's as hard as you make it," Trace told him in his mother's voice. "Sometimes there's nothing anyone can do to make it easier. Sometimes there is."

The door to the room shot open, and Dr. Tachyon rushed in. "What's going on?" he demanded. "A strange joker was seen running out of here—"

He looked around, genuinely puzzled. "What did I miss?"

Brennan looked at him. It was time, he thought, to try to make things easier. He went to Tachyon and took his hand. "The end of an age, old friend, and the beginning of a new."

The Temptation of
Hieronymus Bloat

II

I have a dream.

I have several dreams, in fact. I suppose that makes this teenage governor marginally better than old King, right? They're very odd, my dreams—a lot more hard-edged and surreal than I remember them being before the wild card hit me. But then, I always *did* like the painters who could twist reality and make it their own: Dali, Bosch, Brueghel, Chagall. . . .

Last night I had a dream too.

I was in the Administration Building. (Where else would I be, huh?) But the old place had changed. The stone and brick had changed to glass. It was a wondrous, clear crystalline palace from which I could see out into the world again. The sunlight shattered on it and bled rainbows.

I'd changed too. I was someone else, not Bloat. I stood on my own legs, and my body was a gorgeous, muscular wonder. Kelly, as resplendent and alluring as a fairy-tale princess, stood alongside me. Her thoughts were no longer pitying but full of love and trust for me. Together, we strode up and down inside my palace, marveling at its beauty.

Kafka was kneeling in the lobby as we approached, hooking up that generator he keeps insisting we need. A snarl of wires went all around him.

Then I noticed that the brilliant sunlight had tricked me. These weren't wires. The lobby was filled to overflowing with

jokers, their bodies all pressed together. They were screaming at me, waving hands and tentacles and filaments and
antennae, and shouting, "There's no more room! No more
room!"

I looked out and saw that—Omigod!—they were right.
Through the windows I could see that all the Rox was the
same way—a living, writhing carpet of jokers from end to
end, right into the greasy waves of the bay.

I shouted to them all. My voice was the voice of a King,
deep and charismatic. Not at all the adolescent boy's screech
it really is. "I will make you a new home!" I told them. "I will
do that for you!"

Kelly applauded. The jokers cheered.

But Kafka glanced up at me from the generator. "*They*
won't let you," he said softly.

The massed jokers all howled agreement. I knew that
Kafka spoke of every joker's eternal "they": the nats who hate
us, the turncoat aces who are weapons against their own
kind.

"My Wall keeps them out," I insisted, shaking my head.

Kafka sighed.

I suddenly felt a chill. I looked up to see that the entire
roof of the building was gone. Above, a winter wind flung
dirty wet snow from massed, hurtling clouds. The snow piled
in drifts around and over the mountain of my body—I was
Bloat again. Kelly, disgust on her face, fled the lobby. I was
frightened. I felt more helpless than I'd ever felt, for I knew
that the wall couldn't keep out the snow.

"The wall isn't enough," Kafka told me. "Not enough."

"The jumpers. My joker army."

"Not enough."

The wind howled, a mad laughter. Sleet hissed around
the columns of the lobby, between the supports that held the
floor against my weight . . .

And I woke. My enormous body was trembling so that
the whole building was shaking in sympathy. All the guards
were looking at me, and the smell of the bloatblack . . .

Well, you get the idea.

Hell, dreams are supposed to be escapes. I should be
dreaming of being in a normal body or having some
postpubescent wet dreams about Kelly.

Every joker needs a refuge. I can't even find one in my
dreams.

* * *

I talked to Molly Bolt rather than Blaise because I could hear through the mindvoices that Blaise was busy.

All right, I'll be honest here. That was a lousy excuse. I talked to Molly because I really don't like Blaise.

But even Molly doesn't listen very well to me. She spoke her thoughts, and I heard them twice. *You're a softy, Bloat. Weak. "Power is information." C'mon, that's crap. You know what power is? It's taking the body of some rich snot and humiliating him. Making him run naked down Wall Street jacking off. Having him fire his staff with a goddamn AK-47. Walking him to J-town and having him suck some joker's dick. Making him feel helpless and used. That's power, Governor.*

Molly flung one jean-clad leg over the other as she slouched in the chair in front of me. Details: the knees were out of the jeans. Despite the three inches of snow on the ground outside, she was wearing sneakers without socks and a cutoff T under her leather jacket. She ran a hand through spiked multicolored hair. Her lower lip was out, pouting.

I notice things like that. It's the artist in me.

"Molly, your kind of power is just kicks. You do it because you're a sick, twisted little child. Because you enjoy it." She smiled at that; I chuckled. "But you're worried too," I told her. "All of you are. I hear the thoughts. You're worried because if an assassin can take out a man as well protected as Kien—a man I know Blaise and his friends were supposed to be protecting—then Prime can be killed, even with Zelda watching him. For that matter, so can Blaise or you. The fact you can jump ain't enough."

As I said it, I caught the thought she tried to hide. So I laughed again. "Oh, you wouldn't mind if Blaise were offed, would you? Excuse me, that's 'that fucking son-of-a-bitch cocksucking alien prickhead Blaise,' to be exact. You really need to work on your cursing, Molly. You show a lack of inventiveness. All those clichés . . ."

"Stop your fucking giggling and get on with it, Bloat."

"Information *is* power. For instance, what if I told Blaise what you were thinking just now. Or what if I mentioned your and Blackhead's half-assed plan to get rid of Blaise—"

Molly angrily filled her mind with other images. I chuckled. "You've stirred up a hornet's nest, Molly," I said. "I can hear them buzzing around. So can you. I notice these things. I notice that since Kien died, since Prime's been acting strange, you jumpers have been, well, stupid. You're terrorizing the city like you're in some bad teenage biker movie."

She wasn't impressed. "We're just showing the fuckers we ain't afraid of them."

"Right. What you're doing is playing right into the nats' hands. All you're doing is making them angry, and only blind fools would think that a hundred jumpers and a thousand or so jokers on a little island can *really* stand against 'them.' If they want to just clean us out, they can."

Molly sniffed, though I knew that inside she had listened. "So talk to Blaise or Prime. Since when did you get so fucking political? You ain't no older than me, or any smarter."

"It's because I like you."

I had to laugh at the strange image that put in her head. "Oh, I still have the right equipment for it," I told her. "I think so, at least. It's buried inside. I doubt if it's in proportion to my current body, though. Besides, Kelly's really more my type. Look, I've been studying a lot, Molly—there are minds on this island . . ." I shook my head. The mindvoices intruded even as I tried to talk about them.

"You want power?" I said. "Then you gotta be rich. You gotta play the economic game too. I've been learning all the time, and I've come to certain conclusions. One is that the Rox is too small and too run-down. Kafka's already finding it impossible to keep the place going. 'Infrastructure'—that's the word he uses. The infrastructure is old and antiquated; it keeps falling apart. Yet the jokers keep coming. You keep recruiting more wannabee jumpers. The Rox is crowded now and getting worse."

"You gonna tell me that your idea of taking New York isn't a fucking pipe dream?"

I answered her patiently. "I'm telling you that soon there won't be any choice. They won't let us stay here, not forever. Our own success is going to drive us out, even if they do nothing."

Molly just laughed, and I could see absurd images in her mind. She knew I was watching them and exaggerated them even more for my benefit. "Bloat on a float?" she snorted. "How the fuck are you going to *get* to the city? Your jokers gonna build a goddamn ark? You gonna swim? Jesus, the first whale sighted in New York Bay." She laughed again, throwing her head back and exposing that long muscular neck.

"There are ways, Molly Bolt," I told her. "With enough

money, with enough *power*, there's very little you can't solve."

She wasn't convinced. "Sure. And your fucking wall's gonna go all around Manhattan too."

"Hey, I'm still a growing boy. My powers are expanding with me. The Wall's already a hundred yards farther out than it was six months ago, and it's stronger than ever. That's part of the equation, too. What's going to happen when ships can't get up or down the Hudson from the bay? What will they do when the Rox begins to hit housing in Jersey? They're already changing the air-traffic patterns for Tomlin and La Guardia. Power is *economics*, Molly my dear."

She didn't believe me and said so.

I thought of the dreams.

It won't be enough . . .

I became lost for a minute in the memory of my dreams, in the mindvoices. When I came back to reality, Molly was staring at me. "Look, Gov," she said. "I know you. You got some plan, don't you? That's why you're boring me to death with all your yapping."

I grinned. "I want to *use* you, Molly, you and the rest of the jumpers. I want to use your abilities to make us fucking *rich*. If you want to *really* humiliate someone, you have to know where it will hurt them most when you hit them. And I also know what would scare them the most. I'll organize it; you jumpers be the muscle. I tell you, I'll make us rich, rich, rich. Let me tell you how we do it. . . ."

Lovers
by
Melinda M. Snodgrass

I

"MONSTER!!"

Doctor Tachyon dodged a raking blow from her claw. Acid tears were rolling down her ruined cheeks, eating new wounds in the already suppurating mess that was her face. The joker shook her head violently. As the tears flew in all directions, small burns appeared in the cloth curtain that provided what passed for privacy in the emergency room of the Blythe Van Rensselaer Clinic. One tear struck Tach on the ear, drawing a yelp of pain.

"You did this. YOU. I'll *kill* you."

There was no mistaking to whom this threat was being directed. "TROLL!" bellowed Tachyon.

The nine-foot-tall joker didn't waste time on niceties. The curtain came down with the scream of outraged metal rings. The security chief of the clinic plucked the shrieking woman over the examining table and held her kicking, clawing, writhing form at arm's length. The acid in her spittle and tears had no effect on the horny plates that encased Troll's body.

Tachyon ran for a dispensary cart. Cursed the artificial hand as he struggled to hold the sedative bottle steady without breaking the fragile glass. Filled a hypodermic.

As he hurried back, Troll tried to warn him off. "No, Doc, don't. You'll get burned."

"I deserve to," grunted the Takisian. He ducked in close,

grabbed one of the flailing arms, and pulled it up tight behind the woman's back. Acid burned his hand and face, but he jammed the needle in and pushed the plunger home.

"Now back off!" ordered Troll, and this time Tachyon obeyed.

Two minutes later, and the joker's struggles subsided. With a sigh, she slid into a drug-induced sleep. Tach slumped down onto a stool as Cody came hurrying through the doors to the ER. As befitted the chief of surgery, she was dressed in drab green scrubs. There was a spray of blood across the front of the surgical gown, and that, combined with the black eye patch, gave her a deadly look. She came to rest only inches from Tach and bent in so close that their noses almost touched.

"Frau Doctor Frankenstein, I presume," said Tach lightly. The militant light did not die from her one good eye.

"What in the *hell* is going on down here?"

"Just another typical day in the charnel house."

Concern replaced the anger. "What's wrong? What happened?" Tach made a weary gesture. Cody whirled on Troll. "Is he all right?"

"Physically. He's got a few acid burns. But she cut him . . . deep," Troll said.

Cody's hands closed on Tach's shoulders. "Talk to me! I get this bulletin over the fucking loudspeaker—this damn hysterical nurse screaming that you're being killed down here."

"Nothing so dramatic." Tach sighed and pushed to his feet. "Just another victim taking the author of her misery to task."

Cody followed his gaze to the now supine joker. "When did she transform?" the woman asked.

"Jumped."

"Christ." A tiny shudder took her tall slender form.

Tach understood. With the advent of the strange new wild card power, the sanctity of one's soul was now in jeopardy. A roaming gang of teenagers had suddenly developed the ability to trade bodies with any individual. And they used the power with the vicious playfulness of the very young— committing acts of brutality, atrocity, and humiliation before jumping back to their own bodies and leaving the victim to deal with the often tragic aftermath of a jumper's spree.

Tach sighed again and swept the back of his hand across his eyes as if the action could somehow banish weariness. "I must now call Mr. Nesbitt and inform him his wife is here— but not the wife he recalls."

"Come to Jokertown and lose yourself," said Cody bitterly.

"It's no wonder we've been virtually abandoned by the nats. They're terrified. Hell, even I'm worried as I walk home at night. How long until some covetous joker decides she'd like *my* body?"

"Hush," cautioned Tachyon.

"I don't care if they hear. It's a dirty little joker secret. Some of them know how to get to these kids, and rather than tell us or the police, they'd rather take care of themselves first."

Tach looked sadly at the collection of protoplasmic nightmares that filled his emergency room. "Can you blame them?"

Cody shuddered, and Tach caught a wisp of memory. Once Cody had come terrifyingly close to jokerdom. And Tach himself carried the wild card, twined in a loving, latent sleep about his genes. At any moment the virus could manifest and turn him into a hideous monster or grant him the blessing of death. He didn't even consider the third, golden option—that he would beat the odds and become one of the lucky few—an ace, blessed with metahuman powers.

"Not so easy to be righteous, is it?" he asked softly, and Cody blushed.

"In our dreams we're all heroes," the woman replied. "I would like to hope I'd be strong, tough it out—"

"And you probably would be. I'm the coward who could not face life as a joker."

"What are you doing tonight?"

"I had a date."

"Cancel it. I'll cook dinner." Tachyon stared at her. Then, surprisingly, the lashes dropped to veil the single eye. Gruffly she added, "Chris is going to a friend's . . . slumber party. I'm enjoying it. By next year, I'm convinced, such innocent pleasures will seem tame, and he'll be looking for girl action."

"Cody, you're babbling. Why?"

"You're the telepath. Figure it out!" And she left with an aggressive click of high heels.

Jay Ackroyd caught him on the steps of the clinic. Ackroyd was a moderately successful private detective who at times annoyed Tachyon worse than fleas and on occasion could actually be useful—due more to his ace power as a teleporter than any real brains was a secret opinion that Tach held. Jay was too glib, and Tach did not think it was a mask for a serious mind.

The minute the thought manifested, Tachyon felt guilty. After all, it was Jay who had saved the alien from an assassin a year and a half ago. The Takisian realized that some of his waspishness was due to Jay's having caught the alien doing a silly little hop-skip step up the stained concrete steps.

"Get lucky last night?"

Tach's frowned deepened. Had he spent the evening with any one of his normal complement of female companions, he might have responded with the obligatory leer and nudge. But this was *Cody*. And though their passionate kissing last night had not lead through the bedroom door, Tach was beginning to nourish passionate hopes. What happened behind *that* bedroom door was no one's business. Tach frowned at the nondescript human in front of him.

"Did you come by just to annoy me, or has my money actually garnered a few results?"

"You think what I do is easy?"

"No, tedious—which is why I do not do it myself. Besides, I'm out of the law enforcement business. I tend to my clinic now, and—"

"—cultivate your garden," concluded Jay, startling Tachyon with his knowledge of Voltaire.

"By the Ideal, you read," said Tach as they stepped through the front doors.

"Yeah, it impresses babes."

Tach nodded a friendly good morning to Mrs. Chicken Foot and crossed to the elevator. As they rode up the four floors to Tach's office, the alien could feel the human's mood sobering as he mentally marshaled the information he had obtained. Tach's good mood drained like water sucked into desert sand. In another, more impatient time, the Takisian would have yanked the knowledge from Jay's mind, but this was something he preferred to delay—forever if possible. Unfortunately an ostrichlike response to Blaise was dangerous.

In the office Jay lounged on the couch. Tachyon stood with his back to the room, gazing out the window at Jokertown laid out before him like a pustular sore on the body of Manhattan. Was it age or depression, or had the vista actually grown shabbier and dirtier over the past twenty-five years?

"It's so ugly," Tachyon murmured.

"You just noticed?" Jay's tone offered no comfort. Tach turned to face him.

"Perhaps I have less stomach for it now."

"Then you better get a barf bag because what I've got to tell you doesn't qualify as pretty." Jay pulled out a notebook, flipped it open, and began to read. His voice had lost much of its joking edge. "Blaise is running with a jumper gang."

The desk chair was a welcome support to legs suddenly gone shaky. Tach longed to clasp his hands, but the plastic monstrosity at the end of his right arm offered no comfort. Instead, his left hand cupped his right elbow, both arms drawn protectively across his aching stomach.

"Ideal . . . now he's far too powerful."

"It gets better. He also has ties to the Shadow Fists. . . ." Tach's head jerked up. Jay didn't miss the reaction. "Got friends there too?" asked Jay dryly. Tach mutely shook his head, waved to Ackroyd to continue. "Look, Tachyon, you haven't got a priest, and if you can't trust your private dick, who the hell can you trust?"

"No one," said Tachyon softly.

Jay watched him for a moment longer, then shrugged and resumed. "While running with the jumpers, your charming grandson has engaged in the usual round of fun—beatings, muggings, robberies, nights on the town courtesy of the victim's credit card." Jay hesitated.

Tach leapt on it, imperious and demanding. "What?"

"Everything seems to point to Blaise being the jumper who took over Ira Greenstein's body, and—"

"I know what happened to him." His tone was shrill. Tach regained control of his voice. "Ira has been my tailor for twenty years. How many other people whom I have patronized are in jeopardy?"

"You know Blaise better than I do."

"No, I only thought I did."

"The alien delinquent has graduated from brutality. He's in the big leagues now—murder. Couple of my sources say he blew away a small-time Shadow Fist soldier named Christian."

"Murder's not new to Blaise. He killed when he was in that revolutionary cell in France."

"No, he *mind-controlled* other people to kill. It's a big step to holding the gun yourself. I personally wouldn't know—I hate the fucking things—but for Blaise it's a turn-on. He kills for fun and kicks, and likes every moment of it. That was the one thing my informants agreed on. That, and that they were terrified of the little bastard."

"Is he . . . is he in Manhattan?" Tach hated himself for the hesitation that made his voice as ragged as a broken saw. It revealed his fear, and he didn't like to admit, even to himself, that he was afraid of his grandson.

"No, I think he's based on the Rox, but he and his gang of delinquents make raids into the city."

"You *think*?"

Jay correctly interpreted the added emphasis on the final word as censure. "Look, you hired me to get information on the kid, not recover him. And while I'm not a coward, I'm also not stupid. People who go to the Rox generally don't come back."

"And if I hired you to bring him back?"

"I'd say no. I'm a private eye, not a one-man commando unit."

For a long time they sat in silence. It was hard for Tachyon to ask the question that was battering impatiently at the back of his teeth. Over the years he had been threatened by enemies far more terrifying than Blaise—the Astronomer, the Swarm, Hartmann. Why, then, was he so afraid? Or did a surfeit of love translate into a greater sense of betrayal and terror when that love died?

"Am I in danger?"

They locked eyes. "I don't know. Given your past history, yeah, you're probably in danger. You imprisoned his father, and killed his guardian, sacrificed his tutor to save your neck. Not to mention dressing him in puce and lace—"

"You also bear some responsibility in this. What about Atlanta, when he was possessed by that creature? He mind-controlled that poor joker, made him tear himself to pieces."

Jay shrugged. "Okay, neither one of us are prime candidates for father of the year. The point is, what he thinks will hurt you most. Maybe he'll just be content to fuck over everyone around you."

Tachyon stood, began to pace. "I can't live with that burden."

"I don't see that you've got any choice."

"There must be some other option."

"I can think of one—deal with Blaise."

Tach's stomach felt as if lead shot had been dropped into it. He shook his head. "I can't deal with him."

"Why not?"

"That would require killing him."

Jay's eyes flicked in reaction to that bald statement.

"Jesus Christ, what is it with you Takisians? You've never heard of psychiatrists?"

"Do you want to capture him for me?"

Jay had the grace to blush. He looked down. "Not particularly."

Tach turned away. "I am wounded, Jay, wounded in ways which can't even be seen. I just want to be left alone."

"That's not an option that's open for you." There was a grimness, a seriousness to the detective's expression that Tachyon had never seen before. It was a little frightening. "There are people who are actors on history. They can't step off the stage no matter how much they might like to. You're one of those people—you poor bastard."

There was no answer to that. Again silence held the room. Tach finally crossed to the bar, and poured out a brandy.

"A little early in the day, isn't it?"

"Don't nag. You have unalterably depressed me, now you must take the consequences."

"Hey, it ain't my problem. You can go to hell anyway it suits you. Just don't try to blame me."

Tach set aside the snifter, untasted. "And what of Mark?"

"No trace. Oh, I know he's somewhere within the environs of greater Manhattan, but I don't know where."

"Why is this so difficult? Mark Meadows is a lovely but totally ineffectual person. How could he evade you this long?"

"He's had some help. The jokers seem to be protecting him, and most important, he doesn't want to be found."

"His protectors must know that we can be trusted."

"Look, if we get the information, how long until the cops have it? Meadows is a wanted fugitive. Don't forget that."

"All this fuss over a child-custody hearing. They've ruined a man for nothing."

"They've ruined him for being an ace. His little girl was just the excuse."

"What lovely times we live in." Tach sighed. "Well, keep looking."

Jay rose. "And Blaise?"

"You've told me what I needed to know. Now it's just a matter of warning my friends and protecting myself."

Jay hesitated at the door. "You won't . . ."

"He is my grandchild. The last of my blood. The only heir I will ever have. I can't . . ." His voice, too, died away to nothing.

"I think you're a fool."

"So you have said before."

Jay left. And Tachyon drained the brandy.

The shrilling of the telephone dimly penetrated the thunder and rush of the shower. Tach heard the answering machine kick in. He continued to shampoo his long red hair as his own familiar voice droned through the message. There was the nasal squeal of the signal, and then Cody's voice.

"I've rented us a room at the Ritz." Sputtering, Tach shut off the flow of water. "There comes a time when you can't hide from sex anymore. Meet me."

Tach just stood as shampoo ran down his forehead, and a sudden rush of testosterone brought his cock to rigid anticipatory attention. The soap hit and burned his eyes. Cursing, he switched the water back on, and quickly rinsed. He hurried but seemed to be scarcely moving. His fingers had become clumsy with surprise and nervous expectation. He picked his finest outfit. He wore it only to Hiram's annual Wild Card Day dinners, but tonight merited such elegance.

As he fingered the soft material, he wondered at her choice for a rendezvous. The hotel seemed rather sterile. But her son, Chris, was a factor at her apartment, and to enter Tachyon's would seem like too much a capitulation for this proud woman.

After dressing, he critically surveyed his reflection in the mirror. Short, yes, by human standards, but very slim. The riot of red curls brushed the shoulders of his coat. The lines about mouth and eyes were too deep for his ninety-one years, but the years on earth had not been kind. The worst flaw was that ugly extrusion on the end of his right arm. He wanted to be able to caress her with all the mastery of a Takisian mentat prince.

The front door bell shrilled. The boy with the flowers. Tach grabbed his wallet, and forced himself not to run.

At the hotel door he gave one final twitch to the gold-tipped lace at his throat, adjusted the roses, and gave one quick peremptory knock with the artificial hand.

"It's open, come in," called Cody.

Tachyon entered. There was a room-service cart at the foot of the bed. Caviar, petits fours, a wedge of camembert cheese, and most important, champagne cooling in a silver bucket.

Cody stepped out of the bathroom. There was something hesitant, almost awkward about her stance. Tach understood. He felt damnably nervous and awkward himself. He found himself focusing on the black negligee she was wearing. It revealed her charms in startling ways, and Tach was a little surprised that she would wear such a sexy gown. But then, what did he really know of this woman and her fantasies? He had always seen her as the perfectly cool, incredibly professional surgeon. Perhaps she liked to be a houri in the bedroom to offset that rather severe image.

"I want you to promise me something."

"Anything," said Tach as he proffered the roses. They were like splashes of blood against the black of her gown.

"Don't read my mind."

Tach was puzzled, a thread of suspicion curled in his mind. But his cock was demanding instant attention, and if he refused he might never bed this woman. "All right," he said slowly. "But might I know why?"

"I need to feel . . . safe."

He laughed to off-set the sense of hurt and the taint of disappointment that had wormed its way into his libidinous pleasure. "That's funny, I always feel safer when I can join— completely—with my lovers."

"Well, do this for me. Promise me."

"I promise."

She seemed vastly relieved because she suddenly smiled. The bouquet of roses went sailing into a chair. "Do you want to waste time with all this romantic bullshit?"

"Did you have a better suggestion?" He felt like he was enunciating past a mouthful of cotton balls.

"Uh-huh." She walked to him, pushed his jacket off his shoulders.

As he wriggled and jerked to free himself from the confining material, Tach leaned forward and kissed the hollow at the base of her throat. He kicked off his shoes, and suddenly got a lot shorter without the benefit of the two-inch heel. His eyes were now exactly at breast level. It was an attractive vista. Her hands were at his belt now, opening the waist band of his pants, pulling them down. They snagged at his ankles, and he tottered trying to regain his balance. She chuckled far back in her throat and gave him a push that toppled him onto the bed. Reached down and grabbed his pants, pulling them off as if she were shucking an ear of corn.

His jockey shorts came with the pants, and he felt rather vulnerable and silly in his stockings and shirt, his erection rampant among the coppery hairs of his brush.

Cody tumbled onto the bed with him, and pulled him over on top of her. Tangling her hands in his hair, she pulled his face down and kissed him hard. Her tongue slipped between his teeth, and it was that clumsy adolescent sucking, coupled with the faint *snick* of a door opening, that alerted him to the danger. He tried to roll away, but the false Cody's fingers twined and clutched at his hair like thorn branches.

A quick mentatic check revealed that there were *seven* opponents in the room, counting the woman in the bed, and a terrifying ice wall of mental shielding that could only be Blaise. Tach's mind control lashed out. The false Cody dropped into slumber and one other assailant. The Takisian was then busy fending off a mind attack from Blaise. A heavy weight landed between his shoulder blades, knocking the wind from his body. He sucked desperately for air like a failing pump billow, then tried to exhale violently as the chloroform-soaked cloth covered his mouth and nose. It was hopeless. The fumes from the drug ate at his control, at consciousness. Tachyon managed to roll onto his back. His finally vision was of Blaise pouring out a glass of champagne and raising it in an ironic salute.

When the first jolt of electricity arced through his testicles, Tachyon thought he would die.

He had been climbing slowly toward consciousness, dimly aware of a musty, moldy odor, a too-full bladder, the dull headache that was the legacy of a drug-induced sleep, then . . .

PAIN! A scream ripped like acid from his throat, and Tach's body flopped like a dying fish on the decrepit old mattress upon which he rested. A crushing vise closed about his mind. Tachyon tasted Blaise. Panicked. Fought back with everything he had. The pressure retreated. He could focus now—nightmare vision—Blaise wielding a cattle prod. This couldn't be real, a dreaaaam. Another blast of soul-searing agony. Nobody could hurt this much and stay alive. The jaws were back. Teeth penetrating the perfect crystal sphere of his mental shields.

NO!

Pain, the shattering of self, a cacophony of jabbering, excited, hungry, needy, angry minds. And then one mind.

One mind alone. A familiar, terrifying mind holding him like a bug in amber.

Hello, Grand-père, crooned Blaise.

Tachyon beat feebly at the awesomely powerful mind control that gripped him.

"Now," said Blaise.

Now what was all he thought before the world went mad.

For one wild distorting moment Tachyon was staring down at his *own* body. Another shift and tilt, and a second of wrenching nausea. Tachyon fought for control, fought to stay conscious. Succeeded. Barely.

He realized he was sitting on the stained linoleum floor. There were hands beneath his arms, yanking him to his feet. Tach stared up into Blaise's exulting face. Lips skinning back in a snarl, the Takisian psi lord tried to gather his power and found—*nothing*.

Blaise laughed in great gusting whoops. It was a maddening, terrifying sound.

"Oh, Grandpa." Tachyon was swung up into the teenager's arms. "You're going to wish I had only killed you."

Fury exploded behind his eyes, and Tach swung hard at Blaise's face. Connected, and then froze in shock: *There was a hand at the end of his right arm!* Chipped pink polish created an odd piebald effect on the nails. Bile clawed at the back of his throat.

Blaise flung him down on the mattress. Tachyon fought to remain conscious. The very deepest part of himself. That which was *Tachyon* ran screaming and yammering about his head. Searching for what had been lost. Found only silence, darkness. *My power*, he wailed.

A tearing sound, and cold air struck Tach's chest. Rough hands gripped the waistband of the blue jeans, broke the button, ripped open the zipper. Blaise's nails gouged into his legs as the boy yanked down the pants. They snagged. Muttering oaths, Blaise crawled backward and started to pull off the tennis shoes. It was involuntary. Later he would regret it, but Tach kicked Blaise square in the face.

Blood from Blaise's broken nose spattered on Tachyon's bare legs, on the filthy tiles. Blaise twined a hand in Tach's hair, pulled him up, and slugged him in the face. Tachyon tried to defend, to respond, but he felt weak, disoriented. He knew he had been jumped, one part of him even acknowledged to *what*, but acceptance was impossible.

This isn't happening. This can't be happening. Not to me.

He hurt too much to keep fighting. Tears and blood made a slimy mixture on his face. Blaise stood up. He seemed a colossus towering spraddle-legged over Tach's prone body. Slowly he unzipped, pulled out his rigid penis. Tachyon thought he had endured the worst this or any world had to offer. He was wrong.

Muscles shivered with strain, but still she held him at bay. He had not yet managed to violate her. Blaise was muttering curses as he gripped the soft flesh around her knees and tried to yank her legs apart. She tried to claw his eyes, but he was too quick for her.

Suddenly Blaise pulled her upright by the hair and drove two punishing blows into her gut. Air gusted out like a deflating balloon, and Tachyon wretched. Her legs went flaccid.

"Hold him," ordered Blaise.

Two boys jumped to obey. One on each leg, they played make-a-wish with the shuddering pain-racked body.

With a coarse grin, Blaise raked his nails across the breasts, cruelly twisted the nipples. Involuntarily, Tach yelped. Gentle now, the fingers trailed across the waist, the slight curve of the belly, brushed the mons.

Tach screamed, and Blaise was on him like a wild animal. Teeth tore at his lips and breasts. Methodically Blaise pounded at Tachyon, driving deeper into her.

The room was echoing with his screams. With the cheers of the onlookers.

"NO, NO! STOP IT! *STOP IT!*" The girl in his body screaming her protest.

How odd, Tachyon thought as consciousness slipped from her. *I hadn't realized my voice was so deep.*

The Temptation of Hieronymus Bloat

III

There are times when life is good. . . .

Sometimes the pleasure even comes from odd sources. I've had only a few conversations with Prime. He isn't on the Rox much; when he is, he tends to avoid me. It's because he knows that I can see through his iceman facade. It's because he knows that I see all the deepening cracks behind the smooth cold exterior. He knows that I see the obsession that torments him and titillates him all at the same time.

All the pressure, pent up for years and years and years behind his emotionless wall (not as good a wall as mine), and David—poor David—cracked it with just his presence. David's death was a jackhammer blow. Walls: I have mine; Prime has his; and his is crumbling as the Berlin Wall crumbled last month.

Or. . . I've thought of it another way, too, sometimes. Prime, if you watch him, is like a dormant volcano all covered with snow, but steaming through fumaroles that hint at the turmoil underneath.

That's a better image, overall. And I wonder when he's going to explode. I worry, too, because Prime holds Blaise in check. Without Prime . . .

I was about to witness the unveiling when Kafka came rattling into the lobby, all excited. He hardly glanced at the huge draped package set before me. All out of breath, he just asked where it came from.

73

"It's a present from Nelson Dixon."

Latham—Prime—stood next to the drapes. He sniffed, still playing iceman. Blaise wasn't there, though Molly Bolt and K.C. were. The laughter of my jokers drifted down from the balcony and around the lobby. Peanut beat his one arm against my side, guffawing. I beamed down at the dimwitted joker in affection. Shroud, Marigold, Vomitus, Video, Elmo— maybe a half a hundred all told in the lobby area, and all their thoughts crowded into my mind.

No wonder I'm so big. I have to hold so many people.

Kafka looked as bewildered as a roach can look. He repeated what I'd just said, obviously confused.

"Well, Dixon *signed* the check," I told him. "Nice of him, wasn't it?"

Kafka blinked several times. "Well, I don't know where he got it, and I certainly don't have the foggiest notion of why it works, but it's humming right along. I hooked it up."

Sometimes even mind readers are confused. Belatedly, I looked at the images in Kafka's head and realized we weren't talking about the same thing at all. *He* was talking about a generator. I told him that I was glad he'd finally managed to get his hands on one to bring over to the Rox.

Kafka just shook his head (well, his whole body, actually). "You didn't buy it, Governor?" More confusion radiated from the joker. He looked at me, at Prime, at Peanut and the rest of the jokers gathered around. "It was sitting there in the subbasement, and it wasn't there two days ago. It doesn't look like any generator I've ever seen."

The picture in his mind looked exactly like a generator to me, but Kafka sighed. "I have *no* idea what's fueling it or *why* it's running, either," he continued. "I checked out the readings, and it's pumping out the amps, nice and steady. I ran the west wing's circuits to it. We have lights, heat, and power..."

About then, he stopped, noticing Prime's present to me for the first time.

Prime waved his hand toward the drapes. "A little gift to the governor from us," Prime told him. "The first royalty statement. Bloat's suggestion to myself and the other jumpers has worked out well." He yanked at the covering, and dirty canvas rippled to the floor. All the jokers gasped.

It was beautiful. More stunning than any of the plates I'd seen in the high school art history texts or in the poster I used to have taped to my bedroom wall. The painting—the triptych—stood five feet high, maybe four wide, in an ornate wooden case. On the front were scenes of the Taking of Christ and the Carrying of the Cross, but what I really wanted to see was on the interior panels. I gestured to Peanut and Elmo, telling them to hurry up and open it.

They opened the outer panels, revealing the brilliant fantastic landscape inside. Around the room I felt waves of admiration and surprise rippling out.

"*The Temptation of St. Anthony*. Hieronymous Bosch," I said for the benefit of those who didn't know the work. "Previously at the Museu Nacional de Arte Antiga in Lisbon and now appearing exclusively in the Rox."

I chuckled, loud and long. It was indeed glorious. Bosch didn't know it, but he was painting the post-wild card world before it ever existed. I've often wondered if it wasn't a flash of prescience—no one else in his time was doing anything like this. I can imagine it as my Rox. It would be a wondrous place, a glorious vision.

You know Bosch, don't you? In his head grotesqueries abounded; his brush gave forth a torrent of human forms misshapen, altered, and tormented; his imagination overflowed with all the demons of hell and the icons of a superstitious age—at least that's what my teachers said.

In the midst of a twisted medieval landscape, the characters of Bosch were playing. Jokers. They cavorted everywhere you looked. The triptych is a celebration of jokerhood: fox-headed demons, a merman riding a flying fish, another fish crawling down a road with a castle on its back, a skating penguin, a stag-headed man in a red cloak, another with grass growing on his back, a half-naked woman with a lizard's tail, a toad-man, a monkey-man—hundreds of them, roiling in a dark, stormy world.

Like my Rox. Very much like the Rox I see in my dreams.

The Rox I might build if they'd let me.

Kafka was staring at the Bosch like all the others, captivated. The joker we call Headlamp had turned bright, bright eyes on the triptych, so that it stood bathed in crystalline illumination. Jokers cavorted in egg tempura brilliance.

I laughed gaily. "We've found the way to make the Combine pay us back." The jumpers laughed at that, hearing

K.C.'s phrase for the nat authorities. "They'll pay quite well to be allowed to stay in their own little bodies. Quite well."

For that instant, looking at the *Temptation*, I forgot the tragedies in New York. I forgot the scorn of Prime and Blaise toward the jokers and my dreams. I forgot the nagging torture of all the jokers within my wall.

I forgot it all.

"The Rox has benefactors now. People in high places. People with money. Lots of money. No one will ever be hungry here again."

I laughed again. The voices of the jokers laughed with me. The jokers in Bosch's painting danced in sympathy.

There are times when life is shit. . . .

The day after Prime delivered the Bosch, Blaise did something I still can't believe even he would do.

In one horrible stroke, he has taken Kelly away and wounded the one man who has always helped the jokers. It isn't *fair* what Blaise has done to Kelly. It isn't fair to her *or* to Tachyon. I listened as Blaise brought Tachyon to the Rox. I listened, and I couldn't do anything, for most of the jokers here no longer trust Tachyon, not since he betrayed Hartmann. Still . . .

It makes my stomach—*all* of it—turn to listen to Tachy's pain. Worse, I can't shut it off like I can someone else's voice. I felt it as soon as they pierced the wall. Maybe it's because of my infatuation with Kelly, maybe it's some remnant of Tachyon's telepathy, but we are linked.

He's so loud in my head. He hurts so much. . . .

Burning Sky, please help me. . . .

She hurts so much. She makes *me* hurt.

I was outraged, even though several of the jokers laughed when they heard about it. I sent Peanut to Blaise with a message that I wanted Tachyon returned to his own body. I told him that I understood Blaise had his own reasons for wanting to hurt Tachyon but that the doctor had done more to help the jokers than anyone else. For that, I said, I wanted Tachyon released now. Blaise had had his vengeance; he'd proved how strong he was. Now let Tachyon go.

I'm the governor, right?

Blaise sent Peanut back with Polaroids: Kelly's—Tachyon's—body, naked and spread-eagled, her eyes wide, haunted and hopelessly defiant. Tachyon exposed helplessly, the picture snapped between her spread legs. Tachyon covered by Blaise's body. Tachyon afterward, weeping.

I . . . well, I didn't do anything.

I mean, what *could* I do, really? Was I going to send a squad of armed jokers to the jumper side of the Rox? I could've done that, but Blaise'd just mind-control them, or his followers would jump them. It'd start a civil war here. There are things I have to consider, after all. It's not just a simple thing.

The jumpers bring in money, they bring in the rapture and other drugs that half the jokers here are addicted to. The fear of them is at least part of what keeps the authorities away. I need the jumpers as much as they need me.

There are things I can't do. Really. I just . . . I just wish I didn't feel so bad about it. So dirty. I keep hearing myself, and I sound like fucking George Bush making excuses about how all his promises about 'no new exotic laws' have had to be forgotten.

Do you understand?

. . . *please help me* . . . I still hear her, and she's calling for me.

It hurts. It really does.

I had Peanut burn the pictures, but I kept seeing them.

Kelly, poor Kelly. *My* Kelly. This isn't the way a romance is supposed to go.

Lovers

II

A lifetime ago, Tachyon had been thrown into the Tombs. He had thought he knew despair when the heavy barred door slammed shut behind him. Now he realized that had been only a pale shadow of true wretchedness.

His head pounded in time to the beating of his heart. Breath seemed to rip like shattered glass across a throat made raw from screaming. Blood still trickled sluggishly from his vagina, and he wondered what internal damage had been done.

The incongruity struck him. One should not use male pronouns with female anatomy. *But he was a man. Wasn't he?* He was suddenly aware of a painfully full bladder. He reached down, touched blood matted hair, and *smoothness*. No, he was no longer a man.

It seemed the final straw. As she stared with dry, aching eyes into the darkness, Tach longed to cry, to bathe her burning eyes with warm tears, to release the anguish filling her chest like crushing weight. But she could not cry. It was as if her emotions had been carefully gathered, and packed away in some deep and secret part of her soul. She was suffering, but she couldn't express the pain.

The darkness seemed to have substance. Hands stretched out before her, Tach made a circuit of her prison. Six feet by five feet. Bare concrete underfoot. Brick walls that oozed damp like a sweating fat man. As she made her journey of discovery, her bruised toes tried to cringe from any possible

78

obstacles. They needn't have worried. The room was utterly, totally barren.

Tachyon was discovering that it was much harder to hold urine in a female body than in a male one. She found the door again. Beating desperately on it with her palms, she gathered a breath and shouted, "Hey! Help! Listen to me! HEY!"

There was no response.

As she squatted in a corner and relieved herself, Tachyon realized that in addition to being the most desperate moment of her life, it had become the most humiliating.

Eventually she slept. What woke her was a raging thirst, the clammy cold, and the sound of the door closing.

"No! Wait! Don't go! Don't leave me!"

Her toes struck something. There was a flat tinny sound as metal skittered across the floor. The aroma of oatmeal wafted to her nostrils. Shaking with hunger, Tach dropped her knees and groped blindly for the scattered silverware.

Minutes passed without success. Finally, with a faint *mew* of fury, Tach gathered the bowl in her hands and lapped down the cereal like a starving dog. It dented but did not banish the hunger. With her index finger, Tachyon scraped the sides and bottom of the bowl and sucked off the last bits of oatmeal.

A little more reconnaissance, and she discovered a pitcher of water and an empty bucket. She instantly availed herself of the bucket.

She had lost track of time. One day, three days, a week? How much time had elapsed in the world of light, in a world where people didn't go hungry or live with the stench of bowel movements or strain for even the faintest sound of another living creature?

At first Tachyon had been terrified that Blaise had taken Cody too. After all, the boy had been fascinated with the woman. It was his jealousy of Tach and Cody's relationship that had led him to run away in the first place and set him on this course of vengeance. But Blaise was as unsubtle as he was unstable. If he had held Cody, he would have tortured her before Tachyon's eyes. Thank the Ideal that he did not yet understand the power of suggestion, the agony of *not knowing*.

At least he's transferred his obsession with Cody to me, thought Tach. *Now she will be safe.* And though the thought comforted, Tachyon still had to clamp her teeth together to stop their chattering.

And Cody would be able to identify Blaise as Tachyon's kidnapper. The brief comfort afforded by that thought took a sudden plummet. She was on the Rox—and nobody sane came to the Rox.

Then the final crushing realization: Blaise could not allow Cody to reveal her jump and Tachyon's kidnapping. Had he killed her? Or simply removed that section of her memory with his mind powers? Fear gripped her, for while Blaise possessed the most awesome mind-control power Tach had ever faced, it was like a bludgeon. There was no mentatic subtlety. His clumsy mental surgery might have destroyed Cody's mind. Desperately, Tach prowled the darkness, but it could not match the stygian blackness within her mind and soul. From their first meeting, he and Cody had formed a telepathic bond that Tachyon had shared with only one other human woman. Surely that power would tell her if Cody lived. But the power was gone. So the darkness was filled only with silence and her grim fears.

Six times they had fed her. Did that mean three days had elapsed? Impossible to tell. At times her hunger was so great that it felt as if a small animal were chewing at the walls of her stomach. So perhaps they weren't feeding her every day. It was a blow to discover that her method of telling time proved to be as useless as everything else she had tried. This final loss of control over even the most meager part of her environment had her blinking back tears.

More time elapsed, and eventually the silence became too much. One day she found herself talking to herself. Silverware was the catalyst for this latest bizarre behavior. She had been hoarding it, and she now possessed three spoons and a fork, which she obsessively counted and rearranged a hundred times in the hours between each sleep period.

"In an adventure novel or a cheap spy movie, our hero always constructs some devilishly clever device from ordinary household utensils," said Tach aloud. "But our hero's been reduced to a heroine, and she doesn't have a clue." The laughter hit the low ceiling and fell dully back on her ears.

Tach clapped a hand over her mouth to still the hysterical sound. Exhaustion dragged at her limbs.

Forcing herself to her feet, she made six quick circuits of her prison, and in time to her steps she recited: "A constant and overwhelming desire for sleep. Unspecified attacks of anxiety. Mind-numbing exhaustion. Bouts of hysterical laughter. All classic symptoms of acute depression." She paused for a moment, conceding that this rambling oration was also abnormal behavior. Then, with a shrug, she shouted at the invisible ceiling. "But you won't drive me crazy, Blaise. You may imprison me, starve me, destroy my eyesight with constant darkness, but you will *not* drive me crazy."

It helped to say the words. But then she went to sleep.

Somber reflection in the cold blackness of morning left Tachyon with the decided feeling that she had to do *something*. Waiting for rescue hadn't worked. She had to find a way to communicate, to inform *someone* of her plight. There was only one way she knew, and that would require an intimate study of the fleshy prison in which she now found herself.

For several minutes she paced the length of the cellar. She hated this body as much as she hated the damp concrete walls of the basement. But now she *had* to inspect the primitive mind. Search for the connections that might be trained and honed in mentatics.

It could be done. Long ago, she had trained Blythe to construct bulky unsophisticated mindshields. Granted, Blythe had been a wild card, but her talent had not affected the physical linkages of her brain, and she had learned. So this body could learn.

"*Will* learn," Tach growled.

She settled herself comfortably on the floor. Closed her eyes, began with the feet, tried to make her cramped muscles relax. And behind the darkness of her lids her mind began to whirl like a frenzied animal chasing its own tail: *What have they done to my clinic? Why is no one helping me?*

Furious at her own lack of discipline, Tach sat up abruptly. "If you train this body," she said aloud, "the possibility exists that you can communicate with Sascha, or Fortunato, or some other as yet undetermined wild card telepath. You can escape and come back with many, many powerful aces, recover your body, and level this miserable island."

She spent a few moments picturing the scene. The images of death and destruction had a very salubrious effect. As Tach lay back down, she decided that despite forty-five years on earth, she was still a Takisian to her fingertips.

She was walking in the mountains. The mountains looked Takisian, but the sky was earth's. A flying fish skimmed the tops of the dark pines like an intricate Chinese kite, but for some reason none of this was confusing.

"Does this count as a meeting?" a young man's voice was asking.

Tach searched for the source but saw nothing but grass, flowers, trees, and that damn fish. She did notice that a castle had suddenly appeared on one of the hilltops.

"I suppose so," Tachyon replied cautiously.

"Good. I've always wanted to meet you, but I wanted you away from that place. Do you like it here?"

"It's very. . . lovely."

She had reached an energetic stream. The water was rushing, chuckling over the rocks and parting around a gigantic gray boulder that squatted in the center of the streambed. Tach couldn't resist. Lifting her long skirts, she leapt lightly from rock to rock, feeling the chill touch of the spume of her face and hands. Quickly she clambered up the side of the granite behemoth. The sound of the water was very loud, and mist from the rapids occasionally kissed Tachyon's face.

"So, who are you?" asked Tachyon with studied casualness as she picked gray-green lichen from a crevice in the rock.

"A friend."

"I have none in this place. All my friends live in another world, another time."

"I'm here. I'm real."

"You're a voice on the wind. The whisper of a cloud. The murmur of water. A dream construct of a maddened mind." She shivered and hugged herself. The long sleeves of sea-green gauze snagged on the rough surface of the boulder. "Give me back my world. I can't live in madness, no matter how pleasant."

And suddenly she was back in the cell. The darkness

pressing in on all sides, the concrete cold and rough against her bare bottom.

"Yes," she said on a sob. "*This* is real."

"Oh, Princess, I'm sorry. I'll help. I swear to you, I'll help."

She woke with the passion of that promise still echoing in her mind.

"Well, *friend,* not to sound cynical, but I'll believe it when I see it," she called aloud.

The sound was wrong. The food trap rattled like pebbles in a can as the bolt was pulled back. This sounded like a road being graded. The light struck her eyes like a lance, and tears began to stream down her face. Squinting desperately, she made out a manlike shape against the glare. And then the smell struck. Baked chicken. Saliva filled her mouth like a geyser springing to life.

Tach clambered to her feet, her nakedness forgotten, consumed by the lure of *food.* Now that she was closer, she recognized the manshape. And *manshape* was the only way the joker Peanut could be categorized. His skin was hardened, puckered like the shell of a peanut, hence the nickname. His eyes were almost lost in the scaly mask of his face. One arm was missing, and Tach noticed that he had a blouse and a pair of jeans flung over the stump. Peanut struggled to bend, to set down the tray. Tach leapt to his aid lest the joker spill that wondrous banquet.

"Thanks, Doc." His voice was a heavy rasp forced past lips that could scarcely move. "I brung you some food, and some clothes, but you gotta eat fast so *he* don't find out."

Tachyon didn't miss the subtle emphasis nor the way the joker's eyes flickered nervously back over his shoulder. So everyone feared Blaise. It was not just spinelessness on her part.

"Peanut, let me out," said Tach as she pulled on the jeans.

A stiff headshake. "No, we gotta be careful. *He* said we was walkin' a tightrope." Different emphasis this time. The timbre of respect.

"Who? Who is this person?" She completed the final button on the blouse and felt confidence return like the growth of a second skin. It was amazing what lack of clothes did to one's morale.

Peanut's eyes were shifting nervously. "I've said too much already. Eat, Doc, eat. And he'll help. He's helpin' all of us."

Tach squatted and stripped the meat from the chicken with graceful slender fingers. She ate in quick little gulps but was careful to rate her intake. Too much too fast would send the stomach into a spasm, and it would be criminal to vomit up this bounty. There was a tomato on the plate. She bit into it, the juice oozing over her chin. Replete for the first time in weeks, she sighed and rocked back on her heels.

She seemed relaxed. In reality, she was measuring the distance between Peanut and the door. Testing the strength of her muscles. Suddenly she sprang and darted for the exit. But the weeks of imprisonment had taken their toll. Clumsily she staggered forward on trembling legs. The horny surface of Peanut's arm connected painfully with her face, flinging her backward.

He was stuttering with shame. "I'm sorry. I'm sorry, Doc, but you made me. I gotta think of the others." Peanut swept up the tray and fled. The slamming of the door had a certain grim finality. Tachyon began to weep.

Wait, wait, my love.

It was telepathy, but telepathy like a half-seen shadow in the darkness, a firefly's path observed from the corner of an eye, the sigh of music blown on the wind. She reached for that elusive telepathic sense with both hands.

"Help me!" she screamed aloud.

I will not fail you.

The contact was broken, but the sincerity of that promise warmed Tachyon with the comfort of an embrace. *Someone cared.*

With dawning wonder, she stroked the material of the blouse. *Silk.* To what care this mysterious benefactor had gone.

"Thank you. Thank you!" she whispered into the darkness.

His eyes turned down at the corners when he smiled. It gave him a crafty catlike look, and it always made Tisianne laugh when she saw it. When Shaklan got that look, it meant work would be put aside and some pleasurable outing was forthcoming.

"Papa, where are we going?"

"Ice-sailing."

"But it's past my bedtime, and I'm hungry . . . and cold."

"What you'll see is worth more than sleep."

His arms were clasped about his father's neck, and the fur and lace at the older man's throat tickled Tis's nose. He sneezed. The sound blended with the crack of boot heels on the marble floor.

The aurora borealis was dancing like a shaken curtain of jewels across the star-strewn blackness of the night sky. The cold was intense, and each breath hurt like a rake of claws across the lungs. The glacier that crowned the peak of Da'shalan was cracking and groaning. The crunch of snow beneath booted feet, an occasional muffled cough from the bodyguards. Tis kept his eyes closed, his face buried against his father's neck. Shaklan smelled of ambergis and musk and the sharp pungent scent of gunpowder.

Glittering like a mirror, the lake threw back the colors of the borealis. A ice-sailor skimmed across the surface of the frozen water. It was accompanied by a delicate ringing of bells. It heeled over and skidded to a stop with a hiss. Ice fragments stung Tis's face. He licked his lips and tasted the sharp taste of mountain water as the ice melted in the heat of his mouth.

They were aboard, and the wind was stinging his cheeks as the ice-sailor swept across the lake.

"Take the tiller, Tis."

"I can't, Papa. The wind . . . it's too cold."

A man stepped forward. The borealis formed a halo behind his dark head. A cloak of white and silver lay across his arm. The texture of the fur was so delicate, the tips sparkling in the starlight, that it seemed as if it had been formed of snow. He bowed.

"Ma'am." His tone was so reverential, deepened in the way a man had when he was indicating to a woman that he found her beautiful. Tachyon was disoriented. The little boy looked in confusion to his father.

Shaklan smiled, nodded. "The Outcast will care for you now."

Tachyon looked back to this stranger, and disorientation birthed a different and more familiar emotion for a Takisian—suspicion. The man's coloring was all wrong. Black hair? Tach had never seen the color except as a dyed affectation among the House Alaa until he/she had come to earth. And his clothes. Plain brown leather—no style at all. And the final proof that this interloper in her dream was no Takisian—the name. A Takisian of the psi-lord class wore his or her moniker with more than pride. It was a shout, a scream for attention. A thousand, five, ten thousand years of careful breeding was represented in a name. Can you match it? Can you equal this pedigree? Of course you can't. I'm matchless, peerless. I am Tisianne brant T'sara sek Halima—he could continue in this vein for nearly an hour. But she didn't have the time. Danger had entered his haven of sleep.

Tach backed up, until she was brought up short by his father's knees. "No, Papa, don't leave me." It was a frenzied whisper.

Shaklan chuckled, shook his head, then bent over Tachyon's hands. The strands of his golden hair caught the light and seemed to glitter like spun wire. Tach pressed her mouth against Shaklan's ear and continued to plead. But the words seemed to be reduced to mere puffs of air, and Shaklan's hair caught in the cracks of Tachyon's lips.

"You will be as safe in the Outcast's hands as you are in mine."

Shaklan placed a quick kiss in the palm of each hand, then folded Tach's hands together as if the child were holding and protecting the kisses. It was a beloved ritual, and Tach smiled mistily up at his father, the fear forgotten. Shaklan led Tachyon close to the Outcast.

The man placed the cloak gently about her shoulders. Somewhere in this confusing interchange Tach's sex had gotten very confused again. The long white-blond hair mingled with the fur. Tach frowned. Even her hair seemed to have developed tiny diamond lights. It reminded her of the illustrations in the more flamboyant, romantic Japanese comic books Blaise had been wont to leave strewn about the apartment.

"This is silly. Have my eyes been invaded by stars as well?"

The question seemed to rattle the Outcast. Fingertips lightly touched the brim of his black cloth hat, fluttered to the hilt of the rapier hung on the leather belt with the air of a man trying to reassure himself that he had not forgotten his trousers.

"Princess, I'm the whisper of a cloud, a voice on the wind."

"You!" Involuntarily, her hands closed on the soft leather of his jerkin. "Help me."

"Soon."

The Outcast leaned in, his lips just brushing the back of her hand when there came a raucous scream of laughter. They jerked apart, and Tach stared in confusion at a penguin with ironic human eyes wearing ice skates, gliding along with the skimmer.

The crash of the door being thrown back brought her awake. Blaise had returned. The glare of the flashlights left Tachyon blinking like a mole as the light pulled tears from her sensitive eyes.

"Grandfather. I should have come—" He broke off abruptly, a thunderous frown wrinkling his forehead. "Hey! Where did you get the fucking clothes?"

"I went to Saks for them. What do you think? They were shoved through the door along with my slops."

"I see I've been away too long. People are getting soft with you. But I'm back now, and you'll be pleased to hear I've wrecked the clinic. You're really disappointing a lot of people over in Jokertown."

Each word seemed to strike like a splash of acid. Tach blinked frantically, trying to focus. Eventually she succeeded and flew at Blaise like a fighting cock. "You monster. You evil, parentless bastard! What have you done to my people?"

Blaise knocked her down easily, then blew a kiss at Tachyon. "You're beautiful when you're angry."

The five youths accompanying Blaise laughed. They were all drunk, and they gusted whiskey-scented remarks (outstanding only in their crudity and banality) back and forth between them like men playing shuttlecock.

The rasp of the zipper on Blaise's slacks cut through the babble and banter. "Get him out of her clothes," said Blaise, hopelessly tangling his pronouns.

Even as terror closed her throat, Tachyon noticed that Blaise's voice had deepened. He was becoming a man. Apparently he was again determined to prove to Tachyon just how much of a man. "Blaise, don't do this. This is the action of an animal. How can you assault a woman in this way? How can you touch *me*," Tach pleaded.

The young men were advancing. Tach backed away from them. A step in time to each desperate word. The wall arrived with startling suddenness. There was no place left to run.

They grabbed her and ripped the clothes off her. Then she was down, her legs wrenched open. There was a grinding ache in her hips, and the concrete was cold beneath her bare buttocks.

Blaise was undressing with elaborate flourishes. He handed his sweater, shirt, and slacks to another young man, who folded them with almost reverential care. Tach craned to see, as if facing the horror that approached were preferable. Blaise's cock was rearing rampant from his red brush.

Tach's head hit the concrete with a sharp crack as she began to struggle wildly. She had thought she could lie back and take it. She was wrong. Takisian upbringing went too deep. This was rape. A crime virtually unknown on her world. An act so heinous that it was viewed as a form of insanity.

A last inane little thought passed through her head as Blaise lowered himself slowly onto her cringing body: *We will kill a woman without compunction. But the Ideal forbid we should rape her. Which society is more insane? Human or Takisian?*

It went on and on. Blaise was deliberately withholding his orgasm. Battering at her. Alternating the punishing assault with nibbling little kisses to her breasts, lips, and ears. Somewhere during the ordeal Tachyon began to plead. "Please, Blaise, please."

"What's the matter, Grandpa?" Blaise crooned softly in her ear.

"Don't hurt me anymore. Give me back my body. Let me go."

"You're still too proud, Granddaddy. You're still giving orders, even when you say please. Ask nicely, Granddad. Beg."

Blaise pulled out of her, and stood. "Let him up."

The boys released her.

"Now kneel to me, Grandpa, and beg."

Tach got to her knees. She was staring down at Blaise's bare feet. There was dirt beneath the large toenails. It sickened her in some perverse and bizarre way. And she realized that no self-abasement would soothe or satisfy the demon creature before her. She sprang to her feet and spit in Blaise's face. There was a gasp like a sighing wind from the watching teens. Numbly, Blaise reached up and wiped away the spittle. Studied his fingers. His face was blank, expressionless. Then suddenly it twisted into a hideous grimace, and he backhanded Tachyon. She flew across the room, and came up hard against the far wall.

Blaise was on her. This time, as he drove into her, beat her unmercifully about the face and head. His ejaculation when it came was like a hot tide in her abused body. Blaise gave her one final cuff, but the sexual release seemed to have spent his fury. Without a backward glance, the boy stood up and dressed, and he and his entourage left the cell.

For a long time Tachyon just lay on the floor.

The Temptation of
Hieronymous Bloat

IV

Two weeks later, and I *have* tried to get her out. I knew it wouldn't do any good to talk to Blaise, so I didn't. But I knew Blaise's thoughts. I knew that he had a grudging respect for Prime, even possessed a fear of the man who could create a jumper and couldn't be jumped himself, and so I tried that way.

I had to. It was bad enough that I had to hear Tachyon's mindvoice. But now. . . now she is in all my dreams too. I have them every night. She waits for me in my sleep, patiently.

It hurts. It makes me want to take Blaise and throttle the bastard.

I did try. Really. I talked to Prime—Latham.

Latham folded his hands on the new pair of Dockers he was wearing. Zelda made muscle-magazine poses behind him. He waited, filling his mind with old contracts and legal briefs, so that I had a difficult time knowing what he was really thinking. "I'm a busy man, Governor, and I really can't stay here very long," he said. "What is it you want?"

"I want your assistance," I told him. "Blaise has done something stupid and dangerous. I assume you know what I'm talking about, or do I have to draw you a picture of a certain red-haired alien who has had an involuntary sex-change operation?" I grinned down at him. "I used to be able to draw pretty well. I *could* have drawn a picture."

Latham only blinked. The dense contract language in his mind parted just long enough for him to speak—he really was very good at hiding his thoughts. "What Blaise does is his own business, not mine," he said.

He gave me a smile that belonged on a codfish. The events of the last month had taken their toll on Latham, but he still had the cold act down well, if a little cracked around the edges.

"Kidnapping Tachyon was dumb," I continued. "Even if Blaise hadn't brought his grandfather here, I would've said that. I supposed Blaise gets the stupidity naturally. Tachyon's certainly done some idiotic things himself—backing out on Hartmann comes to mind—but overall, we jokers owe Tachyon a hell of a lot. I don't want him hurt."

Zelda just snorted. "Why," Latham asked, "should I do anything at all?"

"Because," I said, a little bewildered that he could even *ask*, "a man like Tachyon doesn't deserve what Blaise is doing to him." That seemed clear enough to me.

Latham just pursed his lips and nodded. He sniffed, delicately. "Sympathy," he said at last, "is more foolish than revenge as a motive for doing something." He waited. "In my opinion."

I gave him all the rest then. "Look, you don't have to do it out of common decency if that offends you. Do it because Blaise has made the situation for the jokers a hundred times worse. You've heard the news reports. Bush has told Congress he'll consider a revival of the exotic laws if they'll put the legislation on his desk. The courts are playing hardball with any joker accused of any crime. Two states have already passed bills for mandatory sterilization of wild card carriers. The editorials in the papers are full of hatred and venom. Jokertown is a police state, and Koch's making noises about 'no more tolerance of scofflaws and squatters who take over public property'—he always did have a way with words. The jumpers have the entire city paranoid and armed. Kelly isn't going to be able to masquerade as Tachyon for long. Taking someone with his high visibility will force the authorities to look at my Rox."

Zelda pursed her lips in sarcastic sympathy. Latham just sat there, hands steepled under his chin.

"I know you, Prime," I continued. "You hide your thoughts well enough when you're sitting here in front of me, but not always. I know everything you know. All I have to do is whisper the right things to the Egrets, or maybe just tell the authorities what a certain prominent city attorney is up to . . ." I left the sentence unfinished.

Zelda had gone alert and tense. The legal script in Latham's mind shredded like tissue paper. In Latham's mind, everything was cold. So cold. "Let me give you some advice, Governor," he said as softly as ever. "Never bluff with blackmail. It is always a very weak hand."

"It's not a bluff. I'll do it. I will."

Latham almost smiled as guards came to attention all around us. He glanced at them slowly, calmly, then looked back at me. His hands didn't move. Not a muscle twitched in his face, and his mind stayed blank.

That frightened me more than anything he could have said.

I couldn't follow through. He was right. Kafka was right too—bluffing really is a dangerous game.

So I'm sorry, sorry because the Rox needs the jumpers. We need Prime and Blaise and all the rest.

Latham knew it. I knew it.

But I promise you. I will find another way.

Madman across the Water
by
Victor Milán

The boys from DEA paid a visit to the New Dawn Wellness Center just after morning rush when a few last late-running yuppies—if that isn't a contradiction in terms—were polishing off their bulghur-wheat doughnuts and the center's famous low-cal, low-cholesterol, vegetarian "fried eggs," with tofu whites and whipped-squash yolks. Enough onlookers to be duly impressed, but not enough to get underfoot or in line for serious hurt. In the last winter of the 1980s, America's drug warriors could do no wrong in the eyes of the press, the public, or the law, but the powers that be felt that if the shithammer came down—as every member of the strike team devoutly hoped—it wouldn't do to have too many punctured civilians bleeding on camera.

Especially at the scene of what, if it came off, would be the media bust of the decade: the DEA versus a renegade ace.

While agents in civilian garb secured the customers and the single brush-cut, stocky, grumpy female clerk, a three-man element of the Covert Lab Enforcement Team dashed through the restaurant in their black Darth Vader togs, CAR-15s with fat suppressors shrouding the barrels clutched in their black-gauntleted hands. One of them paused to bang his Kevlar-helmeted head against the jamb of the door to the back before dashing upstairs.

"We're waiting on you, Lynn," his buddy Dooley said as he came highstepping up to the second floor. Dooley's mask muffled his words, but Lynn knew he was grinning, with the ESP that came from being pals since eighth grade. Lynn grinned back and bobbed his head.

He and Dooley pressed backs to either side of the door while Matteoli slipped the rubberized tip of a big orange wrecking bar between the frame and the door and popped it open. The other two wheeled inside, Lynn low and left, Dooley high and right.

"*DEA! Covert Lab Enforcement Team! Freeze, mother-fuckers!*"

It was a fairyland, a fucking *fairyland*. It wasn't very big, but neither of them had ever seen anything like it outside a government facility or university. This was their eleventh lab bust, and they'd never even seen half the equipment in here.

The only things out of place were the two men standing in the middle of all that gleaming technology. The CLET strike force had been briefed to expect the kind of scum that would hang around an overage hippie. Not a middle-aged black guy and a leaner younger Hispanic dude in jackets and ties.

The Hispanic was in motion already, reaching inside his jacket in a motion that could mean only one thing. Dooley tracked him with his muzzle.

"Hold it right—"

The big vent-ribbed Colt Python roared as it came on-line, chopping Dooley off in the middle of his sentence. The bulky armor encasing his body would definitely have stopped even the high-speed .357 slug, the face plate might have turned it. But the jacketed hollowpoint nipped neatly between the lip of his helmet and the top of his mask, punched through his right eye and right out the back of his skull.

"Dooley!" Lynn screamed, and held back the trigger. Like everybody else in CLET, he'd had the three-round burst regulator on his assault rifle disabled the moment he'd been issued the thing. He let the whole magazine go on full rock'n'roll, felt the ripple of high-velocity slugs in passing as Matteoli did the same from the doorway.

The Hispanic dropped the Python and did a little jitter-bug dance as the white front of his shirt came all over red. The black guy dove out of sight.

Lynn spun and dropped with his back to a lab table that would never stop a bullet but would at least hide him from sight. He dropped the spent magazine, fumbled another from a belt pouch, and rammed it home.

"Matty, pop a stun grenade on the puke!" he yelled.

"Backup!" Matteoli screamed back. "We gotta call for backup!"

Fuck that, Lynn thought. His eyes stung with tears. *Payback's a mother.* He jacked the charging handle and rose.

To see a black arm waving from the midst of all that mechanism, brandishing a black leather holder with an all-too-distinctive gold shield inset.

"Narcotics Enforcement. *We're NYPD, you dumb sons of bitches!*"

TWO DIE IN SHOOT-OUT AT ACE DRUG LAB, the headline said, or screamed. The subhead read, *Drug Czar Calls Illicit Lab "Most Sophisticated Ever"; Nationwide Manhunt Declared*.

Dr. Pretorius sighed and looked over the half-moons of his old-fashioned reading glasses. "So a couple of your cowboys came off the handle and shot it out with New York's finest. What does this have to do with my client?"

The youngest of the three came out of his leather-covered chair with an incoherent scream of rage. Pretorius raised an eyebrow.

"Lynn," the eldest said, not loud but with a certain attack-dog-trainer snap. "Maybe you'd better wait outside."

The young man with the shock of black hair falling into wild eyes turned and pounded the heel of one fist against a wall, making display cases with exotic insects inside dance. The he ran out of the attorney's office.

"Whatever was that about?" Pretorius asked.

"Agent Saxon was involved in the incident you so insensitively spoke of," said the third man. He was in his early fifties and in all ways average except for the expensive cut of his lawyerly three-piece and the bland smoothness of his face. A man for George Bush's America. "His partner was killed." He settled back, apparently looking for expressions of regret or sympathy.

"My question still stands," Pretorius said.

The third man's face hardened momentarily. "Under New York law, Dr. Meadows can be held responsible for violent deaths associated with his crimes."

"We're talking capital here," the attack-dog trainer added.

Pretorius began to laugh. The two of them stared at him as if he'd sprouted great big white wings like Peregrine's. "That is the farthest-fetched interpretation of the law I've heard in a long time," he said, taking off his glasses and wiping his eyes. "Is there no limit to the arrogant disregard you people have for concepts like 'rights' and 'due process' —not to mention common sense?"

Kinder-and-Gentler smiled. "Given that seventy percent of the American public believes any measures at all are justified in combating the drug menace," he said, "no."

The trainer pulled a sheaf of papers from an inside pocket of his sport coat. "We have something for you, too, Pretorius." He slammed a packet of official-looking papers on the desk and smiled up at Pretorius with satisfaction glinting in his steely gray eyes. Pretorius gave it a 6.5.

"As you're no doubt aware," Kinder-and-Gentler said, as smooth as his face, "under the Racketeering-Influenced and Corrupt Organizations and Continuing Crime Acts, all property belonging to drug dealers is liable to confiscation. As you're also aware, I'm sure, recent interpretations of the law permit us to seize the property of attorneys who represent such scum. We can't permit the enormous sums commanded by drug dealers to deflect justice, now, can we, Doctor?" And he smiled too.

My, we're a happy group today, Pretorius thought. He reached for the telephone, pressed a button. When a voice answered, he said simply, "Go."

His guests stiffened. The Attack Dog Trainer was leaning so far forward, he was in danger of toppling over and splitting Pretorius's desk with the blade of his face. "What are you trying to pull?" he barked.

It was Pretorius's turn to try his hand at smiling, and he gave it his all. "Your latest little perversion of due process does not precisely take me by surprise, gentlemen. I was just speaking to an associate of mine waiting at the federal courthouse. If you'll be patient a few moments, a court order voiding your seizure should shortly arrive by messenger."

They stared at him with eyes like boiled eggs. He reached into a drawer of his desk. The Trainer stiffened, and his hard right hand started inside his suit coat.

Kinder-and-Gentler put a hand on his arm. "He's not going for a gun, Pat. Act your age."

"At the very outset of the Meadows custody case,"

Pretorius said, "I foresaw you gentlemen and your modern Star Chamber tactics might become involved. And I personally have no need for money."

"You can't weasel out of this by waiving your fee, bunky," the Trainer said.

"Nor did I." He trumped the trainer's sheaf with his own embossed legal envelope. "I charged Dr. Meadows my full hourly rate—payable, under the terms of this contract, directly to the March of Dimes for research into mental retardation. And if you wish to try to confiscate *their* assets, gentlemen, I wish you luck."

"We're the future, pal!"

An open-hand slap cracked across the yellow stripe dyed down the center of his close-cropped skull. Trash-clogged foreshore and sagging graffiti-crusted buildings swam in stench thick as heat haze, or maybe from the blow. The tall man hunched his shoulders and raised his arms defensively across his face.

He'd ridden to the Rox in a giant jellyfish in search of shelter. It didn't surprise him much to find there was no shelter there, either. It did made him kind of sad.

He wasn't sure how many joker boys were on him. He'd never had much head for detail on a macro scale. It didn't really matter. *Make Love Not War* were the words he'd always lived by.

In his proper person, anyway. Which was all he had to help him now.

An attacker slammed the scarred pale Hormel ham he carried instead of a hand into the midriff of the tall man's faint paint-dappled Pendleton shirt. He whoofed and doubled and staggered back, and the empirical part of him noted that there had to be at least two assailants since another was, sure enough, down on all fours behind him to take him behind the calves and send him sprawling. That trick had been a constant companion in childhood and early adolescence. Made him nostalgic, almost.

Coughing and sobbing for breath, he tried to remember what the survivors of the Czechago Convention had told him: Curl up, get small, try not to give them a crack at your joints or skull.

Mayor Daley's disorder preservers had had nightsticks. These boys had body parts à la wild card. Like the calcareous hoof somebody was slamming rhythmically into the small of his back, aiming to pulp his kidneys.

"Hey, nat! You ain't gettin' any younger. And maybe (*kick*) you ain't getting (*kick*) any older either!"

The others laughed their jackal laughs, and as painspikes jolted up his spine and down into his scrotum, the tall man wondered if he was actually going to survive. And he thought the thing he'd always sworn he never would: *If my friends were here, you'd never dare treat me like this!*

Laughter. "Hey, old dude, you got no friends! Or didn't you figure that out yet?"

There. It was out. He'd even spoken it aloud without meaning to. Shame as much as anger and pain and fear made his eyes run suddenly hot with tears as the impact of their limbs and their laughter redoubled.

And then a voice, cutting like a busted-off car antenna. "What the fuck is going on here?"

The blowstorm stopped. He rolled over and sat up, curiosity overcoming caution.

A woman—a girl—stood facing the joker quartet. Her hair was short, moussed into a nondescript-colored spike palisade to guard her scalp. Silver bangles and skull-and-bones swung from one ear. "I said 'What the fuck?' Don't try to hide from me, Foureyes," she added to the smallest, who had maneuvered himself behind his companions.

"Hey, hey," the joker said defensively, blinking his name-sakes furiously. "Just trashin' this old nat, you know? Passin' the time."

"Whofuck *you* tellus wha'do?" the biggest one said, the one with the premium ham for a hand and a face that was all fissures and flanges, like a leaf-eating bat. Saliva shot from his face like Silly String when he spoke. "Juzda dumb cunt."

"Cool it, Tyrone," Foureyes said urgently. "She's a jumper."

A slim black kid, normal-looking except for the hoof with which he'd tried to do street surgery on the tall man's kidneys, put a sneer on his chiseled handsome face. "She big time. She *his* squeeze." He added a head flip on *his*.

A quick steel veronica: *balisong*, a butterfly knife, unfolding its wings very pretty, like in the movies, and then just the tip stuck up the black kid's right nostril. "That's K.C. Strange to you, Footloose. And I don't need anybody's help to fuck up a bunch of detached assholes like you, *capisc'*? And don't be trying to circle around *behind* me anymore, Zero, or your friend here's gonna start looking lots more like Tyrone. In fact—"

Stung, or thinking he'd seen an opening, the gigantic Tyrone had begun to roll forward. K.C. smiled.

Footloose stepped back, looked Tyrone dead in the eyes, and laughed shrilly. Then his face changed, and he tried to take a step forward. The hoof didn't want to move. He pitched facefirst into sand caked with something dark, sticky, and sweetly fetid.

Tyrone stopped dead. He raised his hands to his face. The clubbed hand blundered heedlessly into his eye.

He screamed.

Zero was dancing around the perimeter. "What? Foureyes, what's going on?"

"Oh, fuck, oh, Tyrone, you useless fuck!" Foureyes moaned. Footloose raised his head to stare at him. Foureyes began to kick him. "She multiple-jumped the stupid bastards, swapped their fucking minds."

K.C. smiled and made her knife disappear. "You're not as dumb as I thought you were."

"Shit! Shit, we gotta get outta here," Zero gobbled. He grabbed Footloose—his body, anyway—under the arm and dragged him upright as he began to roar incoherently. Foureyes caught hold of the weeping Tyrone-Footloose and hustled him away along the stinking beach.

"Come back tomorrow and ask nice, I may sort your little minds out again," she called after them. Then she shook her head. "Damn. The way we fight each other, all the Combine has to do is wait. We'll do the job on ourselves, and they won't have to worry about how to crash the wall."

She looked down at the tall man. He slumped there, rubbing the ache in his face while the filthy waves of Upper New York Bay shot needles of sunlight in through his eyes and up to the roof of his skull. A twitch of breeze sent crinkled Ding Dong wrappers and styrofoam cup shards skittering like small animals to the shelter of his thin haunch.

"So who are you?" she demanded.

"M-mark," he said. His lips felt big as basketballs. He saw no reason to lie to her. "Mark Meadows."

But she was looking away across the water, at the Circle Line ferry beyond the cordon of Harbor Police boats that surrounded the Rox, chugging toward the foreskin tip of Manhattan.

"Wha—" he gagged, spat sand that tasted like stuff you flossed from between your teeth, "what's the Combine?"

She tossed her pointy little chin after the ferryboat. *Them.* The straights, the nats, the outside world. The government. Everybody but us wretched refuse huddled here on the Rox, brother."

Oh. *That* was nothing new . . . a light dawned.

"Hey, man, I remember now. Randall McMurphy! He's the one with the Combine. Like, Nurse Ratched and them."

She laughed. "You're the first person I've met on this damned island who knew that." She walked away whistling.

Some social worker had given her the small pink-plush elephant, back at another of the dim cold places with echoing halls. Now it lay on her metal-frame bed, slashed open, its cotton entrails strewn everywhere.

Tears filled her eyes. She didn't *understand.* Didn't understand the jeering taunts of the other girls, the make-believe caring of the doctor people, the rough unconcern of the people who actually took care of her, to the extent anybody did. She had grown up with love and warmth and a constant glow of happy safety. Now, in only a few months' time, she'd learned to treasure being ignored. She began to gather up the fragments of the stuffed toy.

She didn't understand what she was doing here. The other girls said they were here for doing bad things, but she had never done anything bad. Her daddy always said she was a good girl. The doctor people said she was *special.* When she asked if that was why she was inside, they told her no, it was because her daddy was a bad man.

She sniffled. Her daddy wasn't a bad man. He was *Daddy.*

She threw herself down on the bed. Her roommate wasn't in. She liked this roommate. She didn't pick on her, didn't pay any attention to her at all.

The tears were overwhelming her now. Most of all, she missed her daddy, tall and strong and always there for her. He wasn't a bad man. And she knew that he wouldn't let her stay here forever. Someday he'd come for her. No matter what.

And a voice inside her head told her, *You're what the other girls say you are. Just a stupid. You're going to be here forever and ever.*

Alone.

She gathered the sad empty head of the elephant to her cheek. Its black-disc pupils rolled up in its plastic-button eyes. She hugged it to her and drifted into sleep, weeping for the death of her friend.

Head thrown back to let the dawn wind ruffle his red brush cut with bloatblack-stinking fingers, Blaise walked through the Rox's gray huddle. He was just in via the Charon Express from a night run with the jumpers. Just a casual cruise to see how some of their investment properties over in Manhattan were doing, and he was on top of the world.

You always lectured me about the proper uses of power, grandpère, he thought, and his smile turned edged and ugly. *And I must hand it to you, you have indeed taught me to use it*.

It came to him then that it might be time to go down below the medical building for a new lesson in the use of power. He was still fairly fresh, with a sixteen-year-old's endurance, and these little jaunts into town tended to leave him unsatisfied and maybe a trifle bored. His jumpers were too simple, too American. It wasn't that he didn't enjoy the same things they did. Only not as long.

And he wanted more. Putting the expensively cultured body of a millionaire's daughter through its paces while its owner looked on had its rewards. But mostly it served to draw his appetite thin and tight like the skin on a starving man's ribs. He could taste *real* power. That was what their victims commanded, why they were chosen.

He was tired of tasting it at one remove. It was like eating soup through a straw.

He came around a corner. To his right the river licked the beach like a wound. A knot of assorted seedballs was drifting though the wet cold sand toward the food tables, gray shapes half distinct in the false light. He paid them no mind. They were the basic flotsam that that fat fool Bloat got such a charge of clasping to his bosom, or whatever you called it: jokers, monstrous to the Takisian sensibilities Blaise had picked up as much despite his grandfather as because of him, nat trash not a lot more tasteful. The sort of scum he would've gotten a kick out of finding asleep in some alley, soaking down with gas, and lighting off if he'd been born a mere groundling.

Then Blaise saw *him*.

In cognition's ground-zero flash he went from a gangly shape stilting head and shoulders over the trash stream to a terror that yammered in Blaise's skull and pounded on the temples like a mad thing trying to get out. With a martial artist's backward leap, Blaise put the cold block of a building between him and the awful apparition. *Burning Sky, could he have seen me?*

"Blaise?"

Like a soft knife, the voice cut through the hammering in his temples. He looked up and saw K.C. Strange framed by his knees, realized he'd sunk into a sort of fetal crouch with his back to the chill cement wall.

"Blaise, what's the matter? You look like you're about to throw up."

He felt a stab of fury, a yellow ice pick through the purple throbbing fog in his brain. *How dare she intrude? How dare she question?* But the anger flickered and vanished like sparks from an oil-drum fire.

From the other jumpers he got fear and deference and awe—even from Molly Bolt, who hated his guts. From K.C. he got *concern*. He had never had people really care about him for his own sake before—he didn't count his grandfather or the one-eyed bitch. Tach's only interest was to keep him from becoming what he was truly meant to be, and Cody was only playing with him. In that last few years he had come to realize, to acknowledge, that for his beloved "Uncle George" he had never been more than a means to an end, and he'd been a kind of revolutionary mascot to the terrorist cells who raised him before that, before his accursed grandfather stumbled across him. K.C. of all the people he'd known gave a fuck for *him*.

Maybe that was why he kept her around in spite of her mouth. She was cute. But with his shoulders and attitude and sculpted looks, most of all with his power, he could have *cute* any time, any way.

He let out a long sobbing breath. "It's him. He's come for my grandfather."

"Who?"

"*Him*. He's cut his hair, he dresses differently, but it is him. I can smell him. I can feel his mind. He is here to rescue Tachyon."

"Don't be ridiculous."

He shot her a hot-eyed look, which she ignored.

"Nobody knows about Tachyon except us—and Bloat, because he knows everything that goes down on the Rox. But Bloat's got a bigger hard-on for the straights than we do. He'd never spill."

"It doesn't matter," said Blaise. "He is an ace. He has his ways."

"Now go back to the beginning and tell me just who this *he* is."

"Mark Meadows," he said in a voice that rang with adolescent *Sturm und Drang*. "Captain Trips."

"Mark *Meadows*?" She laughed. "You're working up a sweat for nothing, lover boy. Why, I met him yesterday. He's just a harmless old—*who* did you say he was?"

"Captain Trips. The ace who has the friends. Jumpin' Jack Flash, Starshine, Moonchild—I am not sure how many more. He was one of Grandfather's best friends." He looked up at her with a face drawn like a Greco martyr's. "I must stop him. He will destroy us."

K.C. laughed. Blaise's face froze. She ruffled his hair. Her fingers did a better job than the wind. As she teased and tickled his scalp, he relaxed slightly, knew again why he tolerated her.

He also knew that one day he would pay her back for each and every impertinence, with interest. But he was learning to defer gratification, sometimes. *Grandpère* would be so proud.

"Relax. He's just a harmless old geezer."

"He's an *ace*, I tell you—"

She laughed again. "He may have *been* a big ace, babe. He's nothing now, *capisc'*? When I tripped over him, he was in the process of getting his skinny butt kicked by Tyrone and Foureyes and company. Righteous dweebs. They were about to stomp his brains out through his big beaky nose until a little tiny teenage girl with a toy knife turned up to the rescue." She squatted beside him and played with the braided tail that hung down the back of Blaise's bombardier's jacket. "Some ace, huh?"

He shook his head clear with a flip of irritation. "He is undercover. He has to hide his powers. You never lived underground. You would not know."

"No, hey, I just lived out on the streets since I was

twelve years old, I wouldn't know *anything* about that, and anyway I'm just a girl."

"That's right."

She reared back, ready to spit at him like a cobra. At the last instant before she said something he would have to destroy her for, he showed his teeth in a feral grin. She blinked, grinned back, hung her hands around his neck, and shook her head. "You son of a bitch."

This is our game, he thought, smiling complacently. *I push her to see how far she pushes back. She pushes back to see how far I'll go.*

And the stakes are her life. Wouldn't that surprise her?

He remembered Mark, then, and lost his taste for games. He pushed her arms off his neck, only half roughly, and started to stand. "Enough of this, *chéri.*"

"Ooh, I love it when you talk dirty."

He shook his head sharply, like a ferret with a mouse. She took the hint. "Your Mark Meadows has played a foolish game and lost. It's time to take from him the price—"

"Andrieux."

He looked up. Mustelina and Andiron stood there. Mustelina cradled an AKM assault rifle in her furry paws—not one of the semiautomatics the liberals were so spastic about, but a *real* assault rifle, full auto as issued to a Baltic conscript with the Warsaw Pact in Poland, who had sold it for a lid. Andiron wasn't armed. He just tapped his blunt greenish-black forearms together gently with a ringing like weights dropped on a carpeted gym floor.

Blaise snapped upright, heels together, and performed a mock bow, half Takisian, half French. "To what do I owe the honor?"

Monsters, he thought, and his skin crawled.

"Governor wants to see you," Mustelina said.

Blaise smiled his beautiful smile at the ferretlike joker. "Ah, but I regret, urgent business requires me—"

Andiron's handless arms pealed like a bell. "Now," he said.

Blaise's eyes became slits. "I could make you dance a waltz into the river and drown."

"Sure you could," Mustelina agreed easily, "but you won't."

Blaise stood a moment longer, his lips stretching across

his teeth so tightly he feared they'd tear. "*Someday*," he hissed.

Mustelina levered the AK from *full auto* to *safe* with two loud clacks. "Someday," she agreed.

Blaise turned to K.C., gripped her by the arms. "Go find Meadows. Get to know him. Find out what he wants."

She nodded and slipped away.

He turned to the two Bloat guards, straightened, pulled back his shoulders, and adjusted the fit of his leather jacket. "Well? We burn the daylight."

Mark settled down with his rump propped on a mostly horizontal slab of asphalt, part of a stack of paving chunks piled at the tip of the southern arm of the blocky U that was Ellis Island, next to the mouth of the tiny little harbor. It was a crisp, clear morning. His breath smoked like a dragon's as he tried to get comfortable with his plastic plate of lukewarm beans perched on his knees.

"Hey there."

He started at the voice, looked up furtively, prepared to run. He still wasn't sure he was *entitled* to eat. The food-distribution system on the Rox was pretty rough and ready: Some plundered steam tables out on the sand, where a pair of truly horrible-looking puswad jokers in stained paper hats ladled out crud to queues of shabby, surly residents. Another joker, as big and as ugly as any two of the bunch who'd hassled him yesterday, stood watch with a pair of lean mean kids, not jokers—which meant they probably were jumpers—armed with bats. They scrutinized him when he took his place in line behind somebody with a head like a burn-victim mushroom growing out of a black leather jacket, but didn't challenge. He guessed the drill was if you looked too familiar, they figured you were trying to jump seconds and thumped you accordingly.

For a moment he feared they'd belatedly decided he didn't look familiar *enough*, but the shadow between him and the sun rising over Manhattan was small. Also familiar.

"Mind if I sit down?" K.C. Strange asked.

"No, no. Uh, like, go ahead."

She hunkered down next to him. He tried hard not to notice the contours of her black Spandex pants. This wasn't the time or the place or the person. He was an outsider. Just an old nat.

He proffered his plate. She waved him off. "You like the water?" she asked.

"I never thought the smell of the Hudson would be a relief."

He regretted it immediately. She seemed to be a big Rox booster. But she laughed.

"Well, it isn't your white-bread world here, that's for sure." She glanced down at him. "Sleep okay?"

"Done worse." Right after the trial he'd spent a few weeks on the street, just wandering, sleeping in alleys or the occasional midnight mission, while Pretorius did all he could, which unfortunately wasn't much. That had been in summer. The makeshift dorms of the Rox smelled so bad, the stench was like a weight, and the debris rustled constantly with small unseen things, but they kept the winter wind off. He didn't care that some of the bodies pressed against his were human only by ancestry; they were warm.

"Thought I'd check on you. After all, it isn't everybody out here I can talk about *One Flew Over the Cuckoo's Nest* with."

"Not even your, uh, your boyfriend?"

Why did you ask that, you nitwit? the little guy who sat in the peanut gallery of his mind asked. It used to be Flash and the Traveler who sat back there and gave him a hard time. Now it was just a little gray guy, anonymous as everybody else in New York. Mark didn't have a ready answer anyway.

She looked at him from the sides of her eyes. They were gray eyes, pale, almost silver. "He doesn't read much. What brings you to the Rox?"

"Had a little . . . run-in with the law."

It was funny. Here he'd been a member of the counterculture most of his adult life, even when the original countercultural heavies were all joining brokerage firms or flogging diet plans and self-help seminars on paid-programming TV shows. And now that he was at last genuinely, authentically *underground*, it embarrassed the hell out of him. Also, he understood in an inchoate sort of way that it wasn't exactly survival-positive to trot out his personal problems in front of strangers. It's 1990, and, as Gilbert Shelton used to say, government spies are everywhere.

She laughed. "Come on. It had to be more than that." He stuck out his lower lip, mulish, and she laughed louder.

"Give me a break. We don't have informers here, even if President George is coming to town to encourage us all to turn in our neighbors. Take a look over there."

She pointed with her chin. A shape was just breaking water out in the miniature harbor, streaming water thousand-colored like an oil slick: a translucent glabrosity, a Portuguese man-o'-war the size of Godzilla's piles. "That's Charon. Making a late run; he usually doesn't like to surface by daylight. He's how you got here, right?"

"Uh, yeah."

He didn't know it—*he*—was called Charon. All he knew was what the joker who looked like a clump of seaweed in an Orioles cap and Coors Light jacket and oozed into the record store to warn him the DEA were on their way had told him: If he thought he might need the sanctuary of the Rox, he ought to blow what roll he carried on a bag of groceries at some late-night bodega, go down to the river, fire up a flashlight, and think real hard about how bad he wanted to go there. It smacked to Mark of clicking his tiny heels together and chanting "There's No Place Like Home," three times, but the drug-war dogs were on his track, and if they took him, he'd never get Sprout free, and so he did what he was told.

And the damnedest thing of all, it worked.

"He's how most people get here. Now look real close. What do you see inside him?"

Mark squinted into the spindrift sun. From this perspective, Charon looked like a grotesque exaggerated glass Oliver Hardy–shaped Christmas-tree ornament; you could just see a hint of face, up near the top. With the late-dawn light shining through his body, you could see—

"Nothing."

"Good answer. But think about this. Charon never makes dry runs."

He felt the greasy congealed beans he'd choked down start becoming buoyant. "But—"

"Yeah. And when you come to the wall—Bloat's Wall that surrounds this place—you start to feel Big Fear. And then you better want to get here *real bad*. Because if you don't, you *stick*—and Charon never stops, either. So the wall holds you in place, and he just sort of oozes out from around you and leaves you on the bottom. Osmosis, like."

Mark bit his lip and put his plate down on the damp

sand. But he took care not to spill it; his appetite might come back in a bit. He'd learned to be practical that way these last few months.

K.C. shaded her face with her hand and looked at him. She was quite pretty, once you got past the crown-of-thorns hair.

"So what're you really doing on the Rox? You're not just on the run for knocking over a 7-11."

"It's my little girl. My daughter. I need to get her back."

"She's on the Rox? Joker or jumper, let me tell you, dude, if she's here, you don't really want to see her. *Capisc'*?"

"No. It isn't that. She's in a juvenile detention center. I don't know which one. I need to find her and get her out."

Something passed behind her ice-fleck eyes. Then her face hardened. "A middle-class wimp who's spun out on the ice past thirty-something, run a jailbreak? Give me a break. You wouldn't know the first thing about it."

"Hey, I can do it!" he exclaimed, outraged. "I can do something, anyway," he mumbled, coming all over uncertain.

"Yeah. Like what?" Her smile taunted him.

"Uhh—" His ears got hot. Aware he'd said too much, he turned quickly away.

"So tell me," she whispered, right by his ear, "where *are* your friends, Cap'n Trips?"

When he spun around, she was gone.

"Now, Blaise," the creature called Bloat said, and tittered. "I heard you thinking bad thoughts about one of our guests here on the Rox. That won't do. It won't do at all, at all."

Blaise let his nose and upper lip contort in disgust at the stench that washed off the shimmering translucent maggot mass as palpably as the evil black crud that cascaded endlessly down its sides. It wouldn't do any good to hide his reaction, even though K.C. said it made him look like a fruit bat. Bloat could read his mind.

Blaise hated that. He let the nausea shine back like a beacon, filled his head with images of throwing up, great yellow geysers.

Hovering in attendance, the big cockroach Kafka made a set of sounds like knuckles popping. Kafka was kind of grand vizier to Bloat and was always trying to make sure his boss got the treatment merited by his position as governor of the

Rox, and not that earned by his appearance. Kafka didn't much like the jumpers. He liked Blaise least of all.

"I suppose you're going to try to tell us what to *think* now," Blaise said, very brassy. "Authority has gone to your head, wherever the hell you keep it."

"No," Bloat said, and he forgot to titter. "I wish I could tell you what to think. Better yet, I'd like to tell you *not* to think. But you can't help thinking, any more than I can help . . . hearing you."

He faltered a little, because Blaise had conjured up a vivid memory of going down on K.C. Strange. Her pubic hair was sparse, dark blonde and very fine. Her flesh was pink, and when he moved his tongue, she moved with it.

"Then why did you send your pet monsters to drag me here?" Blaise asked.

"*Ahh*. Mark Meadows. The man who once was Cap'n Trips. You plan to harm him."

"What of it?"

"He is a victim of the straight world's hatred and fear. I choose to offer him refuge. If he still has his ace powers, he will be an invaluable ally when the nats try to crush us. If he does not . . . his body is still warm. He can still attract bullets that might otherwise find homes in joker flesh. I forbid you to touch him."

Blaise laughed. "What gives you the right, fat thing?"

"He's the governor of the Rox," Kafka hissed, his voice like a snake in dry leaves.

Blaise started to give back static, but Bloat had pulled it from his mind already. "Give me a break. We've had this discussion before. You need the Rox, which means you need me. And if you think you're going to change that, Latham might have a few different ideas."

Latham. That cold fish. He felt a memory of pain deep in his belly and shuddered. He was not ready to square accounts with Latham. Which meant settling Bloat had to be deferred—and worse, the monster knew it.

"Very well, *Governor*." He performed a mock bow. Bloat just giggled. "I bow to your authority . . . *on the Rox*. If Mark Meadows takes action against me here, I claim the right of self-defense."

"Please, Blaise, don't make this difficult. You have that right. But Meadows isn't going to move against you. He doesn't know what you've done with his friend, your grandfather. I read his mind, remember?"

He's an ace, remember?

"He thinks you're his *friend*, Blaise."

"Be that as it may, I have other scores to settle with him. Should he leave the Rox, he leaves your domain, and then he is mine."

"The mainland is a dangerous place," Kafka rasped. Blaise frowned at him. He wasn't naive enough to take the cockroach's agreement at face value. "Even you could have an accident there, Blaise."

To his own surprise, Blaise's reaction was amusement, not anger. "If anyone was going to lay hurt on me, I'd read it. And I'd hurt them *worse*." He was bluffing, of course. It was always good to keep the monsters off balance. And even if Bloat had the perseverance to endure the image of K.C.'s lean thighs wrapped around Blaise's head, he would be able to read only that Blaise was bluffing. Not to what extent.

"Your power is great, Blaise," Kafka said, "but what's its range? There's a thing called a Barrett Light Fifty. A sniper's rifle. It fires the same round as a fifty-caliber machine gun. It has a range of over a mile. Does your power reach that far, Blaise?" He moved his chitinous limbs in the gesture that served him as a shrug. "I'm afraid somebody might take it in mind to pick you right off the Rox with a shot from the mainland. Meadows has lots of friends among the jokers, Blaise."

Tight-lipped, Blaise glared at him. Anger seethed, but there was still Latham. "Don't threaten me," he said sullenly.

"He's not threatening you, Blaise," Bloat said earnestly. "I don't tolerate threats. He's concerned for you. You're one of my people too."

Like hell I am. "You look to use him, don't you? You think he'd be a big help when the nats come for you."

Bloat said nothing. Nameless sounds rumbled from the depths of him.

"All right. But what if something happens to Meadows that I don't have anything to do with?" God, he hated truckling to these beasts. "He's a fugitive. He's wanted by the authorities."

"You're being clever, Blaise," Bloat said. He almost sounded sharp. "I hate it when you're clever. But if Meadows falls afoul of circumstances beyond your control, there's no way we can hold you to account."

"Then we are understood. Mark Meadows is safe from me." Blaise bowed again, much lower than before. "Gentlemen, I wish you good day."

A furry joker and a nat with his hair shaved in sidewalls and a coiled dragon tattooed on either side of his skull were going at it ankle-deep in the sludgy water. Somebody cranked up the Butthole Surfers on a box by way of sound track. Mark ducked his head reflexively between his shoulders and just walked on with his hands deep in the pockets of his Goodwill windbreaker. Other residents of the Rox, living less in the shadow of the Summer of Love, thronged like so many seabirds on a rock and watched with interest.

He hadn't brooded as much about K.C.'s being in on his secret as he thought he would. He was too full of the need to do something for Sprout to give much room to other emotions. What he *could* do he had no idea. Having been all on fire to get here to the Rox, having gotten here alive only because he wanted to so badly, he now was all on fire to get off again. But he had nowhere else to go.

A change in the crowd noise made him stop and look up. A squad of nat-looking youths were moving in on the fight, led by a tall kid in black T-shirt, tight jeans, and a leather jacket. His hair was a startling rich red, blood red, and cut in a brush. He looked somehow familiar.

The spear carriers stopped and cracked their knuckles a respectful three yards away. The redhead walked, not quickly but purposefully, between the combatants. A braided tail hung down the back of his jacket.

Words changed hands. The joker squalled and aimed a roundhouse punch at the interloper. He blocked with a forearm, doubled the joker with a fist in the gut, dropped him with a hammerhand to head, right in the surf.

The tattooed nat lunged at his back. The newcomer half turned, drove a thrust kick into his solar plexus. Dragon Boy staggered back. His antagonist stepped in and kicked, stepped in and kicked, driving him back deeper into the filthy slog of the water. Finally he spun a balletic backkick into one dragon tattoo, his tail scything behind his head, and walked ashore, leaving his opponent bobbing gently.

"You asked about my boyfriend," a voice behind him said. "There he is."

He turned as the jumpers ran to fish out the tattooed kid. She was perched on the prongs of a rusted-out front-end loader, squatting with elbows on trim thighs. "You may have noticed things don't run so smoothly around here," she said.

"They don't seem to run at all."

She jutted the chin. "He's trying to put a stop to that. Start getting things a little organized."

"Looks like it's weighted kinda heavily in favor of head busting."

"A lot of these wags don't *capisc'* much else." She shrugged. "He's kind of like an ace, too, he's got very advanced mental powers. He does things this way a lot, though. To show he's *real*. That's the kind of leadership the Rox needs."

"'Meet the new boss, same as the old boss.'"

She dropped light to the sand. "I don't need tired old hippie shit."

He grinned at her. For some reason he was enjoying this. "I'm a tired old hippie."

"Yeah. Gone prematurely orange, like Ron Reagan, except more electric. And it's more maybe pineapple, on the sides, anyway. What made you do that to your hair? You look like a total dick."

They were walking now, along a line of makeshift structures jumbled together of fiberboard and plastic. A couple of kids—whether nat or joker it was impossible to tell under the grime—cooked what Mark hoped wasn't really a cat on a metal rod over an oil-drum fire.

"It was for the custody trial over who got Sprout—that's my daughter—my ex–old lady or me. She's gone real Park Avenue, and my lawyer told me to cut my hair or I'd get blown out of the water in court. So I did."

"So what happened?"

"I got blown out of the water."

She spat. "Combine justice. Where'd you get the two-tone head?"

"I figured nobody in the *world* would connect Cap'n Trips the federal fugitive, with his long flowing locks and his goatee, with some trashed-out punker." He stopped and looked down at her. It was a long way; at six-four, he was a good foot taller. "But you did," he said. "How'd you recognize me?"

"I—I read the papers sometimes. And you told me your *name*, for Christ's sake. You still have a lot to learn about security."

"Oh," he said, crestfallen. "But, I thought—I mean, you said I was among friends. . . ."

"Yeah, which is why you were getting your skinny ass kicked in when I found you."

Suddenly the knife was in her hand, its sharp little point poking under his chin, tipping his head back. "There aren't *any* friends, any *where*. *Capisc'*?"

He nodded, gingerly. The knife hilt parted and snapped around, devouring the blade.

"Learn that and you've gone a long way toward surviving on the streets," she said, walking on. He followed a beat late, still shaken by the crazy intensity he'd seen in those silver eyes.

"Tell you the truth, I didn't make the name at first. It was only when you got that about the Combine. I suddenly thought, who else but an old flower child would know about Ken Kesey? Then it clicked."

"How'd you know, then? You're no flower child. You're hardly any older than Sprout."

"She's thirteen, and I'm a lot older than that. Centuries, maybe. Don't look surprised; I've been checking you out."

She laughed, a sound brittle and edgy as old copper. "Tyrone and his butthole buddies would be shitting live rats if they knew who they'd been messing with—you got some *powerful* references among our heavier jokers. They still remember what you did for Doughboy, like you're some kind of martyred hero or something."

He looked away, embarrassed. He'd heard a few things along those lines, never taken them too seriously. Still, there was the joker who'd warned him to blow the record store. . . .

"On the other hand, we have a few prominent citizens right here on the Rox who might be even happier to have their hooks in you than your friendly local DEA. Might be some of them remember the Cloisters—and don't go all pale and shaky and start having a coronary on me. You've still got your secrets. I don't make a habit of running my head. As I may have told you, snitches ain't welcome on the Rox."

"Does your . . . friend know?"

"Hey, Blaise is my main man, honey. You're just some bum I picked up on a beach. More'n that, he's the main man for the Rox, in a way poor Bloat can never be. If I think he needs information, he's got it. Okay?"

It wasn't, but he didn't see what he could do about it. He had his head cocked, as if listening for an echo. Something she had said . . . Sometimes it seemed as if he were walking along a slope with depression hanging over him like snowdrift cliffs, and every once in a while it'd land on him in an avalanche, muddle his thinking more than years of constant marijuana buzz ever had.

Whatever bond there'd been between them seemed broken now. He looked at her. "What did you say your boyfriend's name was?"

"Blaise. Blaise Andrieux. He's—"

Mark's head snapped around. The red-haired boy was walking along the beach toward them, and Mark wondered why he hadn't recognized him at once.

He jumped to his feet and lurched into an ankle-deep run. "*Blaise!* Blaise, how are you doing, man?"

Blaise walked with tight-butted dancer's grace through the clinging reeking sand. A satisfied smile was fitted tightly to his face, even if it was taking some effort to keep from shaking his right hand in the air. He'd caught the kid with the dragon tat wrong with a backfist knuckle to the cheekbone and it stung something fierce. But he couldn't show pain. It wouldn't do to have his bannermen getting the idea he was *human*.

He'd bulked up amazingly in the months since he first ran away from his grandfather. His body was just a volcano of boiling growth hormones, and the hot adolescent anger that ran in his veins like live steam had kept him keen on the martial-arts exercises and weight training his grandfather had insisted he maintain. He was already larger than almost anybody of Takisian stock had ever been—anyone who grew so far beyond the classic somatotype would be destroyed as a monster—and his Takisian-derived muscles were denser and more efficient than a human's, his neurons firing and recovering quicker.

All of which was to say that while he'd grown a bit bored with the effortless control his mind power gave him, he had discovered the existential pleasures of kicking ass.

He told K.C. it was to set an example for the others, of course. To show that he wasn't just some effete egghead ace,

just a wimp, like—well, like his grandfather. That was because K.C. wasn't tough, even if she was smart and, when the
mood hit her, as happily savage as any of the jumpers. She
liked to rationalize Blaise's violence by imagining that he was
crafting a New Order of some sort out of the Rox rabble.
Since she amused him, it amused him to play along.

Meanwhile, he was enjoying the animal pleasures, the
morning light almost warm on his face, the breeze blowing
stiff enough from seaward that he could smell the ocean over
bloatblack and New Jersey, the tingling muscle memory of
flesh-on-flesh impact, his bannermen murmuring respectfully
behind him: "Did you see the way he straightened those
fuckers *out*?"

He heard someone calling his name. He looked up. The
sensual mood turned to dust and blew away. The hated stilt
figure of Mark Meadows was running like a horrible scarecrow with an orange do, right along the beach, right at *him*,
waving his arms and calling his name.

Blaise was stupefied. *He must be some kind of monster.
How can he be so bold?*

"Blaise! Blaise, man." Meadows stopped a few feet away,
looked him up and down. "It's good to see you. How long has
it been? A year?"

"I, uh. I think so, Mark."

Merde! He makes me feel thirteen again.

"You're lookin' good, man. Growin' up and fillin' out."

*I should have fucked your daughter in the ass the way
Latham fucked me. She was a beautiful little vegetable. She
could have been a marvelous toy, and I could break her and
throw her away if I wished. . . .*

"Thanks," he said. His lips tasted like paper.

Mark's watery gaze flicked past Blaise at the bannermen,
then back to the boy. "So what, uh, what brings you to the
Rox, man? Pigs come down on you too?"

"Yes. Yes, Mark, I guess they did."

Meadows nodded sagely. "Nail that stands out must be
hammered down, huh? These're tough times to be different,
man."

Yes, they are. And I'll show you just how tough. . . .

"So, have you seen your grandpa recently, man? I, I
really need to talk to him about something."

Blaise felt himself smile. It wasn't feigned. "Real recently.

He's doing very well. What do you need to talk to him about?"

"It's kind of personal, man. I'm sorry."

Blaise gave a petulant little flip of his shoulders.

"Hey, I'd tell you if I could, you know that. But you're young, and I just hate to involve you, y'know?" He glanced around. "Well, I guess I'll catch you around. Good seeing you again, man." Meadows turned and walked away.

Incredible, he thought at the narrow retreating back. *Such arrogance. Tell me now he doesn't wish me harm, dear Governor.*

But he's still safe from me. Oh yes, so very safe.

K.C. was still hunkered on the sand where he'd left her. Her arms were around her knees, and her eyes were hooded.

"Tell me one thing," she said, "and tell me straight. Is that true what you said, that the reason you came to the Rox, the reason you blew off your store, your being an ace, your whole comfortable little fantasyland *life*, was all for this daughter of yours?"

"Yes."

She stood. "You're a real case, buster. See you around."

He didn't see her the next day. He didn't expect to, and was disappointed anyway. In the chilly, fetid, humid dorm that night he reflected that he always seemed to be attracted to women who didn't see him the next day.

Ha. Attracted to her. There's a thought. For a moment, the voice in his head sounded like the familiar banter of JJ Flash, Esquire. But sharp-edged as he was, Flash was never quite that gratuitously nasty. And Mark's *friends* had dwindled away to nothingness within weeks after the trial. Actually, they'd drowned in booze for a few weeks, like the rest of his mind, and when he got a grip on himself they were gone. He wondered if he'd ever get them back.

Maybe he didn't deserve to. He had deserted them, after all—flushed them down the john on his lawyer's advice, to avoid a holding rap that would scuttle his chances of hanging onto his daughter. He had kept five vials, one for each persona. Three had been broken, one had sufficed to save the life of a child—at the cost of his secret, his life aboveground, and Sprout. The final one had gotten him out of Family Court just as the DEA was closing in on him. He had abandoned his friends. Maybe he had murdered them. And it hadn't done one damned bit of good. He wouldn't come back if *he* was one of them.

He went to sleep.

She caught up with him the next day, just after noon. They went for a walk again, and just talked. About books, about the fucked-up world they lived in, about the things Mark had been through, as an ace or beyond. Never about her, though; the times he asked she went quiet and spiky, and he quit after a while. She was a bright, bitter, and all-too-knowing kid, cynical and vulnerable by random turns.

She was also beautiful. He tried not to think about that.

He settled into the routine of life on the Rox. Or nonroutine. Aside from the steam tables, which came to life sometime in the morning and sometime toward sunset, the only rhythms the Rox knew were the sun and the tides and what people felt like cranking through their ghetto blasters.

Mark was going mad. Somewhere his daughter was trapped in a nightmare she couldn't possibly comprehend. He had to help her. But not even Pretorius—sticking his neck way out—had been able to turn up clue one to her whereabouts.

"I can't tell him."

The night wind unreeled flame and light from the tiki torches like a kid jerking at a roll of toilet paper. Pairs of jumpers sparred with one another on the landfill margin behind the Admin Building in the uncertain light.

Blaise paused in mopping his forehead with a towel. He always insisted on clean fresh towels being brought over from the mainland for his showers and workouts. He got them.

"What do you mean, you can't tell him?" His voice took on a dangerous edge.

"It means so much to him. I feel like I'm...like I'm using him."

Anger hit him. Trembling anger. She saw it in his face and stepped back.

You bitch. You bitch! Are you beginning to feel loyal to him?

"You haven't used people before? You haven't used people *up*? Think, K.C. Think hard. You're a jumper, remember? Jumpers use people. Especially burned-out old nat pukes."

"He's not a nat, he's an ace!" She stiffened as if expecting to receive a blow. "Besides . . . besides, I'm through with that. You know that. We need to build something out here, something strong that the Combine can't just sweep away like a kid knocking down a bunch of blocks."

"You're starting to sound like Bloat."

"I thought I was sounding like *you*. You with your talk of a New Order. Is that all that it is, just talk?"

I should kill her now. But the thought fell like a dead leaf through his consciousness, without heat, without weight. He already knew he was through with her. But instead of destroying her here and now, he would use her. Use her up in the destruction of Captain fucking Trips.

I'm learning patience, Grandpère. You'll be so proud of me when I tell you.

"No. And that—that's why you're going to tell him. We need his help. We, we need his ace power when the Combine comes to call. Besides, you'll be giving him what he wants most in the world, won't you?"

She looked at him a moment, eyes glinting like coins in the firelight. She stood tiptoe to kiss his cheek. "Yeah," she breathed huskily in his ear, and kissed him on the adolescent down of his cheek. "Sometimes, Blaise, you're almost human."

She turned and ran away.

I'll pay you for that one too, he thought.

"She's in the Reeves Diagnostic and Development Institute, in Brooklyn. Borough Park area. It's a Kings County joint; there's some kind of deal down between the city, the state, and the counties to share custody, so they can keep her circulating."

He was sitting with his butt planted in damp frigid sand, squinting at the occasional stab of a patrol-boat spotlight. It was cold as hell tonight, but you had to be flat desperate to retreat into one of the crumbling turn-of-the-century buildings crammed together on Ellis. She hunkered behind him, seemingly inured to cold in her thin jacket and thinner pants.

"'Diagnostic and Development'?" he said.

"Yeah. Combine sure talks purty, don't it? Pig Latin for 'kid jail,' pal. It's in a pretty decent neighborhood, never run too far down, starting to maybe catch a case of the yuppies. Not too bad. As hellholes go."

He turned and looked at her, disbelief struggling with the will to believe on the battlefield of his face. "How could you find out, when the best lawyer in Jokertown drew a blank?"

"Best lawyer in Jokertown is by definition not a juvenile delinquent, darlin'. *Capisc'?* 'You wanna find a missing kid, ask an outlaw,' or words to that effect."

He jumped up, walked toward the water, walked back, sidestepping a drunk or drugged joker face down in the sand. He began to pace in front of K.C. "I have to make plans. I have to do this right. Think now, Mark. *Think.*" He plumped down in the depression he'd made before, feeling heavy and overwhelmed.

"Maybe you should get some sleep first." She bent over and kissed him lightly on the forehead, then melted into black.

Mark stood on the sidewalk in front of the Blythe van Rensselaer Clinic with tears standing like small hot crowds on his face. Tachyon wasn't in, the surly and unfamiliar face behind the desk of the strangely deserted reception room had told him. And when the doctor was in, he wasn't receiving visitors. *Any* visitors.

Cody was dead. The news lay in Mark's stomach like a gallon of ice. That lady had meant so much to Tach, had done so much to bring him back from the terrible events of the Atlanta Convention.

Sprout had always loved her. And now she was gone, apparent victim of Tachyon's enemies.

Tach had crawled back into the bottle. As he had when honor had forced him to destroy the mind of Blythe van Rensselaer. It would not be easy for him to escape a second time.

And that was tough.

Mark rubbed spidery hands over his face as if scrubbing his cheeks clean with the tears. As he closed his eyes, he saw his daughter's hand reaching out for him again, while he as– Cosmic Traveler sank through the floor of the courthouse and the bailiffs closed in.

I'm sorry, Doc. She needs me worse than you do. No matter what's happening to you.

I'm sorry.

He raised his head. A patrol car prowled by. The flat black face of the cop on the passenger side seemed to track him through the chicken-wire mesh that covered the win-

dows of all the cars from the Jokertown precinct as it slid
sharklike through the sightseers huddled in schools against
the strangeness of the scene.

Time for my boot heels to be wandering, his nascent
street-sense told him.

He stuck his hands in the pocket of his army jacket and
walked away. But not too fast.

The Demon Princes had shot out the streetlights again.
The man walking home from swing shift down the Jokertown
side street paid no mind. It would take more than cracks in
the sidewalk to disrupt the *primo ballerino* grace with which
he walked, as it would take more than the chill of a New York
January evening to require him to add the threadbare windbreaker thrown over one shoulder to the black Cinderella
T-shirt. Besides, he saw in the dark like a leopard.

His chest and shoulders were those of a much taller
man, swollen with muscle. His head was small and narrow,
the features almost elfin. His eyes were slanted, the color of
lilacs. He diverged far enough from the human somatotype to
be considered a joker. Yet he carried no trace of the wild-card
virus.

He wasn't a nat, either. He wasn't human at all.

"Hey, man." The voice came from the dark alley, a few
feet away to his right: a sick-crow caw. The lilac eyes never
wavered. He had no time for importunate groundlings. And if
it was more than a panhandler...

Seventeen months ago, a nat youth had attempted to
mug him at gunpoint on a street much like this one. The
youth was unduly confident in the superstitious terror in
which the denizens of this vast, reeking, unaesthetic jumble
of a city held their primitive firearms, or perhaps his confidence was chemically enhanced. He had been so little challenge that the man with lilac eyes had been merciful. There
was a *chance* the boy had received medical attention in time
to keep from bleeding to death after having his arm torn off at
the shoulder.

"Durg," the voice said, quieter now. "Durg at-Morakh.
It's you, isn't it, man?"

He froze, turned slowly. The tall gaunt figure that shuffled toward him from blackness into mere darkness did not
much resemble the owner of that voice as he remembered
him. Still, the pale eyes of a being shaped by gene engineer-

ing and training to be the consummate bodyguard were not to be deceived by a few alterations in silhouette.

"Dr. Meadows." Durg performed a brief bow, accompanied by a hand gesture.

The taller man stood there in a posture of helplessness. Durg waited, legs braced, head up. He would maintain that pose all night or all week: awaiting orders.

"Uh, how's life, man?"

"My job as a stevedore provides adequate exercise. The pay affords me such comfort as this overly warm and insufficiently civilized world can provide." Thin lips smiled. "Should I require more funds, my coworkers are ever eager to wager on contests of strength and dexterity. Some of your people are dismally slow learners, lord. I would hope your own fortunes have changed for the better."

"No. Not really. Except—except I've found my little girl."

"I rejoice that the Little Mistress has been discovered. Does your government still hold her captive?"

"Yeah." Mark bit his lip and shuffled his feet. "I—I have to get her back. God only knows what she's going through."

"You mean, then, to employ force?"

Mark's gaze rummaged among the fissures in the pavement. He nodded. "You know I'm not comfortable with this kind of thing. But I'm desperate, man. I'm really strung out. I need to know, will you help me?"

"Does the sun yet shine on Avendrath Crag?"

"Beg pardon?"

"A Morakh saying, lord. So long as the sun of Takis shines, so long as the great rock of Avendrath shall stand—so long shall the loyalty of a Morakh run true."

"It'll mean breaking the law."

The elfin head tipped back, rang laughter like the pealing of a big silver bell. "I care as much for the laws of your kind as you care what legislation dogs might pass. Had you listened to me, you would have defied the law long since and fought to keep your daughter by force or stealth."

"I wasn't ready, man. I—I still believed in justice."

"Your world entertains many quaint superstitions. What now, my lord?"

"Now I'm gonna get Sprout back," Mark said. "Whatever it takes."

*   *   *

Bloat said he hated pity. His visitor pitied him, and he found it oddly pleasurable. What the man didn't feel was *repugnance*. That made all the difference.

"Dr. Meadows," he said, "welcome."

Mustelina and Andiron took their cue and left. Meadows stood blinking up at Bloat's bloatblack-slimy sides. "Thanks, uh, Governor. Like, to what do I owe the honor?"

You're dying to know what's become of your friend, Bloat thought, and couldn't help but giggle. *The poor man. Should I tell you where he is?*

"I understand you have a project in mind."

The tall man swallowed. Bloat heard him turn up the *deception* card and toss it away without hesitation, as if he were unused to its use. How rare that was.

"It's my daughter, Governor." He glanced at Kafka. "I have to get her back." *With or without your permission*. He didn't speak the words, but of course Bloat heard them.

"You don't need my permission," Bloat said, and tittered at the way Mark jumped to hear his own thoughts quoted. "But you have it. My blessings, even. More than that, Doctor. I want to offer my *help*."

"What—what do you mean, man?"

"You want to see if you can bring your friends back. Don't look so surprised, Doctor; you've got to know I can read your mind. I know what you need. You need certain drugs and a safe place to work. I can offer those things."

"What do you want from me?"

Bloat clucked. "My, my. The Last Hippie has gotten cynical."

"It's just the way the world works, man."

"Exactly. Dr. Meadows, you've felt the anger of the straight world—the anger and the fear. We've offered you shelter from it."

"Yeah, thanks, man, like I really appreciate—"

"Wait. That's understood. I want to make sure you understand that this can't last. The nats—the straights—won't let us defy them forever. They have to reassert their power. To destroy us for being different and daring to hold our heads up and not be ashamed."

Meadows nodded. "You think the Combine will move in on you. Makes sense."

"The Combine? Oh, you've been talking to K.C. Strange. Yes. We're inevitably going to be attacked, and we will fight.

What I ask in exchange for my help is that you fight beside us when the time comes."

He read Meadows's hesitation and, stifled his own feelings of disappointed anger and *I thought you would be different.* "I know it's a big step. Asking you to cut yourself off completely from the nat world. But it's really a fait accompli, isn't it, Doctor? The straight world's rejected you. It's hunting you like a vicious animal. Do you really have anything left to lose?"

"No," Meadows said quietly. "Like, I guess not." He raised his head. "I'm with you, man."

Bloat giggled happily. "Marvelous! And now I have something—"

"Just one thing. When I get Sprout back, I have to find out what's happened to Tachyon. If he's in trouble, my friends and I will have to get him out. Then I'll, like, be happy to help you."

Uh-oh, Bloat thought. He switched in mid-sentence. "—something to ask you. What do you think of Hieronymous Bosch?"

Meadows's eyes lit. "I *love* him, man. He's my favorite. Him and M.C. Escher. And, uh, Peter Max."

When Mark had left, Kafka said, "You should have told him to go to Blaise for help hunting Tachyon. It would have been amusing."

Bloat's jellyfish sides heaved. The black ran glistening down. "I need them both," he said. "I need all the help I can get."

"You toyed with the notion of telling him, though, didn't you? About Tachyon."

"Blaise is—he's like a force of nature. I don't dare challenge him. He'll destroy us all. It's all I can do to get him to keep a lid on his taste for atrocity, and that's only here on my island."

Kafka produced clicking sounds with his chitinous joints.

"Someday, Kafka. Someday we'll face down the nats and win. Then maybe Mark Meadows will hear a few things that'll raise his eyebrows. And then maybe Jumpin' Jack Flash will burn pretty Blaise fucking Andrieux down to a cinder.

"*Someday.*"

"We're all secure here," K.C. Strange said. "Bloat's people are keeping the gawkers away."

Mark swallowed, nodded convulsively. He didn't look up from his work. "Ready in a minute, man. Don't rush me."

The metal table was rickety, its washers rattling at every random gust that bulled its way into the fiberboard shack. The light from the alcohol lamp was thin and thready as a dying woman's pulse. Conditions were not ideal. But Mark in his way was an artist, who knew how to work around the limitations of his surroundings and his media. And this was a familiar task, even after so many months he didn't care to count. In the doing of it, he was even able to take a certain shelter: from thought, from demands the world and he laid upon him that he realized he in all likelihood could not fulfill.

K.C. sat down and drew her knees under her chin. Her eyes glowed like coins in the lamplight as she watched Mark measure powder into glittering mounds of color.

Something passed behind Mark's eyes. His hand faltered, but none of the precious powder fell from the scoop. Even Bloat had only been able to obtain a fraction of the substances Mark needed. Enough to summon two of his friends for perhaps an hour apiece. Not necessarily the two he would have chosen.

He let his hand rest on the cold thin-gauge tabletop, suddenly uncertain. "I think there's something wrong with Tach," he said.

K.C. shifted her weight with a mouse rustle.

"This isn't like him. He'd never give up the clinic. He's stronger than he was back in the Forties. The clinic *made* him strong. It gave him something to live for."

"Fucking *give it up!*" Her voice rang like brass knucks on a steel surgical table. "He's ditched you. He's ditched the jokers and you and every fucking body. Sometimes people just turn their back and walk away from you, *capisc´*?"

He lowered his head and shut his eyes in pain. Instantly she was by his side, hand on arm. "I'm sorry, babe," she said. "I've gotten some pretty rough licks from life. Made me pretty cynical, okay? I don't have to lay it off on you."

"No," Mark said. "No, it's okay. I still can't believe he's abandoned me. I think something's happened to him."

Her nails dug into his arm. "What are you going to do about it?"

"Nothing." The word fell to the tabletop with scarcely more sound than a drop of sweat. "Not now. I hope he's okay.

I'll do anything I can to help him—later. But Sprout—that's stronger than friendship. I'm sorry."

She ran her hand up to his shoulder. He started to shy away, then relaxed with an audible sigh.

"You got nothin' to apologize for, babe," she said, low in her throat.

He emptied the contents of the scoop into a tiny vial, then stoppered it quickly, as if expecting the orange powder to escape. "Let's go."

K.C. followed him out onto the reeking beach. Mark stood with his feet spread wide in the sand, twisted the plastic cap off and tossed the orange powder down his throat. He sighed explosively, lowered his arm.

Then he burst into flame.

K.C. screamed and threw herself forward. Furnace heat threw her back. She smelled her eyebrows scorching.

Reeling back, she saw that Mark was not fighting the flame. He had staggered several steps away from her, but now he seemed to be letting the fire have its way with him.

"God, oh God, Mark, what have you *done*?" He was charring down to a mummy right before her eyes. She had read that happened when you burned. She never thought it could happen so fast. *God, he's already down to my size!*

The mummy spread its arms.

K.C. screamed. The flames began to die, seeming to be sucked into the burning man. Astonished, she saw a flash of unburned skin, and then a small man in an orange jogging suit was standing there, grinning, while a final few flames chased each other through his shock of red hair.

"So you're the kind of babe Mark's hanging with these days," he said. "Bit less Park Avenue than the last one, but I'm not sure that's not an improvement."

Her first attempt at speech failed. She swallowed and tried again. "Who are you?"

He laughed. "Jumpin' Jack Flash, at your service, dear." He spread his hands and a tiny fireball arced from palm to palm. "It's a gas-gas-gas."

"Then it's true. He really was Cap'n Trips."

The fragment of fire sizzled and died on the upturned palm. Its echo still glimmered in his eyes as he raised them to hers and said, "He still *is* Cap'n Trips, doll."

He twisted left and right, the locked his hands, held them up over his head and back, stretching.

"Let's do it," he said. An orange glow sprang up in the air around him, without apparent source.

K.C. looked around nervously. "Jesus, do you *have* to do that? We don't need to advertise the fact that Cap'n Trips is back to the immediate world."

"Yeah, you're right. When you're right, you're right. I don't *need* the F/X. It's just been so damn long, and I'm used to going in style...oh, well."

He flexed his knees and leapt into the sky.

Half an hour later, Flash touched down again, flipping a finger at the white foam wake of a harbor patrol boat churning outside the wall a few hundred yards away.

"Officious fucks. Don't even let me have a final flourish. 'Scuse me just a moment, hon. My exits aren't quite as stagy as my entrances." He stepped around the end of the shack.

K.C. stood, brushed wet sand off the taut seat of her black leather pants. "I've seen some scaly shit," she said, "I've *done* some. But this could take some getting used to."

She heard a strange *whump* like gasoline lighting off, and then a moan. She ran to find Mark Meadows lying in the fetal position in a depression in the sand, buck naked and turning blue.

She helped him sit up. Inside the shack was an army blanket. She brought it, wrapped it around Mark's shoulders. "Come on," she said. "Let's get inside out of the cold."

K.C. threaded one of Mark's arms around her shoulders, urged him to his feet. He lurched into the shack like a radio mast that had come to life and decided to take a hike. Inside she sat him on a second blanket thrown over a pad of old newspapers.

Mark turned his face toward the wall. His shoulders shook. "You're crying!" She touched his shoulder. He shrugged her off. "Why? What's the matter?"

"I can't do it," he sobbed.

"What? What are you talking about? You're an ace again. You *changed*. You got to fly. How long has it been, babe?"

"Too—too long. I don't know." He sat up shaking his head. Tears streamed down his wasted cheeks, glinting like melted butter in the yellow lamplight. "I don't think I can handle it."

"What do you mean? You ought to be high as a kite right now. You've *won*."

"No. You don't understand. *They* won. I'm not innocent anymore, man. I've lost the purity. Lost the dream."

"It's the drugs. You're just crashing." She put her arm around him. "You'll be okay in a while."

"*No!*" He tore away, lunged to his feet. "You don't *understand*. I'm no good any more."

"You'd do anything, right? For her?"

He nodded.

"Mark. Listen to me. That's love. That's loyalty. I've seen aces, dude. I know plenty of people who can do weird stuff. Shit, I can chase people out of their own heads and party hearty inside, bust up all the furniture if I want to. But to have that much loyalty to a person, to love her that much—" It was her turn to move away. "Nobody's ever felt that way about me. *Nobody*."

He slumped to the floor. "Yeah. I let you down too. I let everybody down. And now Sprout—shit, man, I can't even help her."

"*What?*"

"I can't do it any more. It just isn't right. I wanted to be more than an ace. I wanted to be a *hero*. But that's all just illusion." He hung his head. "At least for me it is."

"What the *fuck*?" She grabbed him under the arms, hauled him to his feet with a strength she didn't know she had. "Listen to me, you son of a bitch. You don't think you got what it takes to be a hero? Then be a fucking *villain*.

"The world thinks you're fucked up. The world thinks you're evil. The world thinks it's a good idea to stick your little girl in kid jail where the other girls can use her for a punching bag. Where sooner or later some counselor is going to get the idea how very pretty her blonde little head would look bobbing up and down on his needle dick. Decide that's just the therapy she needs."

"Don't say that!"

"Don't tell me you don't know! It's the only thing that kept you going all these months. What brought you out of the gutter and onto the Rox. It's real, Jack. I can tell you it is. Okay? We are not talking hearsay. This doesn't just happen in Linda Blair movies. I know. *I fucking know*."

She had backed him into the wall. He slid slowly down. "But what am I gonna do?"

"Welcome to the jungle, babe. You're on the Rox now.

You're an outlaw. The first thing you do is accept that. The second is, kick some ass."

He stared at his hands. "Yeah. I guess so."

Her leather jacket slumped down beside him. He jumped, looked up at her.

She was skinning her *Jane's Addiction* T-shirt off over her head. Her breasts were small and conical. The nipples stood up into points.

"I lied," she said, undoing her fly. "There is something else you're going to do first."

He was instantly hard. To his horror, his erection tented up the front of the blanket he had wrapped around him poncho-style. He tried to edge away.

"But, uh, Blaise—" he stammered. "But Bloat—"

"But nothing." She covered his mouth with hers.

There were eight million stories in the naked city. Most of them were about assholes. The Great and Powerful Turtle looked over the monitor screens around the control console of his shell and thought pissed-off thoughts about how there was never anything good on television.

He canted his shell and slid down for a look at the crowds by Madison Square. "Imagine," he said aloud. "I'm up here looking out for that asshole, George Bush."

The president was in town to confer with the new mayor. A number of the more prominent public aces had volunteered to help ensure there were no incidents, with the grudging acquiescence of police and city officials. It wasn't that they *liked* Bush. The very idea that anyone might think he did pissed Turtle off no end. But this jumper thing was getting way the hell out of hand. It was more than mere media hype.

Given the country's current mood, anything that happened to Bush was liable to be blamed on aces and the Medellin cartel, a connection George had done so much to establish in the public mind. And if an ace, even a jumper, had anything to do with actually *harming* the president . . .

It would be easy to call the consequences unthinkable. But they were all too thinkable. They'd make McCarthy look like the *Phil Donahue Show*. So the Turtle was up here farting around to watch over a man who'd just as soon see him in a concentration camp. Great. Just fucking great.

A disturbance below. A stout black woman, hat askew,

sat on the sidewalk. A skinny youth elbowed his way through the tourist throngs clutching her handbag by a strap.

"Don't these assholes ever give it a break?" Turtle asked the air. He punched up the megaphone. "Okay, dickweed, this is the Great and Powerful Turtle. Hold it right there or I'll spoil your whole damn day."

The purse snatcher looked left and right, but not *up*. "What a weenie," Turtle said, and winced as he felt his amplified words reverberate through his armor plate. *Forgot to dump the mike*. Great.

He reached down with his teke hand and grabbed the kid by the ankle, swooping him into the air. While the crowd gawked and pointed—"git a picture o' *that*, Martha, or the folks'll never believe us back in Peoria"—he carried the kid, the top of his head ten feet off the pavement, back to where the stout black woman was picking herself up. He shook the kid up and down until he let go of the handbag. "Oh, thank you, Mr. Turtle," the woman called. "God bless you."

"Yeah, lady, anytime." He stuffed the kid in a dumpster and flew off.

"George fucking Bush," he said. "Jesus." Fortunately he'd turned the microphone off.

"This is never gonna work," Mark Meadows said, feeling his head again. The Grecian Formula he'd doused his head with to cover the punk racing stripes had reacted funny with some of the dye, and now it felt as if he'd been moussing with old paint.

Up front in the driver's seat, Durg impassively kept his eyes on the road and his hands upon the wheel, just like the old song. His head looked odd sprouting from his collar and broad, suit-coated shoulders, like some narrow vegetable.

Frowning, K.C. scrunched herself farther down next to Mark. "Quit fussing, will you? Jesus."

Mark plucked at his tan corduroy sport coat and improbably wide maroon tie, and ran his fingers under the harness of his shoulder holster. There was nothing *in* the shoulder holster; Mark had a terror of guns, and like a good modern liberal knew for a fact that if he carried one, it would instantly take possession of his mind and cause him to rush into a subway and start shooting black teenagers. But K.C. insisted he at least wear the holster so he'd have the appropriate bulge under his left arm.

"I'm never gonna pass for a cop. I look like a total geek."

"You don't know much about cops, do you? We should have got you a bad hairpiece too. And maybe strapped a pillow to your stomach so you'd look like you'd put in your time on a Dunkin Donuts stool. Besides—" she turned and stretched quickly to kiss his cheek—"you *are* kind of a geek, babe. Lucky for you I got kinky tastes."

He shuddered. "I don't know what I think I'm doing. I got no right to involve you and Durg in this."

K.C. fell back against the seat, bounced briefly. "You don't have a gun, sugar, so you couldn't hold one to my head."

"I live to serve," Durg said.

Mark's loosely strung-together collection of features twitched in irritation. "That's just a cliché, man. Your life is your own."

"Perhaps it is a cliché among your kind. To the Morakh, it is biological fact. For me, a master is like food—I can go without, but only for a short period of time. Then I must weaken and die."

"Things work different on our world, man."

"My genes are not of this world. They make me what I am."

"You must hate what they've done to you," K.C. said. "The people who created you."

He glanced over the butte of his shoulder. The look in the lilac eyes was amusement. It hit her like a blow. "What *they* have done to me, lady, is give me life. And strength, and agility, and skill. They have given me *perfection*. Among your kind I am an ace. Among Takisians I am an object of awe, even terror. Are these things not glorious? All they ask of me in return is that I do what I am uniquely equipped to do. I see no disparity."

"A man who knows what he wants." K.C. leaned forward and breathed in Mark's ear. "I think I love him."

She nipped Mark's earlobe. He blushed furiously. She giggled.

Durg cleared his throat. "We approach our objective."

"All right." K.C. subsided in her seat. "I'm back to being a bad little prisoner girl now. Kind of like a skinny, mean Michelle Pfeiffer."

Her short neutral-colored hair had been washed and combed out wet into bangs. She wore a scuffed leather jacket over tight black pants and a white T-shirt with three defiant transverse slashes across the belly. No spikes; when they committed you to the juvie justice system, they relieved you of props like that. She *did* look like a skinny, mean Michelle Pfeiffer.

"So, how'd you get this gig, anyway, Durg? What's a Takisian doing hanging out with a skinny Earthling biochemist kind of guy?"

"I came to this planet with Prince Zabb of House Ilkazam, cousin and blood-foe of the being you know as Dr. Tachyon. Dr. Meadows, more loyal a friend than Tachyon deserves, fought to aid him. In one of his avatars he bested me in single combat, thereby winning my loyalty. I have found him a good master, if somewhat prone to forget his servant."

"Sounds kinky," K.C. said.

They topped a hill, rolled down a block of shabby-genteel stone buildings with plenty of wrought iron at ground level. On the right, Reeves showed the street a blank high wall looped with strands of razor tape, a gate of wrought-iron spikes.

"Why are you slowing so soon, man?" Mark asked as Durg braked.

Durg nodded his narrow head. "That sedan at the head of the next block. It has two occupants in the front, more perhaps in back. I am disquieted."

"The windshield's so dark," K.C. said, "how can you see anything?"

"He can see, man," Mark said.

"Should I drive on?"

"You're being paranoid, Durg," K.C. said.

They were almost at the gate, which stood open. On the far wall a small bronze plaque proclaimed RICHARD REEVES JUVENILE DIAGNOSTIC AND DEVELOPMENTAL CENTER through patina and soot. On the near wall a sign said DO NOT PICK UP HITCHHIKERS IN THIS AREA.

Beyond those walls was Sprout.

From what Tach had told him of Takis—a pang of guilt here, over possibly leaving his friend in a tight place—a tendency to err on the side of caution would be a highly desirable trait in a Morakh. *K.C.'s right*, he told himself. "No. We go in."

Durg turned his head a fraction to the right, flicked Mark with his lilac eyes. Mark swallowed. Years of association with the alien told him that was the closest a Morakh could come to open mutiny. He set his jaw and tried to look determined.

Reeves occupied an outsize lot with a paved courtyard. Durg cranked the wheel to bring the car around in front of the cement steps behind a station wagon with heavy wire mesh in the rear windows—

And abruptly slammed the stick into reverse, Mark's chin bouncing off the front seat back as the LeBaron accelerated backward.

Not even Morakh hearing and Morakh reflexes were quite quick enough. The long sedan with the tinted windshield was already blocking the gate, trapping them.

"Daigla bal'nagh!" Durg braked to a bucking stop and reached inside his dark suit coat. He *did* have a gun in his shoulder holster, a Colt 10-mm auto that would shoot through an engine block and knock down a man in body armor.

K.C. dug nails into his arm like talons. "No! Look."

Men in flak jackets, dark blue baseball caps, and identical aviator sunglasses were pouring out of the building and around the brick sides, pointing shotguns and M16s at the car.

"Holy shit," Mark gulped. His hand dived into the inside pocket of his sport coat.

"Come out of the car with your hands up," Lieutenant Norwalk said through the megaphone. He stood tall at the head of the front steps, ignoring the SWAT team's frantic signals to seek cover. He knew these New Age wimps. Mark Meadows would never hurt him. Norwalk bet he didn't even carry a gun.

As he lowered the loudspeaker he cheated his face slightly to the right, so that the *Action News* team on the roof opposite would be sure to catch his best profile. He was a rangy man who really and truly thought he looked like actor Scot Glenn.

The LeBaron's windows were tinted, so that he couldn't see clearly inside. But he thought he saw movement, and a ripple of tension among the crouching SWAT men confirmed it.

The rear passenger's side door nearest Norwalk began to open. He put his head back and waited, conscious that even the way the late-morning bluster ruffled the sandy hair brushed across his balding crown was reminiscent of Scot Glenn.

Out of the car stepped . . . George Bush.

"Hey, kid," the SWAT cop yelled from behind the trunk of a cruiser blocking the street above Reeves. "Get back. Get out of here."

The boy kept coming. A tall athletic-looking red-haired kid in a leather jacket, who obviously thought he was Major Bad News.

"Fuck," the policeman said under his breath. They could have the fucking news teams set up to cover the big event, but they couldn't detail enough people to keep civilians from wandering into the line of fire. Too much danger of alerting the quarry. *Oh*, yeah. He should have stayed in the army.

He stood up, flipping on the safety of his Remington 870 riot gun. Then he stopped, leaned the shotgun against the car, and began taking off his uniform.

Blaise knelt beside a pair of officers behind the sedan parked across the gate into Reeves. The policeman's uniform was a couple of sizes too big, especially in the gut, but that wasn't too overt. With his riot helmet and dark glasses and his tail tucked down inside his flak jacket, nobody spared him a glance.

He was filled with wild hot energy, the energy of repletion, like taking a woman for the first time, or mind-controlling a man into cutting his own throat with a razor. The kind of energy that needed occasional venting so it wouldn't get the better of him. It was coming down payback time on Mark Meadows and K.C. fucking Strange. He knew how to savor these moments.

Thanks to New York regulations, when you dropped a dime on someone, you still actually dropped a dime. Bloat would suspect. At Blaise's first unguarded moment, Bloat would *know*. But he would never take action any length of time after the fact. Bloat needed the jumpers, needed their drugs, needed their numbers when the Man came to call.

More than that, Bloat was too cowardly to burn Blaise in cold blood. He was too sensitive. The ultimate eighties kind of guy.

Blaise giggled. A couple of cops briefly turned faces hidden by sunsplash on visors toward him, but their body language showed neither surprise nor concern. Giggling is more common on the firing line than jackboot-opera cop shows want you to believe.

Then the cops' body language changed to stone confusion.

"What is all this here? What is this? I approve of men on the front lines in the war against crime in our streets showing initiative, but don't you think this is taking things too far?"

No, Lieutenant Norwalk thought, *bullshit—no way. This cannot be the president*. But still—he *looked* like Bush, and he *acted* like Bush, and he had that prissy little mouth . . . and Christ knew he *talked* like George Bush.

The SWAT troopies were back on their heels, lifting weapons off-line in confusion. They couldn't quite believe it was Bush either, but if it was, their nifty Hard Corps vests with *SWAT* in big tape letters on the back were not going to keep their asses out of Leavenworth on a long-term lease if they pointed fucking *guns* at him. And it would be just like the weenie to pull a spot inspection of some chickensquat D-home on zero notice.

No, no, where's the Secret Service? Reality got hold of Norwalk's brain again, and he opened his mouth to give orders to grab the impostor. Then a small nasty-looking number in black leather stuck her Michelle Pfeiffer snub nose out the door behind the pseudopresident. Her pale eyes met his.

"Put down your guns, men," Lieutenant Norwalk rapped. "Can't you see it's the president? Dammit, move when I tell you!"

The SWAT men eyed him dubiously but obeyed, straightening up from behind the station wagon, rising out of the empty flower beds. Norwalk had a rep for liking to chew ass. If he said this was George Bush, that made it official.

The little cupcake in black sagged against the car with drool trailing from the corner of her mouth. Since she was a lot more fun to look at than the president, several of the team noticed her open her mouth as though about to scream. A plainclothes cop who looked like a compressed Jean-Claude van Damme slid around from the driver's side and caught her arm just above the elbow. No sound came out of her.

George Bush strode up the steps. Lieutenant Norwalk

held the door for him. The squat cop and his prisoner followed.

In the foyer George Bush looked left and right. No one in sight. He stooped slightly to honk the girl's left butt-cheek.

"No one can say I don't take an active interest in today's young people," he croaked.

"If I was in my own body, I'd break your arm for you, you asshole," Lieutenant Norwalk said, stumbling slightly.

The president gave the policeman a horrible stroke victim's leer. "It's nothing I haven't done before, my child."

"That was Mark. I don't even know who you *are*, you creepy blue thing, so just fucking watch it."

"I'm your salvation, you ungrateful little—"

"*Shh*," Durg said pointedly. He gave the captive a quick slap on the side of the head, enough to scramble whatever wits she had been able to gather. Or he, actually. Most people who were jumped were incapable of doing anything meaningful for a while, but he was taking no chances.

In the reception area a couple of uniforms stood, making sure the staff didn't go pressing their noses to the front door and giving away the show or getting in the way of any stray slugs. They gaped at the intruders.

"Mr. President," the black cop said.

"Just a moment," a heavyset black woman in a mauve dress with an outsize collar exclaimed. "That's not really the president."

Durg pushed K.C.'s body to the scuffed hardwood floor. His arm whipped out with the big black Colt in his fist. "But this is really a gun. Nobody move."

K.C. guided Norwalk's body past him. Keeping clear of his line of fire, he relieved the black cop of his sidearm, tossed it to Durg. He caught it one-handed, pointed it at the other cop as K.C. disarmed him.

"Oh, my," the man who looked like George Bush said. "I don't approve of firearms. People might use them to defy the law."

"Shut the fuck up," K.C. Norwalk said. To the administrator in the mauve dress she said, "Sprout Meadows. Where?"

"I won't tell you."

K.C. pointed the second officer's pistol at her. "If I kill you, maybe somebody else will be a little more sensible."

"*Lieutenant Norwalk*," the white cop breathed.

"Blow me, Patrolman. Now, where's the girl?" She cocked the pistol. "*One*—"

"Rec room. Annex in the back, second floor."

Turtle blinked and stabbed a finger at the control of his police-band radio, overriding the automatic scanner. He punched it back three channels, to the broadcast that had belatedly caught his attention.

"—*tell you it's the president of the United States!*" a voice was insisting. "*George Bush. The weenie himself. He's on some kind of cockamamy spot inspection*—"

The Turtle frowned. Bush was supposed to be under massive guard, addressing a Turn-In-Your-Parents rally somewhere in Harlem. He looked at the digital readout, checked the freek against a dog-eared looseleaf notebook hung beside his console. *Brooklyn.*

The voices were still arguing about whether the president could possibly be at something called the Reeves Institute. He turned his shell east.

Sprout Meadows sat to one side looking at the pictures in a magazine with a yellow cover. She liked to look at that magazine because it always had nice animals in it. Sometimes it almost seemed she could tell what the words said. But never quite.

Fine Young Cannibals were on the television high on the wall. A couple of girls were arguing over whether to keep watching MTV or switch to *Santa Barbara*. It sounded as if they were going to start hitting each other at any moment. Sprout was getting good at telling things like that. Fortunately the other girls had gotten bored with picking on her; she was mostly left alone these days. That meant the counselors scolded her for not getting more involved in what the other girls did. She hated being scolded. But she hated getting picked on more.

She glanced up. The monitor lady was watching her intently, just as she'd thought. That always happened when other girls got ready to fight. Sprout thought it was because the monitor lady got in trouble if she reported that the other girls were fighting but got rewarded if she told on Sprout. But that probably just meant Sprout was stupid, like the other girls always told her.

The door opened. Two men walked in. One of the girls squealed in surprise. The monitor stepped forward, frowning.

"I'm sorry, you're not supposed—my God, it's President Bush."

"Yes. Yes it is. How perceptive of you to notice." He smiled and nodded at her, then looked around the room. "Sprout? Is there a Sprout Meadows here?"

Cheeks burning, Sprout dropped her *National Geographic* and stood up. She couldn't say a word. Inside she quailed, knowing that he'd never see her because she couldn't make herself talk.

But he did. He smiled and dropped to one knee. "Come here, honey. I've come to take you to your daddy."

The movies notwithstanding, a human being is not physically capable of aiming two handguns at different targets with any degree of accuracy. A Morakh is. Somehow the two police officers sensed it.

They hadn't offered any backchat when he ordered them to drop their trousers around their ankles. Now he'd gotten them to cuff themselves together, back-to-back, and stand to one side, still covered by the Colt, while a nervous staffer pulled the phones out of the wall under the watchful eye of the service revolver. The people outside were still dithering. Everything seemed to be under control.

He knew it couldn't last.

"I can't believe this is going so smoothly," K.C. said as they approached the stairwell. Her voice sounded strange in her ears; *everything* sounded strange in her ears. She was getting antsy to get back in her own body. She'd never liked long-term jumps. They disoriented her, and her borrowed bodies never seemed to respond well to her commands.

"Are you really taking me to my daddy?" Sprout asked George Bush, who was holding her hand.

"Yes, I am. I'm not really the president, you see. I'm one of your daddy's friends. Cosmic Traveler, I'm called."

Her face lit up. "Oh, I know! The blue one. The one everybody says is a weenie."

Black and menacing in his borrowed cop suit, Blaise stalked down the reform-school corridor, head buzzing with fury and the disinfectant smell that forced its way into his

nostrils like probing fingers. He had set the perfect trap for
Meadows: the pigs had the drop on him, and even if Meadows
found the balls to act, no matter how powerful a "friend" the
ancient hippie summoned, he or she couldn't make his companions bulletproof. Meadows didn't have the spine to write
them off and drive for his daughter on his own. Blaise knew
that as he knew he could make a five-year-old skip rope into
the path of a speeding semi.

Yet Meadows had found a way through the jaws of the
perfect trap.

I was right to fear him! he yammered in his mind, as if
Bloat could read him from here. *He's too powerful! He must
be destroyed!*

Ahead of him Blaise saw that the corridor led into a
waiting room of some sort. A familiar pair of legs encased in
skintight black protruded from the left, lying up against a
chest-high wood-sided planter.

He paused, unsnapped the safety strap on his holster. He'd
left the riot gun propped inside the side door he'd let himself
in through. To a European, a shotgun is a peasant's weapon.
He preferred the precision of a handgun, and was vain of the
combat shooting skills his grandfather had drilled into him.

He drew the pistol. It was one of the new Walther nine
millimeters with an ultra-high-capacity magazine. Solid
Euroworkmanship; he approved. He shifted to the right-hand
wall of the corridor and moved forward with the pistol held in
both hands, ready.

The rest of K.C. came into view. She lay with her arms
cuffed behind her. Her head hung listlessly on her neck.
Blaise recognized a common jump reaction. K.C. wasn't
home right now. His pulse raced with hunter's eagerness.
Swiftly, sure, he glided forward into the foyer.

As expected, the monster was there, positioned to cover
both the front door and the white-faced D-home staffers. The
Morakh. The ultimate abomination—a variant Takisian.

Despite the hostility between Tachyon and Morakh,
Durg had often been set to watch young Blaise. The boy had
a nasty way with baby-sitters. But a Morakh mind cannot be
controlled. Try as he might, Blaise had been unable to dent
Durg's mindshield.

But that was then. Blaise had grown, and learned. He
was unique, a new thing beneath the sun of Takis or Earth,
and he knew no rules.

He reached for Durg's mind. It was like grabbing at a wall, massive as battleship steel, friction-free as glass. Yet for just a moment he actually had a grip. The narrow head snapped around, the lilac eyes found his and widened.

The tree-trunk arm swung around. Blaise narrowed his focus, pouring his entire being into a desperate attempt to stop it. It was like trying to keep a tank gun from traversing. The heavy Colt rose inexorably on-line.

For the rest of Blaise's life he would believe he saw the black 10-mm eye of the pistol flash yellow. Only Takisian reflexes saved him then. He felt the hot breath of the bullet's passage as he threw himself back into the corridor, and its miniature sonic boom stung his cheek like a slap.

He hit the right-hand wall with enough force to send the air out of him, went down on butt and shoulderblades. But his training held; he kept two-handed control of the SWAT man's wonder nine, kept the pistol trained generally on the corridor mouth the whole time.

When he stopped sliding, he firmed his aim in the middle of the door where he judged the center of the Morakh's mass would appear. He held there for a dozen high-speed heartbeats, ignoring the trembling in his arms.

The monster did not follow up his advantage. Blaise fought panic like a swimmer in an undertow, forcing his mind to the surface. Durg would *not* pursue him, he realized. To do so would leave the door unguarded, and holding the surrounding police at bay would be Durg's main priority.

Short of a direct threat to his master—or death—there was no force in the universe that could move a Morakh from his post.

The fear receded. Rage took its place. Blaise dropped his eyes to the limp body of K.C. Strange and smiled. With a gymnast's bound, he came to his feet. He flexed his knees slightly, locked his arms into the isosceles triangle of the Weaver stance, drew a deep breath.

The fat white dot of the foresight hovered like a moon over K. C. Strange's sternum. Blaise began to let the breath out. The trigger slack came in.

"Shit! There's shooting!" K.C. stopped halfway down the stairs.

"Well, it can't hurt *me*, at least," read George Bush's lips.

She tossed her pistol to Cosmic Traveler and fumbled a pair of handcuffs out of a pocket of Norwalk's coat. "Put these on my wrists."

"Whatever for?"

"Something's coming down. I've gotta get back to my body."

"But it's too soon! You have to get us *out* of here!"

"You're the ace. If I have to, I can jump somebody else. Jesus, come *on*."

"Oh, this is just *too much*. Trust Meadows to have such unreliable friends. How can you leave me and this innocent child in the lurch?"

"You, easy." She finished snapping the cuffs around Norwalk's knobby ginger-haired wrists. "Sayonara, sucker."

Blaise squeezed the trigger with one smooth pull, felt the sear break crisply.

K.C. raised her head. Her eyes met his above the sights.

"*No!*" he screamed. The gun bucked and roared. The bullet hit K.C. two inches above the right nipple and slammed her back into the planter.

Durg at-Morakh fired three quick rounds into the corridor from which the shot had come. He was firing blind, suppressive fire; the angle was bad, and he couldn't see a target. It was impossible to cover the gaggle of prisoners, the front door, and the side corridors all at once. Even Morakh had their limitations.

Still, he could scarcely believe he had missed his first shot at the intruding policeman. There had been something behind his eyes, a flicker of touch, like nothing he had ever felt before. Perhaps that had thrown off his aim by a fraction of arc.

It was no excuse. A Morakh knew no excuses, only success or death. If his lord demanded his life for K. C. Strange, it was his.

For now, he still had duty.

Cosmic Traveler and Sprout had just reached bottom when the shot hit K.C. The Traveler cringed as Durg blasted shots in return. His impulse was to go insubstantial and melt through the floor into the basement. It was the sensible thing to do. He could keep himself insubstantial only so long, and then bullets would be able to hurt him, cops would be able to lay heavy coarse hands on him. He couldn't tolerate that risk.

But something—residual influence of the baseline Mark persona perhaps—made it impossible for him simply to vanish and leave Sprout to her fate.

Durg saw him, waved him back. "Go. I'll catch up with you."

Traveler rabbited up the stairs with Sprout in tow.

Tears stung Blaise's eyes as he stumbled down the corridor. *Oh, K.C., K.C., why did you have to choose* that *moment to jump back?*

She was hurt too badly to muster the mental concentration needed to jump to safety in another body. She was lost to him, lost. Rage and grief rose up and threatened to overwhelm him.

Now I'll never get to torture you to death! Oh, Mark Meadows, you have much to answer for.

Durg ignored his captives' screaming. He was focused on the front entrance now. The police outside would have heard the shooting.

Bulky in his flak jacket, a SWAT man hit the outer door, popped it open, and rolled in, leveling a shotgun from the hip.

Durg had orders from his lord to avoid violence if possible, to avoid killing at all costs. Durg had mentally amended that to not killing anyone except to preserve the life of Mark or his daughter. He could always atone with his life later if Mark would not absolve him of guilt for disobedience; to preserve the life of one's lord was a higher imperative even than to obey. But Durg felt confident he need take no lives. None of these groundlings was a big enough threat.

Without seeming to hurry, he pivoted, bringing the Colt around. He fired as it came on-line.

The Kevlar jacket was guaranteed to stop anything up to a .44 Magnum. The 10-mm was slightly less potent, equivalent to a .41 Magnum. As advertised, the vest did stop it. But the copper-jacketed bullet delivered a lot of energy right through the vest into the patrolman's solar plexus. He went down gasping like a grounded carp.

* * *

"Ohh," Cosmic Traveler moaned at the pistol crack that chased them up the stairs like Fate hounding a classical Greek hero. They popped out the top, and there at hand was salvation, the Traveler's ultimate refuge: a broom closet. He tried the door. Locked, of course.

"Shit," he said.

Sprout gasped. Heart in throat, he whirled, expecting to see fifteen hundred SWAT cops and federal agents thundering down on them like a herd of buffalo. Instead, the girl was staring straight at his face, and he realized he'd resumed his preferred form, a blue and hairless humanoid with a black cowl.

"Wait here a moment, honey," he said, and stepped through the door.

Once inside, he thought, *why open the door? It will only let them know I'm here. And they'd never hurt a mere child. I—*

The universe seemed to vibrate to a single plangent chord. A chasm opened beneath his feet. *"No!"* he screamed. "It's not possible! I'm supposed to get an hour! Oh, God, the fool will get me killlllled! . . ."

He plummeted into black infinity.

"Something's going on here," SWAT lieutenant Dixon said to the pencil neck from plainclothes. "I'm assuming Lieutenant Norwalk has been taken hostage. I'm taking command here." He pumped his neck and shoulders a little, hearkening back to lineman days.

The honkie from Serious Crimes kind of fell on himself. "Okay."

A couple of officers had dragged Torres from the doorway, and he was unloading breakfast into what winter and half a hundred booted feet had left of a rosebush.

"All right, we're going in again, but this time we're gonna do it right. Connelly, take your men around to the left. Washington, you go right. Kelly, you get three and take the back. The rest of us are going right through the front door."

There was no one in view down the corridor when Durg got there. He waved his Colt back at the terrified staffers. "I'm letting you go now. Out the front door."

The captives just stared at each other and trembled. He fired a round into the wall over their heads. It sounded like a howitzer going off.

"*Now!*"

They stampeded for the exit just as the cops were coming *in*.

For a moment, Mark Meadows stood in the dark with his hands braced against the door and his head hung between them. It had been a long time since he'd been the Traveler. He'd almost forgotten what this concentration of Lysol and ammonia smelled like.

Cosmic Traveler's final fading plaint still echoed in his skull.

I never promised you an hour, man. That's just the max.

He was pleased to have thought of filling a vial with a sixth of a normal dose for just this kind of emergency, and by chance his timing had been perfect. Maybe he *could* do something right. By accident at least.

"*Sprout*," he breathed. He fumbled at the door, got it open, got his feet tangled, and fell on his knees in the front of his daughter.

Without a word, she lunged forward and wrapped her arms around his neck.

At the foot of the stairs he found Durg. The Morakh had his Colt jammed up in the notch formed by Lt. Norwalk's jaw and his ear, and was winding duct tape around the officer's head to hold it in place. Mark looked past him and yelped. "K.C.!"

She was lying against the wall. The front of her T-shirt was scarlet. She was breathing with difficulty. Her eyes were half closed and looked at nothing.

He knelt beside her. "Baby," he said.

"Don't touch her," Durg said. "She's badly hurt." There was a band of duct tape diagonally across her chest, holding down a gauze compress, now dripping red. Durg believed in being prepared.

Mark touched her cheek. She moaned. Blood bubbled from her lips.

Durg finished taping the dazed policeman. "We must move. The groundlings in front will eventually compose themselves enough to act."

Mark looked a wordless appeal at him.

"I can bear her," the Morahk said. "You take the young mistress and *go*."

"Come on, honey." Mark grabbed Sprout's hand, and they raced back up the stairs.

At the top, Mark turned to his daughter. "Stand back," he said. He reached into the inside pocket of his cord jacket, brought out a tiny vial full of orange powder, raised it to his lips.

From the far end of the corridor, a voice screamed, *"Meadows!"*

From thirty feet away, he could see Meadows's mouth fall open. "Blaise?"

Blaise laughed.

What he was about to do was fantastically risky. He was beyond caring. Besides, he was young, and he was Blaise, and he was immortal.

He seized Meadows's eyes with his, coiled his soul like a panther, and sprang.

Sprout looked from the strangely familiar man dressed like a policeman to her daddy. Her father was wrapped in flames. The expression of calm happiness and love on her perfect features never flickered. Sprout took it for granted that *everybody's* daddy periodically caught fire and turned into somebody else.

Roiling red and black surrounded Blaise, suffused him. For a moment, he saw his own now-vacant body through a roaring curtain of flame. And then his soul exploded outward, went spinning into an endless treacherous dark where shadows went to die.

JJ Flash rocked on his feet. It was as if he were whirling around and around inside his own head, surrounded by a maelstrom of shrieking blackness.

The whirlpool effect subsided like water gurgling down a drain, carrying with it a dying shrill keening like nothing Flash had ever heard. "Wow," he said. Bloat must've gotten burned with some impure shit. JJ would like to hunt up his supplier someday and return the favor—just a bit, teach him better business practices. Guys like that gave the free market a bad name.

He opened his eyes to see a SWAT cop collapsing like a

marionette with its strings snipped at the far end of the hall.
"What the fuck?"

"Hi, JJ," Sprout said shyly.

"Babe. What's happening?" He gave her a quick hug and
hung his head over the stairwell.

"Durg. Go for it."

Durg kicked the back door. He put a bit too much
English on it. The heavy meshed-glass-and-steel door popped
right off its hinges and went spinning out into the small
blacktopped yard to bounce off the eight-foot wall that separated
the institute grounds from the street.

He stopped, slung K.C. over his shoulder as gently as he
could. Then he thrust Norwalk out into the cloud-filtered
light, holding the Colt with his left hand.

"Everybody get back," he commanded. "I'm holding the
hammer back with my thumb. If I release it, the lieutenant
dies."

He gave them a few beats to mull that over, then
stepped outside. He could see four squaddies hunkered in
pairs, covering the door from either side. He walked deliberately to the back wall. Then he looked up at the second-floor
window of the annex.

JJ Flash kissed Sprout on the forehead. "Stick tight,
honey. Back in half a tick."

He rolled his hand onto its back. Flame leapt forth,
played against the window. Glass and steel wire shimmered,
puffed away. Flash followed.

"You *can't* use tear gas," the therapist said. She was a
redheaded woman with saddlebag thighs and thick horn-rim
glasses. "That kind of brutality would devastate our developmental strategies—"

"Screw your strategies," Dixon said. "I'm talkin' *lives*
here—"

"Yo!" a voice said. "Down there. Pay attention."

The babble of voices in the courtyard stopped. Everybody looked at one another, then up.

There was a small red-haired man in an orange jogging
suit hovering just above the peak of the roof. "You might want
to stand back away from the LeBaron, there."

"Nail the bastard!" Dixon roared.

Guns came up. Flash let his hand loll out. A jet of fire flashed to the top of the car Mark and company had arrived in. Just enough to melt through the roof and start the vinyl inside burning nicely.

"The gas tank!" somebody screamed. "Get back!"

Cops and institute staffers scattered. Now that somebody'd had an idea, JJ Flash turned up the heat. The LeBaron exploded with a very satisfactory *whoomp* and a ball of yellow flame.

Explosion! A quarter mile ahead, Turtle saw a fireball blossom into the sky.

"Here we fucking go again." He tipped his shell into a shallow dive and accelerated.

The four cops in back turned to stare at the big black ball of smoke rising from the far side of the building. Leaving K.C. balanced on his broad shoulder, Durg rammed his right fist into the wall.

Brick gave. Powdered mortar drooled away.

He punched the wall again. It bowed outward.

JJ Flash shot out the second-story window, holding Sprout in his arms.

Durg spun a back-kick into the wall. A man-size section exploded outward as though struck by a cannon shell. Nodding politely to the SWAT men, he backed through, dragging Norwalk with him.

Fire has a wonderful effect on people. The fear of burning is immediate and deeply ingrained. Flash enjoyed burning things but not people, so the psychological effect of his fireballs was very convenient.

The Brooklyn cops hadn't forgotten all about the back wall. They thought it unlikely the fugitives could make it out that way, so they'd just stuck a patrol car and a couple of uniforms there on general principles.

By a remarkable coincidence, both uniformed patrolmen remembered urgent appointments when JJ Flash burned through the roof of the car's backseat. Took off down the street in opposite directions.

"It smells icky in here," Sprout complained as she slid in back.

"Be better once the car gets moving," Flash said.

He helped Durg ease K.C. in beside her, then fired a blast back through the hole in the wall to keep the SWAT boys on the other side from getting too curious. Durg broke pistol and gun hand free of Norwalk's head, shoved the still-stunned detective lieutenant in the passenger seat, then ran around to slide in behind the wheel.

"I'll catch up with you later," Flash said. "Want to make sure our friends on the other side have their minds right —*whoa!*"

He was snatched straight up into the sky. A voice boomed down, "FLASH? JJ FLASH? WHAT THE HELL DO YOU THINK YOU'RE DOING, YOU NITWIT?"

"*Run!*" Flash shouted. "I'll handle him."

Without a backward glance, Durg put the car in gear and floored it.

Flash tried to dart away. An invisible hand seemed to be holding him fast, pinning his arms to his side. He couldn't move. "Don't make me get rough with you," he said.

Turtle chewed his underlip. "Have you gone nuts?" he asked his microphone.

"Just a little stir-crazy," came back through the audio pickups mounted in the hull. "Look, it's great schmoozing with you, Turtle, but the boys in blue are going to get sorted out down there and start shooting at me in a minute, and I've got things to see and people to do."

"You're a federal fugitive, for God's sake. Why are you—" He stopped. "I get it. It's Sprout."

"You definitely win the Bonus Round. It's Sprout. Now let me go."

"Jesus, Flash, this is jailbreak. I can't let you get away with this."

"So you're lining up with the pigs? Battle lines are being drawn and all that sixties stuff—is that the side of the barricades you're comfortable with?"

A shot popped off from below. Turtle winced. Flame darted from Flash's hand. An especially bold SWAT man yelped and dropped his M16 as if it were red-hot, largely because it was.

"You people down there stop that," Turtle said. "I have the situation under control."

"My ass you do."

"It's your ass that's gonna get extra holes shot in it if they

don't think I can handle you. Come on, Flash, don't you see
this isn't the *way*?"

"We're fresh out of other ways."

"Flash, I feel for you and Mark, and especially Sprout.
But we can't do things this way anymore. And not *now*, for
God's sake! George Bush is in town. The whole country
thinks aces are arm-in-arm with the devil. What's a scene like
this going to do to wild cards everywhere?"

"Not a fucking thing, you complacent tin-plated son of a
bitch! If they're going to let the lynch mobs loose, they'll find
an excuse sooner or later. They'll make one up if they have
to. Let me *go*."

"No," Turtle said primly. "The welfare of everybody
touched by the wild card's at stake here. I'm taking you in."

"A little girl's *life* is at stake, you bastard. And Mark
Meadows isn't going to rot in federal slam!"

Flash set his jaw and forced flame out through every
pore of his body. The unseen grip did not slacken. "So I can't
singe your telekinetic fingers, eh?"

"THEY'RE ONLY IMAGINARY, YOU KNOW."

"Yeah? Well what can they do to me, then?"

"THIS." Inexorably, the hand began to crush the air out of
him.

He looked around. The cop car was already out of sight.
Durg had instructions what to do if Mark was captured, in whatever persona. The mission was a success if only Sprout got away.

And K.C.

*Damn, that's a fine one. And Mark really loves her. But
there's nothing I can do for her.*

His vision began to swim. Blackness gathered around the
edges. He knew Turtle didn't want to kill him, just black him
out. But he had a higher metabolic rate than a nat, used air
more quickly. Old Ironsides might hold on just a little too
long, and then it was going to be JJ Flash, Turnip. And he
knew that wouldn't do Meadows much good either.

Besides, he was Jumpin' Jack Flash. No pansy who
wouldn't go out in public without his fat ass wrapped in armor
plate was going to take *him*. He began to rotate his left hand,
slowly so that Turtle wouldn't notice. The Turtle hadn't
bothered to immobilize him totally, and Flash was fairly sure
he could. Slowly, slowly—*there*. Palm outward.

"It's not—that—*easy*," he gritted. Fire shot from his palm and splashed against the underside of the Turtle's shell.

"GIVE IT A REST, JJ, ALL RIGHT? THIS IS BATTLESHIP PLATE. IT'S DESIGNED TO STAND UP TO SIXTEEN-INCH SHELLS. YOU THINK A LITTLE FIRE'S GOING TO DO ANYTHING?"

The hand squeezed tighter. Flash gasped in pain, blackness flickered across his brain, the fire jet sputtered.

"Go—ahead—and—squash me. But you're gonna—be Great—and Powerful—Turtle—*soup*."

The flame got brighter. The roar was like a blast furnace in full throat. Flash felt his chest being crushed, felt ribs give and squeak as they reached the breaking point.

He screamed. And put all the force of his pain and fury into the fire.

A tentacle of smoke ran up Turtle's nose. He froze. His control panel lit up like a crash scene on the Triboro Bridge, and the display from his forward vid pickup popped and died from the heat.

"Shit!" Turtle yelled. "*Shit!*"

A klaxon began its cat-in-a-stamping-mill yammer as the fire-suppression system—the same as the M-1 Abrams used, surplus production from FY 1988—flushed the interior with halon gas. He freaked.

The teke hand crushing the life from Jumpin' Jack Flash, Esquire, became sudden nothing.

Bullets hit the hull like hail as the policemen on the ground cut loose. It was too late.

The shell plummeted toward the peaked roofs of the neighborhood. Fear hit the Turtle like a cattle prod in the nuts. For a rare moment in his life, it was a *focusing* fear, a fear that overrode the reflex panic induced by heat-noise-light-smoke: fear of collision with the planet.

Like a man about to be hanged, Turtle found his mind wonderfully concentrated. The shell wobbled, sideslipped, knocked over a chimney with a sliding clatter of yellow brick, and rolled out to a flat hover just below rooftop level.

By that time, even the afterimage of Flash's blazing departure had faded from the watchers' eyes.

For a moment, Blaise just lay there. He felt like a man drowning in rapids who had abruptly fetched up on the bank. He had been spinning, spinning in a roaring sunless void. Reaching out for something he could barely remember, reaching and feeling and desperately trying to force himself toward that familiar shard he sensed in a place without time and space and things.

Home. He was back in his body, his splendid body. *Burning Sky, that was close!* he thought.

Any other jumper would have been lost when he was bounced out of Mark Meadows's body during the phase-shift to JJ Flash. Would have spun forever, or until his consciousness had unraveled and diffused and gone, become one with ever-black. Only the supreme power of Blaise's mind had saved him. It was a test he alone could meet, and he had met it.

Exaltation filled him like a gush of semen. *I have triumphed. I am Blaise!*

Then he remembered what he had come for, and it turned to bile in his mouth. Meadows, his idiot blond brat, Durg, K.C.—all had escaped. He had failed. *Blaise.*

He rolled onto his belly and began to pound his fist against the floor.

Round sunset, this stretch of New Jersey was just like Disneyland, if your tastes ran to industrial. Car corpses strewed fields to either side of the road, inorganic fertilizer spread perhaps to foster the growth of the squat tanks and pipe tangles that hovered in the shimmering petrochemical haze of the horizon. The sun swelled like a huge red festering boil as it fell into the pooled gray-brown crud. It made World War III look like not such a bad idea.

K. C. Strange lay on her back on a dirty old blanket next to the station wagon they'd stashed a few blocks from Reeves and collected when they ditched the cop car and a grumpy, groggy Lieutenant Norwalk. Her breath was coming quick and shallow now, and pink froth bubbled her lips at each exhalation.

Sprout Meadows bent over her, trailing tears and long blond hair in the jumper's upturned face. "Don't die, pretty lady. Please." Her father stroked her hair with the hand that wasn't cradling K.C.'s head in his lap.

Durg stood a discreet distance down the road, keeping watch. A rose-gray Toyota Corolla had been parked there since yesterday, all full of blankets and nonperishable food and stuffed toys for Sprout, to ensure they began the cross-country leg of their escape as clean as possible.

"Blaise did this?" he repeated wonderingly.

"Blaise." K.C. repeated.

He shook his head. "He tried to do something to me—jump me, I guess. Why, man? You were his—his lady. I was his *friend*!" He bit his lip. "It wasn't because we—"

She laughed, winced. "He was through with me. He...hated you. Thought you were...threat. Tell you his dirty secret, babe...mine too. He has his grand—"

He pressed a finger to her lips. "Cool it. No time for that now." It was cold as hell out here on this long-forgotten county road, and his breath came in puffs of fog. He didn't notice. "We're away from the city. You gotta let us take you to a hospital. Nobody'll recognize you."

Her fingernails dug into his arm through the thin cotton of his Brooks Brothers shirt with a strength he didn't think she still had. "*No!* Ahh!"

She clung, eyes shut, until the pain spasm passed. "No," she said again, a whisper now. "Don't give me up to the Combine."

"Nobody's looking for you, babe. We'll tell 'em you got shot when somebody tried to rape you—"

She was shaking her head, slowly, as if each movement tore her further open. "No. I'm wanted. Hospitals, pigs...all part of the Combine. Too late, anyway—I'm...about out of air time." Her eyes came all the way open and looked way back in his. "I'd rather die free than live in a cage."

"You don't have to die."

"No," she said, and her voice was clear. "I don't."

She reached up and grabbed his head with both hands. Mark cried out in alarm as blood welled up around the edges of the tape Durg had wound around her chest, almost black in the orange dusklight. She pulled his face close to hers. Her eyes held his like pins through a butterfly's wings.

"I don't have to die." The blood-froth static was back now, and her voice was sinking under it. "I'm a...jumper, remember? I don't have to—go down with this ship. But I can't touch the alien. I won't touch the baby. And you—"

She forced her shoulders up off the mottled blanket, forced her mouth to his. "I love you, Mark," she said, falling back. Her eyes met his again. "Remember...me..."

Something passed behind his eyes as the light went out

of hers. And then her blood was on his mouth, and she was dead.

The three shots were startlingly loud. They seemed to race clear to the horizon, where a thin scum of day's last light lay like self-luminous chemical waste, and rebound in a heartbeat.

The smell of gasoline from the station wagon's ruptured tank crowded Mark's nostrils as Durg slowly lowered the 10-mm. Mark held the highway flare before his skinny chest desperate-hard for just one moment, so the tendons stood out on the back of his hand. Then he pulled the tab.

"Good-bye, K.C.," he said. "Rest easy, babe." He tossed the hissing magenta spark into the dark pool spreading below the vehicle.

It went up in a rush and a shout of yellow flame.

Mark stood there staring until the heat got so intense that even Sprout backed up, tugging her daddy's hand with gentle insistence. He stayed put. Durg took hold of the back of his shirt and drew him irresistibly back until his eyebrows were in no danger of crisping.

"It is done," the alien said. "We must leave before someone comes to investigate the fire."

They walked to the Toy, soles crunching quietly in the cinder berm.

Mark unlocked and opened the passenger door, then walked to the other side. Durg awaited him.

"The bike we stashed for you is still all right?" Mark asked.

The alien nodded. "You intend to leave me, then," he said flatly.

"We talked about this before, man. The three of us together are, like, just too distinctive."

The fine narrow head nodded. "Indeed. But later . . . may I not join you?"

Mark felt tears crowding his eyes again. *I thought I'd run out of those.*

"No, man. I'm sorry. I've put you through too much already."

"It is what I am made for."

"No. I *can't*. People can't *own* people, man. It doesn't work that way here." Like a man breaking through a membrane wall, Mark abruptly leaned forward and wrapped scarecrow arms briefly around Durg's shoulders. It was like hugging a statue. "Don't be so sad. It's *freedom*, man. It's the greatest thing in the world."

"It is for you."

Sprout hugged the Morakh. He smiled then, and hugged her back. She and Mark climbed into the car.

"Look, man," Mark said out the window, "maybe you should, like, try the Rox. I can't go back, not with Blaise there. But it's me Blaise is mad at, you were just like incidental. Talk to Bloat. He can help keep Blaise off your back if he tries to come down on you, and you can help him out like I was supposed to. Do that, yeah. The Rox."

"Do you so order me, lord?"

Compassion struggled with principle in Mark. As it sometimes should, compassion won. "Yes," he said, not meeting the lilac eyes. "I so order it."

Durg stepped back. "I thank you, lord."

"Good-bye, man, I'll never forget you."

"Nor I you," said Durg at-Morakh.

The Toyota rolled away through crackling gravel. Sprout leaned out the window and waved.

Mark looked back himself, once, as the tires took the cracked, neglected blacktop. For a flicker, he thought he saw something glistening on the alien's high cheek. But it had to be a trick of the light from K.C.'s pyre.

Sprout began to sing a song, something of her own, with words that made sense only to her. The road curved. The alien and the burning car were wiped from sight, and nothing remained but a glow in the sky that gradually faded as the Toyota pulled west for California and freedom. Eventually it was gone.

The Temptation of Hieronymus Bloat

V

He was a lacuna in the fabric of the mindvoices. A vacuum. A null.

I'd never encountered a mindshield like this one. It was a hard round shell that I couldn't quite grasp. Tachyon's mind might have been that way once, but her mind powers were now weak and diffuse. Blaise's shields, as I knew, were erratic and poor, emotions dribbling around and underneath them.

But this one... He had to be an ace, and I don't like aces. I had Kafka send Shroud, File, and Video to meet Charon at the docks.

Video came back a little ahead of the others with images that disturbed me: Our intruder was a man about five feet tall and oddly wide, moving too fast for a mere human and lifting the front end of a jeep as easily as someone picking up a pencil. "He says his name's Doug Morkle. Says he's a Takisian, being hunted by the Combine. The demo's supposed to prove to you that he is who he says he is. He wants refuge. He also wants to meet Blaise."

A little stab of fright shuddered through me, setting off an avalanche of bloatblack. They were walking in the front door now, the Takisian between Shroud and File, neither of whom looked to be so much guarding Morkle as hoping that if he made a move, he'd go for the other. Looking at Morkle, I had no doubt that he could disable both of them before they could move to stop him.

But what I couldn't do was read his thoughts. Their absence roared in my head. I didn't realized just how much I depended on that hearing—I felt like someone suddenly deaf. The Takisian, already a threat from a simple physical standpoint, was more frightening because of that.

"Why is he here, Governor?" Kafka whispered to me as Morkle came across the lobby. The man didn't glance at the lush tapestries, the gorgeous expanse of the *Temptation*, the new paint and gilt, or the stained-glass windows that were slowly transforming this place into a palace. None of that seemed to matter to him. He stared up at me. Pale eyes. Lavender eyes.

"I don't know," I answered Kafka.

His carapace rattled as he looked up at me, startled. "You don't *know*? . . ."

"It is not your concern, in any case," said Morkle, telling us that his hearing was as enhanced as his strength and agility. His words, coupled with the frustration of not being able to eavesdrop on his thoughts, made me angry.

"You're on the Rox now," I snapped back. "Everything on the Rox is *my* business."

Morkle only gazed at me flatly, like a snake. His nose wrinkled. I thought maybe that was disgust, the smell of the bloatblack, but I didn't know. "It you want to stay on the Rox, Morkle," I continued, "you'd better learn—" I stopped. Another, less complete hole was moving through the mindvoices, very close by. "Damn it."

"Governor?" Kafka asked.

"Blaise. He's here. This might be trouble."

Tachyon's grandson threw back the lobby doors. Molly Bolt and Red came in with him, all three armed with automatic weapons. They fanned out as they entered, making distance between them. Their weapons were aimed at Morkle, who made no move at all.

Blaise was radiating a curious mixture of fear and pleasure. "Durg at-Morakh," he said. "Why are you here? I hope you didn't come here to finish what was started with Meadows. I'd hate to have to kill you."

"Blaise—" I began, but he didn't even glance at me.

The Takisian spoke in a flat, emotionless voice. "Morakh serve," he said. "You have Takisian blood; you lived when I tried to kill you. I came to see if you would have need of me.

He did something then I hadn't expected. He went to his knees, prostrating himself before Blaise.

Blaise's mind gleamed with sudden triumph. The look he shot at me then was terrifying in its contempt. *Mine. My beautiful weapon . . .*, I caught, and then Blaise's paranoia made him pay attention to his mindshields, and the thoughts were cut off. "Let's go, Durg at-Morakh bo Zabb Vayawandsa," he said, and gestured to the other jumpers.

"Blaise." He turned. "I wasn't done," I told him.

He just looked at me. I didn't want to know his thoughts at all. I could see it all, there in his eyes. *You are done. Half of your jokers are hooked on rapture; more and more are coming here every day, and all the supplies that feed and house them are bought with the money Prime gives you. We have the rapture, we can give the jokers the nat bodies they want. We can jump the rich or not. Jokers like you are eating at the jumpers' trough. You remember how the Rox used to be? Do you remember jokers starving and living in tumbledown shacks? Is that the kingdom you want to govern, Bloat?*

I knew. I knew when Blaise walked from the lobby with Durg that any chance I had to rescue Tachyon had just dwindled to almost nothing. I knew that Blaise's grip on the Rox would become stronger and more harsh. I knew that my own influence would be damaged, maybe fatally.

I also knew that if I ordered my people to fire, to mow them down in cold blood and take control back again, they might not do it. I could hear their thoughts. The blue tinge of rapture would make them hesitate, the remembrance of hunger and overcrowding, the hope for a new, normal body . . .

Hell, we were rich now. Everyone had food. Everyone had all the toys jumper money could buy. No one wanted to give that up.

I didn't know what they'd do or what would happen.

I don't hurt jokers. I *won't* hurt jokers.

"You may leave," I told Blaise. "I'm done with you now."

It was a poor exit line. It was also the only one I had.

The pond outside the Administration Building—which was again the Crystal Castle in my dream—was frozen over with a late hard freeze. From the castle's glass expanse, from all the sparkling spires and flying buttresses, long icicles hung.

A penguin wearing a funnel hat was skating on the pond.

"Bosch was just like you, y'know," it said, and its voice was just like Robert Wanda's, the art teacher at my high school. I was outside, too, though I was still Bloat. The morning snowfall had blanketed me in thick damp snow. Jokers were sledding down my slopes in sleds made from everything from garbage-can lids to sheet metal. One joker was shaped just like an American Flyer and was carrying Elmo, Peanut, and Kafka down my sides. They laughed and shouted so that I could hardly hear the penguin.

"What do you mean?" I asked it.

The penguin did a triple axel in front of me and came to a dead stop, showering me with ice flakes. "Well," it said. "Bosch's world was also marked by huge, terrible upheavals. The years of his life were marked by pestilence and unrest: economic, social, political, religious. The writers and artists of his time reflected a nearly universal pessimism. A sour lot, all of them, obsessed with death and violence and decay." The penguin began skating backward, effortlessly. "Like you, big guy," it said.

The penguin turned and glided away under a low bridge. Above it, crossing the pond on the bridge, Tachyon was being beaten by a large toad creature with the face of Blaise who brandished a hugh wooden penis. Durg, looking like a thing of shadow, walked behind them.

Tachyon was wearing a dress but otherwise looked like the Tachyon of old, not Kelly. I could hear the wailing torment in his mind and regretted once more that I hadn't told Meadows about her. Maybe, maybe he could have gotten her out.

Not now.

"That's right, flagellate yourself with the guilt. It's good for you."

"You can read my mind?" I asked the penguin.

"What there is of it." It cackled loudly.

I could not read the penguin's thoughts at all. The penguin was a vacuum in the world, an emptiness. Like Durg.

"'All that happens can be performed by demons,'" the penguin quoted. It winked. "Thomas Aquinas."

"Is that supposed to be significant?"

"Could be. Could mean that if you want to rule in a place most of the nats think of as hell, you'd better get ruthless, asshole." The penguin pointed across the bay. There

I could see Manhattan, but there were no skyscrapers, just millions upon millions of people like maggots on a piece of rotting meat in July. They were fighting, quarreling, killing. Above them, demons with disfigured hateful faces spat fire on them, pissed great floods of acid, or shat streams of boiling pitch. I could hear the faint screams and smell the stench of burning flesh on the wind. The sky was blood-red above them.

"Alchemy and witchcraft were real stuff then," the penguin intoned. I could feel the agony of the people washing over me now, a relentless, thundering, screaming tide of it. I wanted to hold my hands over my ears to shut it out.

"Devils pranced, incubi and succubi prowled the night," the penguin continued. "Monsters lurked in the dark forests."

"Like jokers in the city," I murmured as if answering some damn refrain in church. With the words, I could see a vision of my people in Jokertown, flitting like angry ghosts from shadow to shadow, many of their lips tinted with the blue of rapture. The nats turned their faces away in fear and loathing.

"Bosch's world was a world for youth. Old age began at thirty. By the time you were twelve, you were already doing your life's work." The penguin was spinning in front of me on one foot. "Only the young can be innocently cruel or unintentionally evil. Like a child, Bosch viewed the world through symbols and icons—so did everyone else. When you put on a priest's vestments, you *were* the church. A king was not just the ruler—he was the *country*."

"*I* am the Rox."

"So you say," the penguin replied. "Is that why so many of your jokers are looking to Blaise and Prime as the Rox's leaders? Is that why so many jokers are offering to pay the jumpers to transfer them to a nat body? You're losing it, fatboy. It's all dripping through your useless little fingers."

The penguin's tone was so mocking that I reared up like a giant cobra, ready to slam my entire weight down on the fucking bird. Sledding jokers screamed as I tossed them aside like fragile toys. "I *am* the ruler here!" I shouted. "There is no Rox without me!"

"The human condition in Bosch's world was caught up in pessimism, folly, and evil," the penguin shrugged. "Bosch snared the visions in his fevered imagination and made them real. Can you make *your* dreams real, fatso?"

"*Yes!*" I was shouting, but the heat from the Manhattan fires was stifling now and very close; the flames seemed to muffle my roar. The snow was melting everywhere; the ice thinned underneath the penguin as it laughed at me. The toad-Blaise had stopped his torment of Tachyon to look at me with evil, calculating eyes.

Suddenly, the ice of the pond cracked with a sound like breaking glass. The penguin silently disappeared into deep black water. It waved at me as it did so, unperturbed.

I woke. I was where I'd always been since I'd come here, in the lobby. The building was dark and silent. In front of me, I could just make out the larger darkness that was the *Temptation*. The room was cold on my face, though I felt nothing past there.

I wondered if it was snowing outside.

After the penguin dream, I slept, and woke again a few hours later. I'm not sure what time it was, but it was still pitch black in the lobby. I knew something was wrong, though I thought it was just another dream. But it's not like I could pinch myself to see if I was awake . . . .

I guess I'm joking because I don't know how to say any of this. It's all still so unreal . . . as strange as the nightmares I'd had the last two weeks. But it *was* real. I can't fucking deny that. Every damn bit of it was real. . . .

I felt faint proddings against Bloat's Wall and the first whisper of unknown minds. A massed hatred. A group fear. A common abhorrence. Nats, all of them.

I turned my attention to the Wall. I couldn't tell exactly how many there were—maybe fifty or sixty, from the reports in the *Times* later. Most of the minds I sensed were scared, too, frightened of what they were about to face, shivering because they'd heard about my Wall and the jumpers and the rogue aces and jokers. They'd heard that the Rox was hell given life. Individually, none of them would have made it through. My Wall would have taken their paranoia and used it as a weapon against them. The Wall would have turned their bowels to ice water, set their teeth chattering loose in their jaws, and scattered them back to the city in a panic.

I was hearing all kinds of voices jumbled together:

the kids know something's up with Daddy, even the little one. God, I hope Nancy's not having a bad night with them

I hear that the bay's full of skeletons, all around Ellis. People who didn't make it past the wall. They kill them, the jokers do, send 'em down for fish food

they're just kids. Man, I got a teenager no older than them. The lieutenant can say "shoot to kill" all he wants, but I don't know if I can turn a gun on some pimple-faced kid like my Kevin

Yes. I laughed. All of *them* I could have turned if they'd hit the Wall one by one.

But they weren't alone. That was the problem. That's what made me doubt myself, really it was. They were a big group, all coming at once, maybe in nine or ten boats and two, three choppers, hitting my Wall from all sides simultaneously.

They'd taken one other precaution too. In each boat, in each chopper, there was at least one mind so angry, so dedicated, so goddamn *determined* to kick some joker ass that I could feel the Wall stretching and thinning like a rubber band.

Amy's fucking son was there in that bank when they jumped the woman. They gunned down my own nephew. Man, it's gonna give me pleasure to pay that back

no goddam joker's gonna stop me. I'll show them my forty-five caliber wild card. Shove it right down their slimy joker throats

you want to stop the whole wild card problem, just wipe 'em out. Real simple. Just take the whole frigging useless lot of them and bury 'em

I grated out Kafka's name. I felt the joker's mind shaking off his own dreams. He asked me if I was having a nightmare again. I told him one thing only. *"They're* coming."

Kafka didn't answer, but I knew he understood. He snapped his fingers at my guards, making sure they were alert, then scuttled away. A few moments later, I heard the low growling of a siren from the roof of the building. The wail throbbed along the girders and walls; I could feel it shivering everywhere in my body, like a howling banshee.

In the darkness, I tried to push back with my Wall, tried to bring it under conscious control and focus its strength where it was being penetrated. I think it almost worked too.

But I'd already made my mistake. I just didn't know it. It sounds like something Latham would throw back at me, but, man, I'd never had to run a battle before except when I played D&D. Maybe I should have known better.

But I *am* just a kid.

I could have handled it myself. I still think that. Hey, they were just a bunch of cops and park rangers. They weren't really trained for this; they'd never worked together. They didn't even really hate us—they were just doing what they'd been told to do: Go get the joker squatters and teenage delinquents off Ellis.

I could've sent them back. Yes. Hell, they were just plain people, like my dad or Uncle George or Mr. Niemann next door back in Brooklyn.

I know from the news reports that two of the boats and one of the choppers *did* turn tail. I did that much at least. But whoever was in charge had been at least a little smart. They'd made some plans to get through the Wall. The pilots were those with a strong sense of duty and a violent antijoker prejudice, the ones already boiling mad at the way the Rox thumbed its collective nose at the "normal" world. The pilots were all guarded by like souls, so that even if the cops and rangers panicked, they couldn't overpower those in charge. None of the weapons, from what I understand, were to be given out until the Wall had been breached.

Even so . . . Even so, I don't think more than one or two boats would have made it. The papers said several cops jumped overboard. Three rangers leapt from their copters into the bay. If only one or two made it past the Wall, they would've had to turn back simply 'cause there wouldn't have been enough of them.

It would have been a bloodless rout.

Except that I'd already been stupid.

Kafka's alarm had roused the island. Lights snapped on in the Administration Building; I found myself staring full at the Bosch triptych. Jokers were rushing all over the lobby floor and along the high balcony. There was lots of yelling, internal and external, and all of us could hear the sullen *thut-thut-thut* of the helicopters.

The nats were still circling, though, still hitting the Wall and retreating again, like wasps butting against a glass door. They weren't moving in toward the Rox anymore. They couldn't get past my Wall. I could feel the paranoia and fear rising among them, like some infection. A few more minutes, and they would have turned tail and run back to New York or Jersey or wherever they'd come from.

I wasn't paying too much attention to the voices of the Rox. Look, no one can make sense of hundreds of people all yammering at you at once. No, you have to shut some of it out, or you just go crazy. I'd let the Rox fade to a background static while my powers stalked the Wall.

Another mistake.

I felt it happen behind my mental back, sorta.

"No!" I screamed, startling everyone around me. Someone jumped back at my shout and nearly knocked over the *Temptation*. It wobbled and finally steadied. "No!"

The mindvoice of the park ranger guarding the pilot was suddenly gone. There was only a silence where it had been, and then a new voice was there, one I knew: the jumper called Red. I could hear his thoughts as he spoke to them. *...safety off "Welcome" magazine in "to the" and let 'er rip "Rox, assholes!"*

The mindvoices in the copter came at me all overdubbed and confused.

Christ just let me get back to my family. You can HAVE this crap. I—what the hell's with Johnson? "Welcome to the Rox"? Oh God, Johnson! NO! Please God don't	*turn this damn chopper around, if you ask me. Let 'em have stinking Ellis if they want it. Hey, what's with Johnson? He's looking pretty damn weird*	*hate leaving Angie anyway. God, it'd be good to just be back home with her, snuggling. Huh? "Welcome—" Lord Jesus, he just took the safety off*

I screamed again. Screamed with the sudden death of the mindvoices and their wailing pain, screamed with the nats I knew were dying. Screamed because it was all so useless and unnecessary.

Outside, the jumped chopper lost control in a wail of shrieking metal. It exploded before it hit the water. I saw the glare wash over the buildings of the Rox.

I've never heard so many people die at once.

I heard the other nat squads slowly realize that something was wrong. I felt their outrage and horror as the carnage echoed over their headsets and radios. I felt their fury.

Their sudden surge of will.

My Wall fell in tatters, shredded by nat hatred. They poured through.

I was staring at the *Temptation* again, sightlessly. Everyone in the building was gaping at me. I knew they were waiting for Governor Bloat to do something, but I couldn't think.

I could *hear* them. I could hear everything—as the two choppers touched down in cold tornadoes of dust and vomited their loads, as a boat full of rangers and cops hit the shores of my Rox and scrambled out. I heard screaming and the percussive bark of gunfire. I witnessed the assault through their minds.

It didn't last long. I'd like to claim that it was something I did or that the jokers did, but it really wasn't. I'd already told Kafka to take one of the walkie-talkies, thinking I'd direct him where the nats were. But even as the squad of jokers ran to the compound where the choppers had landed, the jumpers, directed by Blaise, continued to attack. They were taking the cops, making them turn and fire on their own. The nats quickly found that they couldn't trust their friends. It wasn't the damn kids or the ugly jokers who were the enemy here in the Rox. It was themselves.

They died.

I felt them die. I watched the scenes through their minds, through their thoughts.

Leo caught a glimpse of himself in his buddy's visor. He was thinking that they looked like a bunch of damn robots behind the helmets. He even thought it was funny. He was starting to say so to Tom, his partner, when Tom shuddered. *He looks so strange . . . .* Then Tom whipped around his weapon before Leo could move. Tom was shooting at anything and everything, just holding the trigger down and spraying. Leo saw a line of slugs rip open his stomach and spill purple guts into his cupped hands.

He was dying. Cold mud pressed against his face, but in his mind was another image. He was holding a baby wrapped in a Muppet Babies blanket. In his thoughts, I could see him holding the kid up to his stubbled cheek. He kissed her.

"Good night, darling. Daddy'll be back in the morning, I promise. You be good." He replayed that kiss again and again, crying as his life pumped out from the hole in his chest and the vision spiraled away into the darkness of unconsciousness. "Daddy loves you. He'll be back. I promise. I love you."

A park ranger stood on open ground near the docks. I could sense the hot suppressor of the CAR-15 he cradled against his chest. He looked down at the girl he'd just killed. *Just a kid, just a fucking kid, Jesus, not much older than me* . . . Then his thoughts moved away as he sensed someone coming up behind him. *It's Captain McGinnis.* Only I could hear this captain's thoughts, too, and I knew that it wasn't McGinnis but Molly Bolt, and the only thing in *her* mind was a bloodlust.

Blaise's mind was loud in the turmoil, his mindshields carelessly down. *He* thought it was funny. He thought it was hilarious how Durg could kill them so easily.

The battle was a rout. I could hear it. The nats realized that their strategy had been blown to hell and that they were likely to die here. Their retreat was short and bloody and complete. They fled the Rox, not even dragging away the dead and wounded they found in their path. They piled back into the choppers and the boat.

Blaise didn't want to let them go. He wanted to kill them all. I shouted to Kafka through the walkie-talkie, knowing Blaise would be listening. I told him to let them go.

Let them go.

Blaise didn't like it. But . . . Durg said something to him that I could not hear, and Blaise just watched as the choppers wheeled into the gray sky, as the boat cast lines from the dock and careened away from the Rox.

I don't know what I would have done if Blaise had defied me. Nothing, probably.

I could hear the wounded and the dying. Ahh, those I heard very well. Even though jumpers and jokers were shouting and dancing in an impromptu victory celebration all around, I didn't share any of their happiness.

I just stared straight ahead, at the *Temptation* and its bizarre images. I looked at the burning city in the deep background of the painting and the soldiers spilling over the landscape.

I had *felt* nats die for the first time. A helpless voyeur, I watched them, and it hurt. It hurt just as if they were jokers. They had families and friends, and they weren't any better or worse than my own people. Not really. Maybe, *maybe* they could have opened fire on the jokers here. Jokers are ugly and misshapen and not even *human*, if you know what I mean. But they would've had trouble with the jumpers, with the teenagers who look, after all, just like their own kids or nieces and nephews or maybe even themselves a few years back.

Worse, I knew I could've taken care of this myself without any bloodshed if I'd been a little smarter, if I'd just shut up and let the Wall do its work.

I looked at the *Temptation* and begged it to give some solution. So tell me, is this what victory's supposed to feel like? Is it always such a sour, rotten fruit? Does it always leave you feeling so guilty?

St. Anthony, tormented by his own demons, didn't give me an answer.

Lovers

III

She drove the body unmercifully. She knew she had achieved a small measure of telepathy, but no one was listening! Her constant mental cries for help also seemed to be taking a toll on the body. The last seven times she had awakened, she had been overwhelmed with nausea. She was having trouble keeping down the gluey mass of oatmeal that was her first meal and the canned beef stew or canned chili that inevitably made up the second and final meal of her waking time. And Peanut had not returned.

"I ruined everything, by trying to escape," she whispered.

Tachyon wondered what the body must look like. Gaunt from lack of food, muscle tone degenerating with each week of captivity that passed. And a bath. Ideal, she would *kill* for a tub of hot water. It made her crazy even to contemplate washing out the tangled greasy hair, the sluice of hot soapy water across the shoulders and back. Clean pajamas and crisp sheets with the smell of sunshine in them because they had been dried on a line . . .

Nausea shook her, and Tach bolted for her privy bucket. Vomited up everything in her stomach. Shivering, she retreated into a corner. Tach leaned against the wall, pressed her cheek against the clammy concrete wall. The coolness helped, and she breathed slowly and deeply until the spasm passed. Concerned now, she lay her fingertips on her pulse. Without a watch it was impossible to be certain, but it seemed normal enough. Back of the hand to the cheek. No fever. No pain or ache in the extremities. Probably not a flu. Food poisoning?

166

Unlikely—the heaves were mild, lacked that violent, almost projectile quality that accompanied food poisoning. Her mind continued to run symptoms and causes. Hit one, and froze. A vise had suddenly begun to close around her temples.

"*Ancestors, NO!*" The shrill howl bounced off the walls.

How long had she been buried in this living hell? Weeks? Months?

"And not once has this miserable carcass had its menses!" Tach panted.

Her heart was pounding, she could feel it beating in her gut. Or was it that other *thing*, that unspeakable prospect? Her hand thrust down the front of her blue jeans. She drew her palm across the slight swell of the belly.

Too soon to tell.

No, it couldn't be.

What the hell *else* could it be?

Flu.

Nausea after waking.

Nerves.

No menstrual cycle.

"All right," Tach screamed, sick of the argument with herself. "*All right!* The goddamn body is pregnant!"

And in that moment she went a little mad. When she finally returned to herself, she was on her knees by the wall. Her throat was raw from screaming. And something warm and sticky was matting her hair and pouring across her left eye. Tach ran her tongue across her lips and tasted and sharp coppery taste of blood.

Slowly she raised her hand to her hairline. Whimpered in pain as her fingers touched the mangled scalp. She had been beating her head against the wall, a trapped and maddened animal biting off its leg to escape the trap. Death was an escape. But she hadn't succeeded, and now sanity had returned.

She was making a noise far back in her throat that hardly sounded Takisian. Desperately, Tachyon scrabbled across the floor on all fours. Snatched up the spoon. Thrust it into her teeth as she clawed at the button and zipper on the blue jeans. Ripped them down, pulling them inside out as she kicked with frantic haste to free herself from the confining material.

Knees up, a hand resting on the curling pubic hair, fingers ready to part the labia. And she froze. She had no idea where the fertilized egg reposed. She would have to scrape each wall of the uterus. And if she didn't get it all the

resulting infection . . . and if she tore the delicate walls of the
uterus the resulting hemorrhage . . .

The smell of a woman rotting from the inside out filled
her nostrils. A time when abortion had been illegal. A time
when a desperate joker woman had butchered herself with a
coat hanger.

Tach began to shake. *Infection be damned*, she thought.
Consider what you are contemplating. *I have no evidence this
child is defective. I can kill a defective. I can't kill a baby.*

It's not a baby, argued another part of herself. *It's a
collection of several hundred cells.*

"It's going to be a baby," said Tach aloud.

*And you're a man! Are you seriously going to go through
with this abomination?*

"What else can I do?" she cried desperately. "Butcher
myself, and bleed to death?"

"It's a baby," she whispered again.

It will be defective. It's Blaise's child. It will be crazy!
Destroy it now!

"You are arguing to save yourself from this indignity.
Well . . . why? All the indignities imaginable have been heaped
upon you. You have been kidnapped, robbed, assaulted,
raped, and imprisoned. Why balk at this?"

Because I'm a man *damn it! And there's something
growing in me!*

"It is a baby," Tach murmured as exhaustion struck her
like a blow between the eyes. She flung aside the spoon.
Heard its metallic jangle as it struck the far wall.

The temptation was effectively removed. She would have
to crawl laboriously through the darkness to locate the utensil
again, and by the time she found it, she would have again
talked herself out of committing murder.

She groped for her blue jeans. Pulled them onto her
shivering body. The cold sweat that had drenched her had
now left her chilled to the bone. She crawled to her favorite
corner and fell headlong into a sleep that bordered on coma.

The shrilling of pipes and the deep-throated booming of
drums fell on her ears like a killing cloud on a field of young
flowers. She was female again. *Most* annoying. Damn it, it
was her dream. Why couldn't she be Tachyon again—slim and
lithe and *male*? She became aware of movement, an undulat-
ing rocking that made her feel dreadfully insecure. She

pushed aside the curtains and found herself perched atop a palanquin that was in turn perched atop the brawny shoulders of four young men. They paced a trail that wove between green fleshy stalks of daunting height and girth.

Tachyon sidled backwards, away from the threatening vegetation, and found a new threat. Something behind her, following like a shadow. She spun and saw it again. A flash of iridescence. *Wings*. Sweet Ideal, she had *wings*. She explored the contours of her borrowed face. It felt the same until she reached the forehead and her shrinking fingers discovered velvet-soft antennae springing from above each brow and curving back over her head.

She scurried on hands and knees back to the opening, oblivious to the grief she was causing her strong-backed bearers. The little procession was just emerging into a clearing, and at last she got a look at what topped the vegetable behemoths. Irises, giant irises, their petals hanging down like tongues of exhausted dogs. The clearing was dotted with toadstools, and each fungus was serving as a chair for other elfin creatures like herself. Beneath the shade of the mushroom caps were other breeds of creatures. Ugly and twisted, they resembled nothing so much as a mutant's seaside convention, all huddled beneath their umbrellas to hide from the light of the full moon that floated gibbous overhead. Tachyon wondered in what capacity they served their pretty, delicate overlords.

But closer examination revealed her mistake. It was the dainty fairies on top of the toadstools who wore the chains. The palanquin was turned and lowered awkwardly to the ground. Tachyon clung to the roof supports like a wife greeting a long-absent husband. Once the swaying and tilting stopped, she risked a glance and found herself confronted and confounded by the sight of a gigantic toad. It rolled out its tongue like a grotesque red carpet for visiting royalty. Tachyon shuddered and shrank back against the cushions. Two of her bearers reached in and dragged her out. Her bare toes seemed to be cringing away from the flicking tip of the toad's tongue, and as an errant night breeze teased at her gossamer gown, Tach realized that she was much more pregnant than she remembered or had any business being. Oddly, there was no substance to the belly that ballooned out the fabric of her gown.

The toad frowned. Said to one of its twisted minions, "Can I fuck him when she's like that?"

"No, It'll get in the way... block your penis," was the creature's incredibly ignorant reply.

"Then I've got to get rid of it. Mind-rape ought to do. I can make her shove it out."

The toad wrapped its tongue about her head. Mucus dripped from its stinking surface and ran down her cheeks like tears. Tach gave a cry of revulsion that quickly became a scream of pain as stinging needles seemed to enter her mind. Fingers slipping on the surface of the tongue, Tachyon struggled to throw it aside. There was a click like a key turning in a perfect lock, and the pain and the tongue withdrew, the tongue coiling away like a wounded snake. Tach stared at the flames dancing on her fingertips and the fire that formed a shield for her mind.

"Then rip it out in blood," screamed the Blaise-toad, and one of the goblins drew a curved knife and advanced on her.

Tachyon moaned her despair and laid her arms across the swell of her pregnancy. Then, surprisingly, the creature died in a geyser of blood, one clawed hand scrabbling at the knife that had somehow appeared in its throat.

A strong arm slid about Tachyon's waist, and she gasped in relief as the Outcast pulled her against his side. The tip of the rapier was weaving like the nib of a maddened calligrapher in the air before them. "No, Pretender," the outlaw said. "The child will survive to displace you."

There were screams and shouts from the goblins, and the toad let out a hiss like a thousand cobras threatening. Then an enormous wind blew up, the petals of the irises fell like rain, and the whole grand and grotesque assembly went whirling away, carried higher and higher into the sky until they appeared as small black dots against the face of the moon.

Tach sagged in the Outcast's arms, and it seemed perfectly natural to place her arms about his neck to support herself.

"I won't let him harm it," she murmured in a voice gone weak and bloodless from fear. "Help me. Don't let him hurt us anymore."

Placing a finger beneath her chin, the Outcast forced her to look up. His breath smelled sweetly of honey and brandy. Closer, closer—a kiss to be anticipated...

The slamming of a distant door brought her awake. Tachyon pushed up on the palms of her hands. Her hair hung about her like a shroud. Slowly she pushed it back. Dropped her hands until they lay protectively over her belly. And deep within her something female stirred and dropped back into the timeless sea-rocked sleep of the embryo.

How strange that in the space of a dream Tachyon had discovered a skill and an emotional gift, both of which often took a lifetime to achieve and admit. The Takisian had built a mentatic shield that would protect her and her daughter. And the parent had learned that she *wanted* to protect that child. Illyana was no longer something growing inside of her. Illyana was a part of her.

"There, and now you even have a name," murmured Tach gently.

Weeks passed. She now had a rough indicator of time, a clock measured by the changes in her body. The swell of her belly was now pronounced enough to make zipping the jeans very uncomfortable. Her breasts had enlarged and were tender to the touch. At times, humiliation was more than an emotion—it was a taste, a sickness in the belly, wordless cries. What a fool, a laughingstock, she would seem to the world. But Illyana was a presence, a personality, a friend in the darkness. Her thoughts were basic, almost primordial. Food, warmth, comfort. And she responded. When Tachyon was in her bleak black moods, the clear colors of the baby's thoughts became muddied, swirling like angry eddies. And when Tachyon sang the lullabies and ballads of her youth, the baby quieted, and her thoughts became like a tiny harmony.

"You know something, baby dear," said Tachyon as she sat trying to comb through the tangles in her hair with her fingers. "You are like the cockroach or the rat that the prisoner tames and talks with in the solitude of his cell. You're not really a person. You're just an eating, dreaming, sleeping machine. But you are company for me."

And suddenly, miraculously, the baby *moved*. Tachyon felt her *roll over*.

And suddenly she laughed—for the sheer joy of the moment, the reaffirmation of life. She laid a hand over her stomach, whispered, because she was half embarrassed.

"And I do love you."

Apart from being an emotional mainline, there was another effect of Illyana's busy gymnastics: The morning sickness ended. Being able to keep down her meager meals had Tachyon thinking about food again. By her calculations, she was somewhere in her fourth month. And Illyana and Illyana's surrogate mother needed decent nourishment. The Peanut visit had never been repeated, and while her nightly communions with the Outcast might be emotionally satisfying, they did little to succor the body.

To achieve that, she needed to communicate with Blaise. And even thinking about him brought on a fit of the shakes so severe that Tach feared it was a seizure. Eventually, when control and a modicum of calm returned, Tachyon tried to analyze Blaise's possible reaction. It might be amusement for the ludicrous predicament in which he had placed his grandsire. It might be paternal pride. It might be violence. She recalled her terrifying abortion dream. What if he harmed Illyana? Perhaps it was better simply to hide her condition. . . .

Tachyon's harsh laugh cut the thoughts off abruptly. This was not a condition one hid with any degree of success. Eventually, even those lack-witted teens who delivered her meals twice a day would notice.

Two days later, she noticed that her ribs felt like a washboard to her exploring fingers, and when she lay upon her back on the floor, she could feel the stony pressure against each of her vertebrae. And all of this tapered into the fecund swell of her stomach. The decision could be delayed no longer. There was simply not enough calories being fed into the body to sustain both her and the baby.

That night, as the little trap at the bottom of the door rattled open, Tach was ready. She caught the guard by the wrist and hung on while calling shrilly, "Get Blaise. I must speak with Blaise!"

The jumper broke free, and the trap slammed shut.

Again that blinding light. Tach turned away, covered her eyes with her hands until the retina could compensate. Turned back to her captor, her demon, her child. And was struck again at how much Blaise had grown. The young man was dressed in shorts and a tank top.

So, it's summer, thought Tachyon. *Which means Blaise is now sixteen. How the time passes. Is there anything I could have done to have spared us this wretched outcome?*

"What . . . do you want?" Blaise's sharp-toned question broke her reverie.

Tach lifted her eyes to his face and struggled for calm. The light in those violet eyes was *evil*. As melodramatic as that sounded, there was no other word that applied.

When dealing with a wild animal, it was essential not to show fear, to maintain a low, level tone, Tachyon reminded herself. "Congratulations, Blaise." Tach waited, but the teen did not play along. He continued to stare at her from beneath his thick red eyebrows. It was very disconcerting.

Tach drew a ragged breath and continued. "You will no doubt take what I am about to tell you as a testament to your virility, a proof of manhood—"

Blaise took a step toward Tachyon. She couldn't control it. She shrank away.

"Get . . . to the goddamn point."

Silly, trivial things intrude when you're frightened almost to insensibility. Tachyon found herself wondering where Blaise had picked up the odd speech pattern that had him hitting the opening word of a sentence hard, then pausing before continuing.

"I'm pregnant," Tach squeaked.

Blaise slapped her. "Liar."

Cowering, she stuttered, "N-no. I'm t-telling you the truth."

His eyes dropped to her waist. The top button of her jeans was unhooked, the zipper only partway closed, trying to accommodate the aggressive thrust of baby. Blaise's fingers' thrusting into the waistband drew a whimper of terror that escalated into a scream as he tore down the pants. Tachyon now understood the genesis of the human phrase *to have one's pants around one's knees*. Total helplessness, and humiliation.

The skin of Blaise's palm was hot and sweaty as he caressed the curve of her stomach, his head was bowed almost reverently. "This . . . is great." His strange eyes flicked up to meet hers. "How does it feel, Granddad? What are you thinking?"

This was the moment. How she played the next three minutes would determine her fate and Illyana's fate. She cautiously wet her lips with the tip of her tongue. Weighed again the alternatives. Whatever choice you made with a madman was the wrong one. No, that pessimism would freeze her.

So should she be imperious and demanding—food and care for herself and the baby? And hope it did not whip

Blaise into one of his killing moods? Resentful and sulky—get rid of this bowling ball in my belly? And hope that Blaise would do the exact opposite?

And then in an instant she knew. How to win the moment. How to sway her demon grandson. And she didn't know if she could stomach it. The power, the will, the soul that was Tisianne brant T'sara sek Halima screamed against the act she was contemplating. She was Takisian, she was incapable of such abasement.

Illyana kicked softly. Tachyon's hand flew to her belly. Her medical training enabled her to feel and distinguish the baby's head pressed tightly against the side of her womb.

Tachyon took Blaise's hand between hers. Dropped to her knees at his feet. Tears would have helped, would have convinced him of her defeat. But the ability to weep had been lost in a terrifying afternoon of blood and rape. She studied his hand, noting the smattering of freckles across the back, the red hair forming tiny whorls on the knuckles.

Closing her eyes, she pressed her lips against his hand. "Blaise, you have won. Now I am begging you. Take me from this place. I am frightened by the dark, and I am weary and hungry."

"Cody . . . never believed me," said Blaise, and the scorn was heavy in his voice. "But I always was twice the man you were." He grabbed her by the hair and yanked her head back until her terrified eyes met his. "Say it. Call me master!"

Hate was closing her throat, but she finally managed to force it out. "I acknowledge you my master."

He released her contemptuously. Threw over his shoulder to one of his nervous pimple-faced boy guards, "Take him upstairs. Get him a bath and some food, and tell one of the girls to find some maternity clothes." Turning back to Tachyon, he said with a grin, "I'm going to enjoy watching this process. This is so gross. You'll just get fatter and fatter, and when you finally pop out this one, I'll give you another. I can. I'm a man now, and I own you."

The Temptation of
Hieronymus Bloat

VI

I dreamed. I knew I dreamed, but I couldn't wake myself.

I could hear the Princess sobbing, echoing in my head.

The eerie sound of her pain reverberated from the depths of the place I somehow knew was called the Catacombs, and I couldn't bear the sound of it. Even though I knew that this was the Pretender's domain, this time I had to go to her physically.

With the thought, I found myself—the tall, lithe, and muscular Outcast—standing at the yawning, broken archway to the Catacombs, deep under the Crystal Castle where jokers walked. A rapier hung at my wide leather belt; I was dressed in fine supple leather and wore a wide-brimmed hat of stiff black cloth. With one last glance back at the sunlit world, I took the torch guttering in the wall sconce and entered the cold, empty darkness.

There were stairs, leading always down. I could hear the brush of the leather pants against my legs and the weeping of the Princess. Her anguish drew me and led me through the labyrinthine stairwells, among the multitude of corridors leading away right and left. This was a maze, like the dusty tombs I'd followed in my imagination in role-playing games.

Yet this felt like no game in my mind. I was the Outcast, the Hidden One, and I followed the distress of my distant imprisoned love. I moved cautiously, as silently as possible,

since I knew I couldn't risk being seen here by the Pretender
or any of his companions. He couldn't know that I plotted
against him. It was only because I could never shut out the
voice of the Princess that I came here—because I had always
loved her from afar and now she was in pain. Because we
talked with our minds and she knew me.

It seemed hours later that I came at last to a deep
landing. It was cold here. A chill foulness emanated from a
crevice in the wall to my left, though the passageway led
straight ahead. Still, some compulsion drew me to the crevice
first. It was a thin jagged crack from floor to ceiling, too small
for me to fit through easily. From it issued that strange
coldness and a bitter stench. I was glad the Princess wasn't
down there; I didn't know if I could have gone to her. I tried
to see into that darkness. Beyond there were series of caverns. The torchlight glittered from frozen falls of crystals;
shimmering stalactites and stalagmites formed columns leading into the unknown depths. For a moment, I thought I
caught a glimpse of a large dark bird lurking there, a penguin
who looked at me with human, amused eyes.

Then it was gone.

The Princess cried out again, and I turned from the
opening. I followed her compelling sobs until I came to a
thick oaken door banded with great steel straps. A small hole,
stoutly barred, was set in it. I let the light of my torch fall
inside and peered in.

She lay in a pile of filthy straw in one corner of the bare
stone cell, her golden hair spread out around her. She was
more beautiful than my memory of her when I would watch
her walking outside.

"Princess," I called softly.

She turned, gasping at the sound of my voice.

"Yes," I said. "I am the Outcast."

She rose to her feet. Her plain cotton dress was torn, her
face, arms, and legs bruised with the Pretender's abuse, but
she was still enchanting.

She limped to the door and gazed at my face in
wonderment. "So handsome," she breathed, as if voicing her
thoughts. "I've heard your voice in my mind. . . ." She touched
my face with soft warm fingers, wonderingly. The tears began
again, bright crystalline spheres tracking down her cheeks.
"Please. I want out of here, Outcast. I can't stand this
anymore. Please."

Her pleading tore at me in my helplessness. "Princess, this door's too strong; I don't have the keys." I didn't know what to say to her or how to explain. I couldn't help her, not that way.

"I understand," she said, and I knew she did. "You will find a way. You will."

"I'll try. That I promise you. I give you my oath, because I love you."

From somewhere nearby there was the sound of bolts rasping and hinges groaning. We could hear rough male voices, laughing, and what sounded to me like the low grumbling of some monstrous toad. "Quickly," the Princess said. "Go now."

"I'll send someone to help you," I promised her, twining her fingers in mine one more time. "I have friends. They'll help me. I'll be back."

"I know. But now you must go."

The Princess kissed my fingers.

I moved back into the dark maze of stairs, returning to the sunlight above. Long before I reached it, though, I heard her scream.

And the scream woke me.

It was Tachyon, crying in Kelly's voice in my head, over and over again.

Prime looked around the lobby, nodding faintly. Zelda stood behind Prime and my guards, her muscular forearms folded in front of her and the thought *Fuck you if you're listening* rattling through her head like a mantra.

"It's nice to have money, isn't it," Prime commented at last. "Wide-screen projection TV, expensive sound equipment, fine art, tapestries on the wall—you have quite the modern castle here. Very nice, Governor." Prime looked at me with a cold gaze and colder thoughts. "I suppose you know why I'm here," he said.

I did. I didn't like it either. "No is the answer," I told him. "But I suppose you're not going to just take that and leave."

Prime smiled slightly. He pulled one of the Chippendale chairs toward him and sat. Zelda moved alongside him.

"I didn't think so," I said. "But eighty percent of the take is out of the question."

If he was offended by my blatant theft of his thoughts, he

didn't react—but then, Prime *never* reacts. He just crossed his legs, folded his hands on top of the immaculate and neatly creased pants, and shrugged. "My jumpers are doing most of the work in this little scheme," he said.

"The jumpers are the engine, yes," I admitted, "but it's jokers who are the body. Your little gang of juvenile delinquents doesn't like the drudge work of guarding the bodies and keeping the records straight so that we can pull off the blackmail. And you're making a lot of money from the jokers themselves, the ones who want new bodies. I expect you to give some of that back to us. Fifty-fifty was the deal. It was my idea, my setup, and my jokers administer it." I was getting angry. (I knew this was coming; Kafka had warned me that it would happen. "They'll get greedy," he'd said. "You just watch.")

"You can't do it without us, Governor."

"And you can't do it without me," I shouted back at him. "You're forgetting that I'm the Rox. Blaise and the rest of your hoodlums need this place."

Latham didn't say anything. But he thought a lot. *I am going to do you a favor and not say this aloud. Don't threaten me, Governor, especially not with a weak argument like that. Look at the facts. Fact: While you do make the Rox possible, we all know it's not a power you can turn on and off. Fact: The wall is as much for you as the jumpers, and the only way to get rid of it is to kill yourself, which you're not stupid enough to try. Fact: No one is starving here anymore because of the money your jump-the-rich scheme has brought in, which is good, but it also means that no one particularly wants to go back to the old way, which is what will happen if my people pull out of the deal. Fact: A lot of jokers want to keep this going because they want to buy a new body for themselves. Fact: You have a severe population problem. Our success is bringing more and more jokers here, and even with the money and rapture, you're already having problems finding places to put them.*

And the last fact: If I pull out, you not only have lost the jump-the-rich scheme, you've lost your rapture connection. Tell me, Bloat, what would happen to the Rox if there was no rapture?

We don't need you at all, Governor. You had the idea; we're paying you for that. I have plenty of contacts to keep this going myself, and enough jokers in Jokertown who are hungry for a new body and willing to pay for it that I can pull in as much cash as I'd want. If I were you, I'd be happy with the twenty percent I'm offering. I'd be happy to get anything at all. After all, twenty percent will keep the Rox in food and rapture.

The fact is, Governor, that unless you have something else to bargain with, you have nothing to say about this at all.

Latham smiled at me. "So, Governor," he said aloud, "what *do* you have to say?"

I didn't say anything. I couldn't. I looked at Prime, at the grinning Zelda, and the quizzical glances of my guards. "Get out of here, Prime," I said. "Just get out and leave me alone."

He smiled. He smoothed the crease in his pants and languidly uncrossed his legs. "I thought so," he said. "Good doing business with you, Governor."

"Prime," I called as he and Zelda started to leave. He stopped and turned back to me. "I'll find something," I told him. "I'll find some leverage somewhere. Then we'll talk again. You understand?"

"Of course I understand," he said. "It's exactly what I would do, after all. You see, Governor, we're not so different, are we? We just have different agendas."

They'd had to move the Bosch painting since I seemed to be undergoing some new growth spurt. My body was pushing forward into the lobby. Kafka told me that I'd filled two more of the offices in back and that new floor struts needed to be added. I was hungry all the time too. The Rox's sewage system only took the edge off. The bloatblack that rolled off me was lighter in color and less solid, but stank worse.

I guess it was a corollary that the Wall was a quarter mile farther out into the bay now. It was stronger, too; I could push back almost anyone who didn't really *want* to be here. A nice power, if it were under my control, but it wasn't. The Wall just was, as always.

Too bad the Wall can't do anything to the people inside it.

Blaise was in the lobby, with his tagalong assassin, Durg. Tachyon's grandson didn't do much more than glance at the work in progress. Around the lobby and behind the *Temptation*, jokers were busily taking out walls and replacing them with enormous panes of glass. Already the lobby was brighter, and

I could see more of the Rox. When the renovation was finished, when all around me there would be nothing but windows and my body was raised even higher, I'd be able to look out and see the entire panorama of the island and bay. I'd have transformed the building into the turreted, glittering Crystal Castle I'd seen in my dreams.

All it would take was money. Money we had plenty of now.

My body rumbled. Sphincters dilated, pulsed, and more bloatblack sloughed off down my stained sides. The blackers moved in to shovel away the waste. Blaise stared at them, refusing to show on his face the disgust that was in his mind, though Durg openly scowled. The hypocrisy was enough to make me laugh.

So I did.

"You and your stupid giggling," Blaise muttered, then more loudly: "Tell me, Governor, are you going to still be laughing when we start fighting over land on the Rox? 'Cause that's what's gonna happen, real soon. There ain't room here, Bloat. There's too many people coming out here now. Christ, you're going to want to move the fucking Statue of Liberty over here next. 'Give us your twisted, your disfigured, your huddled masses yearning to be normal. . . .' Damn it, be realistic. There's only so much room here, and we're *full*. No fucking vacancy."

Kafka was glaring at Blaise, but in his mind there was some grudging agreement. *That* was a first. Kafka nodded. "Governor, Blaise is at least partially right. I don't know that we can keep up with the demand on services. If we get too many immigrants, we *won't* be able to feed them, no matter how much money we have. We won't be able to clean up the garbage, won't be able to give them water and sewage and power. We'll have fights and arguments over space and facilities. It'll be worse than Jokertown. That's not what you want. Things are good here now."

"What do you want me to do, Kafka? Say to those who get past the wall, 'Sorry, you can't come in'? You want me to shoot them?"

"Sounds like a fucking good idea to me," Blaise said.

Kafka snarled at him.

"Hey," Blaise retorted. "I'm not asking, I'm *telling*. There's no more room. You want rapture, you want money, then close the fucking borders. That's my feeling, that's

Prime's feeling. So do it, huh? I don't care how, just keep the new jokers out, or maybe we'll stop playing ball with you at all. Then where you gonna be?" He challenged me with a stare. "Ain't that what Prime told you too?"

All the time Blaise was yapping, I was feeling something else. I don't know when I first noticed it—not long after the argument began. I could sense an extension of myself, some psychic limb like the wall that was just beginning to bud and grow. I could feel this thing pushing, pushing against something hard and solid.

Inside . . . I don't know how to describe it . . . there was a sense of stretching, of growing . . . Like I was experiencing a dream at the same time I was talking to them.

I was so tired of feeling powerless, you see—with Tachyon, with the growing pains of the Rox, with what had happened during the cops' attack, with Blaise's goddamn superiority complex, with Prime's cold manipulations. I was so deadly tired of it.

Nobody was agreeing with me. They were all saying the same thing: *There's no room anymore. We don't have the resources to waste on new people or new buildings. You gotta send some of 'em back. You gotta stop them from coming here.*

And I kept thinking of my dreams, of what I wanted the Rox to be.

"Look, the Wall's the only immigration policy the Rox needs," I answered.

"Yeah, it sure fucking kept out the cops, didn't it?"

"Hey," I shouted back, "if one of your stupid jumpers hadn't barged in and wrecked things, yeah, the Wall *would've* kept them out."

"You're full of shit, Governor."

Durg, next to Blaise, suddenly became very alert. I knew he expected me to do something in response to Blaise's blatant rudeness.

But I *was* full. I was full of a vision. A vision of space, a dream of dark places and echoing rooms. The dreams inside me were stretching. . . .

A deep rumble cut off our argument. Blaise was shouting; Kafka was chattering; they were *all* shouting, inside and out. I was scared myself.

The whole Administration Building was shaking. I heard glass breaking and saw the ramshackle buildings across the court swaying. A curtain of dust rippled across the courtyard, even though there was no wind. My feeling of extension hardened, became full.

Then it was over. The quiet was very loud.

I knew. I knew even as the tremors died and the plaster dust drifted down like snow from the ceilings, as Blaise and Kafka and the rest picked themselves off the floor.

"What *was* that?" Their thoughts were all confused and panicked. Blaise was thinking it was another attack.

I just looked at them calmly and told them what it was. "It was a dream."

They just looked at me. "Go to the west wing," I told them. "The basement. You'll see. Go on—all of you. Leave me alone. I'm tired and I'm hungry."

They stared at me. Blaise was thinking that I'd finally gone mad; Kafka was puzzling; Peanut was gazing at me trustingly.

"Go on," I told them again. "Then come back and tell me what you've seen."

They were gone for an hour. I followed them, riding with their minds. When they returned, they were quiet, all of them. Blaise was regarding me with a grudging wonder and a touch—just a touch—of fear. God knows what Durg was thinking.

I gazed at the remembered images in their heads, chuckling now. They *were* gorgeous, my caves. Walls of fluted smooth stone rippling from vast ceilings to distant floors; glittering, snowy patches of calcite crystals; deep pits where water roared in the darkness; hidden places where beasts of dreams walked.

Another world. A joker's land. I laughed.

Tachyon's grandson had wrapped his thoughts so I could hear very little of them. Only the barest tinge of his emotions leaked out. He asked me—knowing the answer—if I'd seen the caverns through their minds.

I told him that I had.

Then he asked me the question he didn't really want to ask because he was afraid that he already knew the answer. "Did *you* make them?"

I was too exhausted for anything but honesty. "I think so, Blaise," I admitted. "I'm not sure, but I've dreamed of them. Still . . . there's a lot more there than what I dreamed. I don't control it. I don't *know* what-all is down there."

Blaise gave a brief nod of his head, almost a salute. Confusion radiated from behind his mindshields. He turned and left the lobby without another word.

"You don't think big enough," the penguin had told me. Well, was this the right size?

"It's not possible," Kafka whispered. "I saw it, but it's not possible. Ellis is just old ship ballast. It's not even a real island."

"Then it's the perfect place for a fantasy, isn't it," I told him. I wanted to laugh, but I couldn't.

While Night's Black Agents to Their Preys Do Rouse
by
Walter Jon Williams

I

Darkness masked the street, concealing its face. Those who walked in the Jokertown night wore their own masks, some visible, some not. In the darkness or in the cold unreal color of the neon light cast by the Jokertown cabarets and boutiques, it was possible to believe that no one, no one at all, was quite what he seemed.

Darkness itself rolled along the deserted sidewalks, absorbing heat and color unto itself, hunting...

The Werewolf lay in a doorway, bleeding. His Liza Minnelli mask lay crumpled at his feet. His olive skin was zebra-striped with red pigment, port-wine stains gone mad. One eye was swollen shut. The other two were glazed.

"Hey." The darkness opened, revealing an imperious-looking black man named No Dice. He was dressed in a black leather Pierre Cardin trench coat with matching leather beret, a Perry Ellis sweater, a couple dozen gold chains, two-hundred-dollar high-top sneaks, the kind with the little squeeze pumps, gold-rimmed shades, a palm-sized green-black-gold leather pendant in the shape of the African continent. "Hey." The man knelt fastidiously, touched the Werewolf's shoulder. "You hurt, homes?"

The Werewolf shook his head, focused his two functional eyes on the black man. He spoke through split, bleeding lips. "What happened? Why'd it get dark?"

"No idea, homey. But I heard shots. You been shot?"

The Werewolf shook his head again. He tried to rise, but his knees wouldn't support him. The black man took hold of him, helped him steady himself against the doorway. The Werewolf looked at the flaking green paint on the door. Bewildered desperation entered his voice. "This is where it was going down! I gotta help Stuffy!"

"Police soon. You better shag outta here."

The Werewolf's hands searched through the pockets of his jacket. "Where's my piece? What happened to Stuffy?"

"Somebody hit you, man. Gimme your mask. Get outta here."

"Yeah." The Werewolf panted for breath. "Gotta split."

He staggered away, feet dragging on concrete.

No Dice watched him for a moment. He reached into the pocket of his trench, pulled out a pistol, then put it atop the Liza Minnelli mask that was—this week, anyway—the Werewolves' gang emblem.

Darkness bled downward from the sky and swallowed him up.

The revival house was showing Jack Nicholson in Roman Polanski's *Jokertown*. The last showing had ended three hours ago, and the marquee was dark. The marquee swayed, creaking slightly, in the cold winter wind pouring down the street.

Across the street was a spray-painted slogan, dayglo orange on brown brick: *JUMP THE RICH*.

Beneath the slogan a young woman knelt, hunched over a chalk painting. She was dressed in thirdhand clothing—a shabby baseball cap, a pale blue quilted jacket, and heavy boots two sizes too large. She had to squint in the darkness to see her work, the chalk painting she'd spread across a full slab of concrete sidewalk. It was a bright fantasy landscape—green hills and flowering trees and a distant rococo Mad Ludwig castle, a scene as far removed from the street reality of Jokertown as could be imagined.

A man named Anton walked down the shadowed street. He was a huge man in a large belted canvas trench coat, and he had a drooping mustache. He had a heavy diamond ring

on each and every finger, sometimes more than one. In one
pocket he had seven credit cards his whores had lifted off
tourists in Freakers, in another pocket he had their money,
and in a third he had a small supply of Dilaudid and rapture,
substances his women were hooked on and which he sold to
them in return for their share of the earnings. He wasn't
worried about people stealing any of this because he had a
pistol in his fourth pocket.

"Hey, Chalktalk. Baby. Ain'tchoo got a place to sleep?"

The young woman sprang up from her drawing, faced
Anton in a defensive crouch. The streetlight gleamed on
needle teeth, flexed claws. A stray piece of chalk fell from a
pouch on her belt, rolled unnoticed into the gutter.

"I ain't gonna hurtchoo, baby." Anton maneuvered to
head off the young woman's escape. "Just wanna take you
home and give you something to eat."

The street artist hissed, flashed claws through the air.

"Aw, Chalktalk," Anton said. "I ain't dissin you. I bet you
real pretty when you get cleaned up, huh? Bet the boys like
you."

He had the girl back up against the wall. She was
shifting her hips back and forth, trying to decide which way
to bolt. He reached a hand toward her, and her claws flashed,
too swift for the eye to follow. Anton jumped back, stung.

"Joker bitch!" He shook blood from his hand, then
reached for the belt of his coat. "Wanna play for keeps, huh?"
He smiled. "I can play that way, bitch. Bet I know just
whatchoo like."

And then the darkness rolled over him. The girl gave a
little gasp and flattened herself against the brownstone wall.

"I believe, Anton," said a voice, "I told you I didn't want
you in my neighborhood anymore."

Anton screamed as he was hoisted off his feet. The
darkness was as complete as if an opaque mask had been
dropped over his head. He scrabbled in his pocket for his
pistol. There was a crack as his arm was broken across the
elbow. Another crack, the other arm. Another crack, his
nose. All had come so swiftly, one-two-three, he couldn't cry
out.

He cried out now. And then cold flooded him. His bones
seemed filled with liquid nitrogen. His teeth chattered. He
couldn't summon the strength to yell.

"What did I give you last time?" the voice said

conversationally. "I believe it was second-stage hypothermia, correct? Lowered your body to about—was it eighty-eight degrees? Just made you a little uncoordinated for a while."

Anton was still hanging in the air. Suddenly he felt himself falling. He wanted to scream but couldn't manage it. His fall stopped short. There was a horrible wrenching of his knees and ankles.

"Let's go to the third stage, shall we? Shall we make you eighty-one degrees?"

Heat funneled out of him. He could feel his heart skip a beat, then another. Anton ceased to feel altogether. His breath rattled in his throat, trying to draw warmth from the air.

"I told you to stop stealing, Anton," the voice said. "I told you to stop pimping underage joker girls to tourists. I told you to stop beating and raping girls you meet on the street. And you go *right on doing it*. What does that make you, Anton? Stupid? Stubborn?"

The voice turned reflective. "And what does this make me?" Cold laughter answered the question. "A man of my word, I believe."

The darkness flowed away, revealing what it had left behind. Anton, gasping for breath, swayed in the wind. He had been strung up from a streetlight, his feet lashed to it by the belt of his trench coat. His pockets had been emptied of money. The credit cards and the drugs remained, enough to put him in prison. Or at any rate the prison hospital.

Droplets of blood made little patterns on the pavement as the wind scattered them—each, until chilled by contact with the air, a precise 81 degrees Fahrenheit.

"Chalktalk? Girl? You all right?" Darkness flowed toward the fantasy landscape on the pavement.

The street artist was gone.

The flowing darkness paused, alert to movement in the night, alert to body heat. Saw none, then looked downward.

The fantasy landscape was brighter, as if lit from within. Invisible clouds traced moving shadows on the landscape.

And in it the young girl was running. Up over a green hill, and out of sight.

Night surrounded the phone booth, which stood alone in a puddle of yellow beneath a streetlamp. Despite the spilling light, it was difficult to see just who it was who picked up the receiver and dropped a coin into the slot.

"Nine-one-one emergency. Go ahead."

"This is Juve." (pronounced *Hoo-vay*). His words had a strong Spanish accent. "I heard shots. Shots and screams."

"Do you have an address, sir?"

"One-eighty-nine East Third Street. Apartment Six-C."

"May I have your full name, sir?"

"Just Juve. I want to be anomalous."

Juve hung up and in the instant before the darkness claimed him, smiled. The emergency dispatcher would never comprehend that in his very last statement, he had meant exactly what he said.

The streetlight shone green. Then yellow. Then red. Colors that reflected on the dark chalk landscape drawn on the pavement below.

The wall read: *JUMP THE RICH*. Red light glowed off the orange graffiti, off the little droplets of blood on the pavement.

Anton swung above, his body growing colder with each red drop that spilled from his swinging form.

When No Dice walked into Freakers, the air turned chill. People shivered, shuddered, turned apprehensively toward the door.

No Dice only smiled. He just loved it when that happened.

No Dice ignored the stage show and glided regally to a booth in the back. Three Liza Minnellis sat on its torn red plastic seats. All were wearing black bowler hats, as in the movie *Cabaret*. At least they'd spared him the net stockings.

"My man," said No Dice. He looked from one Minnelli to the next, uncertain whom to address.

"Mister No Dice." A big man rose from the booth. No Dice knew he was Lostboy from his high-pitched voice.

"Lostboy," said No Dice. "My man." As if he'd known all along which Liza to talk to.

No Dice gave all three of the 'Wolves the homeboy handshake—thumb up, thumb down, finger lock and tug, back-knuckle punch. Then he sat down in their booth. His long leather coat creaked.

"Lookin fresh, No Dice," said Lostboy.

No Dice smiled. "Manhattan makes it, Harlem takes it."

"That the truth," said one of the Lizas.

"Order you a drink?" Lostboy said. He grabbed a waitress as she passed. "Chivas Regal. Straight up."

No Dice leaned over the table. "Wanna move *weight*," he said. "Wanna move *kilos*."

Lostboy picked up his highball glass and deliberately threw its contents on the floor. "I always like my man No Dice." Lostboy reached into his pocket and pulled out a plastic bag of blood—fresh from the blood bank and guaranteed free of AIDS. He began squeezing it out into his empty glass. "My man No Dice always wants weight, always pays cash, doesn't give attitude. Got his own clientele up in Harlem, so he never cuts into our action. Never no hassles with No Dice."

"That the truth, homes," said No Dice.

"I'll drink to it."

No Dice's smile turned a little glassy as Lostboy lifted his Liza Minnelli mask and his proboscis unrolled from beneath his tongue into the red fluid.

"Château AB Negative," he sighed. "My favorite vintage."

Whoever answered the phone answered it in Chinese.

"Can I speak to Dr. Zhao, please?"

"Who shall I say is calling?" The switch to English came smoothly enough.

"Juve."

"One moment."

Juve knew the place he was calling, had been in it a few times. The bar-restaurant was on the second floor above a grocery, and it didn't even have an English name, just a sign in Chinese characters on the door. Juve gathered that the gist of the name was simply *Private Club*. Sitting in red leather booths would be soft-voiced Asian men in Savile Row suits and handmade Italian shoes, very probably packing Israeli submachine guns.

"This is Zhao."

"This is Juve. You still lookin' for Dover Dan? The guy with three eyes who stole your product in that apartment down on East Third?"

"Ah." A moment's thought. "Should we discuss this over the phone?"

"Ain't no time to get up-close-and-personal witchoo, man. He's in Freakers with some of his homeboys."

"And you're certain he's there."

"He was there five minutes ago. He took his mask off when he got his drink, and I seen him."

"If this information is correct, you may apply to me tomorrow for my very special thanks."

"You know I'm a man of my word, Dr. Zhao." Juve hung up the phone.

Darkness hovered uncertainly around him. He stared up at the glass front of One Police Plaza. Anything else to do tonight?

Might as well go home.

He buttoned the collar of his black leather trench and headed southwest on Park Row. One Police Plaza glowed across the street. He kept to the shadows.

"Simon? Is that you, Simon?"

The distorted voice wailed out of a doorway. Juve jumped at the sight of a figure huddled under a salvaged old quilt, the sad-faced old female joker whose face seemed to have collapsed into itself, so heavily wrinkled it looked like that of a bloodhound.

Terror rolled through him. He wasn't Simon anymore.

"Simon?" the joker said.

"Not me, lady," Juve said.

"It *is* you!"

Juve shook his head and backed away. The woman lurched to her feet, tried to reach for him.

Her hand closed on air. She stared around her.

The darkness had engulfed Juve entirely.

"*Simon!*" she screamed. "*Help me!*"

The darkness didn't answer.

He was No Dice again by the time he got a cab heading north. He had been Juve wearing No Dice's clothes, he thought, and that had made him uncertain, made him overreact when his identity was challenged.

Who was still alive, he wondered, who remembered Simon?

Some old joker lady apparently. He couldn't remember ever seeing her. He wondered why her appearance had frightened him so much.

The cab left him at Gramercy Park. Darkness carried him up the side of a whitestone building on raven wings. He opened the roof entrance with his key and went down two flights of stairs, then padded on an old wine-colored carpet to his apartment door. The door and frame were steel sheathed in wood. He opened several locks and stepped inside, then pressed the code that would disconnect the alarms.

The apartment was spacious, comfortably furnished. In the daytime it was full of light. Books were lined alphabetically on shelves, LPs and CDs on racks. The hardwood floors gleamed. There wasn't a dust speck out of place.

He put on a Thelonius Monk CD, took off No Dice's clothes, and had a shower to wash off the man's musky cologne. A large bedroom wardrobe, also steel sheathed in wood, had a combination lock. He spun the combination and opened the door, then hung No Dice's clothes next to Wall Walker's, which hung next to Juve's. On a shelf above was a feathered skull mask. Wrapped in plastic, fresh from the dry cleaner's, was a NYPD uniform, complete with badge and gun. There was also a dark cloak he'd once worn during District Attorney Muldoon's ace raids on the Shadow Fists.

In the rear of the closet was the blue uniform and black cape he hardly ever wore anymore, the costume that marked him as Black Shadow. Black Shadow, who had been wanted for murder since the Jokertown Riot of 1976.

He looked at the varied sets of clothing and tried to remember what it was that Simon wore.

The memory wouldn't come.

After a few years, he realized he didn't know what to call himself anymore. It had been years since anyone had called him by his real name, which was Neil Carton Langford. The last anyone had heard of Neil was when Columbia tossed him out for not ever getting around to finishing his M.A. thesis. Black Shadow had been an outlaw for fourteen years. He'd been Wall Walker for a long time—it was his oldest surviving alias—but Wall Walker was too genial a personality for the kind of life he led most of the time. The other masks came and went, transient and short-lived.

Finally he settled on calling himself Shad. The name was simple and had a pleasant informal sound. It was a name that promised neither too much nor too little. He was pleased at finally figuring out what his name was.

No one, other than himself, called him by that name. Not that he knew of, anyway.

When he'd started out, there'd been other people whose

line of business had either intersected his or complemented it. But Fortunato had gone off to Japan. Yeoman was gone, no one knew where. Croyd was asleep most of the time, and he was usually on the other side of the law, anyway.

Maybe it was time for Shad to hang up his cape. But if he did, who would be left to persecute the bad guys? All the public aces seemed to be engaged in lengthy public soap operas that didn't have much to do with helping real people.

None of them had Shad's expertise.

He might as well stay with it. He didn't have a life anywhere else. Not since 1976, when he'd realized what lived inside him.

When he woke, Shad drank coffee and watched the news. The coffee didn't do much for him—no normal food did—but when he was living his normal existence in his normal uptown upper-class apartment, he tried as far as possible to act like a normal person.

The news was enough to wake him up, though. Shortly after eleven o'clock the previous evening, a group of what witnesses described as "casually dressed Asians" walked into Freakers, strolled to the back, drew machine pistols, and smoked three jokers wearing Liza Minnelli masks. Another Werewolf in another part of the bar returned fire, splattering one of the Snowboys in return for being disembowelled by about forty semiwadcutters. One of the Wolves had actually survived in critical condition but was not expected to be conscious and of any use to police for a long time.

No Dice was going to have to contact someone else to get his shipment of rapture.

The news rattled on. A vice president of Morgan Stanley had supposedly skipped town with hundreds of millions of investors' funds. Nelson Dixon, the head of Dixon Communications and owner of the Dixon-Atlantic Casino, had just bought another art treasure, van Gogh's *Irises*, for $55 million, a private purchase from an Australian billionaire who'd run into hard times. He'd also fired his entire security staff and hired new people, complaining that the old people had been lax about the jumper threat.

Good luck, Shad thought.

The military cordon around Ellis Island had been tightened after some jumpers had hopped into the bodies of some coast guardsmen and taken their cutter for a joyride.

Shad's eyes narrowed as he considered the situation on Ellis Island. Maybe it was something he needed to be concerned about. He didn't much give a damn if some idealistic jokers wanted to claim Ellis Island as a refuge from oppression. Good luck to them. But if killers were using the place as a hideout, that was another matter.

There were supposed to be a lot of people on the island, however. And Shad was only one person. He'd always worked alone. And if he got jumped, there was no guarantee he'd ever end up anywhere, or anyone, he wanted to be.

Funny if it ended that way. A man with so many different identities, permanently stuck in somebody else's body . . .

Who, he found himself wondering, still remembered Simon? Simon had been an uptown kind of guy, he remembered, not the kind of man to hang around Jokertown. So why was a joker looking for him?

He finished his coffee, washed out the cup, put it in the dishwasher. He went back into the bedroom and looked at the three suitcases sitting next to the bed. One was filled with forty pounds of rapture, with a street value of approximately a quarter million. The other two valises contained $100,000 in hundred-dollar bills, the stuff he'd taken from the Snowboy-Werewolf deal and blamed on Dover Dan.

A hundred grand. Not bad for a night's work. And with any luck, he'd started a gang war as a bonus.

He'd have to start moving the stuff out of his apartment. Starting, he figured, with the drugs. He'd keep enough to pay his informants and dump the rest in the Hudson.

An image sang through his mind, a distant orchard, peaceful green fields dappled with cloud shadows, a distant castle . . .

Stupid, he thought.

Time to hit the streets.

Summer 1976. Hartmann and Carter and Udall and Kennedy all slugging it out in the Garden, cutting little deals with each other, planting knives in one another's backs.

New York was a city on fire. And everyone, suddenly, was on one side or another. You were with the jokers or against them. On the side of justice or an obstacle in its path. He'd never known a time so hot.

Neil had been an ace for years—it had come on gradually during his early adolescence—but after his parents and sister were killed, he'd never done anything with the power, nothing but disappear into the darkness when the memories got to be too much and he didn't want to be Neil anymore.

Senator Hartmann had been the one who had inspired Neil to become a public ace in the first place. Neil was in the hotel to hear a speech by Linus Pauling, and he wandered into the wrong ballroom by accident. He still remembered Hartmann's words, the ringing phrases, the calls for action and justice. Within a week, Black Shadow was born, born right in Hartmann's office, Shad and the senator shaking hands and smiling for the cameras.

A little problem, Hartmann told him a little while later. A little problem in Jokertown. An honest-to-God Russian *spy*, someone trying to get into Tachyon's lab to learn Tachyon's approaches for controlling the wild card. The Russians were infecting people deliberately, killing the jokers, inducting the aces into the military. They wanted to find a less drastic method and thought maybe Tachyon was working on it.

The night was hot. Marchers were in the streets. Fire seemed to burn in Shad's heart as he found the agent and his equipment—his cameras and developers and one-time pads—and he took the agent apart, breaking bones, putting a chill into his sweating skin. He left the man swinging from a lamppost right in front of the clinic, a placard pinned to his chest announcing the man's, and the Soviet Union's, crimes.

Something had snapped in him, a wildfire that raged way out of control. Hartmann's call for compassion and justice had twisted somehow into a call for burning action and revenge. Shad's heart leapt as the crowd tore the spy apart, as the night burst out in fire and madness. It wasn't until later, when he saw Hartmann fall apart on television, that he knew how he'd betrayed the senator's ideals.

Even after the riot was over, he couldn't figure it out. He hadn't known such rage was in him. He found Hartmann, slipped into his apartment before the man had even had a chance to recover from the disaster of the convention, and asked him what to do.

Hartmann said, plainly and quietly, that he should turn himself in. But anger blazed up in Shad again, anger warring with anguish, and he argued with Hartmann for an hour, then left the apartment. A little while later he did it again, found a couple of homeboys mugging tourists on the Deuce and left them swinging, broken, from lampposts.

The lampposts were well on their way to becoming his trademark.

He was in vague contact with Hartmann after that. Hartmann always urged him to turn himself in but would never call the authorities himself. Shad respected him for the courage it took to do that.

And in answer to the guilt that clawed at him, he left more people swinging from lampposts.

The evil joy, the uncontrollable rage, that he'd first felt was less in evidence now. It hadn't flared up in years. Maybe he was growing up—he'd made a decision around the same time to break with Hartmann. He didn't dare compromise the senator anymore.

Now he just hung people from lampposts because it was what he did. He didn't get much satisfaction out of it. It was an unsatisfactory thrill, like substituting pornography for good sex. Maybe it kept the crime rate down, kept a few people honest. He liked to think so.

But he was getting restless. People like Anton and the Werewolves weren't worthy of his talents.

He wanted to work on something big.

Shad went to a safe house in Jokertown and dressed as Mr. Gravemold, the joker who smelled like death. He put on Gravemold's feathered deathmask and doused himself with chemical stink.

People around him shrank from the smell. Shad liked that. It gave him privacy. But he didn't want to smell it himself. When he was Gravemold, he chemically numbed his nasal passages and taste buds, and he'd tried a lot of substances over the years. By far the best proved to be high-quality cocaine he took off dealers. He could get used to the stuff, he figured, except he had much better ways of getting high.

The hallelujah chorus rang through Mr. Gravemold's sinuses as he walked around Jokertown looking for the hound-faced lady. He asked everyone Gravemold knew: Jube, Father Squid, people in relief agencies. People told Gravemold everything they knew, just to get rid of the smell, but nobody had seen the joker who had asked after Simon.

He walked beneath the lamppost outside the Jokertown Clinic as if it were any other lamppost. As if it were a place that had no meaning for him. It didn't. To Mr. Gravemold, it was just a lamppost.

A chalk landscape, its colors faded and scuffed, occupied part of the sidewalk. A kind of lagoon with odd-shaped boats on it. He found himself watching it to see if it came alive.

Nothing happened.

After nightfall, Mr. Gravemold bought some lemons in a fruit and vegetable store, went back to the safe house, dumped his smelly clothes in a trunk, scrubbed himself with the lemons to kill the scent, then took a shower. He still had to use some of No Dice's cologne to cover what remained of the stink.

He tried to figure out who he was going to be. No Dice had no business in Jokertown tonight. Simon had been gone for years. People might be looking for Juve. This was the wrong neighborhood for Wall Walker, for the Gramercy Park identity, and for the cop. Maybe he could just be Neil Langford. The thought came with a rush of surprise.

What the hell.

He looked at the clothes in the wardrobe and wondered what Neil would wear for a night in Jokertown.

It came to him that he had no idea. He'd been playing all these parts for so long, he'd lost track of who he really was.

He decided finally to dress in jeans, shirt, and a midnight-blue windbreaker. The cocaine was still making him sniffle, so he put some tissues in a pocket. He pulled a watch cap down over his ears and set out into the night.

He made a businesslike quartering of Jokertown, starting with its southern tip around One Police Plaza. His senses were abnormally acute, and he was highly sensitive to body heat—he didn't have to walk down every alley or look in every doorway.

John Coltrane ran long arpeggios in his head, working on McCoy Tyner's "The Believer."

He moved down the street like a cool breeze, feeding as he walked, taking little pieces of body heat that no one would miss, pieces that made him stronger, made him glow with warmth. The mellow buzz of all the stolen photons zoomed along his nerves and were far more satisfying than the cocaine could ever be. People shivered as he passed, glanced behind them, looked wary. As if someone had walked across their graves.

As he walked, he found old chalk drawings, faded with

time or rain. Fantasy landscapes, green and inviting, smeared or beaten by pedestrians. Urban scenes, some that Shad recognized, some so strange as to be almost impressionistic. None of them signed. But all of them, Shad knew, from the same hand.

Chalktalk. The perfect name.

JUMP THE RICH.

He found her across the street from the graffito, under the theater marquee advertising Polanski's *Jokertown*. She had paused there, an old brown blanket around her shoulders, her stuff in a white plastic shopping bag. She paused in the theater's glow and glanced around as if she were looking for someone.

Shad couldn't remember ever having seen her before. He wrapped darkness around himself and waited.

The joker paused for a while, then shrugged her blanket further around her shoulders and walked on. The top of one of her tennis shoes, Shad saw, was flapping loose.

Darkness cloaked him as he walked across the street. He put out a hand, touched her shoulder, saw her jump. Took a little body heat as well. "What do you want with Simon?" His voice was low, raspy, faintly amused. Black Shadow's voice.

She jumped, turned around. Her hound eyes widened, and she backed away. He knew she was looking at . . . nothing. An opaque cloud of black, featureless, untextured, taller than a man, a nullity with a voice.

"Nothing," she said, backpedaling. "Someone—someone I used to know."

"Perhaps I can find him." Advancing toward her. "Perhaps I can give him a message."

"You—" she pushed out a breath, gasped air in, "you don't have to—" Her wrinkled face worked. Tears began to fall from her hound-dog eyes. "Tell him Shelley is, is . . ." She broke down.

Shad let the darkness swirl away from him, reveal his upper body.

"Simon!" Her voice was almost a shriek. She held out her arms, reached for him. "Simon, it's Shelley. I'm Shelley. This is what I look like now."

Shelley, he thought. He looked at her in stunned surprise as her arms went around him.

Shelley. Oh shit.

*   *   *

He took her to an all-night coffee shop and bought her a watery vanilla shake. She chewed on the plastic straw till it was useless, and tore up several napkins.

"I got jumped," she said. "I—somebody must have pointed me out to them."

"How do you know that?"

"Because whoever jumped me marched my body to the bank and cleaned out my trust fund. I'd just turned twenty-one and got control of it. Almost half a million dollars."

JUMP THE RICH, Shad thought.

"I went to court," she said, "and I proved who I am, but it was too late. Whoever was in my body just disappeared. I never went back to drama school—what's the point? And I got fired from my job at the restaurant. I can't carry trays with these hands." She held up padded flippers with fused fingers and a tiny useless thumb. Tears poured from her brown eyes. Little bits of paper stuck to her furry face as she dabbed at tears with bits of torn napkins.

"Why did you go away?" she wailed.

"That was a bad scene you were in. I told you it was time to leave."

She stirred her shake with her useless straw. "Everyone started getting killed."

"I told you."

"You didn't tell me they'd start *dying*."

"I told you it would get as bad as it gets."

"*Why didn't you take me* with *you?*"

He just looked at her while guilt planted barbed hooks in his insides. He'd done what he'd done and just walked away, as if Shelley had been no more to him than one of the freaks he left hanging from lampposts or as if she were as invulnerable as she seemed to think she was.

He hadn't thought he could save her, a little rich white girl stuck in a scene so evil, so decadent, so glamorous that it probably would have crumbled into violence and madness even without his prodding. But she hadn't seen it coming—she led a charmed life, like everyone in her set, protected by her beauty, her trust fund, her sense of life as something to be devoured, *inhaled*, like the drugs she and her friends bought from the smiling, menacing street hustlers who saw them only as victims, as people to be led, step by step, into a place where a temporary and frantic safety could be acquired only by giving away their money, their bodies, eventually their lives. He didn't think he could have saved her. In his best professional judgement at the time, it was impossible.

But then he'd never know. He hadn't tried.

She took another napkin from the dispenser and began to tear it into shreds. "Bobbie's dead. Somebody beat her to death with one of her sculptures. And Sebastian's dead. And Niko."

"I'm not surprised." He'd killed Niko with his own two hands, snapping the man's neck with a quick, practiced twist. He'd never met anyone who deserved it more. Left him on his bed with his head facing the wrong way, gazing into the nodded-off face of his junkie chicken, Rudy—Rudy, who used to appear in Sebastian's little art films, telling stories about his life and shooting up between his toes and talking about how much he wanted to fuck the cameraman.

"Violet threw herself off a roof. Or maybe the police pushed her. That's what Sebastian said, anyway. And Rudy's on the streets. Maybe it was Rudy who pointed me out to them. The jumpers. But he wasn't the guy who contacted me."

Shad looked down into his coffee. It was cold, and he hadn't used any of the heat. His reflexes were singing a warning, telling him not to ask the next question, that whatever the answer, it was going to lead him into another pit of tragedy. "Who contacted you?" he said. "Why?"

"A lousy twenty grand," she said, "and I get out of this body." She looked up at him, and her mouth twitched up in a smile. "You wouldn't happen to have twenty thousand dollars, would you?"

He looked at her, the sense of horror deepening, widening, ready to swallow him in. "Twenty grand?" he said. "Maybe I could get it."

He bought her a room in a Jokertown hotel and said he'd come the next day with more money. Then he slipped away, walking north, toward his building off Gramercy Park.

He'd met her at a dope deal. He'd been following this guy with the stunningly original name of Uptown Brown, brown being the color of the bad heroin he sold in Harlem in order to support a more fashionable existence on Fifth Avenue east of Central Park, brown also being the color of his victims, who shot the stuff and then went into respiratory arrest from whatever it was—Drano, battery acid, whatever—he cut it with.

Shad had arrived at the address he'd been given and walked up the outside of the building to peer in the windows. He'd been expecting the usual meeting, guys in overcoats and shades carrying suitcases and shotguns, but what he saw was a party. Young white people drinking spritzers or imported beer while someone banged out a lot of furious, clashing chords on a cream-colored baby grand. And among them was Uptown and a couple other guys who didn't fit into the scene at all.

He just walked in the door and said he was Simon. That was how he met Sebastian, the poet-slash-filmmaker; Bobbie, the sculptor; Shelley, the actress; Violet, the composer; and Niko, the director, a man who liked to direct other little dramas besides those on stage and intended to direct everyone in the room straight into hell so he could watch them flare and burn.

Shad found out his informant wasn't wrong. It *was* a dope deal he was part of. Everyone in the room was hustling someone or something, drugs and art, drugs and money, or drugs and *real life,* this last being something this little set craved and had never, to hear them tell it, experienced.

If it hadn't been for Shelley, he would never have come back. These people weren't his problem. People dying back in his old neighborhood were his problem, dying from Uptown's bullets and bad drugs. Now he knew why Uptown was peddling bad junk. He'd found another class of people he could move among, and he didn't care what happened to his old customers.

But for some reason Shad found himself returning . . .

He saw something duck into an alleyway ahead of him, and his nerves went on the alert. He cautiously called the darkness down and moved toward the entrance.

Looking down the length of the alley, he could see at the other end a small figure running in heavy boots and baseball cap. Chalktalk, he knew, the street artist.

"Hey," he called, but Chalktalk kept running.

He looked down at his feet. Drawn with careful attention to detail was a picture of him, of Shad, dressed in his windbreaker and watch cap, leaning in the doorway and reading the *New York Post* by the light of a streetlamp.

Shad ran after her, but Chalktalk was gone.

*   *   *

"Simon. It's almost noon. I was afraid you weren't coming."

"I thought I'd buy you breakfast. Then some clothes. Okay?"

Shelley looked at him carefully. "I've been thinking, Simon, you know?"

Shad looked at the shabby hotel room—the thinning carpet and broken venetian blinds. "Let's get out of this rattrap." Pimps in the hallways, junkies shooting up in the back rooms. Jokertown. "I'll get you a nicer place tonight."

"I could stay with you."

He frowned. "I'm sort of between lodgings at present."

He bought her breakfast at the same coffee shop they'd been in the night before. "Here's what I think," he said. "You contact the jumpers. I'll give you the twenty grand. Then we see what they want you to do."

She pulled some of the wrinkled flesh off her eyes and looked up at him. "Who are you, Simon? You're not just some student, like you told me."

"I'm just somebody who wants to do you some good, okay?"

"Are you the longbow killer? Is that who you are?"

He raised his arms. "Do I *look* like Robin Hood to you? Where's a homeboy going to learn to shoot a *bow*, for God's sake?"

"You're no social worker, that's for sure." She bit off a piece of toast. "Harlem Hammer?"

Shad gave a laugh. "I wish."

"Black Shadow."

"You're reaching, Shelley."

"Black Shadow." There was a glow in her eyes. "I should have known!" Her voice was excited. "When I saw you just come out of the darkness like that, I should have *known*."

"Keep your voice down, will you?" Shad looked furtively at the other diners. "I don't want anyone taking this seriously." He turned to Shelley. "Can't you just believe I'm someone you never heard of who wants to do you some good?"

"Black Shadow." Her eyes glittered. "I can't help thinking about it."

"Let's talk about the jumpers," Shad said.

He kept trying to find the Shelley he knew beneath the mask of wrinkled joker flesh. She'd burned so brightly that he, with his frozen heart, had been attracted to the light and heat, had circled it like a sinister icicle moth.

The second time he'd met her, it was to sit with her friends to watch a film she was supposed to star in. The film was in grainy black and white and consisted of Shelley lying naked on a bed and reciting lengthy monologues, written by Sebastian, largely on the subject of orgasms. Occasionally Sebastian himself, also naked, would wander into the frame, face the camera, and recite an ode to his cock. Shad, looking at the organ in question, could not comprehend what the fuss was about.

The wretched film came alive only through the medium of Shelley. She disarmed the worst lines with genuine laughter; the best were said with glowing sincerity. Life bubbled out of her as from an artesian spring. Shad found himself enchanted.

Now he could only find bits of her wrapped in the tired joker skin. Memory kept digging sharp nails into him. Her familiar words and gestures sent waves of sickness through his belly.

Twenty grand, he thought—*maybe she'd be Shelley again.*

She was supposed to establish contact by putting an ad in the *Times*. He got her a new wardrobe and a room in an uptown hotel that was so classy, they wouldn't turn down even a dog-faced joker. He rented the adjoining room for himself. Then he placed the ad for her.

He said he had someplace to go and split.

He called all of Croyd's numbers from his hotel room. There was no answer, and he left messages on the tapes, specifying date and time so that if Croyd woke up in a month's time, he'd know not to bother answering.

When he got to the safe house, his answering machine was blinking with a message from Croyd. Croyd had apparently awakened as a joker this time, because his voice had turned into a high-pitched honk. He sounded like a goose with a cleft palate. Shad had to play the message twice to understand it. He returned the call at the number Croyd had given.

"This is Black Shadow," Shad said. "Are you looking for work?"

"I don't know if I can help you this time around," Croyd

said. "I'm just planning to go back to sleep as soon as I can and forget I ever woke up looking like this."

Shad understood maybe half the words, but the meaning was clear. "Can you do anything at all?" he asked.

"I'm sort of like a giant bat, except without hair. I've got a membrane between elongated fingers and thumbs, and I have sonar, and I—" He hesitated for a moment. "I have this craving for bugs."

"You can fly, though?"

"That's the only good part, yeah."

"I think you're just what I need. Can we meet?"

"I don't feel like going out."

"Can I bring you anything?"

"A box of bugs, maybe. Assorted sizes."

Shad thought about it for a moment. If you could buy a box of bugs anywhere, you could buy them in Jokertown.

"I'll see what I can do," he said.

He found a box of fried locusts in an exotic food store on Baxter and took it to his meeting. Croyd was repulsive, even for a joker, a three-foot-high pink-skinned homunculus with fleshy wings. Money changed hands, and locusts got eaten. Things were arranged.

After a visit to his Gramercy Park flat for some gear, Shad slipped back into his adjoining room at the hotel a little before ten o'clock, knocked on the door to make sure Shelley was okay, and found her in bed watching a movie on TV. He carefully bugged Shelley's room, including a video camera that he aimed through a fish-eye lens he installed in their adjoining door.

"Here's what happens from this point on," Shad said. "We don't see each other till the meeting's over. They may be watching your room. You take the money now, you make the meet, you do what they tell you. Afterwards you come back here, and if things are clear, we'll talk."

"What if they ask me where I got the money?"

"Tell them you stole somebody's jewelry, then sold it."

Shelley pulled her wrinkles up out of her soft brown eyes and looked at him. "Who are you? Why are you doing this?"

"I don't know."

She gave a nervous little laugh. "Which question did you answer?"

Shad looked at her. "Both."

The jumpers called Shelley at four-thirty in the morning. Evidently they'd got an early edition of the paper. They ordered her to meet them at eight, standing right out in the traffic circle at Chatham Square, with the twenty grand in her handbag. Shad watched her leave on the TV screen, called Croyd, turned on the VCR, and headed downstairs. He got on his motorcycle—a Vincent Black Shadow, natch, restored for No Dice by the Harlem Hammer—and headed for Chatham Square.

He wished the jumpers hadn't set the meet for broad daylight.

Before eight, he was on the rooftop of an apartment building on Baxter Street with Croyd. He could see Shelley standing nervously in the traffic circle a half block away. The morning rush-hour traffic was almost gridlocked around her.

"Can you fly with one of these around your neck?" Shad asked.

Croyd eyed the walkie-talkie carefully. Shad looked at the pink hairless body and wondered where Croyd's excess body mass had gone.

"I don't think so."

"I'll leave one here, then. After you're done, you can report."

"Walkie-talkies don't work so good around here. Too many tall buildings with metal inside."

"These are police walkie-talkies. There are repeaters set up everywhere."

"Where'd you get police walkie-talkies?"

Shad shrugged. "I dressed up as a cop, walked into Fort Freak, and took a couple from the charging rack."

Croyd gave a nasal honking laugh and shook his head. "Gotta admire your style, homes."

"Shucks. Ain't nothin."

He went down the stairs, then walked past where his motorcycle was parked. He put on a navy-blue beret, settled in a doorway where he could keep an eye on Shelley, and chewed a toothpick for a while.

Black men hanging out in doorways are not unusual in America's teeming metropoloi. He concentrated on not being unusual. He concentrated on being Juve, and Juve was checking out the scene, with long Yardbird Parker riffs, all staccato, in his head.

Juve tried real hard not to notice the little pink guy flapping through the air about five hundred feet up.

It was almost eight-fifteen when he saw the powder-blue Lincoln Town Car easing through the gridlock a second time. His nerves started humming. Nouveau-riche criminals, he had often observed, often gave themselves away when it came to personal transportation. But the Lincoln went out of sight, and then Shad's attention snapped to Shelley. She was moving, walking with the light in the direction of the East River.

Damn. She wasn't supposed to leave yet.

Juve ambled out of the doorway, straddled the Black Shadow, and kick-started it. Shelley was disobeying instructions, and this couldn't be good. It wasn't until he eased the bike out into traffic that he realized what had just happened. His nerves began to sizzle. He cast a wild look down Worth Street, then Park Row, just in time to see the blue Lincoln turn right on Duane.

Shelley was in the Lincoln. She'd just been jumped. Croyd was following the wrong body, damn it.

Shad clutched and shifted, and the Vincent's engine boomed in synch with his thrashing heart. He raced down St. James Place, elbows and knees tucked in as the bike dived between stationary gridlocked vehicles. Leaving a trail of booming decibels, he performed a power slide behind One Police Plaza, then crossed Park Row without waiting for a break in the traffic, and felt as if he were saved only by some abstruse corollary of particle physics: He wasn't in the same state, particle or wave, long enough for anyone to hit him.

Once onto Center, he saw the Town Car in the distance and throttled back. Center joined Lafayette, and the powder-blue Lincoln turned right on Houston, then made another right on First, heading back into Jokertown. The streets were choked, and Shad had no trouble following.

The Lincoln made a few more turns once it entered Jokertown, then turned off into a nineteenth-century brown-stone warehouse with its tall windows closed off by more recent red brick. The electronic garage door closed behind the Lincoln, and Shad passed slowly on the motorcycle, turning neither left nor right, an odd prickling on the back of his neck. He wouldn't show up on this block again, certainly not on the bike. He'd be someone else entirely by the time he came back.

He turned, positioning himself to see the Lincoln if it headed back east, then pulled over to the curb and tried to contact Croyd—nothing. He searched the sky for a flapping pink figure, saw no one.

Time passed. Juve jacked a set of earphones into the radio and bobbed his head to a Kenny Clarke beat.

Two Werewolves stood on the corner, wearing gang colors but only ski masks, which gave them a better field of vision than Liza Minnelli or Richard Nixon, a precaution in case any Asians with guns showed up. The gang war seemed to be proceeding nicely. They scoped Shad out, offered him procaine cut with baby laxative, were ignored.

"Yo. Homes. This is Wingman."

Juve straightened, reached for the police radio. The tw dealers saw him raise it and split.

"Homes here."

Undercover cops used the same sort of elliptical language, Shad knew—he hadn't been challenged with these radios yet, even though the police were listening. If anyone questioned him, he planned to be Detective-Third Sam Kozokowski of the Internal Affairs Division, and what was your name and badge fucking number? Which should shut them up in a hurry.

"She just wandered around for a while," Croyd said, "then passed her handbag to a boy on a scooter. Then she wandered some more. Now she's in a restaurant, eating an Egg McMuffin. Anything I should do?"

"She's been jumped. There's somebody else in there."

"Shit."

"I need you to follow a powder-blue Lincoln Town Car."

"Snazzy wheels."

Shad paused. This was the first time he'd heard the word *snazzy* in decades. He told Croyd where the car was, then went back to being Juve. A little shift in the infrared spectrum showed him where Croyd was hovering.

It was almost one in the afternoon before Shad saw Croyd begin to move. Shad paralleled him on the bike. The zigzag course took him and Croyd back to Chatham Square. The dog body waited on the traffic circle. Shad pulled up behind the Lincoln, memorized the license plate, then parked where he'd been that morning. He went into the doorway and became Juve again.

There was a new chalk drawing there, right on the stoop.

It showed Shad and Shelley having breakfast in the Jokertown coffee shop. Shad looked at the picture and felt an eerie wind crawl up the back of his neck.

He forced himself to stay in the doorway till he saw Shelley hail a cab. Then, checking behind himself constantly for tails, he headed for the hotel.

"Yo. Wingman."

"Hi, homes. The dog-faced joker I was following earlier collapsed—I think she got jumped again—but I saw her getting up as I followed the car. The Lincoln went back to the warehouse."

"Thanks. I'll talk to you later."

"We'll do some beer and bugs. Wingman out."

Shad sped back through the tape he'd made of Shelley's room. Two people had scoped the place. They were in their late teens, by the look of them, the boy in stylish leathers, the girl in denim and an eye patch. She seemed to have only one hand. The boy had got them through the lock with a raking gun. The one-eyed girl put something on top of the tall cabinet that held the TV. Then they both left the way they had come.

At least neither of them had been Chalktalk.

Shelley showed up a few minutes later, looking as if she'd been through a lot.

Shad reached for the phone. "Hello?"

"This is the front desk."

"Oh. Hi. Front desk, right."

"Say that yes, you want to stay another day."

"Yes. I want to stay another day."

"You still want to pay cash."

"I still want to pay cash."

"You'll have to come down and do it in person."

"I'll be down in a few minutes."

He met her at the elevator and pushed the emergency stop button to halt it between floors.

"I thought you were going to have a new body," he said.

"Yes. They've promised me one." She licked her pendulous lips. "The thing is, I get to pick."

"Oh."

"They've got a catalog. Just like L. L. Bean."

"Tell me what happened."

"I got jumped again. They put a bag over my head. They drove around for a while, then took me into a little room. It was fitted out like a prison cell—metal walls, a heavy door with big locks and a barred window. There was mesh overhead and a guy with a gun walking around."

"Okay."

"There were other cells. I could hear people talking. Some were crying and screaming." She gave a strange little smile. "I didn't care. It was *wonderful*. I was human again. Young! And beautiful. They showed me my face in a mirror. I was gorgeous."

"Who showed you?"

"Two kids. Boys, maybe fifteen. Zits, but real good clothes. Rolexes, jewelry. The gold chains must have cost fifty grand. And there was a joker." She gave an expression of distaste. "Brown, with a carapace. Looked like a cockroach."

"Did they call him Kafka?"

"Yeah." She pulled her wrinkles back and looked at him. "How'd you know?"

"He was around a few years ago. I knew him slightly when I joined the Egyptian Masons."

Her eyes widened. "The Egyptian Masons? You mean the—the ones who—"

"Yeah. Those guys. I'd only just joined, then somebody blew up their temple with me in it. I barely got out, and I didn't know there were any other survivors until they started trying to toss people off Aces High."

She looked at him, her lips twitching in what might, under the wrinkles, be a smile. "You *are* Black Shadow, aren't you?"

"My name's Simon."

"Uh-*huh*. Sure."

"So what happened in this cell?"

"Somebody else came in. Dr. Tachyon."

Shad's mind whirled. He forced himself to speak. "You sure?"

"Who wouldn't recognize Tachyon?" She gave a shiver. "Jesus, I never expected that. I was scared he'd read my mind or something and figure I knew you."

Maybe he did, Shad thought. "Did you see a one-eyed woman?"

"No. Why?"

"Never mind. Just tell me what happened."

"Tachyon made a speech. About joker rights. Now I had a chance to experience life as a member of the oppressed, and so naturally I'd want to join him in his great work."

"And the great work?"

She shrugged. "They're jumping the rich. If I agree to do what they want, I get jumped into a new body. I clean out the bank accounts and the family silver. Half goes to Tachyon and the jumpers, and the other half I get to keep to set up a new life somewhere. Unless—" she hesitated, "I decide to do it again. And again. He made that offer. I build up a nice nest egg, then they jump me into whatever body I choose when I want to retire."

"What did you say?"

"I said I'd have to consider it."

"What are you going to do?"

She looked at him. "What do you *want* me to do?"

"It's your call. I'm not going to make you do anything."

She took a breath. "I hate this body. I don't want to hurt anyone else by jumping somebody into it. But"—she shook her head—"I have to think about it."

"This thing gets settled, maybe we can put the victims into new bodies."

Why had he said that? he wondered. He didn't really believe it. He wanted Shelley back. That's why.

He made himself think about Tachyon.

"It'll take a few days," she said. "I have to familiarize myself with the target out of the catalog, know what moves to make. I stay in the cell the whole time."

She'd made up her mind, he realized. The thing was going to happen.

He remembered an old film he'd seen, *The Third Man*. Orson Welles had taken Joseph Cotten up on a Ferris wheel, pointed at all the tiny little people below, and said, "If you could have a million dollars, but one of those little people dies, would you do it?"

Some stranger, some little antlike speck below the Ferris wheel, was going to end up in a dog's body and have her bank account plundered.

"When you're free of them, call me," he said. "The number is 741-PINE. *P-I-N-E*. There will be an answering machine. Leave a message where I can find you."

"Okay."

"The number?"

"741-PINE."

"Good."

He started the elevator again and got off two floors down.

He had things to do.

Shad decided it was time to find out a few things about Tachyon. He had to start somewhere, and where he ended up was the public library and the back-issue newspaper files. The responsible papers were too discreet about what they knew to be of much use, but the tabloid made a lot more of it all.

TACHYON QUITS! BROKEN HEART CITED. That was the headline on the *Post*. Shad looked at the inevitable pinup on page 3: "Happy Holly" was said to like "professional wrestling, baby ducks, and naughty nighties for that Someone Special," a strange summation that had Shad picturing her displaying herself for a slavering Haystack Calhoun in a frilly negligee with little yellow ducks on it.

Then he turned to the article on Tachyon. Dr. Tachyon, it said, had resigned his position at the Jokertown Clinic. "Intimates," the article said, reported that Tachyon was frantic about the disappearance of his "one-eyed Jill," Cody Havero, and had been unable to concentrate on work. There was a strong implication that he'd been spending his days in an alcoholic coma. Dr. Finn, whom Shad knew both as Wall Walker and Mr. Gravemold, hinted gently at Tachyon's breakdown and also praised Blaise Andrieux, Tachyon's grandson, who had been a "tower of strength in this ordeal." Which didn't much sound like the Blaise that Shad had heard about, but maybe the kid had grown up some.

There was also a lengthy rehash of Tachyon's history, concentrating on his "drunken peregrinations" following the death of Blythe van Rensselaer. There was also a description of Dr. Havero's "controversial career," along with more speculation to the effect that Cody had been assassinated by a CIA conspiracy anxious to cover up something they'd done in Vietnam. The paper hadn't found anyone reputable to report this last, which came from a "professional psychic known to the police." *I'll just* bet *she's known*, Shad thought.

Shad narrowed his eyes and looked at Cody Havero's picture. The scarred, one-eyed face looked interesting. Maybe she was someone he ought to concern himself about. He could put money out on the street, maybe hear something that the police and FBI hadn't.

He spent the rest of the day doing just that and came up with zip.

"I've been trying to sleep," Croyd said. "But it's no good. I'll probably be awake a couple days at least before I can drift off."

"I could use a flyer around that warehouse. I want to track who goes in and out."

Croyd gave a peculiar nasal sigh. "Come by and bring more bugs. We'll talk about it."

"Yo. Homeboy."

"Homes here."

"New arrivals at the warehouse. Three people in a limousine. One of them's a lady with a bald head. Then there's a bodyguard and—you're not gonna believe this."

Shad, whose feet were planted to the vertical surface outside Tachyon's window, was at this point prepared to believe anything. "Try me."

"St. John Latham. You know, the mouthpiece."

"Yeah. I know who he is."

"Some other people showed up just this minute. Some kids in a van."

"Don't let them see you. They're probably jumpers."

Shad couldn't be certain if the following squawk came from Croyd's throat or from careless use of the *squelch* button. Finally Croyd's voice came back. "Funny company you're keeping."

"The entertainment never stops."

Croyd signed off, and Shad relieved a cramp by shifting his stance outside Tachyon's window. Thus far, the evening had been pretty dull, consisting of Tachyon and Blaise polishing off a couple of microwaved TV dinners and a six-pack of Rolling Rock. Shad had always thought of Tachyon as having a more refined palate, but on the other hand, Hungry Man Dinners weren't exactly the mark of a criminal mastermind either.

Blaise popped a cassette into the VCR and sat down in front of the set. Tachyon opened a bag of Fritos and sat down with him.

Shad couldn't catch more than a fraction of the film from

where he sat, but he saw enough pink flesh and heard enough
moaning to be convinced of its nature. Whatever the man
was doing to the woman on the film seemed insignificant
compared to what the sound track did to "Cherokee."

Blaise seemed enthusiastic about the action and gave
Tachyon a running color commentary on the film. Eventually,
Tachyon rose from his chair and kind of wandered around the
apartment for a while, then went to the liquor cabinet, mixed
bourbon, gin, Cointreau, vodka, and brandy in a tall cocktail
shaker, then gulped the lot. He passed out on the bed, got up
to stagger to the bathroom and vomit, then returned to the
bed and passed out again.

Blaise took note of all this but did not intervene. So
much for Dr. Finn's pillar of strength.

Hypothesis one: Shad thought: Tachyon was the mastermind behind the whole jump-the-rich scheme. He'd cracked
when his girlfriend had disappeared, or earlier; and he'd
decided that justice for wild cards was too long in coming,
and he'd become a terrorist. He was, after all, the man who
when threatened by the Snowboys and the Syndicate, had
raised a private joker army—Mr. Gravemold had been in
it—then led them into combat twirling pearl-handled six-
guns. Looking at it that way, it didn't seem like Tach had been
too tightly screwed together in the first place.

Hypothesis one-point-one: He'd become a terrorist, and
he'd killed his own girlfriend because she'd found out.

Hypothesis two: Tachyon and the grandkid have been
jumped. That's someone else in there. This theory explained
everything very neatly except for where was Tachyon's real
mind?

They Stole Tachyon's Brain, Shad thought. Next on the
Tachyon triple feature.

If they'd had any sense, the bad guys would have killed
Tachyon, the real Tachyon, right away—as they'd probably
done with Cody Havero, who was in a position to spot the
switch.

If Tachyon was jumped, Shad wondered, when had it
happened? Could it have been two years ago, at the Demo-
cratic Convention in Atlanta? Tachyon had made a sudden
political turnabout, and there were plenty of rumors of aces
hidden among the delegates.

Shad didn't think it too likely. No one had heard of
jumpers until long after the convention, though that didn't

mean they hadn't existed. But it had only been recently that Tachyon's behavior had changed radically.

There was no evidence either way so far, at least from Shad's fly-on-the-wall perspective. Though if that *was* Tachyon in his own body, he'd been keeping his taste in cinema well hidden.

The thing was, what was Shad going to do about it?

Whoever was in Tachyon's body, he was an evil son of a bitch. He's stolen Shelley's body and Lord knew how many others.

He thought that Tachyon was going to have to simply disappear. And Blaise was going to have to go with him.

Ten minutes later, Shad had about decided to join Croyd at the warehouse, but at that point Blaise got up and turned off the TV. He shook Tachyon awake, and the two started getting ready to go out. Blaise moussed up his hair and put on a stressed-leather jacket and enough gold chains to make No Dice jealous. Tachyon looked disinterestedly through his wardrobe and more or less donned things at random. Which was probably what he normally did anyway.

Shad slipped down the face of the building and got on his bike so that he'd be ready when Tachyon left.

"Homey." A voice honked in his ear.

"Yeah, Wingman."

"People are moving out. Looks like a whole convoy. The limo, the van, that blue Lincoln, some other people on motorcycles."

"Stick to Latham. I want to see where's he's heading."

"Roger, wilco. Look, I can't carry this radio on the wing, so it'll be some time before my next report."

"I'll be waiting."

Tachyon and Blaise left the apartment building—Tachyon wasn't walking very straight—and went to the garage around the corner where they checked out a black Saab Turbo. Blaise drove. Shad followed them to the offices of Global Fun & Games. When he got there, he could see Croyd overhead.

Shad chained his bike and went up the back wall of the office building. He perched atop the penthouse, and Croyd flapped to a landing near him, panting for breath.

"I'm not in shape for this," he said.

"You should climb more buildings."

"The whole convoy came straight here. I don't know where they're all headed, but—"

"The penthouse would seem indicated."

"Yeah."

"Fly over to the other building, and catch your breath. When Latham leaves, I'll give you the high sign, and you follow him."

"Man. I sure hope I'm awake when this all comes to a head. I'd like to know what's going on here."

Judas Priest began to thunder from beneath Shad's feet. He could feel the bass rumble through his soles.

Croyd took a few wheezing steps to the parapet and launched himself off into the night. Shad cloaked himself in darkness, then peered over the edge into one of the windows.

Van Gogh's *Irises* sat on the penthouse mantlepiece, vibrating to the heavy metal booming from eight-foot-tall speakers. Nelson Dixon, the painting's new owner, strutted up and down on the boardroom table in two-thousand-dollar handmade shoes. Jokers, including Kafka, hung around a boardroom table, not mixing much with a bunch of kids who were probably jumpers. A well-muscled bald woman stood in the corner and watched everyone with an expression of cold contempt. Near her, Shad recognized the lawyer St. John Latham. Shad wondered if Latham had been jumped but decided not—no jumper could possibly imitate that frigid manner. Shad also recognized the comptroller for the city of New York, a famous Wall Street bond profiteer, the curator of the Metropolitan Museum, and somebody from the old Reagan administration whom he couldn't otherwise place. Then Blaise came in with Tachyon, and the boy jumped up on the long table with Nelson Dixon, and the two exchanged high fives. Tachyon swayed to a chair and seemed to pass out again.

An interesting start to the meeting.

Shad took pictures through the window with a pocket camera and wished he had eavesdropping equipment.

The bald woman came forward and called things to order. The music faded away. People spoke. File folders were produced and passed around. Party bowls of cocaine and rapture moved up and down the table.

Shad wondered where Constance Loeffler was. The new head of Global Fun & Games had to be a part of this scene.

The meeting went on for several hours. Nobody thought to look out the window and wonder what a piece of darkness was doing poking its head below the sill.

When things broke up, Shad had decided whether to

follow Tachyon or the Van Gogh. The art attracted him more—he wanted to see where they were keeping the loot. He followed it to the same brownstone warehouse in Jokertown.

Damn. Still, he had a good start. All he had to do was follow people around. Connect the dots.

Then do what he always did.

Later that night, he slipped into Shelley's hotel room, just to see what it was the one-eyed girl had put on top of the tall cabinet. He picked the lock and slid in silently, wrapped in darkness. Shelley was breathing easily on the bed. Shad walked up the wall and peered at the top of the cabinet.

His mouth went dry.

What the girl had put there was her own eye. And her hand. The eye was looking down at Shelley's sleeping figure. Apparently Shad had not caught its attention.

He got the hell out of there.

Next morning, following instructions, Shelley set her window shade to the angle that meant yes.

And the jumpers came and got her.

Two nights later, Croyd collected his last payment of cash and bugs. Between the two of them they'd collected a large dossier, following and photographing every person and every car they could connect with the jumping scheme. Shad's files bulged with data.

Tachyon. St. John Latham. Curator of the Metropolitan Museum. The city comptroller. Shad had been in and out of each of their apartments, though without finding much incriminating. Nelson Dixon. Probably Connie Loeffler. Maybe even Donald Trump, who the hell knew? Trump had sure been going through a lot of changes lately. Hell, he'd gone and fired his wife. Nelson Dixon had fired a lot of people, too, including his entire security network. He bet the new security people were part of the scheme.

It wouldn't be the jumpers in their bodies, Shad figured. Fifteen-year-old street punks couldn't pull off impersonations this complex. Jumpers were just the means of entry. Shad guessed that the new tenants were probably well-educated jokers from Ellis Island, people who might have been Nelson Dixon or Donald Trump themselves if their wild cards hadn't been stacked against them.

How many millions were going into that warehouse?

Along with guns bought with converted bearer bonds, medical supplies from the Jokertown Clinic, drugs from the Snowboys, paintings from the Metropolitan collection...

The question was how to bust it open. His usual method was to infiltrate, then turn the bad guys against each other. But this was too damn big. And infiltration would be difficult. He wasn't a jumper, wasn't a joker, wasn't a Snowboy, and he certainly wasn't whatever the bald woman was.

The third night, he followed Tachyon to the warehouse. The Saab couldn't get in because there was a navy-surplus deuce-and-a-half sitting in the open main door. Blaise and Tachyon conferred inside for a few minutes, and then the Saab led the truck onto a pier on the Lower West Side.

Shad remembered himself as Mr. Gravemold, fighting a paranoid albino Croyd and a near-invincible Snotman on this same pier. It seemed the pier wasn't keeping any better company since that time.

He slipped through the pier rail and walked inverted over the water. He stopped when he heard the truck brakes squeal, then the slam of doors and the sound of voices. The water near the pier began to bubble. Shad's nerves gave a leap. He summoned darkness to cover him.

Something broke surface, a gelatinous hemisphere streaming with cold Hudson water. Shad's mouth went dry as he saw the bulbous eyes, up top like a bullfrog's, and the leering twisted mouth. He was used to jokers but he wasn't used to *this*.

"Let's hurry it up," the thing said. "I got dinner waiting."

Its veined skin split open, and another joker stood up inside. The joker was built along the lines of a beer truck, with a heavy armored exoskeleton to strengthen him, and he began to take heavy crates from those above and stow them carefully inside the shimmering dome.

The crates seemed evenly divided between food and munitions.

"My aching back," said the aquatic dome. "I hope you're ready for a slow ride home."

"Anything to give Granddad a kick in the teeth," Blaise said. Tachyon and the jokers looked uncomfortable.

Granddad, Shad thought. *Tachyon* had *been jumped. And he was on the Rox.*

Tachyon and Blaise lay flat on a case of antitank rockets.

The big joker stepped out, the dome sealed, and in complete silence, it vanished from sight beneath the river.

The deuce-and-a-half rumbled as it started up.

Shad decided to burglarize Tachyon's apartment again. Maybe he'd find something incriminating this time.

On the pavement below Tachyon's window he found a chalk drawing of himself, dressed as he was just now, his feet planted to the wall. Shad's head swung wildly, his ears alert to the sound of laughter.

He heard nothing.

He found nothing in Tachyon's apartment.

He wondered, as he scuffed the drawing away with his shoe, if his role in this was ordained by someone not himself. If he was a pawn.

And he wondered if that someone had chalk dust on her fingertips.

741-PINE.

"Hi. My name is Lisa Traeger these days. I'm calling from the trust officer's desk while he's off converting about half a million dollars to bearer bonds. I just thought I'd let you know I'm still among the living. I'll call back later, when I get some free time."

Lisa Traeger. He knew the victim's name now.

He heard the phone call hours after it was recorded. He'd seen the jump after having followed the Lincoln from the brownstone warehouse, but he hadn't known Shelley was a part of it. Shad was waiting by the phone when it rang again.

"Yes?" he said.

"This is, ah, Miss Traeger. I was wondering if you would care to join me for a night on the town."

"Are you free?"

"Nobody's watching. They trust me. I'm a criminal now, just like them."

He wasn't completely certain he believed that.

He met her at Tavern on the Green, in the Chestnut Room, which was one of the few rooms in the restaurant where people lurking out in Central Park couldn't watch them through the glass walls. He had taken a few circuits of the building before he'd gone in, just in case, and seen nothing, not even a detached eyeball.

Shad wore a blue blazer, gray wool slacks, and regimental tie. Lisa Traeger was in her late thirties, white, dark-haired, dark-eyed, and handsome. She carried a leather briefcase that Shad suspected was stuffed with bearer bonds. She wore a black off-the-shoulder Donna Karan evening dress and a Georges Kaplan fox wrap with the price tag still on it. Emeralds shone at her throat and ears. She ordered champagne and a warm chicken-salad appetizer with bacon and spinach.

"Brilliant," she said. "It went without a hitch. Traeger'll be held till tomorrow morning, and then I'll have to get the hell outta town."

"How do you feel?"

"Glorious. That joker body was *old*. I'm young again—well, younger. And my senses are much better. I can taste things again." She laughed as champagne went up her nose. Her skin glowed against the background of polished brass and rare wormy chestnut.

Sadness whispered through Shad's bones. "Traeger's hurting," he said. "Wherever she is."

Shelley considered that for a moment. "She'll make them the same deal I did. Wouldn't you?" She gave him a shaky smile. "I don't want to think about that anymore. I just want to be human again." She gave a brittle laugh. "I want to be safe for a little while, okay?"

She ordered the Muscovy duck in juniper sauce. Shad, to be polite, ordered the veal *escalope* and ate a few bites. He hadn't had solid food in days, and his stomach griped at him. His nerves kept giving little jumps as new people entered the room, as he checked them against his mental files of people connected with the jumpers' scheme. He saw nobody he knew. She ordered a bottle of Puligny Montrachet Latour '82, and Shad sipped a glass. Alcohol danced warm spirals in his head.

Outside, a cold winter wind flogged at the trees of Central Park. Shad put on No Dice's leather trench coat and got on his bike. Shelley gave a laugh and climbed on behind him, her hose-covered thighs gripping him. They sped up Central Park West, heading uptown. He danced the Vincent left and right, eyes straining, awareness reaching out, trying to make sure he wasn't followed. He stole heat from the cars and buildings they passed, a degree or two at a time, until his body roared with fire.

Shelley took his shoulders, leaned forward, spoke into his ear. "Wherever you want to go."

Wherever. Right.

Wherever ended up being a suite at the Carlyle. Shelley paid with Lisa Traeger's Gold Card. She hadn't been human for a long time. She wanted to do the most human thing of all.

Blindly, he reached for her. Her eyes glowed in shadowed sockets, and columns of flame pulsed in her throat. "You'll keep me safe, won't you?" she said.

He felt masks sliding away one by one. He felt less safe than he had in years.

"I'll do what I can," he said.

Shelley slept like a baby. Shad prowled the two-room suite, trying to work things out in his head. Strange little Miles Davis études sang through his thoughts. He kept hoping the situation would define itself, that he'd look out the window and see a human eyeball on the sill outside staring at him; then he would know what needed doing.

No eyeball. No clue.

He kept thinking about that green landscape glowing on the sidewalk. There, maybe, people wouldn't need masks.

In the pale predawn Shelley woke with a laugh. She threw up her arms and rolled across the Carlyle's sheets, giggling like a girl. Then she glanced up at Shad, who sat on the edge of the bed. Her eyes narrowed. "What's that on your shoulder?" she said. She reached out, touched the skin.

"It's the CBS eye," Shad said.

Her face wrinkled in puzzlement. "You had it done? Why?"

"Scar tissue," Shad said. "Somebody carved it into me when I was little."

Shock rolled across her face.

"I don't want to talk about it," Shad said.

She sat up in bed, put her arms around him. "I can't understand how somebody could—"

"Somebody did. And somebody jumped you and put you in a joker body."

And some people string others up from lampposts. "People do these things," he said.

She rested her cheek on his shoulder. "I can't believe I

didn't see those scars before." Her eyes narrowed. "Is that another one around your throat?"

Where the garrote had sawn into him and the tracheotomy had gone into the windpipe. Shad nodded. "The light's at the right angle or something. It happened years ago. It's hardly visible anymore."

She looked at him. "So what do you do with your time? You just live in hotels and carry a lot of cash with you and help people feel safe?"

"What are you going to do?"

She seemed surprised. "What do you mean?"

"I mean, what are you going to do? You've got money, a new body. A credit card that's probably good for a few more hours. So what's your plan?"

She lay back on the sheets. He looked at the dark nipples atop her soft mature breasts, and he couldn't help remembering the breasts of the old Shelley—smaller, firmer, with a dusting of freckles.

"I don't know," she said. "I feel too good to think about it right now. All I know is that I want to be safe again."

"People are going to start looking for Lisa Traeger in a little while, and I don't figure you want to be found."

"No." She leaned forward again, propped her chin on her knee. "I can pay you back your twenty grand. I've got enough with me."

"You don't have to. It wasn't my money anyway."

"You steal it or something?"

""Yes." Looking at her. "That's exactly what I did."

"Anyone get hurt?"

"Lots of anyones."

She frowned at him. "You're not making me feel safe anymore."

He shook his head. "I've never been what you'd call safe, Shelley."

She signed. Carefully her eyes queried his. "I know how to be safe if I have to."

"Yes?"

"I take the jumpers up on their offer. And I do the jump again and again, until I'm rich beyond my wildest dreams of avarice. And then I get jumped into a body more my own age—you know this Traeger body is all of thirty-eight?—and I live happily ever after in the Bahamas or wherever it is that retired jumpers go."

He looked at her. "I think you should quit while you're ahead. You don't want anything more to do with those people."

"I've lost twenty years. This body is going to be wanted by the police. And you say I'm ahead?"

"You're ahead of where you were a week ago. I'd settle for that."

"Twenty years." He saw tears in her eyes. "I've lost damn near twenty years. I don't *want* to be thirty-eight."

"Shelley." He reached out, took her hand. "Bad things are going to start happening to those people."

"Bad things. Meaning you."

"Me and about two hundred million other people. They can't keep this up. Not all those impersonations. Not people like Tachyon or Nelson Dixon or Constance Loeffler."

"Connie Loeffler?" Shelley sniffled, then shook her head. "She isn't being ridden."

"Then what does she have to do with all this?"

"They did jump her, yes. Put her in a joker body, one of the really disgusting ones, for a few hours. That was all it took." She shrugged. "She was a pretty young woman, okay? A pretty young woman with money, like I used to be. She *jumped*—heh, sorry—she jumped at the deal they offered. She pays fifty grand a month protection and allows them use of some of her cars and facilities. And she's living in L.A. now, to keep away from them, but that won't keep them away if they want her. The only way to keep safe from these people is to do what they want."

"That's not safe," Shad said.

"It's as safe as I'm going to get."

"Listen," Shad said. "I can make you disappear. I can get you new ID, a place to live, whatever it takes . . ."

"And I put my new money in a trust fund, right? And then someone in the trust department gets jumped, and—"

"It doesn't have to be New York."

"There are more jumpers all the time, right? It's a mutant wild card—like what that carrier spread a few years ago, only slower. In another few years there won't be any-place safe. The only way to keep safe is to keep on their good side."

A melancholy warning bell tolled slowly in Shad's heart. "I told you once," Shad said. "I told you bad things would start to happen. You didn't listen then."

"What about my missing years? How do I get them back?" Her voice was a wail.

"Think of the years you've got left. Make those the important ones."

"Shit! Shit!" She turned away and beat a pillow with her fist.

He reached for her, tried to stroke her shoulders and back. "You're ahead of the game. You've got lots of options."

"I was *young!*"

She clutched a pillow to her. Tears spilled from her eyes, and Shad's nerves twisted. "You were a joker," he said. "You're not anymore."

"I want to be safe."

"There isn't anyplace safe. The Rox least of all."

A vision of cool green fields passed before his mind.

Shad held her till she stopped trembling. Then she jumped up and went to the bathroom to find some tissues. A few minutes later, she was back, red-faced and red-eyed, and began to pick up her clothing.

"I should think about getting out of here," she said.

"I can hide you."

She frowned, considered, shook her head. Stepped into her underpants. "I want to be free," she said. "Free to make up my mind without any pressure."

"Don't hurt people, Shelley."

A little muscle in her cheek jumped. She gave him a resentful look. "The worst that'll happen to them is to end up in Lisa Traeger's body. You seem to think that's a good place to be."

"That's not exactly what I said."

Shad watched her dress and felt hope trickling out of him. He reached for his own clothes.

Leave her alone. Let her make up her own mind. He couldn't tell her what to do—he'd made too many wrong decisions himself to tell anyone else how to behave—but he knew that decisions had consequences, that karma worked on that level if no other, that nothing good could come out of any of this.

But he couldn't really think of any way to make it better any other way, either. What had happened to Shelley was like what happened to people in prison. You got fucked up. It didn't matter if you were in for an unpaid traffic fine and were the best prisoner in the world, because prison fucked you

over anyway. What you learned there was only good for
survival in prison, and what you learned was only how to
manipulate people and keep everyone at a certain distance
and play the game to get what you want and not care about
anyone else. And you couldn't help it, because that was what
you had to do to survive the slams. And when those reflexes
carried over to the outside, bad things would happen.

He buttoned his shirt, looked up at her. "Don't tell them
about me."

Her look was scornful. "What kind of person do you
think I am?"

"I'm here to tell you I'm not going to hurt you, okay? I
know you're not the enemy."

"Violet wasn't the enemy. She went off the roof anyway."

"I didn't push her."

"That doesn't mean it wasn't your fault."

Shad didn't have an answer for that one. "741-PINE," he
said. "Leave messages. I'll get them eventually, and I want to
know you're okay. But I don't live by the phone. You can't
trust it in an emergency." He looked at her hopelessly. "If
someone pushes you off a roof, I can't help."

Her look was slitted, hidden. Like someone gazing out
from behind a hundred years of hard time. She sighed,
reached out, touched him. Became Shelley for a little while.
"I won't shop you," she said. "You helped. I'd still be a joker
if it wasn't for you."

He put his arms around her and held her close. Her life
had turned nightmare, and she wanted it all back, the youth
and beauty and trust fund. Maybe she'd get it.

What she would never get back was that miraculous
innocence, the racing exuberant joy.

And they both knew it.

Two days later, Shad was ready. He had the jumpers
scoped out, knew their movements, knew that things were as
ready as they'd ever be. Shelley hadn't called him, but every
day that went by was another day in which she could decide
to rejoin the jumpers, and he wanted to make his move in the
interim.

The only delay had been caused by the building's alarm
systems. The warehouse had new state-of-the-art alarms, but
the building had first got electricity a century ago, and the
junction box in the alley out back was a spaghetti maze of

hundreds of different-colored dusty old wires. It had taken
Shad nineteen hours of work, crouched twelve feet off the
ground as he worked with his meter and alligator clips,
before he had the proper wires isolated. He was lucky it
hadn't taken weeks. All he had to do, come the proper
moment, was bypass the alarms with current from a six-volt
battery, and then it would be time to rock and roll.

He decided to move early the next morning, when any
guards would be tired and maybe asleep. He went to his
apartment off Gramercy Park and watched the news and
played Cannonball Adderley's *Savoy Sessions* and tried to
sleep.

At four in the morning, he got up, went to the wardrobe,
and unlocked it. He got out a heavy belt and a bunch of gear
and laid them out on the carpet. Then looked at the clothing,
all the identities lined up on the rack awaiting his habitation.
His eyes drifted to the Black Shadow costume: the navy-blue
jumpsuit, the black cloak, the domino mask.

The costume sang to him of readiness, and he felt his
soul answer.

There was a chalk drawing on the wall next to the
junction box. It showed only the junction box blown up to
enormous size, its mass of wires rendered in bright, almost
surrealistic detail, with a giant pair of hands working with
alligator clips and a voltage meter.

Shad found his nerves keening again, his head gymballing
madly as he looked for the street artist, but he knew she was
long gone.

The cloak floated about him as he crouched on the wall
next to the junction box and attached his homemade bypass
box to the alarm system. He took a cellular phone from his
belt, dialed 911, and told the police that there were jumpers
holed up with their loot in the warehouse and that they had
captives in there. He finished by saying that he'd heard shots
fired and that they'd better cordon off the neighborhood and
get a team ready to send in.

"Give me your name, sir," the operator insisted.

"Black Shadow."

Why the hell not?

Shad hung the phone on his belt and walked up the wall
of the warehouse. Night spilled from his cloak, raced through
the sky. He sucked photons until the darkness billowed out

ten yards in all directions, until his nerves sang with pleasure. He picked the lock on the roof access and went down a fluted nineteenth-century cast-iron staircase. Torn, graffiti-scarred wallboard revealed crumbling red brick and slabs of unreclaimed asbestos.

Below, on the upper floor of the warehouse, were the tiger cages.

It looked like a brainwashing academy out of *The Manchurian Candidate*. Solid prefabricated metal-walled cells had been built and riveted together, each with a single steel door and a slot though which food could be passed. The cells were open on top and screened with metal mesh. Catwalks lay atop the mesh so that sentries could march along them and peer down at the inmates. Each cell was equipped with a cot, a mattress, a washbasin, a pitcher of water, and a slop pail. February cold filled the place; the prisoners were wrapped in blankets and secondhand winter clothing. Spotlights jury-rigged to the graceful brick arches of the roof kept the prisoners in perpetual daylight. Cameras peered down from above. There was a stairway and a pair of empty freight-elevator shafts that led to the floor below.

The smell was not good.

Shad saw two guards, both jokers. One, a slouched figure in a hooded cloak, paced atop the cages and carried an AK complete with bayonet, while another, a slab-sided gray-skinned elephant man, drowsed naked in a chair to one side of the cages, sitting in front of a collection of electronic equipment that looked as if it had been kludged together by Victor von Frankenstein: video monitors, rheostats, switches, red and green Christmas-tree lights, Lord knew what. Both sentries were wearing shades against the glaring light.

The thing Shad found most pleasing about this setup was that there were a lot of photons to rip off.

He covered himself in darkness, inverted himself, and walked along the ceiling until he was over the cages. Most of the people in them were lying down, trying to sleep, arms thrown across their eyes to cut off the incessant light. Most were jokers, many badly deformed. One of them wore a straitjacket and was chained to the door of her cell. Little rhythmic moans came from her slitlike mouth.

The ones they couldn't afford to let go. People like Shelley they could release after a few days, but not Nelson

Dixon or the city comptroller. Not the ones with access to accounts they could loot forever.

Shad looked down at the joker guard and felt certainty filling him like a swarm of buzzing photons. He'd hidden himself away, turned himself into other people. No Dice, Wall Walker, Simon, other phantoms of his imagination or of the street. All dealing with penny-ante shit. Now he was himself again, working on something worthy of his time. Readiness filled him like a welcome draft of springwater.

Photons dopplered along his nerves at the speed of light. The joker guard was right below him. Shad dropped from the ceiling, turned himself upright in air, and landed just behind the guard. The wire mesh boomed. One hand twitched the hood off the joker's head and jerked him backward, the other drove a palm heel into the joker's mastoid. There was a nasty sound of bone caving in. The joker fell onto the mesh with a crash like a falling tree. Shad didn't figure he was dead, but of course skull fractures were unpredictable. And Shad was already on his way to the other guard.

The elephant man had come awake and was staring at Shad, blinking hard, shading his eyes against the glaring light and trying to make out what had just happened in the boiling cloud of darkness that had dropped atop his cages. It was far too late to do anything by the time he realized that the cloud of darkness was heading for *him*.

The cape crackled in Shad's ears as he sprang off the tiger cages and landed on the joker's chest with both booted feet. The chair went over backwards, and both Shad and the joker spilled to the floor. Shad rose to his feet and considered his handiwork. The elephant man was flat out of the picture, half his ribs broken, blood oozing from a scalp wound where the back of his head had hit the floor.

"Hey! Hey! Let me out!" The voice boomed in the huge room. Apparently one of the captives had noticed that his guard had been flattened right over his head.

"Put a lid on it!" yelled someone else.

The darkness swirled away, revealing Shad's form. He looked at the scarred homemade plywood desk that supported all the electronic gear. There were a series of numbered switches that Shad concluded operated electric locks in the cells.

"Let me out! Let me out!"

"Shut up, fuckface!" Another weary voice.

Shad peered toward the cells. "Which number are you?" he shouted.

"Six! Six!"

Shad pressed number six. There was a loud buzzing sound, a door slammed open, and a yellow-skinned, round-bottomed bipedal dinosaur, wearing nothing but a polka-dot necktie, flung himself out, looking wildly left and right, and started heading for the stairs leading down into the warehouse.

"Not that way!" Shad yelled. "Over here!"

The dinosaur reversed direction and started running again, heading for the stairs to the roof. Shad intercepted him and grabbed him by the necktie.

"Hey! Lemme go!"

Shad started dragging the dinosaur toward the console. "This way," he said. "We're letting everyone out."

"Me first!"

"What you're gonna do is push buttons. And then maybe I'll let you leave. Okay?"

Shad got the dinosaur in front of the console, then walked toward the first of the tiger cages. The door had 01 stenciled on it. Inside was a purple joker with flippers for hands.

"Hit one!" Shad said. He pulled the door open and turned to the joker. "You're free. Take the stairs to the roof, then down and out of here. Tell the police."

The joker ran for the stairs as if he were afraid Shad would change his mind. Shad walked down the line of cells, opening one after the other. Captives moved toward the exits. The woman in the straitjacket had to have her chain torn off the door by main strength—Shad sucked a lot of photons and boosted his muscles—and then she ran, hooting, for the stairs without waiting to have the canvas jacket unbuckled.

"Hit eight!" The door buzzed and Shad looked up into Lisa Traeger's eyes. She seemed a more privileged class of inmate; she wore an opaque sleep mask propped up on her forehead and had an electric blanket for her cot. She was dressed well in Guess jeans and a cashmere rollneck. A delicate gold chain winked around her neck.

There was a dossier open on the bed, with photographs and xeroxes of bank statements. She was studying her next target. They didn't let their people out after they knew who the target was. A good piece of security, Shad thought.

"You're free," Shad said. His mouth was dry. "Follow the others to the stairs."

She made a nervous gesture with her hands. "I left you a message earlier."

"I forgot to check."

"I haven't told them anything."

He opened the door. "Better get out of here."

She took her blanket and left without looking back. Shad walked to the next door. Peering out the window was a scar-faced woman in an eye patch whose distinctive features he'd last seen in the *New York Post*.

Dr. Cody Havero.

"I've been looking for you, Doc," Shad said, and turned to the dinosaur. "Hit nine!" The lock buzzed, and Shad pulled open the door.

"Listen," Cody said.

"You're free," Shad said. "Take the stairs to the roof, go down the fire escape, and head for the police station."

"No. Wait. My name is Cody Havero."

"Hit ten!" Shad looked at her. "I know who you are. The whole city's been trying to find you. Hit eleven!"

"Listen." Following him. "I know things. A lot of what's going on, here and on the Rox. I know a lot of the people they've lined up as targets. And—"

Shad heard one of the freight elevators start up and put a hand over Cody's mouth. Night rose from the floor, covered them both. Cody gave a little shiver as her vision darkened.

The elevator platform rose, and Shad could see through the old-fashioned folding elevator door that Tachyon was on it. He looked pale and about a hundred years old. Even the plume on his hat drooped. He was carrying a tray with plastic-wrapped sandwiches and paper cups of coffee.

Shad was already moving, a memory flaming in his mind of Shelley in the hound-joker body, little bits of tissue sticking to her fur as she wiped away tears...

Tachyon slid open the elevator door before he noticed anything was wrong, and Shad turned everything to night, reached into the elevator, and grabbed Tachyon by the throat. Hot coffee spattered the floor. Shad slammed Tach's head into the side of the elevator, then swung him around and out of the elevator and smashed him into the brick wall of the main room. Tachyon went limp.

Shad reached down, took the alien's collar in his hands,

applied an X-hand choke hold, pressing not only on the windpipe but on the blood vessels on either side of the neck, cutting the arteries that fed the brain. Whoever was inside Tachyon was going to have to die before he jumped out.

He tightened his hold. The darkness fell away, and Cody screamed.

"No! Leave her alone!"

Tachyon was moving feebly, trying without success to tear Shad's hands away. Cody ran to him, grabbed one of Shad's arms in both her own, tried to haul him off the alien.

"That's not Tachyon!" she said.

"Either way," said Shad, and tightened his grip, pressing hard. Tachyon's eyes rolled up. Shad remembered the way the garrote had sliced into his throat when he was a boy, the way the police had to give him a tracheotomy after they kicked down the door, dug a hole in his windpipe, and how he didn't understand what was happening and tried to fight them, thinking they were trying to kill him too.

Cody tugged on him. "It's just some girl named Kelly. She's not really *anybody*."

Shad looked at her. She took a step back, her eyes widening as she saw his expression, and then determination entered her face, and she yanked on his arm again. "She's Blaise's girlfriend. That's all she is. She does what they tell her."

Shad looked down at the alien body, its face turning purple, and released his hold. Tachyon thudded to the floor, clutched at his throat.

"Blaise is the bad one," Cody told him. "He's behind the whole thing. He's *evil*."

"Didn't think he was a choirboy," Shad said. His throat ached as if in sympathy with Tachyon's.

"He killed the real Tachyon months ago. Blaise told me."

Tachyon's not dead, Shad thought in surprise. *He's on the Rox.*

He was about to tell Havero that, but suddenly the room was filled with the flat unmistakable boom of a Kalashnikov. Shad's nerves screamed as he dove forward and rolled, willed his opaque black cloak around him. He flattened himself against the metal wall of the prison complex.

The overhead mesh rattled. Cody, he saw, had reacted well, throwing herself flat, and she was now low-crawling toward cover. Her Vietnam reflexes seemed intact.

The AK boomed again. Shad extended his opaque field and climbed up the wall of the cage complex. There was a fountain of sparks from the control console, and the yellow dinosaur fell back, arms waving.

The joker was crouched, the AK shouldered and leveled, and there was a ripping sound as the guard unloaded a full magazine in the direction of the escaping prisoners.

Shad screamed in anger and ate every photon in the joker's body. It took several long seconds. Shad's heart seemed to swell with sudden heat. The joker pitched forward, frozen; there were little crystalline sounds as bits of him broke off and rattled downward through the mesh. Shad ran for the table, saw the dinosaur lying splayed with his brain oozing down the brick wall behind him, the yellow body twitching in its final throes. Shad looked wildly for Shelley and saw her—saw Lisa Traeger's body—running up the iron stairway, panic stamped on her face but otherwise unharmed. Two more of the prisoners were down, wounded. The rest of the swarm of bullets had only pocked the red brick walls. Either the guard was a bad shot, or he'd been seeing triple from his head injury.

Cody Havero ran forward to render first aid, her hands snatching automatically at her pockets as if for medical instruments.

A telephone on the control panel began to purr. Shad picked it up. His eyes tracked to the stair.

"What's happening? Who's shooting?" The voice sounded female and young.

"What's happened—" He felt himself smile. "—is that I just killed your guard. The question is, what do you think you can do about it?"

He put the phone down. "Everybody out," he said, and hit the remaining switches. Jokers burst out of cells and staggered for the exits.

"Help your friends!" Shad said, pointing to the two wounded. "Get 'em out."

Out of the corner of his eye he saw Tachyon rise to an unsteady crouch, then fall headfirst down the stairs. Shad suppressed an impulse to pursue and instead hit the switches labeled *floods* and managed to kill most of the floodlights. An alarm buzzer began its cry, repeating its grating message every three seconds. Shad walked toward the stairway, darkness swirling off his form like dancing mist.

The first two jumpers bounded up the stairs with UZIs in their hands. Shad dropped night around them, watched the panic grow in their eyes, then drew heat from their bodies till they went unconscious and stumbled back down the stairs. He heard someone scream down below. Shots bounced up the stairway, fired blind by someone out of sight.

Shad jumped over the barrier to the freight elevator that Tachyon hadn't used, then walked down the side of the elevator shaft. Peering around the corner, he saw a cold-eyed mastiff of a joker and a chubby-faced young white girl braced behind some packing crates, the joker with another AK and the girl with a Dirty Harry revolver far too large for her hands. Both were staring at the stairway with its two blue-faced figures. A white boy in a flash Italian jacket and Bart Simpson T-shirt was trying to kick-start a vintage Triumph motorbike, but in his panic he'd flooded the engine.

Shad didn't see Tachyon anywhere.

Van Gogh's *Irises* hung on one of the walls under a row of track lights. The warning buzzer was still crying.

Shad took them all out, dropping them with hypothermia, one after another. It took a long time because Shad's body had already absorbed a lot of energy, but the targets were helpless, and he took all the time he needed. When the boy dropped with the Triumph on top of him, the joker began firing wild, bullets whanging off brick, and when Shad began consuming his heat, he held the trigger down and emptied the magazine into whatever crates were nearest him.

Shad slipped from out of hiding, searched the area for Tachyon, and didn't find him. The red metal fire door in back was open; maybe the Tachyon body had simply bolted. Shad handcuffed each of the shivering victims, cuffed their feet as well, and put a garbage bag over each head. A hand-lettered tag attached to each bag identified each as a jumper. The police or emergency-room personnel would remove the bags at their peril. The jumpers couldn't jump anyone they couldn't see.

Shad wandered for a moment amid the stacks of loot. There were lots of paintings, some of which had just taken some 7.62-mm rounds. More prefabricated detention facilities, German in manufacture, designed to be ready for use in any insurrection, revolution, or instant concentration camp. Enough weapons to start a revolution, each labeled in its packing crate—grenades, mortars, antitank weapons. Some of

the lettering was Cyrillic, some Chinese. Most seemed to
have been transshipped from Texas. Medical supplies. Bearer
bonds. Gold bars. Serious amounts of drugs, presumably not
for use, rather an investment. File cabinets filled with reports
from lending institutions, credit-check companies, credit-card
companies, and private detectives hired to scour the neighborhood for new victims.

It was bigger than Shad had imagined. His heart blazed.
This was the kind of thing he was meant for.

Well. Time to be a hero. He got on the Triumph, started
it, heard the tail pipe boom off the echoing warehouse walls.
He drove to the loading dock, opened the door, rolled the
bike out. The cold street waited. Shad accelerated, cape
snapping out behind him, and turned the corner.

A turreted NYPD armored car sat like a squat insect on
the eroded city asphalt. Police in helmets and flak jackets
were setting up sawhorse barriers and stretching out yellow
tape.

The Triumph's headlight rolled over them, and Shad saw
them start nervously, a general movement toward weapons.
Shad decelerated and held up a peaceful hand.

"Chill," he said. "I'm on your side."

A tiny Asian woman in a flak jacket—Captain Angela
Ellis, he knew—gave him a narrow look. She had never met
Shad, but she'd met one of his identities who had worked out
with her in the same karate school. She was talented, Shad
judged, but impatient. From her look, maybe the bells of
memory were beginning to chime. Her M-16 was pointed
slightly to the right of Shad's heart.

"Who are you?"

"The warehouse is full of loot," Shad said. "Gold bars,
paintings, drugs, and a whole lot of guns. There are some
kidnap victims I've let go—"

"We've picked up some." A flat declaration.

"Some are wounded."

Captain Ellis nodded, raised her walkie-talkie, spoke a
few words.

"I've subdued the kidnappers and bagged them for you.
Some are jumpers, so be careful."

Ellis nodded again.

"They've been jumping the rich," Shad continued. 'The
city comptroller, Nelson Dixon, other people with access to

cash. There are files in there that should give you a lot of names."

She looked at him with unforgiving jade eyes. "You never answered my first question. Who the fuck *are* you?"

Shad's smile broadened, and he couldn't resist a low, calculated laugh. "Call me Black Shadow," he said.

She stroked her chin and nodded.

He laughed again, exultant. This was, all of it, what he was born for. He looked at her, the laughter still rolling from his throat. "Somebody else got jumped," he said. "Somebody important."

Her eyes were most unfriendly. "Who?"

What should have happened was that he spoke the name of Tachyon, ate every particle of light for about ten yards around, gunned the Triumph, and disappeared like the Lone Ranger into the night, trailing triumphant laughter. What happened instead: The world suddenly spun in his head, and then he was looking up into a starless New York opalescent night, and he could feel his own limbs twitch and spasm as if they were not his own. Shelley looked down at him with a sneer on her face. She was wearing a lot of mascara and the wrong-colored eye shadow. Her breath was warm and smelled of gin.

"Asshole," she said. "Son of a bitch. I should blow your brains out." Brandishing a chrome-plated .38 revolver.

Shots banged off hard brick walls. Shad could hear shouts and screams. Shelley grabbed him by the collar, jerked him left and right. He couldn't seem to make his body do what it wanted. Roof asphalt and pebbles grated on his back.

It wasn't Lisa Traeger doing this to him but the old Shelley, the young girl he'd first met. He recognized the bridge of freckles across her nose.

"Hear that?" Shelley said. "That's Diego in your body, and he's kicking police ass." She laughed. "Cops are gonna come looking for *you*."

He had been jumped. The thought pierced Shad's mind like an icicle. He gasped for breath and tried to rise, arms and legs thrashing.

Shelley laughed contemptuously and shoved Shad back onto the roof. Police shotguns boomed out. "Relax," she said. "You'll be back in your body real soon, and you won't like it."

Shad's mind whirled. He had just worked out who he was, and now he wasn't himself anymore.

The hell he wasn't.

I am Black Shadow, he thought. There had to be a way to make this body work for him. He lay back on the cold roof and concentrated on making one finger move. It seemed to do as he commanded.

Okay. A start.

I am Black Shadow, he thought.

Shelley went to the roof parapet and looked down. "Diego, shit!" she said. "Get outta there! Jump! You've made your point."

She wore a white evening dress, a fur wrap, and an incongruous pair of battered red sneakers. Her hair was longer and punked up with mousse. She and her friend had probably just come back from a night of club-crawling and seen the police setting up their barricades. You needed a twenty-one-year-old body to get into the kind of clubs where jumpers probably wanted to hang out. Shelley had provided one. Maybe that's all they really wanted her for and the trust fund was just a bonus.

Shad tried to move his left foot, was successful, and managed to move the left leg a few inches. More or less as he intended. Then he tried the right leg.

I'm Black Shadow. Black Shadow. The words becoming a mantra.

More guns fired. Shelley paced back and forth at the parapet, muttering. Shad wondered if the police were winning.

"Yeah! Yeah!" Shelley chanted. "Run for it!"

A storm of fire erupted. Shelley leaned out over the parapet, apparently following someone escaping around the corner, and then she sighed. "Good." She came back to stand by Shad's side and looked down at him. "You're gonna get yours, asshole."

Black Shadow. Black Shadow. I'm Black Shadow.

He looked at the woman next to him. *And you're not Shelley.*

Shad moved. His coordination wasn't very good, so he chose a move that could be done without any real precision. His *kenpo* teacher called it Sticks of Satin. He dropped his right leg against the front of Shelley's ankles, then slammed his left leg against the back of her knees. His accuracy was none too great, but the leverage was still good enough to pitch Shelley forward, landing hard on hands and knees.

Shad lunged upward and grabbed her gun arm by the

sleeve, then dragged her toward him. He clubbed one fist and tried to bring it down on the back of her neck, but his accuracy was wretched, and he hit the back of the head instead. He kept hitting. Shelley struggled, almost got free, but Shad lurched atop her and bore her down to the asphalt.

"I'm Black Shadow," he said. "*Black Shadow.*" His arms wrapped Shelley's head, right forearm folding across her jaw, left cupping the back of the head.

"No," Shelley begged. "Don't." Shad's heart twisted.

"*Black Shadow!*" he screamed, and snapped Shelley's neck.

He pulled the .38 from twitching fingers and staggered to his feet. The sky whirled around him. He tottered to the parapet and looked down.

The Triumph was on fire. Angela Ellis was on the pavement, moving feebly as police figures crouched over her shouting into their radios. Other officers lay sprawled across the pavement, some in pools of blood.

They'd blame Black Shadow for it, he realized. How could they do anything else?

There was a noise on the fire escape, and Shad spun to face the sound. Dizziness almost brought him sagging to his knees. Black Shadow rose from the darkness. He looked at Shad and the sprawled figure of the lifeless jumper.

The cloaked silhouette approached. He was carrying a police M-16. "Man. I thought I was cornered there for a second. I musta jumped twelve times before I ended up back in this body." He dropped the rifle and grinned. "Turns out this guy can walk up walls. Lucky for me." His look turned puzzled. "Why are you in my body?" Thinking Shad must be his friend. He looked from one to the other again, then alarm entered his eyes. "What are—"

Shad lurched toward him, swinging up the pistol on the end of his right arm. "I want my body back, motherfucker."

Black Shadow looked uncertain. Then he smiled. "Maybe," he said. "If you drop that gun."

"Bullshit." The gun swayed. Shad grabbed it with both hands.

Black Shadow's eyes narrowed inside the mask. "Maybe I can cross that distance before you pull the trigger."

"Just try it, motherfucker. I know I ain't faster than a speeding bullet, and neither are you."

The jumper hesitated. Apparently he didn't know that he

could hide himself in darkness or freeze Shad solid, because he didn't try it. Maybe he hadn't been alive to read *Aces* magazine in 1976.

Shad blinked sweat from his eyes. The gun jittered in his hands.

"You don't seem too coordinated, asshole," said Black Shadow. "Why don't you put the gun down?"

"I want my body back," Shad said, "and if I don't get it, I'm gonna hurt you."

Black Shadow looked at him. "How you gonna do that?" He grinned insolently. "I'm in *your* body. You aren't gonna hurt *this* body, are you? Look at yourself. You're fifteen years old. I'm a grown-up."

Bang.

Black Shadow's eyes widened as the bullet whipped over his head. "*Shit!*" he said. "Will you put that thing down?"

Shad blinked eyes dazzled by the muzzle flash, a problem his regular body didn't have. "If you give me my body back," Shad said, "you can have this body. *This* body has a gun, motherfucker. Maybe you can kill me with it before I snap your fucking neck."

Black Shadow hesitated, licking his lips. "Let me think."

Bang.

The bullet clipped him in the leg, and he went down with a yell. "*Stop that!*"

"Give me my body back!"

"Fuck you!"

Bang.

The bullet took Black Shadow in the torso somewhere, and he went down, suddenly limp, hands clutching at the roof. "You're crazy!" he shouted.

And then his eyes narrowed as he looked at Shad. Triumph sang through Shad's veins as he realized what was about to happen. He gave his hand a command to drop his pistol, but suddenly the world was spinning again, and he couldn't be certain if the command was obeyed.

Asphalt hit him in the face. *I'm Black Shadow,* he thought, and laughter rang through his mind.

He ate every photon he could reach. Heat blazed through him. He rolled across the roof as blind pistol shots snapped out.

The jumper loomed in his awareness, a flaming infrared target that staggered around the roof, blinded by darkness.

Shad's body had been exercising hard, and it was starved for energy. Shad concentrated on the figure and drank in its heat.

The jumper swayed, staggered, collapsed.

Shad gasped for breath and tried to rise to his feet. The wounded leg seemed willing to support him; the bullet had gone through the fleshy part of the thigh. The other bullet had gone through the right shoulder, and Shad could feel bone grating as he tried to move it. Blood was soaking the jumpsuit, coursing warm down Shad's right arm.

The wounds were in shock, and there was no real pain yet, just little crackling twinges of what was to come. He was going to need a doctor real soon. Except that the police had fired a lot of bullets at him, would have no idea whether they'd hit, and would be searching the hospitals for him. The jumpers too, probably.

He'd have to find a doctor he could trust, a junkie or alcoholic or someone who would want his cash and not turn him in. He searched his mind.

Nothing. Shit. He'd settle for a vet.

He could hear police shouting, the pounding of boots on pavement. They'd heard the shots and figured something was up.

Time to leave. He squatted over the jumpers and Shelley's body, and ate every bit of heat in them, feasted on photons until the two lay with frost covering their glassy eyeballs.

Shad rose and headed off the roof. A tornado of heat swirled in his heart. Blood drizzled on the cold pavement below as he eased himself over the wall.

I'm Black Shadow, he thought.

A glowing green landscape burned in his mind. The night covered him with its velvet mask.

He collapsed two blocks away. He panted for breath, ate photons, tried to gather himself together. He became aware of someone moving cautiously across the street, watching him with dilated cat's eyes.

"Wait!" He called the darkness, staggering toward her trailing a boiling black shroud and a trail of red. She hesitated, then began to retreat. "I need help." He sagged against the wall and slid to the pavement.

Chalktalk turned. Her dilated cat's eyes seemed big as the moon.

A bolt of pain shot up his arm. "I've been shot," he said.

"I need to get out of here." He sagged against a brick wall. Chalktalk stood, undecided, five long yards away. "Can you take me somewhere?" Shad asked. "Someplace where I can... get better? I can't have police involved."

She said nothing.

Shad tried again. "You've been following me, okay? I know that. So you know what I've been up to. I don't know what your reasons were, but—" Pain crackled through his body. He gasped. "Help me now, all right? Like I helped you with Anton."

She walked close to him and knelt, her bulky overcoat obscuring her work as she reached for chalk and began to draw.

Shad shivered. The girl's warmth called him, but he didn't take it. The chalk made little scratching sounds on the pavement. Shad became aware that he was sitting on wetness.

"Hurry," he said.

The girl looked up at him. Her famished wide-eyed face was lit from below, as if the pavement were glowing with light. He crawled toward her, and she ducked her head toward him and kissed him, and before he had a chance quite to absorb that, he was suddenly aware that he was falling.

Falling into another place.

The phone rang twice. 741-PINE. The answering machine picked up.

A woman's voice spoke for a few seconds. "I've called a dozen times," she said.

There was no one to answer. The little Jokertown room was empty, holding only a narrow bed and a footlocker with an odd assortment of clothing.

"I don't know what to do," the woman said.

There was a click. And then there was silence.

The Temptation of
Hieronymus Bloat

VII

Blaise had torn down the Administration Building around me, replacing it with a gigantic cage of steel. I stared out forlornly through the bars as Blaise and Prime rounded up all the jokers from their houses and the caves below, herding them into a great mass before me. Tachyon-Kelly was there, too, standing beside Blaise and cradling the great mound of her belly. Blaise kissed her savagely, his eyes open and staring at me, not her. Prime applauded the gesture—Latham had taken all the money from the jokers; the bills in an enormous green pile before him.

"Now, Durg," Blaise said, and I heard a rumbling. An enormous bulldozer the size of a house came into view, and instead of grillwork, the front of it was Durg's face. Dozer-Durg churned the earth of the Rox, driving inexorably toward the jokers, who screamed with rapture-blue lips, cowering and backing away from the mechanical horror until the water of New York Bay lapped at their heels.

"Stop!" I yelled to Blaise from my case. "This is the joker homeland! This isn't your place; this is the Rox!"

Blaise only laughed. Prime smiled coldly, sorting the stacks of bills before him. A cold wind was blowing, a dark wind, and it scattered the money. Latham ran after the flying bills, shouting and grasping, but the wind took them all out into the bay. Prime-Latham jumped up and down on the shore, cursing.

"Prime!" I shouted to him. "You have to help me! I'm the governor!"

Blaise was laughing at Prime, laughing at me. Dozer-Durg herded the jokers, forcing them deeper into the water.

"Well, Fatboy, they've got you trapped, but then you already know that."

I looked down to see the penguin grinning up at me. A huge key ring was hung over the funnel hat; an ornate ancient key dangled from the ring. "Shut up. Go away," I told it.

"Whassamatta, Gov? You afraid?" The penguin *tsked* softly, shaking its head. The key rang against the ring with a dull chiming. "You have so much potential, so much power."

"I don't have *any* power," I raged. "Nothing. The caves just came; I don't know how I did it or how to do it again. It's all a sham. Damn it, I could make this place something wonderful if they'd just let me."

"You certainly could," the penguin agreed. "If you'd get off your big ass and use that power. But you won't. You don't really believe in it."

I began pacing the perimeter of my cage. I was the Outcast now, with an empty scabbard banging against my hip as a reminder of my impotence. I shook the bars; I raged.

None of it did any good. Blaise laughed, Latham ignored me. Dozer-Durg drove the jokers out until the waters of the bay closed over them with black finality.

Blaise's arm snaked around Tachyon's swelling waist and walked her over to my prison. "You see," he said to her. "He's nothing. He's powerless to help you. He's lost every-thing." He pointed at me, low, and chuckled.

I looked down. Blaise was right. I was naked, and where my genitals should have been there was nothing but smooth unbroken skin. I began to scream. . . .

I was still screaming when I woke up.

"You'll take the message to Latham?" I asked Croyd. "Is it safe for you?"

Croyd shrugged. I could tell he was wired, red-eyed and ready to sleep. He looked like a pink-skinned bat on growth hormones—not a pretty sight. He'd come to the Rox since he didn't feel that Manhattan was safe for any joker any longer. *It's a bitch, man. If I'd known Shad was gonna cause this kinda ruckus . . .* "I can do that much, sure. I still think it'd be a lot easier to just get a whole bunch of us together and bust Tachyon."

"It's not that simple," I said. "You don't know the situation here. I have to be honest, Croyd. I've got a tower room all set up for you—hell, you're one of the joker heroes—but I can't say you're safer here than Manhattan."

"I'll take my chances," Croyd shrugged. Wing membrane rustled. "And I'll pay the rent, too. I make a hell of delivery boy; don't have to fool with traffic. What's in the package?"

"Blackmail."

Croyd grinned. He flew off.

I hadn't been kidding. Whoever this ace was who'd wrecked our jump-the-rich scheme had left me one silver lining. There was now a lot of pressure on the authorities to hang someone for this. I was only reminding Latham that I had a lot of information regarding that scheme that would make his life very, very uncomfortable. Sure, he'd shrugged that aside once before, but there was a lot more heat now. I also let him know that none of that information would ever reach *them* if he could do me just one little favor—convince Blaise to let Tachyon go, or simply spring Tachyon himself. I knew Latham's thoughts, after all; I knew he detested Blaise as much as anyone. I knew that he feared Blaise as well. In my letter, I asked him what might happen to Blaise once *they* heard from Tachyon what had happened. *Blaise,* after all, was the visible head of the jumpers.

Croyd came back several hours later. "It's done," Croyd said. "Latham said that he'd take care of it."

I laughed, happily. *Yes!* I exulted. *Soon, my love! Soon you will be free. It's done!*

I'd done it. It had taken far longer than my worst fears, but at last this injustice would be over. The realization felt so good, so damned good. Even the colors of the Bosch seemed more vibrant.

Croyd looked at the painting, too, sighed, and rustled his wings, folding them around his wrinkled, wizened body. "Now, where can I sleep, Governor?" he asked.

Riders
by
Lewis Shiner

The man was a Shinto priest, but in an attempt to satisfy everyone, he had worn a black suit and black turtleneck. There was enough March sunshine to make the clothing uncomfortable. He had visibly begun to perspire. "Dearly beloved," he said, with some sort of Asian accent, "we are gathered here today . . . to celebrate—" He stopped and looked down at the prayer book, puzzled. Then, looking horribly embarrassed, he flipped forward and started the service for the burial of the dead.

Veronica shifted uncomfortably on her metal folding chair, as did most of the small crowd of mourners. For Veronica, it was an attempt to keep from laughing. *Ichiko*, she thought, *would have laughed*. But Ichiko was dead.

"I did not know Ichiko personally," the priest said, beginning to drone. "But from what I understand, she was a kind, generous, and loving soul."

Veronica wondered how he could go through with it, to stand there next to her coffin and issue platitudes, to sum up the life of someone he'd never met. She tuned him out and looked around once again, hoping to see Fortunato. Ichiko was, after all, his mother. Veronica had sent the telegram herself to the monastery on Hokaido where Fortunato had retreated. There had been no answer, just as there had been no answer to any of the other letters or pleas that had been sent him. All she saw now was sunshine, birds splashing in the puddles left from a morning shower.

In all, maybe a dozen people had shown up for the service. Cordelia and Miranda, of course, who had been with Ichiko to the end. A handful of former geishas. Digger Downs, probably hoping for a glimpse of Fortunato. Three elderly men Veronica didn't recognize. None of Ichiko's famous clients, of course, could afford to be seen at her funeral.

There were lots of flowers.

She looked at the old men again, wondering if one of them might be Jerry Strauss, in disguise. She hadn't heard from him since the previous fall, but it wasn't like Jerry to give up easily. It was Miranda who had told her about his ability to change his appearance, something he'd never let on about in all the time he was paying for her professional services. Still, if one of them had been Jerry, he would have been watching her. These three seemed to have trouble staying awake.

Then again, she thought, *even Jerry might not recognize me now.*

The transformation had started the night Hannah died, a year and a half before.

Hannah had become the thing Veronica lived for, the reason she cared what her body looked like, the reason she was able to wake up in the morning, the reason she went downtown everyday for her jolt of methadone mixed with sickly-sweet orange drink. And Hannah had somehow, inexplicably, hanged herself in her jail cell before Veronica could get to her.

In the process of getting there, Veronica had learned something about herself even she hadn't known. Her sometime lover Croyd, temporarily spreading an infectious wild card virus, had given it to her. She had developed an ability that she didn't fully understand, that she had hardly used. It seemed to cause another person to become weak, helpless, devoid of willpower.

Even that power had not let her save Hannah's life.

She'd left the police station and wandered back to the apartment she shared with Hannah and gone to bed, holding on to her cat and waiting and waiting for sleep. At three in the morning she came violently awake, sure that she was in danger. The police could find her there, and so could whoever had killed Hannah.

It was murder, beyond question. Some outside force had taken possession of Hannah in a midtown bank, while Veronica stood by helplessly. That same force had to be responsible for her suicide.

She packed a suitcase and put Liz in a cat carrier, and phoned for a cab. She waited in the shadows of the building's entrance until the cab arrived, then got in quickly and gave the address of Ichiko's brownstone.

Veronica had to go into Ichiko's bedroom and wake her up, which was more difficult than she'd expected. Finally Ichiko got out of bed and struggled into a kimono and took a few clumsy strokes at her hair with a brush. Veronica had never seen her without her makeup before. She had let herself forget how old Ichiko was, in her seventies now.

"I need help," Veronica said. "Hannah's dead. She killed herself—they say—in her jail cell." It was Ichiko who had sent her to Hannah in the first place, for drug counseling. "But she would never have killed herself. It's not like her."

"No," Ichiko said. "You are right. It is not her way."

"There's something between you two, isn't there?" A sudden pang of loss blinded her for a second. "I mean, there *was* something. You sent me to her, out of all the therapists in this city."

Ichiko nodded. "Years ago, she was part of a group, a feminist group."

"W.O.R.S.E."

"Yes. That one. She had decided to make us her target. She wanted to have her people follow our geishas on their assignments and make trouble for them, draw attention to them, embarrass our clients. There is no doubt she could have destroyed the business this way."

"When was this?"

"Seven years ago. Nineteen eighty-one. She had just joined the group. She had many problems, with her marriage, with drinking and drugs. She was not . . . stable. She came to me and told me what she planned to do. She had not formally proposed it to the group yet."

"And?"

"And I gave her money not to."

"Hannah? You *bribed* Hannah?"

Ichiko held up her hands. "I made her an offer. A hundred-thousand-dollar anonymous donation to the organization. Enough money to keep them going for years. In exchange she would let me take my business apart slowly, in my own time, in my own way."

"I can't believe it."

"She was not the same woman then. When she brought in that donation, it gave her much power. She soon became president. That in turn gave her personal strength, let her conquer her private demons. There is no simple good and bad here."

"So the two of you stayed in touch."

"We shared that guilty secret. The guilt is mine also. I have done little to keep my end of the promise. Little until now. But perhaps the time has come."

"What about W.O.R.S.E.? Are you in touch with them? Could they help me?"

"I will try. But you are not safe here. Check into a hotel somewhere. Pay cash; do not use your real name. Tell no one. Call me tomorrow at noon. I will see what I can do."

Veronica did as she was told. The next day, Ichiko gave her a single name: Nancy. This was the woman who had arranged for Hannah's lawyer. Ichiko described her over the phone with typical precision: five foot three, long brown hair parted in the center, wire-rimmed glasses, small breasts, full hips. Veronica was supposed to meet her at Penn Station at three o'clock, by the ticket windows for the Long Island Railroad.

She stopped off for her methadone on the way. She still had a check from Ichiko in her purse, the check she'd been meaning to deposit two days before, when Hannah . . .

Her numbness had started to wear off. The thought hurt her more than she could have imagined.

Finish it. When Hannah had gone berserk. Taken a guard's gun and started shooting.

The check would have to wait. She couldn't go back into that bank again, even if the cops weren't likely to be looking for her there.

Ichiko had said she was to be ready to travel, which meant lugging the suitcase and cat carrier with her. Liz hated being in the cage and squalled continuously. The suitcase, full of winter clothes, was enormously heavy. She was tired and sore and sweating by the time she made it through the labyrinth of tunnels to the LIRR.

Someone touched her elbow. "Veronica?"

Ichiko's description had been carefully nonjudgmental. It had omitted Nancy's clear skin, her smiling Clara Bow mouth. No makeup, of course. Intelligent light brown eyes. "Yes," Veronica said.

"I'm Nancy," she said. "I'll watch your things. Get us two one-way tickets for East Rockaway. We can just make the 3:23."

Veronica bought the tickets and Nancy carried her suitcase onto the train for her. They got settled and Veronica opened the door of the cat carrier to stroke Liz, hoping to shut her up. "Where are we going?" Veronica asked.

"I'm putting you up at my place for the duration. You'll be safe there. Not even Ichiko knows."

"I don't know how to thank you. I mean, you don't even know me."

"Hannah knew you. That's enough."

Veronica noticed the past tense. "You've heard, then."

Nancy looked away, nodded stiffly.

"I'm sorry," Veronica said. "I don't know you, I don't know what to say to you."

Nancy nodded again, and Veronica suddenly realized what an effort she was making to be polite. "You don't have to say anything at all."

They changed in Jamaica. The wind whistled through the open platform, and Liz huddled in a corner of her cage, crying softly. They boarded the Long Beach train in silence.

When the train stopped in Lynbrook, Nancy suddenly grabbed Veronica's suitcase and started for the doors. "Come on," she said. "This is us."

Veronica got off the train behind her. "I thought..."

"It never hurts to cover your trail. Carrying that cat around—somebody at the ticket window might remember you."

They walked downstairs and crossed the street to Carpenter Avenue. Veronica had never been on Long Island before, and the sense of space made her uncomfortable. None of the buildings were over two stories high. There were lawns and vacant lots covered with trees and grass. The streets were nearly empty.

Nancy led her to a door in a row of tall, narrow wood-frame houses across from the library. There was a dead bolt but no police lock or alarm system. They climbed two flights of stairs to a refurbished attic. There was a bed, a bathroom with a shower, a half-size refrigerator, and a hot plate. A huge leather-covered armchair sat by a lamp and a crowded bookshelf.

"If somebody comes along who's got a worse problem than you, we'll make other plans. Until then, you can

stay. I'll do your shopping for you, at least for a while, until
we see how hard they're looking for you."

"I've got money," Veronica said. Or she would have,
once she could find a way to cash the check. "I can pay for
the room."

"That'll help." Nancy stood up. "I'll get you some food—
and a litter box for the cat—and then I've got to get back to
the city. Will you be okay here?"

Veronica nodded. Her growing despair seemed to make the
wood-paneled walls grow even darker. "I'll be fine," she said.

The priest droned to a close, and the coffin was lowered
into the ground. Ichiko would rather have been cremated,
Veronica suspected. Miranda had refused to hear of it. And
she had come up with this bastard amalgamation of Shinto
and Catholic for a funeral service. Miranda was Ichiko's oldest
friend, and she was Veronica's mother, so she got her way.

They filed past the hole, and each threw in a ceremonial
shovelful of dirt. Veronica's dirt hit the coffin with a hollow
whack. She passed the shovel on and went to stand by her
mother. Miranda had walked well away from the others and
stood with her arms folded, watching the driveway.

"He's not coming, Mother," Veronica said.

"He's Ichiko's only son. How could he not be here?"

"What do you want me to say? I could tell you maybe his
flight was delayed. Maybe he got held up in customs. But you
know as well as me he just decided not to come. She's dead,
there's nothing he can do."

Except, she thought, *use his tantric powers to bring her
back to life*. A particularly nasty thought that she left unsaid.

Miranda started to cry. "It's the end of everything. The
business is closed down, Ichiko's gone, Fortunato might as
well be dead. And you, you've changed so much..."

I must be getting stronger, Veronica thought. *I can
almost handle this*. She put her arms around her mother and
held her until the crying passed.

It had taken Veronica a week to settle in at Nancy's
house. Nancy had gotten her a fake birth certificate, which
they'd then parlayed into a driver's license and a bank
account. Ichiko had rewritten the check with Veronica's new
name on it. With the money Veronica had Nancy buy her a
portable stereo and a TV set for her attic cell.

She also got on a methadone program at Mercy Hospital. This was the biggest risk of all, but there was no way around it. It meant riding the bus up Peninsula Avenue once a day. The hospital, with all its Catholic paraphernalia, seemed comforting to Veronica, an island of her childhood.

More and more she would find herself remembering her comfortable middle-class neighborhood in Brooklyn. Miranda had been making a lot of money working for Fortunato, most of it going into savings. There was enough left over for a good-size apartment in Midwood, new clothes every fall, food, and a color TV. Linda, Veronica's younger sister, lived in the apartment now, with her good-for-nothing husband, Orlando. Between Orlando and the smack, Veronica hadn't seen her sister in two years.

Nancy tried to talk her out of the trips to the hospital. It would be safer, she said, for Veronica to go back to shooting up. The words alone brought back the memory of the rush. The floor seemed to drop out from under her like she was in a high-speed elevator. "No," she said. "Don't even kid around about it." What would Hannah have thought?

On her first Saturday night in the attic, there was a meeting downstairs. People showed up all through the afternoon, and the sound of movement and laughter filtering up through the stairwell only made Veronica's loneliness worse. For a week she had been cooped up there, seeing Nancy for no more than ten minutes a day. She lived for her short bus rides to the hospital, where she might sometimes exchange a few words with a stranger. Her life was turning into a prison sentence.

On Sunday, when Nancy came up to check on her, Veronica said, "I want to join the organization."

Nancy sat down. "It's not that easy. This isn't NOW or Women's Action Alliance or something. Hiding fugitives isn't the only illegal thing we do."

"I know that."

"We only invite people to join us after months, sometimes years of observation."

"I can help you. I worked for Ichiko for over two years." She took a notebook out of the nightstand by her bed. "This is my client list. We're talking some major people here: restaurant and factory owners, publishers, brokers, politicians. I've got names, phone numbers, preferences, personal statistics you're not going to find in *Who's Who*."

There was more, but Veronica wasn't willing to tell her the rest, not yet, about her ace power. She still didn't know how it worked or how to control it. And she didn't know what Nancy's reaction would be. Veronica had been watching CNN there in the room and was just starting to realize how strongly the tide had turned against wild cards. Aces and jokers were even turning on each other, thanks to Hiram Whatsisname, the fat guy's, murder of Chrysalis.

Nancy stood up. "I'm sorry. I didn't want to have to say this, but you pushed me to it. Try and look at it from our point of view. You're a prostitute, a fugitive, and a heroin addict. You're not exactly a good risk."

Veronica's face felt hot, as if she'd been slapped. She sat motionless, stunned.

"I'll talk to the others," Nancy said. "But I can't make any promises."

Ichiko's funeral was on a Sunday. On Monday, Veronica was back at work. At the moment, she was the receptionist at a company that published trade journals: *Pipeline Digest, Catering!, Trout World.* The owner, one of Veronica's former clients, was the only male involved in the business, and he was never there.

When she'd decided to go back on the job market, she'd gone straight to her client files. At her first two interviews, the men who'd once salivated at the sight of her naked body simply stared at her. She'd put on twenty-five pounds in the last four months, and her metabolism, still trying to adjust to life without heroin, had taken it out on her complexion. She wore no makeup, her hair was cut short, and she'd given up dresses for loose drawstring pants and bulky sweaters. The men smiled with faint distaste and told her they'd let her know if something came up. The third interview landed her a cooking job at one of the better New York hotels. After a couple of months, she moved up to a senator's office.

She'd been with Custom Publishing for six weeks. For the first time in her life, she felt comfortable, surrounded by competent women. She had even relaxed enough to stop for a drink with them now and again at Close Encounters, a fern bar across the street.

Which she did on the Thursday after the funeral. It was still only slowly dawning on her that Ichiko was dead, that the most significant part of her life thus far was finally and absolutely over. She needed a little companionship to ease the sudden fits of panic and loss that would sneak up on her. A drink would have helped, but she'd quit that when she quit the heroin.

She looked up from their corner table at the restaurant to see a man standing beside her.

"Veronica?" he said.

She'd gone back to using her own name, but none of her new friends knew about her past. She wanted to keep it that way. "I don't think I know you," she said coolly. Betty, a woman in her fifties with steel-gray hair, stared at the man hungrily. He was young, good-looking in a soap-opera sort of way, wearing an Armani suit.

"We . . . went out together a couple of years ago. Donald? You don't remember?"

There had probably been more than one man she'd forgotten, what with the heroin. "No," she said. "I wish you'd quit bothering me."

"I wanted to talk to you, just for a second. Please."

"Go away," Veronica said. She didn't like the touch of hysteria she heard in her own voice. "Leave me alone!"

People all around them were looking now. The man—Donald?—held up both hands and backed away. "Okay," he said. "I'm sorry."

Veronica saw, to her horror, that her wild-card power was affecting the man, without her conscious control. He had turned pale and seemed barely able to stay on his feet. He caught his balance on the back of an empty chair and walked unsteadily out the door.

Donna, a thirty-year-old blond who wore short skirts all winter long, said, "Are you crazy? He was *gorgeous*. And that suit must have cost a thousand bucks."

Betty said, "This is the first we've ever seen of your sordid past." She turned in her chair, watching Donald move away down the street. "You can't blame us for being curious. You never drink anything but club soda, you never talk about dates or husbands, none of us even know where you live. . . ."

Veronica tried a smile. It was supposed to be mysterious, but she could feel the wrongness of it. "My lips are sealed," she said.

On a Saturday evening, her third week in the attic in Lynbrook, there had been a knock on her door.

Nancy stood in the stairway, looking uncomfortable. "It's okay for you to sit in on the meeting. But for God's sake, don't say anything, okay? You'll just make me look like an idiot."

Veronica followed her downstairs. A dozen women sat around Nancy's dining-room table. They were all dressed casually; most wore little or no makeup. Three of them were black, two Latin, one oriental. One was a joker who seemed to have too much skin for her body; she had no hair, and folds of flesh hung off her chin and neck and hands. She looked like one of those weird wrinkled bulldogs that rich people sometimes had.

Only one of the women was under thirty, and she stood out like a panther in a rabbit hutch. She couldn't have been out of her teens. Even with her bulky winter clothes, Veronica could tell she was a bodybuilder. It showed in her neck and the width of her shoulders, in the way she held herself. Her hair was black, shoulder length, and to Veronica's expert eye, almost certainly a wig.

Veronica found a chair. The meeting started and lurched slowly forward. Every issue was put to a vote, and then only after endless debate. The young bodybuilder seemed as bored as Veronica. Finally she said, "Screw all that. Let's talk about Loeffler."

The joker said, "I can't see that being as important as the joker issue. Wild-card violence is tearing this city apart." She slurred her words, and Veronica found it hard to understand her.

One of the black women—Toni, her name was—said, "Zelda's right. This joker shit could take forever. Let's talk Loeffler."

The joker woman objected and was quickly overruled. Even W.O.R.S.E., Veronica thought, was not completely free of prejudice. As the discussion heated up, Veronica put the pieces together. Robert Loeffler was the publisher of *Playhouse* magazine and head of the entire Global Fun & Games empire. The group intended to confront him and force changes in the magazine's attitude toward women. The problem was, nobody knew a way to get through to him. A slight woman in her fifties named Frances offered to use her locksmithing experience. Zelda wanted to use a bomb.

After a half hour of debate, Veronica excused herself. She went upstairs and copied Loeffler's unlisted phone number and the combination to his penthouse elevator on a piece of paper. She took it downstairs with her, handed it silently to Nancy, and took her chair again.

Nancy, across the table from her, said, "Where did you get this?"

The debate stopped.

Into the silence Veronica said, "I used to fuck him."

The table came to life. In ten minutes they had the outline of a plan. The rush of power went right through the top of Veronica's head, like a hit of crystal meth.

Toni said, "Let's *go* on this. My only question is, how soon?"

Martine, the joker woman, threw her weight behind the bandwagon. "How about tonight?"

"We haven't got time to get set up," Veronica said. "But tomorrow is possible. Sundays were always good for him."

The next night, Nancy and Veronica took the train to Penn Station, and Veronica made the call from a pay phone in the lobby of the Penta Hotel across the street.

"Bob? Veronica."

"Veronica!" His voice was muffled, but he sounded pleased. "Darling, how are you?"

"I'm gorgeous, Bob. And the thermostat in here doesn't seem to be working. It's so hot! I had to take all my clothes off." A gust of freezing air came through the front doors, attacking her legs. The extra weight she had put on in the attic made her feel thick and clumsy, and her nerves were ringing like a switchboard at a radio station. "And one part of me is hotter than all the others. I bet you remember which part that is."

She heard a soft moan. "Don't do this to me, Veronica. I'm a married man now. Don't you read the papers? She was the May Doll of the Month."

"I don't care if you're married to Miss America. It's not *marriage* I'm interested in." At first, Nancy's jaw had dropped in amazement. Now she was starting to crack up. Veronica had to turn away to keep from losing it herself. "I'm freelance now, Bob. I'm offering a special to my very favorite clients. The first one's free. Just to remind you why you should always let a professional take care of your needs. All your *special* needs. Hint, hint."

"Oh god. We can't do it here. Bev would kill me."

"That's why the good lord made hotels."

"Tonight?"

Veronica covered the receiver and mouthed "Tonight?" to Nancy, who nodded. "Sure, baby. I'm just over here at the

Penta, with the heat turned all the way up. Oh! It's really getting damp and sticky in here."

"I'll be there in an hour."

"Call it ten o'clock? I'm ready now, but by ten o'clock I'll *really* be ready. I'll have the room set up just the way you like it. Call me from the lobby."

She made a kissing noise into the phone and hung up, a little uncomfortable at how easily it all came back. She left Nancy to phone for reinforcements and rented a room under her own name.

By ten till ten, they had five more women, including Toni and Zelda and Martine, the joker. Nancy wanted Veronica to get into bed with Loeffler so they could take pictures. Veronica refused.

"It's not like you've never done it before," Nancy said. "How much could it hurt?"

"Leave the chick alone," Zelda said. "I wouldn't want nobody inside *my* body unless they was invited."

"The ends *are* the means," said Toni. "We can't victimize our sister."

"Okay, okay," Nancy said.

"I got a better idea," Zelda said, taking off her clothes. She was not as built-up as Veronica had thought. She was smooth and feminine, with extraordinary muscle definition. Veronica found it a little hard to look away.

The phone rang. It was Loeffler. Veronica gave him the room number and told him to hurry. She left the hall door slightly ajar and took the other women into the darkened bathroom.

"Don't nobody fart," Zelda said, and there was muffled laughter.

Veronica heard Loeffler come in, the door clicking shut behind him. "Veronica?" he said. "Did you bring the pickles?"

One of the women strangled a laugh.

"Get undressed," Veronica said through the door. "I've got a surprise for you."

She heard the sound of a zipper. "Mmmmmm. I *love* surprises." Clothes hit the floor, covers swished back, the bedsprings creaked. "Okay, darling, do your worst."

Zelda was the first through the door. She pulled the sheet down and had Loeffler's erect cock in her hand by the time Nancy got the lights on and the camera focused. Somebody else threw a copy of that day's *New York Times* on the bed to verify the date. It took Loeffler at least three frames to shove Zelda away and say, "Veronica, what the hell is going on here?"

Veronica shook her head. Toni stood at the foot of the bed and presented their list of demands. They weren't asking him to kill *Playhouse* or turn it into a women's-lib magazine. They wanted the Doll of the Month to become Woman of the Month, and feature the occasional professional woman over thirty. Feature articles supporting the ERA and condemning the NRA. Fiction by women. In short, finish out the decade with at least a minimum of social consciousness.

"And," Zelda said, "I want your centerfolds to stop lying about their waist sizes. Nobody has a twenty-two-inch waist. That is such *bullshit!*" Veronica giggled in spite of herself.

Loeffler was not amused. During the lecture, he had gathered up his clothes and gotten dressed. "Do you realize who you're fucking with, here?"

Nancy said, "Maybe you don't realize who *we* are."

"WORSE would be my guess."

"That's right."

"I'm not afraid of you."

"You should be," Toni said. "We can mobilize letter-writing campaigns that will get your magazine pulled from every convenience store in the country. Picket lines to keep your employees from getting to work. Media coverage that will have the fundamentalists all over you like flies on shit." She nodded toward Nancy and her camera. "Not to mention breaking up your marriage."

Loeffler sat down to put his shoes on. "If you'd come into the office like reasonable human beings and discussed this, I might have listened to you."

Martine said, "I've been trying for an appointment for three months. Don't pretend you're interested in our 'input.'"

"Okay, then, I won't." He started for the door, then turned to look at Zelda. She was still naked and had been following him around the room. "And put some clothes on," he told her. "Looking at those muscles makes me sick."

Zelda didn't change expression. She merely leaned back, still smiling, and threw a side kick that snapped Loeffler's neck.

His body hitting the floor was the only sound in the room. Veronica thought of the carnage in the bank and Hannah's swinging corpse. She thought she might pass out. She made herself kneel next to Loeffler's body and reach for a pulse in his throat.

Zelda slapped her hands away. "He's dead. Trust me."

"Jesus," Veronica said.

"Sorry," Zelda said without conviction. "I wasn't thinking."

"Zelda, for Christ's sake," someone said.

"You really are a loose cannon," Toni said.

Nobody but Veronica seemed particularly shocked or upset. Nancy looked at Veronica and said, "*Uh*-oh. Trouble."

Toni took Veronica's hand and pulled her to her feet. "Give me your room key. We take care of this. You get across the street and catch a train home. Can you do that?"

Veronica nodded.

"Shit," Toni said. "Nancy, you go with her. We handle this."

After they were out of the city, somewhere around Forest Hills, Nancy said, "Are you okay?"

"It's so weird. It's like...like it was all a dream or something."

"That's right," Nancy said. "That's all it was. Just a dream."

It was all over TV the next day. Loeffler's body was found in an alley near Penn Station, apparently the victim of a robbery.

That evening, Nancy came up to tell her they were in the clear. "You don't need to know how they did it," Nancy said. She seemed radiant with success. "But they got him out, and there's nothing to connect us with him at all."

"Doesn't it bother you?" Veronica asked. "That he's dead?"

"Look, I'm not crazy about violence either. But you have to remember. The guy was scum. With him dead, his daughter takes over GF&G. It becomes a women's corporation, and that's going to make things better for women everywhere."

Veronica remembered Loeffler's childlike energy, the way he threw himself into sex with unrestrained enjoyment. She remembered the flowers he'd always brought her, his sense of humor. "I guess," she said.

The next Saturday, one of the women brought in photos of Zelda and Loeffler that she'd printed up herself at work. They were passed around to much laughter and admiration. There was a nervousness behind the bravado. Veronica felt it, and the others probably did too, but no one mentioned it.

Veronica left the meeting early, and the next Saturday she stayed in her room. No one came to invite her downstairs, and Nancy never mentioned W.O.R.S.E. again.

*   *   *

Donald—whoever he was—had put Veronica off her feed. She left Close Encounters and went home, put a frozen dinner in the micro, and turned on the news. They had a feature story on the Rox, a follow-up on the unsuccessful park ranger raid back in February.

"Admit it," the reporter said to some man in a ranger uniform. "Those kids could have done a lot worse if they wanted. It was like they didn't even take you seriously. A few people got shot up, but that was all. They made fools out of you."

"Mister," the ranger said, "you don't know what's out there on that island. It's worse than you could ever imagine. Just pray to God you don't ever find out."

Veronica had saved one photo of Hannah. It had been sitting on an end table, but she'd gotten to where the constant sight of it was a reproach. Now she took it out again and sat down with it in front of the TV. She realized she had never cried for Hannah, not once in the sixteen months since her death. With that thought, the tears came.

Jumpers, she thought. They made fools of all of us.

She turned the TV off. She couldn't seem to get herself back together since that man in the restaurant. It was the past come to haunt her. Like all hauntings, it was something she'd brought on herself. It was something she'd left undone. For over a year, she'd been pushing it away, but the questions had been there all this time, fighting to get out.

She walked nervously around the apartment. She wasn't going to be able to sleep tonight, not in this state. She had to do something, no matter how small, to buy off her conscience.

She sat down and dialed Nancy's number.

"Hello?"

"Nancy?"

"Yes?"

"It's Veronica." After the odd terms they'd parted on, she didn't know how Nancy would react.

"Yes?" she said again, this time nervous, reluctant.

"I don't mean to bother you. It's just...there's this question I always wanted to ask you. It's about...it's about Hannah."

"Go on."

Veronica could picture her standing on the faded carpet in the hallway, back stiff, eyes staring straight ahead, waiting for some inevitable ax to fall. "Ichiko told me W.O.R.S.E. paid for Hannah's lawyer. I just wanted to know... I mean... how did you know she was in jail?"

"You mean, did she use her one phone call to call us, instead of you? Is that what you're asking?"

"I guess so. I mean, she told me she was through with all of that."

"She was. She didn't call us. Latham, Strauss did."

"They called *you*?"

"It was Latham himself. He said they would provide Hannah an attorney free of charge, but they didn't want that fact to get out. They wanted us to say we were paying for it. It wasn't an offer I was willing to refuse at the time."

"How did he know where to find you?"

"I have no idea."

"Really? You don't have *any* ties to Latham?"

"We'd talked about targeting Latham for an action. Believe me, it was as much a surprise to us as it was to you."

After a few seconds, Veronica said, "Are you okay?"

"Yeah. Life goes on. You know?"

"I know," Veronica said.

When she hung up, her hands were shaking. Latham. She's seen him on TV: elegant suits, razor-cut hair, eyes as cold as a winter sky. Jerry's brother was the *Strauss* in Latham, Strauss, and he'd told her stories about him. He was so inhuman that Jerry's brother had wondered if maybe he was a secret wild card, that the virus had somehow killed all his emotions. Just the idea that he could somehow be mixed up in Hannah's death was terrifying. It was like opening up a tiny box and finding everything in the world inside it.

There was nothing left to do that night. She went to bed but didn't sleep. Instead she lay awake, seeing Latham and Hannah. And Nancy.

When snow fell on Long Island, it stayed. It had lawns to pile up in and kids to make snowmen out of it. Veronica had sat in her cell that December and listened to the wind howl outside.

On Christmas Eve, Nancy brought her a bottle of white wine with a ribbon on it. Veronica had wrapped an antique silver comb just in case, and Nancy had seemed touched by it.

Later, Veronica heard her crying downstairs.

She had only been in Nancy's apartment for W.O.R.S.E. meetings. She agonized for ten minutes, then went down quietly. Nancy was stretched out on the couch, clutching a pillow. She didn't even look up when Veronica lay down next to her and took her in her arms.

"Nobody should be alone on Christmas," Veronica said.

"Everything, everything just kind of fell apart," Nancy said. "I was supposed to go to Connecticut, and then their kids got measles, and I . . ."

"It's okay," Veronica said.

"I can't believe you're being so sweet to me when everything's gone so badly. I've left you alone up there, night after night . . ."

"You've done so much," Veronica said, trying to be generous.

"No I haven't. I was jealous. Of you and Hannah. We used to be . . ." She didn't seem able to finish.

"You were lovers."

"Years ago. But she got tired of me."

Veronica kissed the top of her head. Nancy looked up at her, helpless and vulnerable. Veronica unhooked Nancy's glasses and put them on the table, then kissed her on the mouth.

They made love awkwardly, with vague passion and no conviction. Veronica was ashamed of her body. With nothing to do all day, her addict's metabolism had developed a craving for sugar that she couldn't control. It took all her strength to stay on methadone and off heroin. There was no strength left to diet. In a month and a half she'd already gained fifteen pounds and was still gaining.

Nancy's body was covered with fine dark hairs, and her skin seemed unhealthily pale. The taste of her vagina seemed odd and sour. Veronica would find herself remembering Hannah, then have to force herself to go on.

Eventually they moved into the bedroom. They held onto each other through the night but didn't try to make love again. Toward morning, Veronica woke to find that Nancy had turned away and was snoring softly into her pillow. Veronica got up a little after dawn and got into her clothes. She came back to kiss Nancy lightly on the forehead. Nancy woke long enough to squeeze her hand, then went back to sleep.

After that, Veronica stayed in her room. She stayed there through the bitter cold of January, into the worse cold of February. One Sunday, the temperature fell below zero, and all of Long Island was covered in ice. Veronica was unable to get out of bed. She thought about Hannah, about the things they'd done together. She thought about the scene in the bank, the change that had come over Hannah's face just before she took the guard's gun and started shooting. She thought about Hannah hanging in her jail cell, dead.

She curled deeper under the covers. She'd gained another ten pounds, and now she felt heavy all the time. Liz settled into the small of her back, and the two of them slept through the day.

By nightfall, Veronica was sick.

It was like nothing she'd heard or imagined. Suddenly she was outside her body, filling the room, lighter than air. Distantly she felt her body begin to convulse. Vomit trickled out of the distant body's mouth, and Veronica knew, distantly, that if the body did not roll over, it would likely strangle. The body did move, fortunately, when a fit of coughing made it double up on its side.

Nancy came upstairs to see what had happened when Veronica fell out of bed and crashed onto the floor. She found a bottle of Hydrocodone and made Veronica swallow three of them, forcing them past her raw and swollen throat.

It was another quarter hour before the spasms passed. "I have to get out from under this," Veronica whispered. "I don't care what it costs."

The next morning, she boarded Liz at the vets and checked into Mt. Sinai's drug-treatment program. It took six weeks. She lost all the weight she'd gained, then put it back on again. Handfuls of hair came out of her scalp, and the crow's feet that grew out of her eyes never went away, even when she finally got clean and was able to sleep again.

She still had money left from her hooking days, enough to get her through the end of the year, as long as she stayed out of the hospital. But she needed something to fill the empty days. No one seemed to be looking for her. She had her hair cut in a pageboy and bought herself new clothes, pants and sweaters, all dark, all loose-fitting.

She found her own apartment, a few blocks from Nancy's.

Nancy only nodded when Veronica told her the news, cried a little when Veronica brought the last of her things downstairs. "I haven't been much help to you, have I?" Nancy said.

"You saved my life."

Nancy squeezed her, then let her go.

Veronica took a job typing and filing at a Lynbrook

insurance office. She made minimum wage and watched while the boss flirted with another of the secretaries, a hardened thirty-year-old who chewed gum. Veronica had less than no interest in a toupeed insurance salesman in a double-knit suit. Still, it was the first time in her life a man had ignored her. And why not? She had taken herself out of the game. Overweight, severe haircut and clothes, no makeup or perfume, her sallow skin broken out from all the sweets.

It was late summer, the summer of 1989, before she saw how the world around her had changed. Instead of going home after work, she sat on the lawn of the library and watched the kids playing in the grass. It was a perfect afternoon, the skies clear, a light breeze rattling the leaves. She was able to look at it and realize, objectively, how beautiful it was. It seemed possible to her, for the first time in years, that one day she might be able to look at a sunset and actually feel it, and not be overwhelmed by Hannah's absence or her own fear of being discovered, or her worries about her weight and what she was to make of her life.

She suddenly wondered what was happening in the world. She hadn't even bothered to plug in the TV at her new apartment. She bought a newspaper, sat on the bench, and started to read.

The headlines were full of something called jumpers.

She had to force herself not to skip ahead, ignoring the buzzing in her ears and the unease in her stomach. Teenage gang members all over the city had developed the ability to somehow trade consciousness with unwilling victims. The teenagers would ride around in the shanghaied bodies, killing and looting and terrorizing, and then would jump back into their own bodies when they were done.

Once more, Veronica remembered the scene in the bank, the handsome blond kid whose eyes had dulled at the same time that Hannah's had changed.

Hannah had been jumped.

The press—and everyone else—was convinced that this was a new manifestation of the wild card. It had cranked the anti-wild-card hysteria in the city to a new pitch. It was a good thing she'd kept quiet about her ace power. All the wild card victims were being treated with fear and hatred. New York State had started a "voluntary" registration for aces. Editorials argued for internment camps, and letters cried out for blood.

Veronica went home and studied herself in the bathroom mirror. In October, less than a month from now, she would be twenty-seven. It seemed beyond belief that so much of her life was already gone. She'd been hiding out almost a year. No one would recognize her the way she looked now. Reading the *Times* had reminded her how much she missed New York. She was strong enough now, she thought, to stay clean. It would be easier, really, once she was back in the city where there were places to go and things to do. The temptation was always lurking in Lynbrook because of sheer boredom.

It was time to go home.

On the Friday after Ichiko's funeral, Veronica got up with bags under her eyes and a feeling of dread in her heart. Before she left for work, she called Latham, Strauss. She asked for Dyan Mundy, Hannah's lawyer. Mundy wasn't in, but Veronica got an appointment with her for that afternoon.

Lunch at Close Encounters was the office tradition on Friday, followed by very little work getting done the rest of the afternoon. Their usual table for six was waiting for them when they got to the restaurant. Veronica looked around the bar nervously as she walked in, afraid she would see the man in the suit—Donald—again. Instead she saw a woman at the bar and froze where she stood.

Veronica could only see her from behind. She had dark brown hair worn loose past her shoulders. She had on a blue lamé dress, cut below the waist in the back, completely inappropriate for afternoon.

It was Veronica's dress.

The woman turned slowly on her stool. Veronica knew, with the certainty of a nightmare, what she was about to see. She was right. The woman had her face, her old face, the one she'd had when she was hooking. Lean, languidly sexy. Lots of makeup. She stared at the firm breasts and trim waist that had once been hers.

The woman stared back.

Okay, Veronica thought, this is clearly not happening. I am clearly dreaming this.

The woman reached into her purse, and Veronica thought, she's going to pull out a gun and shoot me; then I'll wake up.

She waited for the eternity it took for the woman's hand to come up out of the purse. It held a photograph, torn out of a newspaper. It showed a blond boy in a tuxedo—handsome, sensual, smiling with the confidence of money. It was the boy from the bank. The one who'd jumped Hannah.

"What do you want?" Veronica whispered.

The woman stood up, wrapped herself in a shawl. She took a few tentative steps toward Veronica, unsteady on her four-inch heels. "To talk," she said. It was Veronica's own voice. "Will you listen to me?"

Veronica nodded and followed the woman outside.

"I'll make this quick," the woman said. "I know a lot more about what's going on than you do. The kid's name was David Butler. He was seventeen. He was a summer intern at Latham, Strauss. As far as I can tell, he was the one running the kid gang when all this jumping business started."

" 'Was'?"

"He's dead. But the jumping is still going on."

"Who are you?"

"Never mind that now. The point is, this is some kind of wild-card phenomenon. It's not just a coincidence that all these kids developed the same power. The wild card doesn't work that way. Somebody is *giving* it to them."

The way Croyd gave it to me, Veronica thought guiltily. Then, in an instant, her brain flashed from her own infection to what she had learned about Jerry. About how he could change the way he looked. Change *everything*.

The woman was saying, "We have to find—"

Veronica took a step backward. "Jerry? Is that you?"

The woman broke off. "What?"

"It *is* you, isn't it? You bastard, how did you find me?"

"Your mother. I convinced her it was life and death."

"Change back. Change back now. I can't stand looking at you like this."

"I haven't got anything else to wear. I'm not going to stand here as Jerry Strauss in a dress."

"Do *something*."

The woman's features melted and reformed. It was like a coat of facial mud washing off. Now Veronica was talking to the young Ingrid Bergman.

"Oh Christ," Veronica said. "Did my mother give you the dress, too?"

Ingrid nodded, blushing.

"What do you want from me? What am I supposed to do?"

"Help me find who's behind this. Whoever is creating these jumpers is responsible for my brother's death."

"Kenneth?"

"That's right. They killed him. Last fall. They killed Hannah, too. Doesn't that mean anything to you?"

Veronica slapped her, then swung her purse at her head when she tried to cover up. "Don't you tell me what Hannah meant to me. You bastard! Get out of my life and stay out!"

Suddenly she saw the women from the office, watching her out the window of Close Encounters. They'd seen everything, of course. Her life was in a shambles again.

She turned and ran.

It had been Veronica's mother that told her about Jerry. Veronica had gone to see her that past Christmas. She knew at the time she was taking a risk, letting herself make contact with her former life, but she wasn't willing to go on living in fear forever.

The brownstone was dark when she arrived. At first, she thought something drastic had happened, that the Mafia or the Shadow Fists or Global Fun & Games had finally taken over and shut the place down. She rang the doorbell, and after a minute or so, Miranda's voice came over the speaker by the door.

"Yes? Who is it?"

"Mom, it's me." She had even called the week before to warn her. "Can't you see me?"

"Veronica? Is it really you?"

The door opened. Veronica stepped in with her shopping bag full of presents. Miranda hugged her. "I'm sorry, darling, it's just that . . ."

"I know. I've changed."

They had Christmas dinner: turkey in garlic sauce with rice and snow peas. Chinese food was as oriental as Miranda was willing to go as a cook. Ichiko's native Japanese cuisine appalled her. It was just Miranda, Cordelia, Ichiko, and Veronica. "Most everybody you knew was already gone," Miranda said. "Melanie is a translator for the UN, if you can believe it. Adrienne is doing shop windows at Bergdorf's. Everyone has decent jobs, and they all sent Christmas cards. We still get two or three calls a week from clients who hadn't gotten the word."

"They need me to help with the rent now," Cordelia said.

Miranda said, "We have all the money we need, and you know it."

Cordelia shrugged. Her hair was cut short now, very businesslike. "Let me pretend I'm useful. I've got money to burn, now that I'm a producer. Everybody in GF&G moved up after Bob was killed."

Veronica tried not to let her guilt show. She turned to Ichiko. "Have you told Fortunato? About shutting down the business?"

"I wrote him and told him. I got no answer. I write him every so often, but it's always the same. The letters don't come back, but there is never an answer either." Behind the bitterness, Veronica saw how tired Ichiko was. The business was the only thing that had kept her going all these years. Veronica wondered how long she would last without it.

Miranda talked about Linda and Orlando. The marriage, it seemed, was on the rocks. "Pray God," Miranda said.

"Mama!" Veronica said, shocked.

"You were right about him," Miranda said. "He's a good-for-nothing. She's better off without him."

"Give her my love, okay? I really want to see her."

"Maybe you *should* see her. I think she would like that."

It was a thought. It would be good to see the old neighborhood again. Good to patch things up with Linda, to be friends with her. She had another helping of turkey.

"What about Jerry?" she asked. "Do you ever hear from him?"

Ichiko and Miranda exchanged a look.

"Mama? What is it? What aren't you telling me?"

Miranda looked at her empty plate. "Did Jerry ever tell you about... his, uh, special ability?"

Veronica thought she had seen most of Jerry's abilities, and they were pretty average. "What are you talking about?"

"I was afraid of that."

"Mama, don't keep this from me."

"It's just, with things the way they are these days, you don't want to talk about it... see, baby, Jerry is an ace."

"You're kidding. *Jerry?* He never said anything to me." But of course he wouldn't have. Jerry wanted her to love him for himself, as he'd told her more than once.

"Last winter, around the same time as... as that business with Hannah, he was here." Miranda flushed, obviously sorry that she'd mentioned Hannah's name. "Some of those Shadow Fist people were here, threatening us. He... I don't know exactly how he did it, but he's got this ability to change the way he looks. *Everything* about the way he looks. He turned himself into Fortunato. He made his skin dark, and he got all skinny and even—you know. The thing with the forehead."

Veronica couldn't get over it. Jerry an ace. Of course she was one, too, but she didn't dwell on it. As long as she didn't use her power, she couldn't say for sure that it was still there.

"We haven't seen him since," Cordelia said. "I think maybe he gave up on you."

Dessert was fried bananas in honey. Afterward, they gathered around the tiny bonsai pine in what had once been the waiting room. Miranda had bought Veronica a beautiful silk blouse that was now two sizes too small, even if Veronica still wore such things. Cordelia gave her earrings that she couldn't wear since she'd let the holes in her earlobes close. "They can put clips on them," Cordelia said awkwardly. Ichiko gave her a delicate china saki jug and bowls. Veronica didn't mention that she had given up drinking as well. Veronica had bought books for all three of them in a fit of idealism and repressed anger: *The Marx-Engels Reader, The Women's Room, The Feminist Encyclopedia*. There was a moment, when all the presents were opened, when Veronica was sure she was going to cry. Then Miranda said, "Some Christmas, huh?" and started to laugh. Then they were all laughing, arms around each other, huddled on the floor, laughing until they did cry, after all.

And as Veronica had feared, Ichiko hadn't lasted, dying on the last day of February. And Jerry, it seemed, hadn't given up on her, after all.

Close Encounters, and the magazine offices, were on Broadway north of Columbus Circle. When the first burst of energy from her anger and embarrassment wore off, she kept on walking, into Central Park. She found a bench and looked at the bare trees, the little knots on their branches showing the first fuzzy signs of the leaves to come.

A man and a woman, both in their sixties or seventies, shuffled past, wearing knit caps, gloves, and layers of sweat clothes. They seemed to be jogging in slow motion. And how long, Veronica thought, am I going to keep on running? How long am I going to hide my power and let other people make decisions for me?

The sky had started to cloud over, and the wind had turned cool. Veronica walked south, out of the park, and stopped for a cup of coffee at the Cosmic Café, a Greek-run lunch counter. She asked for a phone book and looked up Latham, Strauss. The address was on Park Avenue South.

She took a cab and got there a few minutes early for her appointment. It was an older building, and the wallpaper between the slabs of granite in the lobby was turning the color of nicotine. Latham, Strauss had one of only two suites on the eighth floor. It looked like a movie studio. Behind double glass doors was a reception desk, a single thin sheet of ebony supported by steel legs the diameter of pencils. There was nothing on the desk but a telephone. Behind it was a stunning blond in a white silk blouse, and behind her, on a wall covered in red velvet, was the name *Latham, Strauss* in gold.

Veronica walked in. "I'm here to see Dyan Mundy."

"Ms. Mundy is in conference just now. Do you have an appointment?"

Veronica gave her name. The receptionist directed her to a waiting area to her right, out of sight of the elevators. Veronica was fascinated by her precise, emotionless gestures. "What do you do if you have to write something down?" she asked.

The woman smiled mechanically. "We have secretaries for that."

Veronica looked through the magazines. *Smithsonian, Fine Homebuilding, European Travel and Life*. No *Aces* or *Cosmo* here.

In less than a minute, a woman appeared behind her and said, "Veronica?" She was six feet tall, heavily built, with strong features, glasses, and slicked-back hair. "I'm Dyan Mundy."

She was not the socialite Veronica had expected. It was comforting, but it made things more difficult as well. Mundy led her down wine-colored carpeting, past recessed lighting, toward a huge office with corner windows. Veronica caught a glimpse of someone she felt sure was Latham himself. Then they turned into a side corridor, and Mundy ushered her into an empty office.

As soon as Mundy sat down, Veronica said, "This is about Hannah. Hannah Jorde."

"I don't recall the name."

"You were hired by an organization called W.O.R.S.E. to defend her. A shooting in a bank? There was all this weird stuff about the case. Only it never came to trial because Hannah killed herself in her cell."

"Yes, yes, I remember it now."

"The problem is, W.O.R.S.E. wasn't paying you at all. Latham, Strauss volunteered to defend her. I want to know why."

Mundy swiveled her chair around and scooted over to a file cabinet. "I remember you now. You were . . . personally involved, I think."

Veronica gave her a small shrug.

"Ordinarily, the sort of information you're asking for is confidential. But I can promise you that you're on a wild-goose chase." She pulled an olive-drab hanging file out of the cabinet and opened it up on her desk. "Here's the case file. We show payment in full, by cashier's check. W.O.R.S.E., as I'm sure you understand, is not a chartered corporation with bank accounts and so forth, so that is the form of payment we would be looking for in this situation."

If the woman was lying, it was beyond Veronica's ability to tell. Which meant the answers lay higher up.

With Edward St. John Latham.

From Jerry she knew that Latham worked long hours, nights and weekends. When he wasn't in the courtroom, he was in the office.

Getting a key was not difficult. She called Frances, from W.O.R.S.E., who gave her a wax block in a small plastic case.

"Be sure and get the whole key," Frances told her, "head and all, both sides."

At noon on the following Monday, Veronica rode the elevator up and down in Latham's building. On her third trip, a young guy in a suit got on at the eighth floor. She followed him to the street, then used her power to stagger him. She shoved him face first against a wall and smiled at the people passing by, who all turned their heads away. He didn't seem to notice as she took out his key ring and sorted through them. Two keys looked possible. She printed them both and put the key ring back in his pocket. By the time he turned around, she had faded back into the crowd.

Frances made the keys for her while she waited. "You sure you don't want no help? Been awhile. I'd love some action."

"It's a one-woman job," Veronica said.

"And you won't tell me who you're going after."

"You can read about it in the papers."

*   *   *

She sat in a coffee shop until ten P.M., so nervous that she ate three pieces of chocolate pie and drank four cups of coffee. There was a guard in the lobby when she went inside. She signed Dyan Mundy's name and got in an elevator. The guard never looked up from his copy of the *Post*.

The first key worked. The office was barely lit by a couple of pin spots. Veronica locked the door after herself and retraced the route she'd taken the day before.

Latham's office was lighted, the door closed. Veronica crept down the hall and tried the knob. It turned. She shoved the door open and stepped inside.

Latham looked up from his desk. He was working at a computer, with green-bar paper spread all around him. He didn't seem surprised to find a stranger in his office. "Yes?" he said.

"We have to talk," Veronica said.

"I doubt that."

"It's about Hannah Jorde. She was jumped, and the jumper made her shoot up a bank. The jumper's name was David Butler."

That got a reaction. Latham's mouth twitched, and his eyes lost their focus for a second.

"Butler worked for you. You arranged to have Latham, Strauss represent Hannah in court. That let you send David down to see her in jail. Where he jumped her again—and made her kill herself."

Latham's finger moved a few inches and touched a button on his intercom. Veronica focused her power on him. The hum of the computer drive slowed and made a coughing sound. The lights flickered and dimmed. Before Latham could say anything into the intercom, he blinked, and his hands dropped to his sides.

"Don't touch that again," Veronica said. "Now. I think you're in this up to your neck. What's your connection with David? What do you know about these jumpers? Why are you helping clean up after them?"

"I—" Latham said. He never finished the sentence.

Veronica saw a blur come at her from the right. She ducked reflexively and only caught a grazing blow to her shoulder. Even that was powerful enough to knock her across the room.

"Get rid of her," Latham said weakly.

Veronica focused her eyes. It was Zelda, minus the wig. Her head was shaved smooth. "You," Veronica said.

Zelda smiled. "Veronica. Long time no see." She bent and grabbed a fistful of Veronica's jacket. "You want her dead, boss?"

"Yes," Latham said. "Dead."

"I'll take her out to the Rox to do it. Bloat can find out what she knows."

Veronica felt the room start to spin. "You were working for Latham . . . all the time."

Zelda threw her into the hallway and shut Latham in his office. Veronica started to crawl toward the receptionist's desk.

"Boss had his own reasons to want Loeffler dead. He owed money to some of Boss's friends. Boss likes to keep his options open. Wanted to make sure Tina and her friends didn't come after *him*." She let Veronica crawl, stalking her.

"Let me go," Veronica said. "I'll go away somewhere. You won't ever hear of me again. I promise."

Zelda laughed, and Veronica got up onto her feet, taking a couple of lurching steps. Her right shoulder was dislocated or worse. The sense of betrayal was almost as bad as the pain. Almost. To know that even W.O.R.S.E. had been no more than a puppet of the male establishment. It made everything seem futile.

Stop it, she thought. If she didn't fight back, Zelda would kill her. She had to use her power, quickly, while she still had the chance. She turned and concentrated all her rage and despair against Zelda, burning it into her eyes.

The lights flickered, but Zelda was unaffected. "Trying to scare me, Veronica?" She swung a halfhearted side kick with her right leg, and Veronica jumped backward out of the way. She stumbled against the receptionist's desk, and then the obvious truth hit her: her power was only good against men.

"You'll have to do better than that," Zelda said. "Looks can't kill. Not since Demise bought it."

It made sense, in that twisted way the wild card sometimes had. The only power she'd ever had was over men. Probably had something to do with hormones. Didn't everything?

Veronica's hand touched plastic. The telephone. She lurched forward and swung the receiver at Zelda's head, catching her solidly across the temple. Zelda hopped back half a step and shook her head. Veronica swung again, but

Zelda blocked it and knocked Veronica down with a punch to the solar plexus.

"That actually hurt," Zelda said. She seemed puzzled.

Veronica couldn't breathe. She dropped to her knees, listening to the air squeal in her throat.

"I liked you, you know," Zelda said. "Out of that whole bunch, you were the only one knew who you were. Even if you don't take care of yourself for shit."

"Then . . . let me . . . go."

"Sorry, kid. No can do. You shouldn't have pushed this one."

As Zelda moved in, Veronica saw the cage she'd been in, how no matter how fast she ran, she never got anywhere, just like a rat on an exercise wheel. The never-ending cycle of violence, from Hannah's death to Veronica's own wild card power, from the murder of Robert Loeffler to this. It was so sad and small, and when she looked at it from this angle, it seemed like it should have been so easy to go another way.

But now, of course, it was too late.

She tried to get up.

Zelda smiled and leapt into the air.

The rest was darkness.

Nobody Does It Alone
by
Walton Simons

It was past midnight, and Jerry was about to call it a night. He was in his car across the street from the building housing Latham/Strauss when they carried the body out. Jerry could hear their shoes scraping heavily on the pavement through his directional mike. He pushed the earpiece in and quieted his breathing.

"What did you say her name was?" The voice was female but didn't mean anything to Jerry.

"Veronica. Old acquaintance. Not much of the hero type when I knew her." This voice Jerry did recognize. He'd gotten to know most of the jumpers, and Zelda scared him even more than the rest of them.

"Where do you want to do her?" he asked.

"Let's take her to the Rox and give Bloat or Blaise something to play with," Zelda said. "She's damn sure no interest to me."

Jerry reached into the front seat and picked up one of three guns. This one had an infrared scope and fired rubber bullets. The other two were a high-powered rifle and a tear-gas launcher. Almost any weapon could be gotten hold of if you were a millionaire who could impersonate anyone.

He took a deep breath and sighted in on the larger of the two figures. Zelda had Veronica under the armpits and was walking backward. Jerry centered the cross hairs on her throat, then lowered a bit to her chest. He pulled the trigger. The gun kicked noisily in his hands.

The bullet knocked Zelda backward and free of Veronica. She clutched her chest and went to her knees. Jerry heard her gasp and moan. The other woman looked at Zelda and was gathering herself to move when Jerry nailed her in the back with his second shot. She fell to the asphalt, screaming.

Jerry loaded the tear-gas launcher and fired it. Moments later, the canister exploded in a cloud by Zelda. Jerry pulled on his mask and trotted across the street. He saw a car round the corner and began changing his shape, making his features more angular and his hair pure white. He moved slowly into the cloud, groped around on the sidewalk, and found a motionless female body, which he figured had to be Veronica.

Jerry bent down close enough to recognize her and picked her up under the arms. She was heavy and hard to move. He began dragging her back out of the cloud. A hand grabbed his ankle and squeezed hard. Jerry turned around and brought his booted heel down on the wrist. There was a crack, and he heard Zelda scream, but she couldn't jump what she couldn't see. Jerry hoisted Veronica onto his shoulders and staggered out into the street.

Two cars had stopped, and the people inside stared at him as he opened up his backseat and laid Veronica inside. She was in bad shape, one side of her head bruised and swelling, her eyes watering from the tear gas. Jerry jumped in behind the wheel and started the car, then whipped out into the street and swerved through the parked cars. Someone was sure to get the license-plate number, but he'd ditch them and put on another set. He'd done it before.

Veronica moaned from the back seat. It was ten blocks to the nearest hospital. Jerry hoped she wasn't as bad off as she looked. Jerry had been in love with her back when she was one of Fortunato's geishas, or at least he'd thought it was love. He was focused on driving now and couldn't let his heart distract him. All he could do was drop her off and hope for the best. Latham was still his main concern. If Veronica died, that would be just one more reason to see him dead. One way or the other.

Except for a drunk snoring on a nearby bench, the park was quiet. Jerry crouched behind a row of half-dead shrubs with Jay Ackroyd. Jay had done P.I. work for Jerry in the past, and they got along. Ackroyd was expensive, but then, he was a projecting teleport. His power had inspired the nickname "Popinjay."

"You sure she comes home this way?" Jay asked, shifting his weight uneasily.

"Every night I'm aware of, for the past three weeks," Jerry said. "She's been to the Rox at least three times, so I figure she must be a jumper by now."

"She have anything to do with what happened to Veronica?" Jay's eyes glimmered in the moonlight.

Jerry shook his head and pointed. A teenage girl was walking quickly toward them, her sneakers squeaking slightly on the walk. She had her hands tucked into the pockets of her worn denim jacket. Her straight brown hair was pulled back into a ponytail.

"Now," Jerry whispered. "Don't let her see us."

Jay pointed his first finger toward the girl like the barrel of a gun. The girl disappeared. There was a loud pop. The drunk sat up on his bench and looked around, then lay carefully back down.

"Let's go," Jay said.

Jerry had spent two months and a bundle of cash getting the basement ready. He could see her pacing around inside, but she couldn't spot him through the unbreakable one-way glass. There were handprints smeared on the glass where she'd been looking for a seam. Jay was waiting upstairs. He would probably be better at interrogation, but Jerry wanted to keep the information to himself.

Jerry flipped a switch. "You're in trouble," he said. His voice was electronically distorted to sound like aliens from a fifties science-fiction film.

She took a step back and looked around.

"The speakers are in the ceiling, but there's no way out," Jerry said. "Unless we let you out. And that won't happen unless you tell us what we want to know."

"Who the hell are you?" She rubbed her nose.

"Someone with enough on the ball to trap a jumper." Jerry was enjoying intimidating her, then remembered what had happened to make her into one of Latham's body-switchers. "We don't want to hurt you."

She continued to look around the mirrored room, her eyes hard. "I've been hearing that all my life."

"What's your name?" He asked.

"Valerie." She sat down. "What are you going to do with me?"

"Let you go—" Jerry paused, "as soon as you tell us what we want to know."

"And if I don't?" Veronica started picking at her fingernails.

Jerry sighed audibly. The distortion made it sound spooky. "Then we'll turn you over to the government. They're offering a fortune, under the table, of course, for a live jumper. They need to do some experiments to try to isolate the genetic abnormality that produced you. They sew your eyelids together to make you harmless. At least, that's what I hear."

Valerie's eyes got big, and she bit her lip. "Bullshit. You're feeding me bullshit."

Jerry knew the only way to get anything out of her was really to scare her. "You just don't know about our government, little girl. I hope you get old enough to wise up some. But if that's the way you feel, there's no point in talking."

Jerry left it at that and waited.

Valerie's shoulders slumped. "Are you still there?"

Jerry paused for effect. "What is it?"

"Tell me what you want to know."

"What do you know about Latham?" Jerry asked.

"Who?" Valerie looked genuinely puzzled.

Jerry shook his head, mad at himself for making a mistake. "Prime."

Valerie hugged herself. "He did that thing to make me one of the gang. I've only been in it for a couple of weeks. Zelda and Blaise are the ones you need to talk to."

"You must know something. Plans he might have. Anything." Jerry rubbed his palms together.

Valerie shook her head, then tilted it. "I don't know if this is what you mean, but he likes blond boys. Not to be in the gang, but for other things. At least, that's what Molly says."

"Does the name David Butler sound familiar?" Jerry asked.

"I think so. I don't know." Valerie got up and started pacing. "Please let me go."

Jerry pushed a button, a signal to Jay to come downstairs. "So you can go back to them."

"I can't do that now. You know that." She went back to worrying her nails. "Bloat would know I told." She clutched her hands over her chest. "You don't know what they'd do."

Ackroyd opened the door and stepped into the room. Jerry cut off the audio to the mirrored cage.

"Get what you needed?" Jay asked.

"Nah. But it was worth a shot." Jerry pointed to Valerie. "I guess you can send her back to the park now."

Jay shook his head. "I think you'd be better off telling me everything, but you are the one who signs the checks." He made his hand into the familiar gunshape.

"Trust me," Jerry said.

Valerie disappeared. There was a muffled *pop*. "Mrs. Ackroyd didn't raise any boys that stupid."

"The check is in the mail," Jerry said, smiling.

"You going to be at the memorial service tomorrow?"

Jerry stopped smiling. He'd been trying not to think about it. "Yeah," he said. "Want a lift there? I could use the company."

Jay nodded.

People were taking turns speaking, remembering the man who had been their friend. It had rained off and on all morning but was dry enough inside the tomb.

Jerry looked up at the replica of the JB-1. Jerry hadn't ever been much interested in Jetboy, even after he drew the wild card, and had never felt much about the young flier's death. It was impossible to think about a world without Tachyon, though. Jerry was still trying to get his mind around the idea. If it weren't for the Takisian, Jerry would still be a giant ape. He hadn't been able to help Tachyon any more than he'd been able to save Kenneth. Latham was responsible for the deaths. He had to be made to pay.

The clothes of those attending were a stark contrast to the gray weather. Almost everyone had dressed in outrageously colorful outfits because "Tach would have wanted it that way." Jerry was wearing a lime-green suit with a paisley-print shirt and rainbow scarf. Ackroyd had dressed in an everyday suit. "A man in my line of work can't afford to look stupid, even for a minute," he'd said.

Father Squid stepped forward to speak. "I cannot claim to have understood all that he did, but his was a great heart, full of compassion and understanding."

Jerry glanced over and saw Cody. He eased his way through the crowd toward her. Her bad eye was to him, but she turned just as he reached her side. "Mr. Strauss," she said. "I haven't seen you recently. I suppose I should have expected to today, though."

Jerry fished a twenty-thousand-dollar check from his

pocket and slipped it to her. "I know. It's hard to go near the clinic, now that he's gone."

Cody took the check and tucked it away. "Thanks. Hard as Finn and I have been working to raise funds, we don't seem to be getting anywhere."

"Bad times," Jerry said.

Cody nodded. There was a strain in her face he'd never seen before, something that didn't have anything to do with being a doctor.

"How could Tach get jumped?"

Cody shook her head and looked down. "They jumped me first. Used me as a Judas goat. Tach never could think straight when there was a woman involved."

Jerry could understand that well enough. "I guess there's no chance that somehow he's still alive?" He had an almost blind faith in Tachyon's ability to work miracles.

"He's gone," Cody said, her voice flat, weary.

"But how can you be sure?"

"Blaise used to visit me once a week. He wanted me to know what he was doing to his grandfather. He told me everything. He kept moving Tachyon from body to body. All jokers, each more twisted than the last. He brought me obscene pictures. *Is this what you want to fuck?* he'd ask me. *Is this what turns you on?* But finally he got bored with the game. That was when he killed Tachyon." She looked away. "He brought me pictures of that, too."

"Maybe he was lying," Jerry said. "Trying to hurt you."

"The prisoners were all kept in the warehouse," Cody said. "If he was still alive, he would have been freed in the raid, along with the rest of us. He's dead, Mr. Strauss. Denying it only prolongs the pain."

Jerry figured she was right. He put his hand on her shoulder, then walked back over to Ackroyd.

"Trying to pick up Cody at Tach's memorial service is a gesture he'd probably understand," Jay said, smiling.

Jerry's shoulders slumped. "I wasn't trying to pick her up."

"I know, I know," Jay said. "What is it about tombs that makes people lose their sense of humor? Let's get out of here before someone asks us to make a speech."

Jerry sighed. "How about dinner?" He didn't feel like being alone.

"Now you're talking," Jay said. "Being morose gives me an appetite."

The pair made their way to the edge of the crowd and out onto the rain-slicked concrete. A rainbow arced over Staten Island. Jerry wondered if there would be a pot of gold on his doorstep when he got home. It was the last thing he needed.

Jerry sat alone in the private room of the Haiphong Lily. Half the Gambione family had died in this room, and he wasn't happy about the apparent thinness of the walls, but he could live with it. His look was burly, middle-aged, and Italian. The person he was meeting thought he was a Mafia kingpin from Vegas. He'd been laying the background for the disguise for several weeks.

The door slid open, and the Lily's owner ushered in a young man in a pressed dark gray suit. The man looked more Greek than Italian. His eyes and mouth were impassive and deadly. Jerry studied his face and build. Never could tell when it might come in handy.

The door closed. "Sit down," Jerry said.

"Thank you." The man unbuttoned his coat and quietly took his seat. Jerry passed him the menu. "No, thanks. I'm not here to eat."

"Whatever." Jerry ran a finger cautiously along his lower lip. "You come highly recommended."

The man shrugged. "There aren't many of us left. To still be around, you have to be the best."

Jerry nodded and pulled an envelope out of his coat pocket, then slid it across the table. Inside was everything he'd managed to find out about Latham's habits and associates in the past months and twenty thousand dollars in cash. He'd removed his fingerprints when handling the paper and didn't have any now either. "How soon can you start?"

The man opened the envelope and slowly went through the contents. "Soon as I'm out the door."

"He's heavily guarded most of the time," Jerry said. "Watch out for the kids especially."

"I'll want another twenty when I'm done." The killer carefully tucked the money back into the envelope.

Jerry nodded.

The man stood and took a step toward the door, then turned and smiled. "Want any souvenirs? I do that for free."

"No," Jerry said. "I'll save the news clippings."

The man nodded and left.

*   *   *

Jerry sat in the Tomlin International Airport, fidgeting in one of the plastic chairs. A newspaper was folded across his lap. *Mafia Killer Found In East River* was a front-page headline. Next to the story was a picture of Alex "Buttons" Parylos. Jerry should have known Latham would be too tough for one man, even a professional.

"Delta Flight twenty-three now arriving from Chicago at gate nine," came a soft voice over the public address.

Jerry bounced up from his chair and shouldered his way through to the front of the receiving area. Latham would have to wait; this was more important.

After a couple of minutes, the passengers began trickling out of the plane. After fifty or so had passed by him, Jerry panicked and wondered if he'd gotten the wrong flight number or come the wrong day. He'd made that sort of mistake before.

She was almost in his arms before he saw her. She'd grown her blond hair out several inches and dropped some weight, but her smile was the same.

"Hey, bro," Beth said, setting down her blue overnight bag and giving him a big hug. "Long time no see."

Jerry squeezed Beth hard and kissed her on the forehead. Her touch and smell were both wonderful and familiar. "Too long, as far as I'm concerned. I can't believe Chicago has that much to offer."

Beth took a step back and rolled her eyes. "We're not going to go through how I don't love you anymore before dinner, are we?"

Jerry laughed. "No, before dinner is for your presents. Later on, I had you penciled-in for some serious doting. How long are you in town for this time?"

"At least a month." Beth picked up her bag and tucked her arm under his. "Presents, huh? After the baggage handlers are done with me, you can have me practically all to yourself."

Jerry knew that wasn't really true. Beth still seemed married to his brother, Kenneth, although he'd been dead for months. "After showering you with gifts, it's dinner wherever you want tonight."

Beth nudged him as they walked down the concourse. "Why, sir, you're positively the most generous multimillionaire I know," she said, in a bad Southern-belle imitation. "I'm sure you're going to spoil me for anyone else."

Jerry straightened his shoulders and let his voice slip into Clark Gable. "Frankly, my dear, I don't give a damn."

Jerry pulled the Olds up to the gate and punched in his code. He changed it every couple of days, just in case. The wrought iron creaked and opened. He eased up the drive and pulled up to the garage. The door there had a coded entry as well.

Beth wrinkled her forehead. "Is this going to open up on the Jerrycave?"

Jerry pulled into the garage and waited for the door to close again. "Rich people have been getting jumped, you know."

Beth nodded. "I thought that was mostly high-profile types like Dixon."

"Mostly," Jerry said. "But you can't be too careful. They might decide to go slumming on us old-money types." He got out of the car and trotted around to her side to open the door. "Just one more set of coded locks, and we're in."

"And just in time. I need a shower." Beth ran her fingers through her hair. "This stuff needs help."

"Want any company?" Jerry had made several tame advances, but Beth had always gently declined.

She sighed and stroked his face. "I'd like that a lot, Jerry. That's the main reason I'm here."

Jerry stood motionless for a second. He hadn't really considered the possibility that she'd take him up on it. "Really?" Two syllables were all he could manage.

"Really," she said. "Now get us inside."

Jerry walked up to the door and paused with his hand over the keypad, the combination momentarily gone from his mind. His fingers took over and punched it in. The locks clicked, and Jerry opened the door.

They kept their clothes on until they got upstairs. Jerry watched her undress. Her legs were a little heavy, and she didn't have much of a waist, but he couldn't imagine a more desirable female body.

The bathroom was big enough to pitch a tent in, one of the perks of being fabulously wealthy.

"How hot do you like it?" he asked, turning on the shower.

Beth smiled and gave him a peck on the lips. "Can't stop talking in movie dialogue, can you? I like it really hot to begin with. We can cool it down a bit after a while." She slid open the glass door and led him into the shower.

Jerry picked up the soap. "Want me to do your back first?"

"Sounds good." She leaned forward and let the water run over her head as Jerry began to soap her shoulders.

He worked his way down her back and paused at the base of her spine. "I hope you're not planning on missing any spots," she said.

Jerry slid the soap over her bottom. He almost resented the slippery film that kept him from actually touching her flesh. "Now who's talking straight from the movies?"

Beth turned around and put her arms around his neck. "Kiss me, dummy." She put her lips on his and pushed her tongue into his mouth.

Jerry relaxed and let his hands roam all over her. She twisted her fingers into his damp hair and bit his lip. Jerry closed his eyes and let go completely.

This was going to be as good as he'd always imagined.

He ran his fingers slowly up and down the hollow of her back. Beth reached around and took his hand, then brought it to her mouth and kissed the tips of his fingers.

"I can die happy now," he said.

"Don't say that, even just kidding." Beth rolled over and looked at him, unblinking. "With me it's not funny."

Jerry pulled her close and kissed her neck. "Sorry. I wasn't thinking." This was positively the worst time to make her think of Kenneth. "You know what's weird?"

She breathed heavily onto his shoulder. "What?"

"The better sex is, the harder it is to remember. I think that's why at the beginning, couples don't do much of anything else. You try to have something to keep, but it always slips away like a dream. Doesn't seem fair, somehow."

"Is that a hint?" Beth lowered her mouth to his chest and bit his nipple.

Jerry laughed. "I don't know if I'm up for another take right now."

Beth smiled. "You underestimate me. It's like being a lion tamer." She reached down between his legs. "Enough skill and determination, and the beast will obey you."

Jerry arched his back, pushing his head into the pillow. The phone beeped. Beth looked up at him.

"Let the machine downstairs answer it," he said. "That's what I bought it for."

"I love a man with his priorities straight." She began to nibble and lick him.

"Oh, yeah," he said. "You're one hell of a lion tamer."

He wandered downstairs to get the phone messages. The first one was several hours old. He hoped it wasn't important.

Jerry pushed the button, waited, and heard Ackroyd's voice. "Jerry. I have it on pretty good authority that Veronica is going to be transferred to an institution upstate in a few days. This place is famous for experimental and dangerous methods of treatment. Veronica might not do so well there. I figured you would want to know. I'm busy with other commitments right now, or I'd help you out myself. Keep in touch."

Jerry sank onto the couch, not hearing the other messages. In spite of the problems they'd had, he couldn't abandon Veronica to some nutcase shrinks.

Beth bounced down the stairs in her blue terry robe. She plopped down on the sofa and put her arm around him, then frowned. "Something wrong?"

"Veronica," Jerry said.

Beth kept her arm in place but pulled her hand from his shoulder. "I thought that was over a long time ago."

Jerry sat up straight and took her hand. "It is. That's not it at all. She's in the hospital in a coma or something. I think she's in real danger. It's not like we're close or anything, but I feel like I owe her."

"Jesus," Beth said. "Is there anything you can do?"

"I'm rich—there ought to be something." He chewed on his lip. "You used to be a nurse way back when, right?"

"Yes. Got tired of dealing with doctors and hospital administrators. I've done some volunteer work in Chicago, though."

"Okay." Jerry tapped his fingertips together. "I'll need you to set up my old projection room with all the equipment we'll need to handle a coma patient. All I need to do then is figure out how to get her here."

"You'll have to take me along, you know." Beth turned his face toward hers. "That's my price for doing the rest. You have to let me be there with you."

"Thanks," Jerry said. "I would have asked you to anyway. I need to have someone I can trust around me when I'm scared. If I'm in trouble, I want you there. Mr. Selfish strikes again."

She leaned over and kissed him on the cheek. "I'd do more, but we're going to need our strength for other things."

"Right," he said, standing. "I'm going to get cleaned up, then go down to the hospital to do a little snooping. If you could take care of buying the equipment, I'll help you set it up later on."

"Okay. I hope I can get everything we'll need," Beth said.

"You're rich and gorgeous." Jerry helped her up from the sofa.

"With that combination, anything is possible."

It was three A.M. Wednesday, probably as quiet as the hospital ever got. Jerry strode down the corridor with what he hoped was a weary authority.

Beth was handling the gurney. The nurse's uniform flattered her figure more than he'd expected. "You really look great. Next time I'm sick, I want you to wear that."

"So much for the silk teddies and leather outfits I was going to buy." Beth's voice was nervous and edgy.

Jerry clutched at his doctor's clipboard and leaned close to her. "This will be easy, trust me. I do this kind of stuff all the time. You're in the care of a professional." He thumbed the orange badge on his smock that said *Dr. Evan Sealy*.

Beth gave him a hard glance. "Yes, but you can change your face, which, by the way, looks like too many doctors I've known. I'm stuck with what I'm wearing."

Jerry didn't have anything clever to say to that. He counted down the room numbers until they were outside Veronica's door. He took a deep breath, pulled his glasses down onto the bridge of his bulbous nose, and went in without knocking. Beth followed him, leaving the gurney in the hallway.

The guard was sitting in the chair, engrossed in a well-thumbed copy of *Soldier of Fortune*. He was middle-aged and rounding all over. There were two empty styrofoam cups on the cheap bedside table.

"Morning, Dr. Sealy." The cop nodded once and stared back down at his magazine.

"Morning." Jerry sighed and walked over to Veronica's bed on the side where the guard was seated. She looked terrible. Her skin was broken out, her features sunken, and her breathing shallow. A yellow-and-purple bruise covered one side of her head. Something inside Jerry hurt to look at her. He edged closer to the guard and pretended to take her pulse. Beth moved closer to them. Jerry put Veronica's hand down. He reached into his pocket and pulled out a cotton rag, then jumped on the guard's lap and shoved the rag into his mouth.

The cop bit down hard on Jerry's fingertips. Jerry clenched his teeth to avoid screaming. Beth was backing away with an empty hypodermic in her hand. He hadn't even seen her stick him. "How long?" he asked, trying to tug his hand free.

Beth capped the needle and put the hypo in her pocket, then stepped in for a better look. "He's out already."

Jerry flattened his fingertips and pulled his hand free. "Fucking flatfoot cannibal," he said, rubbing his fingertips.

Beth rolled the gurney next to the bed and quickly unhooked everything but Veronica's I.V. and gently slid her hands under the comatose woman's armpits. "Get her feet and lift her over."

Jerry grabbed Veronica's ankles and carefully hoisted her over.

Beth folded up the metal arm and hooked the I.V. bag to it. "Let's go, Doctor."

Jerry opened the door and stepped into the brightly lit hallway. He motioned to Beth, who wheeled the gurney out next to him. They headed slowly toward the elevator. Jerry marked something unreadable on his clipboard and hoped he looked the part. The elevator was empty, and they both sighed as the doors closed.

"So far, so good," Jerry said. His back and armpits were soaked in sweat.

"Mm," Beth said. It was more a growl than anything else.

The car stopped in several jerky motions, and they moved out into the basement. Jerry could hear someone in Emergency moaning. There were several patients sitting in the hall. One, a bloody hand held to the side of his head, was talking to a police officer. Jerry didn't breathe as they moved past. The cop didn't bother to look up.

"Dr. Sealy?" The female voice came from behind him.

Jerry's shoulders tightened. He turned around slowly. A nurse with sharp eyes and features was looking at him hard. "Yes," he said.

"Is that patient being transferred out?" The nurse looked at Veronica.

"Yes. Why else would she be down here?" Jerry hoped his sarcasm would back her off.

The nurse made a face. "Then I assume you have some paperwork for me?"

Jerry nodded stiffly. "Of course. Once she's situated in the ambulance, I'll be back to take care of you."

"If you don't," the nurse said, "I know where to find you."

"I hope not," he whispered, turning away. He looked over at Beth. Her skin was a couple of shades paler than usual.

They quickly rolled Veronica out to the nearest ambulance and opened up the rear.

"Everything you'll need?" he asked, looking inside.

Beth nodded. They lifted Veronica in, and Beth climbed up after her. Jerry closed the doors and walked around the far side, pulling off his smock. He had his EMS outfit on underneath.

He made his face rounder and changed his hair from gray to brown. Jerry got into the driver's side and tossed the smock onto the floorboard. He softened his fingertip and slid it into the ignition slot. When he felt it fit, he hardened his finger and turned. The engine caught immediately, an echoing roar in the concrete underground. A few blocks away he could stop and hot-wire the ignition, until then he'd have to make do with one hand.

"Shit," Beth said from behind him.

"What?"

"Her heart's stopped." Beth took a deep breath and prepared an injection. "I'll try some adrenaline. Get us the hell out of here. I don't want to get caught now. Move it."

Jerry put the ambulance into gear and drove slowly through the Emergency parking area to the street.

"Is she going to be all right?" he asked.

"I can't tell yet." Beth's voice was shaky. Her face was covered with sweat. "I've got a pulse, but it's erratic. Could go either way."

Jerry drove one-handed for as long as he could stand it. There was no way he could make it through three boroughs to reach the family home in Staten Island that way. He stopped, softened his fingertip, and tugged it, bleeding and swollen, from the ignition. He pulled a knife and electrical tape from one pocket and bent under the dash. "We'll be moving again in a minute," he said.

Beth sighed. "I can't believe I volunteered for this. If we get caught, I'm going to strangle you with my bare hands."

Jerry brought the wires together with a tiny blue spark. The engine kicked to life. "I love you, too."

After taking Beth and Veronica home, Jerry drove the ambulance into Queens and abandoned it. He caught a cab back from there. It gave him a twinge of glee that Veronica had wound up in his projection room. She'd never have come there when they were dating. *You were paying her to fuck you,* he thought. *It wasn't a date.*

Beth was looking Veronica over when he walked in. "This isn't good, bro. They didn't use a gel-foam cushion under her while she was there."

It bothered him a little that she called him "bro," although he wasn't sure why. Jerry knew what a gel-foam cushion was only because it was a squishy bed covering he'd figured might have real erotic possibilities. "What's the problem?"

"She's got some ugly lesions on her bottom, and a couple are starting on her shoulders, too. They weren't looking after her well at all." Beth squeezed some antiseptic cream on a gloved hand and applied it carefully to Veronica's flesh.

"'Lesions'?"

"Bedsores." Beth pulled off her gloves and tossed them into a trash can. "If she doesn't come around soon, we're going to have major complications."

Jerry snorted. "Over bedsores?"

"That's right. If they get bad enough, you have to do skin grafts to prevent life-threatening infections. That requires a plastic surgeon and anesthesiologist at the very least, assuming I can grow a few more limbs to take care of everything else." She walked past him and patted him on the shoulder. "Trust me."

"Shit," Jerry said, turning and following her out of the room. "How do you get somebody out of a coma?"

"You don't, really," Beth said, putting her arms around him. "I guess we'd better get some rest."

"Rest?"

"I'm afraid so," she said. "We'll need our energy to devote to Veronica." She kissed the end of his nose. "This is another reason I stopped being a nurse."

"You're so good," he said. "I don't know what I did to deserve you."

Beth laughed. "For his next trick, Jerry will put all of his self-esteem into a thimble."

Jerry slapped her ass. "Enough. Let's get some sleep."

"Veronica, I love you. You have to come back for me." Jerry stroked her hand, carefully avoiding the area where her I.V. was attached. Saying he loved her was a lie, but he wasn't going to crucify himself for it at this point. "Hannah needs you. We all do." Veronica's chest rose and fell slowly. Her eyelids might as well have been carved in stone.

Beth walked into the room with two plates of food. "Fettuccine for two." She set the plates on the coffee table in front of the couch. "So much for the question 'But can she cook?' Good men have plotzed for my Italian food since the dawn of time."

Jerry stood and stretched. He was glad Beth hadn't heard him telling Veronica he loved her. It would be too much trouble to explain right now. He walked on stiff legs over to the couch and sat down in front of the plate with the largest helping. It was weird having so much normal furniture in the room with a coma patient. "What time is it?"

"A little after seven." Beth took Jerry's seat next to Veronica and began bathing her with a fresh washcloth.

Jerry fumbled for the TV remote control and punched the set to life. "Hot damn. I don't think I've missed much of it. Chrissie is probably dead, though."

"What are you talking about?"

"*Jaws.*" Jerry rubbed his hands together. On the screen, Brody was looking down at the girl's crab-infested remains.

Beth wiped Veronica's forehead. Her touch was light but firm. Like she'd been with him in bed a few nights before. "I thought *Jaws* scared you to death."

"Several times." Jerry paused and glazed-over his eyes. "Very first light, chief, sharks come cruising."

"Enough," Beth said. "It's obviously going to be a long night."

Jerry nodded. "For all the wrong reasons."

He turned back to the TV. It was a commercial break, and a fast-talking salesman had a penlike device at the end of an egg. "Wow. Look at that. You can scramble an egg without even breaking it open."

Beth laughed. "I forget how much you missed in your twenty years as a giant ape. You're Ronco's dream customer."

"It's nice to be somebody's dream something." Jerry bit his lip. He'd been trying to cut down on self-pity, but he had a genuine talent for it.

"God, I'm sick of hearing that kind of shit. If we're going to have a chance, that kind of talk has to start disappearing." She turned away from him. "Even now, you can't believe that I love you."

Jerry rubbed the bridge of his nose. "I'm afraid to. I'm crazy about you, always have been. You make me deliriously happy. I'm not a bad guy, but I just can't imagine you'd ever settle for someone like me. I feel so...insubstantial or inadequate or something."

"I'm old enough and smart enough to know who I want," she said, "and I want you. Maybe you should consider counseling to get over your self-esteem problems."

"Maybe. Couldn't hurt, and at least I can afford it." Jerry took a bit of fettuccine. It was hot and delicious, but he didn't feel like chewing.

"Jerry." Beth sounded upset.

He looked over quickly. Veronica had reached up and taken Beth by the arm. The bedridden woman pulled Beth's face to hers. Beth twisted away and tucked Veronica's arms down beside her. Jerry jumped up off the couch and over to the bed. Veronica's eyes blinked slowly, then opened.

"Veronica. It's Jerry." He brushed a damp strand of hair away from her eyes.

Veronica swallowed and looked slowly around the room. She stared long and hard at Beth. "I hope you're not married to this guy."

Beth squeezed Veronica's hand and brought a cup of water up to her dry lips. "Once you sweep them off their feet, they stay swept, bro."

"I feel terrible," Veronica said.

Jerry smiled. "I feel better."

"Latham's girls were supposed to kill me," Veronica said. She glanced over at Jerry. "I guess you rode to my rescue."

Jerry shrugged. "I couldn't just let them kill you. You'd have done the same for me."

Veronica closed her eyes. "Sure I would. How long have I been out?"

"Latham?" Beth grabbed Veronica's arm. "Edward St. John Latham? He did this to you?"

"Actually, it was Zelda who did the damage," Veronica said. "He just ordered it, as usual."

Beth looked up at Jerry. "And you knew?"

Jerry nodded. "I had a reason for not telling you."

"Kenneth. It was Latham, wasn't it." She put her hand over her mouth.

Jerry held her by the shoulders. "Yes. I knew he was behind it, but I couldn't prove anything."

Beth stood, shaking her head. "You should have told me. You know you should have." She walked stiffly from the room. Jerry headed after her.

"What about me?" Veronica tried to sit up, fell back on the bed.

"You're not going anywhere right now," Jerry said. "We'll talk later."

Jerry caught up with Beth on the stairs. He grabbed her by the elbow. "I'm sorry. I just didn't want you to get hurt."

She wheeled on him, her eyes full of tears. "You think this doesn't hurt. My husband was killed, and you didn't think I had the right to know all the truth."

Jerry's shoulders slumped. His eyes were beginning to sting. "If I screwed up, I'm sorry. We both know I have a track record of doing that. But you have no idea how crazy Latham is. All the things he's into. And he's getting worse."

"What about the police?" Beth dabbed at her eyes.

"There are some good cops, but you can't know who they are. If somebody can be bought off or intimidated, St. John would probably go that way. If not, he'll just have them killed. Like Kenneth." Jerry looked down. "I swore I'd get Latham for what he did. I watched him for months, got to know his mind, his habits." Jerry made a fist. "I had him in the sights of my rifle once, and I just couldn't do it. Who knows how many other people would still be alive if I could have squeezed the trigger."

Beth took his hand. "You're not a killer, Jerry."

He looked up, right into her eyes. "Yes, I am. We all are. It just takes more extreme circumstances to bring that out in some of us. I have to kill him."

Beth shook her head. "For a promise to someone who'll never know you kept it?"

"No. Because he'll get me first. Why do you think I have all this security? He's bound to come after me sooner or later."

"Come to Chicago with me," Beth said. "We can start something for us there. If you go against Latham, he'll kill you. I can't believe I didn't figure this before now, anyway. Who else would want Kenneth dead?"

"It's only obvious in retrospect." Jerry dabbed the tears from her eyes. "No matter where I go, he'll find me. If there's one thing St. John is, it's thorough."

"Don't make me beg you, Jerry. If you try this, you'll only get killed."

"I don't think so." He tried to sound cocky. "I've got Veronica to help me now. If I can convince her to help. With Latham's killers breathing down her neck, that shouldn't be too hard."

Beth opened her mouth in disbelief. "She can hardly move, Jerry. There's no way she's up to any kind of fight."

"She's an ace. Aces heal fast," he said. "Trust me."

Latham made most of his personal calls late at night. Jerry was sitting in a building across from St. John's apartment, waiting for some action on the line. A regular phone bug would have been found in a hurry, so Jerry didn't even bother. But Latham had a cordless phone that operated on a specific frequency. It had taken some doing, but he'd found out what it was and how to intercept it. Most of what Jerry had learned came from the late-night listening.

He stifled a yawn. He still wasn't clear how to get Latham, but he knew he wanted Veronica to do the actual killing. That shouldn't be a problem, since Latham had ordered Hannah killed and almost put Veronica away too. The specifics were just not there, though. Probably he was distracted about Beth. When he wasn't thinking about her, he was congratulating himself for not thinking about her, and then there he went again. Being that happy, even for one day, was a scary thing. All of a sudden, he had a lot to lose.

There was a dial tone. Jerry flipped on the recorder and listened to the numbers being punched in.

Several rings later, a young female answered the phone. "I was wondering when you'd call." The voice belonged to Zelda.

"Yes," Latham said. "I want you to make some arrangements for Friday night. I'll need a companion."

Zelda sighed. "Again? I don't know what you need that for, with me around."

"It wasn't a request, Zelda." Latham was cold, but his voice lacked the total control Jerry was used to hearing. "After letting that woman slip away, you should be eager for a chance to do something right."

"I don't think anyone else would have done a better job than I did." Zelda sounded angry and defensive.

"Blaise would have."

"Fine. I'll get your young blond god, but he won't be David. Even Blaise can't bring him back." Zelda paused. "Anything else?"

"That will be all," Latham said, and hung up.

Jerry stopped the recorder and pounded his fist into his palm. This was the setup he needed. He flipped through his notebook for the name of the escort service Latham had been using. He'd pay them a visit tomorrow as a handsome blond young man. Right now, though, he needed to check on Veronica.

Beth met him at the door. She waited a moment before saying anything. Her face was tight. She forced a smile.

"She's gone."

"What?" Jerry stared hard at her, expecting some kind of lengthy explanation. "So . . ."

Beth walked over to the couch. "She recovered so quickly. I've never seen anything like it. Look, I'm sorry, but I don't know what I could have done to stop her."

You could have gone to bed with her, he thought, remembering Veronica's current sexual preference and the way she'd looked at Beth. Jerry flopped down on the couch and combed the hair from his eyes. "How did she leave? Did she walk? Catch a cab?"

"A cab." Beth sat down next to him, perched on the front of a cushion. "Jerry, is it really that important?"

"Yes," he said, sharply. "Absolutely."

Beth's mouth tightened. "Starline," she said. "That was the cab company." She stood and left the room.

"Beth, wait." Jerry took a couple of steps after her, then stopped. Explaining would take more time than he had right now. He had to get on Veronica's trail while it was still hot.

He absolutely needed her to take out Latham. He'd apologize to Beth later. Get down on his knees if necessary. But there was no safety for any of them until Latham was dead and gone. He checked the cash in his wallet. There was plenty for what he had in mind. He headed for the door.

The back seat of the cab was sticky. Jerry didn't want to know how it got that way. He'd found out the name of the driver at the Starline central office and had him sent down.

The cabbie was young and Middle Eastern. At first, he could barely speak English. But after Jerry introduced him to the Jackson twins—a trick he'd picked up from Ackroyd—the cabbie became more helpful. He told Jerry how he'd picked up Veronica, described her clothing, the way she smelled, and how she behaved. After a little more financial inducement, the cabbie agreed to drop Jerry off at Veronica's destination.

They were in an old part of Brooklyn. The red-and-white stone walls were faded, but for the most part clean. Kids with easy smiles played on stoops or out in the streets. The cab eased to a stop.

"Here. It was on this spot." The cabbie leaned across the seat and pointed through the passenger-side window. "That building. She went into there." The cabbie turned and smiled. "You are grateful now."

"Unspeakably." Jerry peeled off another twenty and handed it over. The cabbie certainly had grasped the essence of capitalism. Jerry got out of the cab and walked over to the stoop. He looked up.

Veronica was staring down at him. "Fuck." He didn't hear it, but he could read the word on her lips.

This wasn't going to be easy or fun. He fingered the door and went in. The paint on the walls was fresh, but the overhead light flickered. Jerry walked slowly toward the stairway at the end of the hall. He could hear kids screaming in Spanish inside one of the rooms.

She met him at the landing between the second and third floors. Her teeth were clenched, her eyes wide with anger. "Leave me alone, Jerry. Just leave me the fuck alone." She said the words slowly. "My family lives here. Do you understand?"

Jerry looked her in the eye and took a step forward, like a kid trying to sneak up on a cat. "He knows who you are,

Veronica. He's going to come after you. Either you help me take Latham out, or you're as good as dead."

"What business is that of yours? Maybe I'm tired of living." She put her hand on his chest and pushed him backward. "There's plenty of high-priced hookers out there. You don't need to mess with me anymore."

"Veronica, look at me. Can you see what's wrong with me? I'm scared, just plain scared. Latham wants me dead too. I don't blame you for hating me. I'm not here to dredge up the past. I used you and I'm sorry. I can't fix what's already happened." He was trying to use her again, but this time it was actually for her own good. "He killed Hannah, and he killed my brother. There's no telling how many others. I've been after Latham for months, but I can't do it on my own."

"Why?"

"Because he's the head of the jumpers from the Rox and runs organized crime in this city, to boot. He's probably the most dangerous, ruthless man either one of us will ever meet." Jerry extended his palms. "I don't want to die yet. If you won't do it for me or yourself, do it for Hannah."

Veronica leaned against the wall and closed her eyes. He could see the beginning of tears. "Leave me alone," she said.

Jerry swallowed hard. He'd never seen Veronica hurting before. She'd always been so tough with him. He went up and put his arm around her. She shrugged it off violently, banging his hand painfully into the plaster.

"Sorry," Jerry said. "You were really in love with her. I just didn't understand that until now. I guess I didn't want to." He thought of how he'd feel if Beth was killed and someone tried to use that as a carrot on him, then backed away, ashamed. "I won't bother you anymore. You should get out of town and make a new start somewhere else. If you don't want my money, I could arrange for a loan."

"No," she said.

Jerry turned and walked slowly down the stairs. He was useless to her now. She knew him too well, and he didn't know her at all. That was probably much more his fault than hers.

"Jerry?" Veronica was looking down at him from the top of the stairs.

"Yes."

"What do you want me to do?"

Veronica was hard and all business again. "I want you to help me kill him."

Veronica was already inside. Jerry had fingered the service door to let her in, then walked around to the front of Latham's apartment building. After a brief conversation with someone upstairs, the doorman had let him in.

According to the old ad campaign, blonds were supposed to have more fun. Somehow, Jerry didn't expect that was going to be the case tonight. He was young, tawny, and gorgeous. They'd almost had to clean their shorts when he walked into the escort service. He was exactly what Latham wanted, a David Butler look-alike with just enough differences to make it believable.

Veronica met him at the elevator, and they stepped quietly inside. She was wearing a freshly ironed white blouse and navy pants. She fidgeted from one leg to the other as the car moved up the shaft to the penthouse. Jerry had been here before, and for the same reason. To kill Latham.

He'd blown it, though. Zelda had jumped him and only when she freaked out in his body had he been able to get away. He felt better about his chances this time, with Veronica along. All he had to do was take out Zelda. He touched the cloth of his shirt pocket, feeling the packet underneath. He was going to need it.

"I'm going to get the door unlocked and slightly open one way or the other," he said. "When I do that, move fast." Veronica nodded.

The elevator glided to a stop, and the doors opened. They stepped out, and Jerry motioned Veronica out of sight. He took a deep breath, let it out slowly, and knocked. Zelda opened the door, dressed in sweat clothes. Her eyes widened when she saw Jerry-David, but she quickly hid her surprise with a nasty smile.

Jerry took off his coat and folded it over his arm, then stepped inside.

"Look what we have here," Zelda said.

Latham emerged from the office, deep in conversation with a hairless pink bat. He looked at Jerry and stopped dead. His mouth hung open for a moment, then he closed it and eased over toward them. He was wearing a black silk robe with silver embroidery, and his hair was carefully blow-dried and combed.

"Perfect," Latham said. "Ideal."

Jerry looked dubiously at the joker. "Nobody told me this was a group deal. I charge extra for bats."

"He won't be staying," Latham said coldly. He turned his attention to the bat. "Tell the governor that I'll take care of it."

The joker half walked and half flopped to the window. He perched momentarily on the sill. "Sorry to miss the fun, guys," he said. "Maybe next time." He dropped out of sight, and Jerry heard him flap noisily away.

Jerry put his arm around Zelda, and licked her neck, then bit it. "There's still plenty of us to make a party."

Zelda grabbed Jerry by the throat and tossed him backward. Jerry's feet came out from under him, and he bounced across the carpeted floor on his seat.

"Don't touch me, whore," Zelda said, wiping her neck, "or I'll break every bone in your fucking body." She turned to Latham. "I'm going back to my workout." Zelda walked from the room.

Latham walked over and helped Jerry to his feet. He stared hard at Jerry's sculpted features, as if looking for something.

"Is your friend some kind of nutcase?" Jerry asked, throwing his coat on the back of the sofa.

"Zelda is very exceptional . . . in her own way." Latham guided him by the elbow over to the couch. "Please, sit down. I'll make us a drink."

Jerry eased back into the soft cushions. They were the only thing comfortable about the situation. "I hope I'm what you had in mind."

Latham smiled thinly. "Oh, yes. Exactly what I had in mind." Latham filled two glasses with liquor and sat down next to Jerry on the couch.

Jerry took the glass when it was offered and took a tentative sip. Whiskey he loved; scotch he detested. The liquor burned but didn't satisfy. Latham tilted his glass up and almost emptied it.

Latham pulled a vial and small spoon from his pocket. He popped the vial open and carefully poured a spoonful, then held it under Jerry's nose. "Inhale," Latham said.

Jerry hesitated, then drew a deep breath. He felt like someone was pulling out his nose hairs from the inside. Something in his brain gave way, and he felt a massive tingle of pleasure. "Jesus," he said.

Latham snorted a spoonful himself and let out a long breath through his thin lips. "I think God will likely be absent from our company tonight. Just as well." Latham bent over and put his mouth on Jerry's, pushing his tongue inside, and ran his hand over Jerry's crotch.

Jerry felt pinned by both Latham's mouth and the unreality of the situation. He tried to think of it as the kiss of death for his brother's murderer. His brain snapped into a memory of Beth's lips. For a moment, he kissed back.

Latham broke off the kiss and sighed. "It's a shame."

"What?" Jerry asked.

"Nothing." Latham stood. "Let's go into the bedroom."

Latham walked toward one of the open doors, his silk robe rustling. He stopped in the doorway and looked back at Jerry. Jerry caved in under the stare and followed. The bedcovers were turned back, and the sheets were clean. A red robe and mask hung in the corner.

"Take your clothes off," Latham said.

Jerry began unbuttoning his shirt. "I forgot my drink in the other room. Back in a minute."

Latham nodded, unsashed his robe, and laid down on the bed.

Jerry quickly crossed the living room and made it to the door. He unlocked it and opened it a crack. *"Now,"* he whispered to the outside.

He could hear weights clanking in the room Zelda had gone into. Jerry padded across the carpet and stepped inside. Zelda was bent over with a large dumbell in either hand, doing flies. She looked up when Jerry came in, her face flushed with exertion. Jerry reached in his pocket for the packet and thumbed it open.

"The man wants to see you," Jerry said.

Zelda continued working her arms. "You're being paid to please him. So do it."

Jerry pulled the packet out of his pocket and threw the contents into Zelda's eyes. She dropped the dumbells and screamed. The powder was finely ground drain cleaner. Jerry had used it once before, in Jokertown. He knew Zelda couldn't jump what she couldn't see.

The kick caught him below the ribs and sent him crashing into the wall. His shoulder smashed through the plaster and Sheetrock.

"Kill you," Zelda said, shaking her head.

Jerry crawled away from her, putting a workout machine between them. The lights flickered and dimmed. Veronica was doing it to Latham. It was all going to work out fine.

Jerry grabbed the machine and pulled himself upright. The barbell sitting on it clanked. Zelda wheeled at the sound and took a step forward. She stepped squarely on one of the dumbells and it slipped underneath her, pitching her forward.

Zelda cartwheeled into the machine, and Jerry leapt out of the way. She slammed into the mass of metal, knocking it over with her on top. The barbell tipped and fell. One heavily weighted end thudded into her back. There was a snap. Zelda opened her mouth. Jerry expected a scream, but there was only a low moan.

He backed into the living room slowly, looking away from her. Zelda was one of his least favorite people in the world, but the suffering on her face was more than he could stand to see.

Veronica was sitting on the couch with a gun in her hand.

"Did you do it?" Jerry asked.

She shook her head. "I couldn't. It's just not in me."

Jerry gritted his teeth. "What about Hannah?"

Veronica looked up and gave him a slow stare. "She wouldn't have been able to either." She handed him the gun. "You'll have to take care of it yourself."

"Fine," Jerry said, hefting the pistol in his hand. "Get out of here. I'll meet you at the car."

Veronica stood and left.

Jerry walked into the bedroom. Latham was lying on the bed. His eyes were closed and his breathing was shallow. Jerry bent over and put the silencer to Latham's head, then paused. He understood why Veronica couldn't do it. After he fired the gun, Jerry would never be the same person again. No matter what the justification, killing a helpless person would leave a big scar. He closed his eyes and squeezed the trigger.

Nothing.

"Can't be jammed," Jerry said, fumbling with the weapon. "Can't be."

The hands were around his wrist before Jerry even saw them move. They twisted the gun from his grasp and sent it bouncing to the floor. Latham bounded up, and put the bed between them.

"Who are you working for?" Latham asked. "Tell me, and you might leave here alive."

Jerry moved around the bed and toward the door. Latham cut him off. "Nobody," he said.

Latham stared at him for a moment, as if weighing the situation. He head a groan from the exercise room. "What did you do to Zelda?"

Jerry thought he saw fear for a moment in Latham's face. "She did it to herself, playing with her weights." He knew that only one of them was going to live. Maybe that was the only way he could turn killer, by counting on his survival instinct. He let his features go and took on his natural face. "Recognize me now?"

Latham sneered. "Strauss the older. In years anyway. I knew there was someone sniffing around the edges of things, but couldn't ever pin you down. Kenneth would be so proud."

At the mention of his brother, Jerry bolted at St. John.

He slammed into Latham, knocking them both to the floor. Latham took Jerry by the neck and began squeezing, his hands hard and relentless. Jerry aimed a knee at Latham's groin, but caught him on the inner thigh. He clawed at St. John's face. The fingers at his throat clutched him tighter. Jerry could feel the muscles in his neck going numb. His vision was blurring. He thought of Kenneth's shattered body lying in a street. Thought of what would happen to Beth and Veronica if he failed.

Jerry put his index finger into Latham's ear, and extruded the bone through his own flesh and into Latham's. His bone snaked through the eardrum and into Latham's brain. Jerry remembered the egg scrambler and whipped the strand of fingerbone around inside the lawyer's skull. Latham made a strangled, hissing noise and began twitching.

Jerry twisted away and reshaped his hand. It felt like he'd stuck it into boiling water. He kissed the tip of his finger reflexively, then jerked back. He spat the brain tissue from his mouth.

Jerry looked over at Latham. He wasn't breathing. He had to be dead. Had to be. Jerry sat down on the bed and took a deep breath. He'd always thought Latham was tougher and smarter than him, but it was St. John dead on the floor. Jerry closed his eyes and put a hand over his mouth, his insides suddenly cold. This was what killing felt like; what it really was. He knew the horror he felt now would be worth the peace it bought down the line, but now all he wanted was to be gone from this place.

He reached over and picked up the gun, tucking it into his pocket. He got up, but turned in the doorway and looked down at Latham. The dead man's face was all pain, without a trace of peace. Jerry staggered out into the living room and grabbed his coat, then left the apartment. He changed his appearance as the elevator descended. He darkened his skin and hair and added a touch of age. But there was no changing how he felt about what he'd left in the apartment upstairs.

They were walking through her neighborhood in Brooklyn. Veronica's skin had some lines, of course, but her color was back. Her hair shone in the sunlight.

"How do you feel? I didn't think you could actually kill anyone. You weren't up to talking about it the other night." Veronica waved at a couple of kids playing with balsa wood gliders. They grinned and waved back.

"Not good. I can't kid myself that murder is okay, but I had to do it. Part of being a grown-up is doing what has to be done. It was him or us." Jerry shivered, suddenly cold. "I don't know. Sometimes I'm okay and sometimes I'm not. Eventually, I'll make my peace with it."

"I hope so," Veronica said. "You're not bad, for a man. You're a fuckup sometimes, but you've got a good heart."

Jerry rubbed the corner of his eye. "Veronica, I wish I'd gotten to know you. I guess it's too late now."

She smiled. "Probably. I need to start all over again. I've spent a lot of years finding out what I hated. I need to find something I can love. I guess that's why I came back to the old neighborhood. It's the last place I remember being happy. I want to be happy again."

"Good luck." Jerry held out his hand. Veronica took it, and pulled him into a soft hug, then backed away. "If there's ever anything I can do," he said.

She nodded and turned away.

Jerry walked to the corner and hailed a cab. He felt like he was going to throw up. He leaned against a street sign and tried to clear his head. A taxi pulled over, and he was in the backseat in an instant. He lay down and wondered about the roaring in his ears. Then he passed out.

The hospital room was as nice as hospital rooms ever get. Jerry pulled the bedcovers up to his chest. He was still cold.

If they didn't have those stupid backless gowns, he might be able to get warm.

Beth walked in and cocked an eyebrow. "Back in the land of the living, finally."

"I died and went to heaven," Jerry said. "It pays to be Episcopalian."

Beth put her hand on his forehead. "I think your fever's down from yesterday." She stroked his arm, carefully avoiding the area near his I.V. "You were lucky not to lose that finger. The bone was pretty badly infected."

Jerry propped himself up on an elbow. "Why did you decide to sleep with me? We didn't really talk about that."

Beth settled into a chair next to him. "Because no other man could make me stop thinking about you. That hasn't happened since I first met Kenneth. Don't know what it is about you Strauss boys, must be good genes. I want you to be part of my life, Jerry."

"Me too," he said. "I want that a lot."

"I'm going back to Chicago, though. I know that now. This town is crazy. It makes everyone in it crazy." She took his hand. "I want you to come with me, but I want you to think about it first. I want you to be sure."

"As sure as I ever get about anything." Jerry looked into her eyes. "I want to come visit real soon. I just might wind up staying for good."

Beth got up and kissed him lightly on the lips. "Get your rest. You don't have to decide on anything today. I'm not leaving until you're completely well."

Jerry closed his eyes. He was too tired to worry about it. He'd worry about it tomorrow.

Tomorrow was another day.

The Temptation of Hieronymus Bloat

VIII

"My army is gathering to me, Princess," I told her. "Every day since we battled the invaders from the great city and won, more and more people have come to me. They're jokers, most of them, but a few are aces..."

"You have too many," she whispered in the darkness. "There are too many people here now. That is what the Pretender has told me. He says there wasn't room in your shared kingdom before the battle and the new caves aren't safe for his people. He says there isn't proper housing for those who deserve it. He says the jokers have too much money, too much room. He hates you, all of you, and the situation is making him angry. He says horrible things about you."

"The Pretender is a fool," I spat out, though I had worried about the same thing. "His words don't scare me."

"If his words don't scare you, then why have you not rescued me, my love?" Her soft, sad smile took some—but not all, not all—sting from her words. "I am in your hands entirely, Outcast. You have the power; I have nothing. I believe you. I...I love you. Please, please take me out of here."

My soul ached. My breath caught in my throat. I stroked the smooth skin of the Princess's hands, glaring at the crude bars and stones that held her as if I could break them by the force of my will and desire. The ground underneath my feet rumbled and groaned in concert with my rage. "You know I will do that when I can, Princess," I told her. "You know that I have pursued several avenues to have you set free. I thought I'd found the way twice now. Both times I've been thwarted. This isn't easy. I must be able to guarantee that you will be safe and that my people will be safe as well."

"When, then?"

"Soon. Trust me. I *will* find a way. I must be careful. You know how powerful the Pretender is. If he knew I was here now, he might send the Silent Guardian." I felt a shiver of fear go through her; the same chill touched me.

But she was right. I couldn't tolerate her torment much longer. The soft swell of her belly under the dress was an accusation. I told myself that I *would* find a way, no matter what obstacles the Pretender placed in my way.

The strength is within you, she had told me. I wish that I felt it were really true.

"I won't let them hurt you anymore," I whispered to her, the Princess with Kelly's face. I said the words, and they became a vow, a resolution. "I will make you a way out. Believe me."

Before she could answer, there was the sound of nearby bolts being loosed. I felt a rush of panic. I kissed the tips of her fingers before I hurried away from her into the darkness of the Catacombs and the long stairs under the Ruined Castle. I began the long climb back to the sun.

The ascent was becoming more difficult every time. The hallways of the Catacombs had shrunk, pressing inward. I seemed heavier and much larger. My body barely fit in the passageway. The stones tore at my leather clothing, holding me back and making it difficult to maneuver through the twisting turns of the labyrinth.

Exhausted and bloody, I paused at the landing where the crevice led to the caverns. The crevice had widened as the Catacombs had diminished. The opening was now easily large enough for me to fit through. I looked into the caverns beyond—there was a figure there. I thought for a moment that it was the toadlike presence of the Pretender, and my heart hammered against my ribs while my breath came harsh and quick. I held my torch high, letting the light shatter on the crystalline walls. I pulled the rapier from my belt.

The penguin laughed at me. "You don't need that here, Fatboy. What a fucking scaredy-cat."

"I'm not scared," I told him. "The Outcast is never scared."

"Yeah. Right. That's why you've let your Princess sit in her cell for so long. That's why she's knocked up. That's why you've always tried to get someone else to do your dirty work. You're scared, all right, or you'd've done something." The penguin cocked its head at me. "You gonna stay out there, or are you afraid of the dark?"

The penguin's scorn made me scowl. I scrambled through the rocky opening into the cool air of the caverns. Shadows fled the light of my torch. This place was vast: I could not see the roof or the far walls. Blackness hinted of openings leading out into secret ways and further caverns.

"What is this place?" I asked.

"It's *your* dream. You fucking tell me. All I know is that it's big and there're places here I wouldn't care to stay, and other places so damn beautiful, it makes me cry. It's a place. That's all. Big enough for everyone and all the horrors and beauty that the Rox can dream."

The penguin looked at me strangely. "So, when you gonna *do* something?"

"When the time is right."

The penguin hawked and spat an enormous glob of spittle at its feet. Centipedes crawled from the rocks and lapped at the moisture. "Bullshit again. The time is now."

"The Pretender's still too strong, even with the death of the Overlord."

"Nope. You're too weak. It's time for you to grow up, Fatboy."

With those words, the penguin sounded exactly like my father. "Just shut up!" I shouted back at him. Shadows moved in the darkness, as if my words had stirred unseen creatures to life. "What the hell do you know?"

"I know that you're acting like a kid afraid of the neighborhood bully," the penguin told me. "I also know that for as big as you are, you just don't think big enough."

"And what is that supposed to mean?"

"You really love her? Then get her out. *Do* something."

"I don't know *how!*" I told the penguin in anguish, and my voice was a wail.

"I'll help you, Governor. Let me help you."

My whole body shuddered. The dream had dissolved. I

found myself in the lobby, and Peanut was looking up at me with trust and loyalty and sadness in his mind. His wide sympathetic eyes, caught in their eternal hard folds of skin, gazed at me.

"Peanut—"

"It'd be best that way. Really. I know the way through the caves to her better than anyone. All you have to do is make an opening into her cell. You can do that, can't you?" He looked up at me with those trusting eyes. "I can lead her through the caves, get into a boat, and take her to where she'd be safe. No one would know, Governor."

"No," I said. I couldn't send a whole contingent of jokers—that would start a civil war here, and the jokers would inevitably lose. I couldn't afford to oppose Blaise directly, and with Latham gone, I had no more leverage within the jumper camp. So many people gone: K.C., Latham, Zelda . . .

I smiled at Peanut. So simple and confident and faithful— he believed that there was always a way. He believed that Good always had to win in the last reel.

And so, I guess, did I.

I felt the same stirrings of *something* that I'd felt when I'd made the caves, and I knew that, yes, I *could* make the door into her cell. I could do that much, I was certain.

"Let me think about it," I told Peanut.

Lovers

IV

The little room under the eaves was a stupendous improvement over the basement cell. There was a narrow window, and she could watch the sun set. She had a cot and folding metal chair, and once a day her guards took her for a walk about the perimeter of the hospital building. The food was no better, but at least there was more of it. But unfortunately she was, for the most part, denied the things most necessary to a breeding female—milk, fresh green vegetables, fruit. But as the days and weeks passed, as she became rounder and rounder, she developed a grudging respect for Illyana even as the baby made her more and more ungainly.

"You are a tough little bitch, aren't you? Fed on next to nothing, and you still thrive. That's your Takisian blood—makes you a fighter."

Tachyon was sitting on the chair gazing out the window at a truly lovely sunset, provided courtesy of Manhattan's smog. It was beastly hot up under the eaves. Tach lifted the skirt of her dress, opened her legs even wider than was necessary to accommodate the bulge of her belly, and fanned herself vigorously. And for the hundredth time she made herself—and the illusory wife she might someday possess, should fate and fortune smile and restore her to her rightful body—the promise that she would *never* force a woman to endure a pregnancy in the summer.

A small knot of jumpers emerged from the door four stories below and walked toward the trees. Tach leaned forward, more from force of habit than any real drive, and studied them. Fell back when there was no glint of copper-red hair. Her body was not among them.

This complacency was a recent development. In the beginning, she had peered from the window. During her walks, she had cast about like a hunting hound seeking desperately for a glimpse of herself, but the Tachyon body remained stubbornly out of sight. Now it was hard to arouse that level of concern. Her focus had narrowed to the room, and more importantly to what was occurring within her borrowed body.

She was content to sit for hours listening to her heart beat, weaving her thought colors through the fabric and colors of the baby's thoughts, singing Takisian lullabies she had thought long forgotten.

The grate of the key in the lock brought her head around, a frown of puzzlement between the blond brows. One of her guards, his mouth slack, drool running down his chin, jerked zombielike into the room. Her body was behind him. The reaction ran like fire along her nerve endings. Tach came to her feet, stared hungrily at her own body.

The girl who wore her skin was dressed in tattered cutoffs. The shirt was the one Tachyon had been wearing at the time of the kidnapping—billowing sleeves, drawstring at the throat. It was open now, revealing a good deal of the chest with its whorls of copper hair. The bones of the clavicle were like stony ropes beneath the white skin, the legs stick thin. Stubble littered the pointed chin and the sunken cheeks.

The sound they both made was surprisingly similar. A tiny whimper of misery, divided by two octaves. Tachyon recovered first. Stretched out imploring hands.

"He raped me." The words were jarring in that husky baritone.

"No, he raped *me*." Furious, Tach gripped the jumper by the shoulders. "Return me. Put us back! I can handle him."

"I can't."

"*Won't*."

"*Can't!* I'm not a jumper. Can't ever be one now."

Before that bit of miserable knowledge could fully pene-trate, the guard let out a choking sound and fell to the floor like a broken puppet. For Tachyon, medical instinct took over. Jerking her eyes from her body, she knelt awkwardly beside the boy and checked his pulse.

Eyes shifting with lightning speed from the prone boy to Tachyon and back again, the body asked, "What's wrong with him? What did I do?"

"A mind-control can be a silken web or a steel trap. Yours was of the latter variety."

"Will he be okay?"

Tachyon looked up at her eerie doppelgänger. "No. His mind has been shredded. Death is only a matter of time."

The body gasped, a sharp little hiss of fear. "I had to see you. You've got to help me."

Tach gave a short bark of laughter. "*Me?* Help you? Isn't that rather presumptuous of you?"

"You've got me pregnant," said the body in a blinding non sequitur.

"Well, no. It's not something I managed all by myself . . . any more than I managed to get your body raped all by myself."

The body was staring in fascination at the curve of her belly. He advanced a few steps, and his eyes jerked up to meet Tach's.

"My head's making me crazy. I can't turn it off. I think things, and they happen."

Tears welled up in the lavender eyes. Tachyon writhed inwardly. How painful to watch *yourself* weep. And for a brief instant she acknowledged that there was more than one victim in this hellish scenario.

"What are you called, child?" she asked gently, feeling unimaginably old.

"Kelly."

Plans began to explode in Tachyon's mind. "Kelly, listen to me. Blaise is no match for my body. I can teach you how to control the power. You can mind-control him. Force him to return us."

She was pursuing Kelly around the room as he retreated before her, desperately shaking his head. With panic shortening his breath, Kelly said, "I can't. I can't. He hurts me—"

The door slammed into the wall. They both cried out and whirled to face Blaise. And both fell back, for they knew the maddened rage that glittered in those dark eyes.

Blaise seized Kelly by the arm and threw him across the

room. " I *told* you . . . you couldn't see him. Don't *ever* . . . disobey me again."

Kelly's teeth were chattering so hard, he couldn't speak. He shook his head frantically, the long red hair flying about his face.

Blaise turned with almost balletic grace to face his grandfather. Tachyon's heart was jumping in her throat. Blaise stepped inclose, cupped her cheek in the palm of his hand. Suddenly his teeth clamped down on his lower lip, and hauling off, he backhanded her across the face. She was flung into the wall, pain exploding in her shoulder and head. With a moan, she slid down the wall. Black spots danced before her eyes. She could hear Blaise approaching. Ponderous footsteps.

A lighter, quicker step. The sounds of a struggle.

"Stop it! Stop it!" the Tachyon voice shouting shrilly.

Tach opened her eyes. Kelly was clinging to Blaise's shoulder, clawing at his face. All the gestures were oddly feminine, jarring to Tachyon. Blaise snarled, and gathering up Kelly's shirtfront, he proceeded to beat the crap out of the smaller man. Kelly's screams filled the room. He subsided into muffled sobbing, curled like a ball on the floor.

Blaise resumed his threatening advance. Tach watched the boy's foot draw back. She knew what was coming, and she managed to get her arms across her stomach before it happened. Her wrist took most of the kick, but even the residual force was enough to set her retching. Illyana's thoughts, pain, and fear were like the beating of wings in the confines of Tachyon's skull.

Blaise backed off, reached down, and hauled Kelly to his feet. They exited, leaving Tachyon with the dying guard.

"I swear to you, by all that I am and ever shall be." The musical Takisian syllables rippled through the room and mingled hideously with the dying boy's moans. *"By Blood and Line. You shall die. And by my hand."*

Then and only then did Tachyon allow herself to faint.

The garret room had metamorphosed into a tower cell. Lancet windows, gray stone walls, a private prie-dieu—ironic considering she wasn't Christian—a curtained canopy bed . . . a romantic's vision of the Middle Ages.

And it irritated the shit out of her. This wasn't fantasy; this was deadly reality. And Tach was sick of the games. Her head seemed to be throbbing in time to her pulse, an outside pressure trying to warp and force the dream to fit his standards. Grimly, Tachyon fought back. What was achieved was a strange hermaphroditic compromise. Tachyon was male again, but pregnant.

Alien man gives birth to human child!

The ultimate tabloid headline, Tach thought, *but then, we live in a tabloid nightmare. The wild card virus saw to that. We took order, peace, security . . . and gave them chaos.*

Tachyon was braiding his-her hair. But it really *was* his-her hair. Metallic copper curls sliding between his-her fingers. Frowning, tip of the tongue peeking from between his-her lips, he-she concentrated, struggled. Suddenly other hands took over the chore. The deft pull, right over left over right, the tug to the scalp was heaven. Tachyon sighed and dropped his-her hands into his-her lap, cradling the curve of their pregnancy.

"You sent for me," said the Outcast.

"Yes."

Tach shifted around to face him. The wide brim of his hat shadowed his eyes but could not match the darkness within those eyes. Tachyon took the Outcast's hand and laid the palm against his-her belly. "Feel her." And Tachyon gathered up his-her child's thought and thrust them into the mind of his-her courtly lover.

The Outcast reacted like a slaughterhouse steer seeing the fall of the hammer.

"She's going to die. I'm going to die . . . if you don't help us."

The man pulled his hand away as if the contact pained him. "I've tried . . . tried to help."

"Here?" Tach gestured. "Well, it's not enough. The time for dreams is over."

"It's difficult. He's very dangerous."

"*I* know . . ." Long pause, then Tach added with poisonous softness, "I'd wager . . . better than you."

The flush rode up in the Outcast's cheeks like a spill of blood. "How do you even know I can do anything?" There was a childish complaining note in the deep voice.

"I don't . . . and you'd probably like me to assume you're merely a symptom of incipient madness. That would let you off the hook. But you sent Peanut. He speaks of you with reverence. No, you exist. And now you have to find the courage to act."

The Outcast turned away. "There are so many...so many of them needing me—"

"And now there's one more," Tach interrupted. He-She touched her belly. "Her name is Illyana. I sing, and she thinks music back to me. She's a trickster because she knows there's one particular place where she kicks and I have to urinate. She knows it makes me mad, and it makes her giggle."

Tachyon could see the tension in her reluctant hero's back. The muscles in his neck formed corded rejection. "That's Illyana," Tachyon continued quietly. "And Blaise kicked me in the stomach. To him, she's just a parasite. A means to torture me. But I know better...she is my daughter...and I love her."

Tachyon rose. Made his ungainly way to the Outcast's side. Lightly touched the man on the back of the hand. "Don't let him kill her."

The man whirled, almost knocking Tach off his feet. "Would you kiss me?"

"What? Now?"

"Now...sometimes...always."

"Well...yes."

"You hesitated!" Accusation and suspicion made the words cut like blades.

"Of course. I don't know who you are. You don't know *what* I am."

"My love."

Tachyon covered his ears and spun awkwardly away. Fled until the width of the circular room lay between them. "Stop it, *stop it*, STOP IT!" Panting breaths punctuated each word. "Why does no one know me? Am I always to be a symbol? The *saint of Jokertown. The faggot from outer space. The Takisian. The drunkard, the prince, doctor, alien, lover, rival.* And now *your* 'love.' Well, dammit, why can't I just *be.*" He was sobbing wildly.

The Outcast crossed the room in three long strides. Took Tach in his arms. Made soothing, shushing noises.

"A kiss," the Takisian murmured wearily as his sobs subsided. "Is that the price of freedom? Then you'll have it. I swear."

The dream was fading. Tach became aware of the sagging cot beneath her body, the pressure of an overfull bladder, the smell of the slops bucket, voices calling outside.

And fluttering through her consciousness like a fading memory, another voice. "You promised. Remember, you promised."

"Doctor. Doctor Tachyon, wake up."

Tach cranked up on an elbow. Pushed back her hair, tried to focus. "Peanut, by the Ideal . . ." The words died into silence as she stared at the joker protruding from the floor like a horny mushroom. Tach blinked and realized that the lower half of the man was beneath the level of a trapdoor—*where there shouldn't be a trapdoor.*

"Come quick. I'm gonna get you outta here."

The joker had a Coleman lantern hung over the stump of his arm. With his other hand he reached out to help her. As Peanut's chitinous fingers closed about her hand, Tachyon felt a thrill as great as if it had been the touch of a lover. *Free, free—she was almost free.*

"It's a long ladder. Can you make it?"

"Not easily," said Tach as her stomach rubbed at a rung. "But I'll manage," she concluded grimly.

"Can you close the trap?"

She stretched, grasped the edge, pulled. It fell with a dull thump. Peanut's terror was palpable in the confined space.

"Sorry," said Tach. "It was heavier than I thought."

"That's okay, but let's hurry."

They began climbing.

"Can you go a little faster?" Peanut asked after several minutes.

"No. I'm a little awkward right now. And a little scared," she added.

"Don't worry, Doctor. I won't let you fall. And anyway, you'd land on me."

"And then where would I be?" She smiled back and down over her shoulder. "You're my guide, Peanut."

At last they reached bottom, and Tach found herself in a cavern. Seven openings debouched into the vaultlike room. Tach pivoted slowly, staring in wonder at the colorful painted glyphs that rioted on the curving walls. Somewhat reminiscent of Mayan art, they also partook of Balinese temple paintings.

"Blood and Line, this is *very* strange," Tach murmured.

"Pardon?" said Peanut politely.

"Nothing... hysteria... relief," Tach quickly added at the joker's look of alarm. "But this can't be real... can it?"

"It is. He's had me down here exploring them. They go all over. Weird places, but okay places too."

Peanut headed toward one of the openings. Tach fell in step with him.

"Places like where?"

"New Jersey."

"Definitely a weird place," said Tach thoughtfully.

The tunnel had started to climb, and Tach knew damn good and well that they hadn't walked to New Jersey yet. She stopped, planting both feet heavily like a balky foal. Peanut looked back questioningly.

"Where are you taking me?" Suspicion sharpened her tone.

Peanut seemed to collapse in on himself. His thickened eyelids blinked rapidly several times. The effect was like watching a stone idol come to life, and Tach imagined that she could hear a sharp click as the hoary lids met and sprang apart.

"I gotta take you to him first. Then we'll go. He just wants to see you."

"Who? The Outcast?"

"The governor."

"Governor? What are you babbling about?"

Wounded dignity descended over the joker like rolling fog. "This is a joker place now. We take care of each other, and he takes care of us. We got laws now and everything."

"I'm sorry, Peanut," Tachyon said contritely. "It's probably a good thing you have a joker place. And I'm very fortunate. You're probably the only people in the world who would help me right now."

They resumed walking. "We're scared of Blaise, but not enough to stop caring for you."

"You didn't feel that way two years ago when I derailed Senator Hartmann's presidential campaign."

"The governor explained why you did that."

That stopped Tachyon in her tracks again. "He did?" she asked in a voice gone suddenly as wobbly as her knees.

"Yeah. He wouldn't give us details. He just said that what you did probably saved us from even worse persu... persecution." Peanut faltered slightly over the unfamiliar word. "He says you do care for the jokers like nobody ever has."

Falling into step with the joker, Tach asked hesitantly, "Is . . . is the governor a joker?"

"Of course."

That stopped her yet again. It was an act of will to kick herself back into motion again. She steeled herself to pay the price of freedom.

A kiss.

A joker.

"You promised . . . remember, you promised."

A joker.

Faceted surfaces seized the light. Broke it into the primary colors of the spectrum. Threw it back in rainbow striations on the white sand floor of the cavern. Tach shook her head. Only on the world of her birth had she seen such gaudy extravagance. A jewel-encrusted door, the gems forming the pattern of a coat of arms.

"Your governor doesn't underrate his importance."

"We didn't build it. Honest. It just happens."

"How?"

"I don't know."

Enchanting ice, the faceted surfaces cool and sharp against the palm of her hand. One of the gems was loose. It formed the eye of an eagle, and beneath her probing fingers, it suddenly tumbled free like a bloody tear. Bewitching fire, as a ruby the size of a plum filled her hand. She couldn't resist. She pocketed the wealth.

"The ability to make dreams manifest . . . energy-to-matter transference," murmured Tach, trying to remove this latest wild card mutation from the realm of fantasy into the workaday reality that was science.

Scientific theories held little interest for Peanut. He threw back the elaborate bolt, the turned to Tachyon. "Wait here. I gotta make sure everybody's cleared out. The fewer people who know, the better."

Darkness fell around her like a storm as Peanut and the lantern passed through the doorway. And carried on its stygian wings was a *stench* that defied description. Tach, her stomach heaving, spun and staggered back a few steps from the door.

What could possibly live and produce such foulness? For

over forty years she'd faced and physicked the worse the wild card had to offer. She could face this too. What she couldn't face was the blackness. Memories of her basement cell scurried like tormenting demons through her mind. Footfalls in the darkness, raucous laughter. Light struck her like a blow, and Tachyon screamed. Blaise was coming.

Peanut's hand across her mouth smothered the sound, yanked her back from the edge of madness.

"I'm sorry... I'm sorry." Her teeth chattered over each consonant like hail on a tin roof.

"Don't be afraid of the dark. We won't let anything getcha. Now come on, but you remember—because he won't, won't want to—you gotta hurry."

They were through the secret door, and her feet recoiled from a sticky resinous substance. The stench made her head reel, made her doubt the evidence of her eyes. That voluminous mass of stained white couldn't possibly be flesh? Could it?

Pipes thrust into the mass like air hoses into an inflating balloon. But this was not so benign. Dried blood flaked from the skin around the punctures like peeling paint, and Tach could see an angry red, the corona of infection, flaring from several of the crudely sewn incisions. And from the pores poured the source of the foulness—liquid shit oozing in perfect beadlike globules, running down the joker's side to join the mountains of waste. Ancestors help the poor creature, it *was* flesh, it *did* live. Stomach heaving like a bucking horse, Tach fought her revulsion and tried to see where in this mountain of protoplasm resided the mind, the soul.

"Get the doctor a handkerchief, Peanut," said a high-pitched voice from high above her. "She's not accustomed to the smell of bloatblack." The boy hit the word *bloat* with the bitterness of a falling hammer.

Tach searched wildly for the source of the voice. Finally located it. Pygmylike, the head, neck, shoulders, and arms of a young man perched like a figurehead on the prow of a massive ship of flesh.

Was there anything in that round fat face reminiscent of her dream phantom suitor? Only the hair color. A nudge from Peanut startled her. He offered a handkerchief. It had been drenched in Lagerfeld. It had been Tachyon's favorite—

"After-shave, yes, I know," said the young man in chorus

with her thoughts. "That's why I got it for you... for this moment."

The damp cloth formed a veil against the stink and Tachyon's horror. "Are you..." She couldn't form the rest of the words.

"The Outcast? Yeah. Now, I suppose, you see why."

They were tuned. He was the first person she had read with her feeble telepathy. They had walked in dreams together. It was easy to slide into his mind. Past the lithe, tanned figure that was the Outcast, the soul's image of his true self. Past erotic visions of Kelly. A simulacrum of Tachyon—heroic, noble, suffering. Down to where the boy-child lived. Encased in fat, eating sewage, lying in shit, and dreaming of beauty. Quick blurred images flashed past—of Teddy, slow and always a little pudgy, but blessed with beautiful hands. Those hands sweeping across the page of a sketchbook. The smell of drying oil, the romantic quirky paintings that filled his room. They were lovely; they added something to a world that dismissed, discounted, and rejected Theodore Honorlaw.

Monster/tired/screaming/hateself/mustlive/mustdie.

Tachyon's spirit wept.

Teddy looked down at her. "You're crying on the inside for me."

"Yes."

"Why don't you cry on the outside?"

"I can't. I've lost the ability," Tach said simply.

"When?"

"After the rape." They studied each other for a long moment. "Now you're weeping for me," Tach added softly.

"Yeah... but only on the inside. Wouldn't do for the governor of the Rox to show weakness."

Again silence fell between them. Tach remembered Peanut's admonition. "Teddy, the longer I stay here, the greater the danger. Peanut and I—"

"Bloat, the name's Bloat. Teddy belongs to another world... and haven't you forgotten something?" Tachyon cringed, eyes flicking guiltily from side to side. "No, you haven't forgotten, you were just hoping I had. I disgust you, don't I?"

Tach just shook her head. She wished she could lie. Knew she couldn't. He was in her mind again. She couldn't hide anything from him. His face puckered like a baby about to cry.

"We've all revolted you. For forty-five years you've been

totally grossed-out every time you touched one of us, cared for one of us." His tone wound higher, fueled by his growing anger.

"I'm sorry . . ."

"I thought you loved me!" The enormous body was quivering, sending shocks through the walls and floor of the old building. Tach tottered, struggled to maintain her footing. Peanut was terrified.

"You're a fraud, Tachyon, a total fucking fraud!"

Her shame collapsed before a wave of indignation. "No—I helped create you—I'll bear that guilt. But I have worked and lived among you, given half my life to your care, your protection, your well-being. I *do* care for you. You are my wounded step-children, but how can you ask me to love you when you can't even love yourselves?"

Snorting, gasping sobs emerged from the boy atop his hideous throne. Unable to help, Tachyon listened to the sounds of woe come falling down the joker's sides like the rivers of bloatblack.

"Somebody's coming," said Peanut suddenly. Tachyon hadn't even noticed him moving to the door.

"Has to be Blaise. My jokers are all under strict orders."

"Ideal," murmured Tachyon, and felt her bowels go to water. The boy's face hardened. He scrubbed at his eyes. Tach dug to her core. Takisian pride would support her. It was all she had left. "This is your moment. Revenge yourself and all your fellows upon me. You have the power."

Bloat stared at her. Fury fell away. He sighed. "I can't do that to you. For months you've cried, and sung, and talked in my mind. You're beautiful . . . I can't hurt you. Climb up."

Tachyon needed no urging. Revulsion gave way to self-preservation. She picked her way through the mounds of fecal waste, placed a foot on one of the pipes jabbed IV-like into the joker's body. Fingers pinching at the skin she hauled herself upward, and fell forward into the folds of flesh. She lifted a flap of skin. It was like handling a sack of wet sand, but sweat made it oily. She slipped beneath it, and pulled it up like a blanket. It was *horrible*.

The sound of the doors slamming open brought back memories. Tach chewed on a corner of the handkerchief.

"How dare you bust in on me like this!" Bloat roared. "This is joker territory, jumpers only come when invited."

"Looking for someone," wailed a boy in a cracking

adolescent's tone. The door slammed again. Tach sagged with relief.

She stood and made her way to the head, her feet sinking several inches with every step. His head reached only to her breast. She pushed his hair off his forehead. It was silky, freshly washed. She caught the thought *in preparation for meeting you*.

Their thoughts continued to dance and weave about and through one another.

"I wish you could come with me too," said Tach in answer to an unspoken question.

"Will you ever come back?" Pleading without ever having asked.

"I must."

"Oh, yeah, your body'll still be here."

"More than that. There's you, and I'll help you if I can."

Tach hesitated. Bloat's dark eyes were pleading with her. He looked away, mumbled, "Blaise knows you're gone, they're hunting... you better go."

Setting her jaw, Tach drew in a hissing breath between her teeth. Took Bloat's face between her hands, bent in for the kiss. His flabby arms wrapped about her waist, drew her in close, and Tachyon began to shake. This had nothing to do with Takisian revulsion for the deformed. This was gut-wrenching terror.

Blaise's teeth drawing blood from her lower lip in his own grotesque and evil version of a kiss. Almost choking her as he thrust his penis down her throat.

Tachyon whimpered as Bloat's hands closed tightly about her wrists.

He forced her hands from his face, pushed her away.

"NO!" The word twisted and vibrated with his emotional agony. "I'm not going to hurt you. You'll never remember me as someone who hurt you."

"I promised!" cried Tach.

"And I want it! But not this way. Not when all you can remember is a rape! Peanut, help her down." The joker scurried up onto Bloat's back, put a hand beneath Tachyon's elbow. "Hurry."

It was harder going down. Eventually Tachyon just sat down and slid. Her dress and hands were stained with bloatblack.

She looked back up the wall of flesh. "No, Peanut, I've

got to do it. I've got to go back. I can't leave him with my word broken."

"No, Doctor, we've gotta go. It'll hurt him worse if you get caught."

They stepped through the secret door. The last sound Tachyon heard was a boy weeping.

Eventually fear can kill you. It starts by sapping the will and turning the body into a shivering sickly husk. Tach had reached that state. Without the support of Peanut's arm, she could never have reached the chamber in which they now stood. In another lifetime she would have shrunk from that rough contact. But she had endured the sweating, stinking, flaccid mound that was Bloat, and she had felt his love and his despair. She had been assaulted by the physical beauty that was Blaise and known his hate.

"It doesn't matter," she whispered as she sank down on the glittering sand that formed the floor of the cavern chamber.

"What, Doctor?"

She looked up at him. The sad, sad eyes, the chiseled wrinkles about that slit of a mouth.

"Peanut . . . you're a very handsome man."

"No, Doctor, I'm a joker." Bending, he held out his single hand to her. "You rested enough? Can you go on? That Blaise . . . he knows we're running."

The tinkling of falling water drew her attention. She looked and located the source. "Let me bathe my face and hands. That will help."

"Okay," said Peanut dubiously.

The water was icy cold, but it revived her like a slap. She looked down at her dress, gave a little *mew* of disgust, and pulled it over her head. Immersed it beneath the tiny waterfall that had first attracted her. The waters of the pool were soon fouled and darkened with the bloatblack. She put the dress back on, shivering at its clammy touch, but at last she was clean, and the stink was gone.

They kept walking. Tachyon slid a hand into Peanut's. He looked back and smiled. Striations of mica in the rock walls threw off a soft phosphorescent glow. Tachyon was no geologist, but she didn't think that mica could do that. Elaborate stalagmites and stalactites yearned for each other from the floors and ceilings of the caverns, their colors shell pink, sea green, amber.

"Peanut, Ellis Island isn't a real island," Tach said conversationally. They were passing another underground grotto, and on a whim Tach kicked a small pebble into the mirror-like water. The reflected stalagmites and stalactites bowed and swayed like stony dancers.

Forehead buckling with a frown that made the horny skin erupt like the earth in an earthquake, Peanut said, "But it's surrounded by water."

"That's not what I mean. It was made from landfill. There can't be caverns like this beneath its surface."

"But they're here," said Peanut with a blunt practicality that made Tachyon's intellectual maunderings seem inane.

Tachyon nodded, shrugged, but only made it through part of the action because she saw the spider. The size of a coffee table, it was stalking deliberately through the caverns, its eight multijointed legs making a horrible creaking sound. A tiny *mew* of fear made it past her blocked throat.

Peanut followed her terrified gaze. Adding a cocky swing to his normally stiff, blundering walk, Peanut strolled over and ran his hand through the body of the arachnid. It broke apart like stirred oil, globules of ectoplasmic spider floating in all directions.

"Don't worry, it's not real. None of 'em are real. You see things down here. Monsters and people, and just plain things. I think this is the place where nightmares live."

"Whose?" asked Tach a little breathlessly.

"Maybe everybody's in the whole world. Maybe just ours—us on the Rox, I mean."

"Then my nightmares..."

"Oh, there're probably a few sneaking around," answered the joker.

It was an intriguing thought, and Tach searched for these fragments of self. There was a strange sense of déjà vu when she finally spotted one because she so clearly recalled the dream that had given birth to this sad-faced phantom. Cody, lost, crying—so strange because Tachyon couldn't recall ever having seen Cody cry. Adding to the grotesquerie—the tears were slipping from beneath her eye patch but not from the normal healthy eye. She was in her green surgical scrubs, a giant bloodstain directly over the crotch.

"Don't let them hurt me. Keep him away from me. Don't let him hurt me again."

The phantom wasn't really speaking. The mouth moved,

and Tachyon supplied the words. Rape dreams seemed to torment her. Her own, of course, but also Cody's. Was she safe, or had Blaise inflicted the most brutal assault and indignity upon her?

Peanut became alarmed at her rigid, white-lipped stare. "You want me to break it up, Doctor?"

"No, don't touch her. Let nothing touch her." Tach resumed her plodding trek for freedom.

Minutes passed, marked by the scuffle of their shoes in the white sand and the hiss of their puffing breath. Tachyon walked diagonally across the path in front of them. Tachyon froze and watched himself pass. The Tachyon phantasm was bigger than in reality. The expression was cruel, the knuckles of the artificial right hand stained with blood.

"I'm glad—" her voice was a low, ugly growl, "glad to know that I'm part of Blaise's nightmares. The Ideal knows he forms a prominent figure in mine."

Peanut rolled a wary eye at her. Shook his head, kept walking. Around a curve, a new apparition waited. A narrow-hipped, broad-shouldered man of indeterminate years. Hair like silver gilt caught the ghostly light from the walls forming an effect like a nimbus about his head. He was dressed in a white and gold uniform that would have been in place at an Austro-Hungarian ball. The man was seated on an outcropping of rock, one booted foot drawn up, nursing a knee. He was very beautiful.

"Wow!" An expression of awe from Peanut. "Like an angel."

Tach laughed. It echoed back from the unseen cavern roof, a strange sound in these dim halls. An even stranger sound in the dim recesses of her burdened soul. Idly, she wondered when she had last laughed.

"Hardly. It's my wicked cousin Zabb. Zabb and several other of my relatives tried to meddle in your affairs back . . . oh, I guess it must be five years now."

"What'd he try to do?"

"Drop a very large asteroid on top of your pretty planet."

The path was beginning to rise. Tach could feel the stress in the muscles of her calves. Her mood rose with the angle of the floor. *Free-free-free-free-free*, sang a jaunty little litany in her head.

"Who stopped him?"

"I did, ably and critically assisted by Cap'n Trips. Yes,

that was certainly one of Zabb's more flamboyant and malicious gestures. On a more personal, less cosmic scale, he's just plotted and tried to kill me several times," Tach continued with great joviality. "I wish I had seen Zabb first. Then I would have known this was all a mind cheat." She answered Peanut's puzzled glance. "Zabb's either dead or several hundred light-years away. I know damn good and well he's not living in a tunnel under New Jersey."

"You've had such an interesting life," said Peanut wistfully.

Tach saw Blaise slipping through the rock formations to their left. She shuddered, and increased her pace. "The Chinese curse. Don't long for it, Peanut. Embrace, caress, cherish the mundane—"

Hands closed around her hips just below the curve of her pregnancy, lifted her into the air. Tach screamed.

"Going somewhere, Granddad?" crooned Blaise in her ear. Spittle wet her lobe, and his stubble rasped across her cheek. "But the fun's just begun. You can't leave until you've popped . . . and I've given you another one. You wouldn't cheat a father out of his firstborn, would you? It's not a very fucking Takisian thing to do." The words dripped with venom.

Jumpers were emerging from the rocks and shadow. Poor Peanut was splayed on his stomach, held down by several young men. Blaise casually tossed Tachyon into the arms of one of his lieutenants. Sauntered over to where Peanut lay supine and shivering. Tachyon realized she was making a horrible little mewling sound in the back of her throat. She had never heard a sound like that out of a human or a Takisian before—only out of dying animals. She bit down on her cheek to still the shocking sound.

"Okay, Peanut, now you're going to tell me all about who put you up to this."

Before Blaise exercised his mind-control power, he always set and shot his jaw. Obviously Peanut knew the habit, knew what it signified. Peanut's fingers crawled across the sand, moving carefully, subtly, toward the boot of one of his captors and the large bowie knife that rested there.

Peanut, NO! The mental scream echoed about the confines of her skull, and Tachyon felt Bloat stir, a huge stretched presence on the edge of her consciousness.

Peanut's hand closed about the knife, yanked it free. Twisting wildly, he managed to get the blade beneath his chin. He drove his head down, and blood gouted first from beneath his chin and then from his eye as the tip of the blade emerged through the socket like a moray eel nosing out from its rock cavern.

Grief raced through her, fused with Bloat's feelings of disgust and relief. Together they mourned for the dying joker. Blaise was quivering with fury, and his jumper minions stepped hurriedly away, trying to escape the parameters of his power, trying to blend with the rocks.

Mother . . . fucker," spat Blaise, and rounded on his grandfather. "So *you'll* just have to tell me. Bloat was behind this, wasn't he?" The demand was shrill.

Tach shook her head. "No, only poor Peanut. While exploring the caverns, he found my basement cell. He brought me food, and eventually I convinced him to help me."

"I think you're lying. Peanut wasn't smart enough to cook this up."

"He didn't. *I* did. And as for lying—" ever so sweetly, she continued, "you can always read my mind and find out."

It had the desired result. Blaise's face twisted with fury as he considered this void in his power. He could control, but he couldn't read. The secrets of the soul and mind were forever beyond him.

"The only advantage telepathy gives is that people don't know they've been fucked with. Well, I prefer for you to *know* I'm fucking with you."

It didn't take a genius to figure out what was coming. He would mind control her, and force her to talk. Tach broke free from Bloat. She needed all her concentration to marshal her feeble shields.

"I've put up the deathlock," Tach warned.

Blaise understood the significance. The deathlock was the ultimate Takisian mindshield. It could be broken, but only at the cost of the victim's life.

"You don't have shields. You're just a human now."

Was there hesitation in those purple-black eyes? This was high-stakes poker—very high stakes—lives and minds hung in the balance. Could she risk everything on a bluff? Tach considered that gargantuan lump of fat, supine and helpless in the Administration Building. Pictured Blaise with a gasoline can, pictured Teddy burning, dying.

"Try me," Tach invited.

Power lanced out, struck her shields, was repelled, and withdrew. And her shields crumbled like a sand castle at high tide. But Tachyon had won the bluff. Having been repelled, Blaise did not come back for another try.

Shoulders hunched, hands balled into fists, the teenager turned away. Suddenly spun back, fist lashing out in a punishing backhand. Only the support of her captor kept Tachyon upright as the blow landed hard on her temple.

Blaise was unlimbering his belt. "It's time you learned the price of disobedience, *Granpère*."

It was Tachyon's phrase. How many times had Blaise heard it? Resented it, hoarded it while waiting for this moment, savored it as he threw back the words like a challenge.

Then Tachyon forgot all about thinking as Blaise raped her again.

The Temptation of Hieronymus Bloat

IX

There are things that a person shouldn't have to remember.

Peanut's martyrdom was still reverberating in my head, driving out everything else. *Governor, I won't talk. I won't. Don't worry...*

I could feel the knifepoint against his throat, could feel it through his mind. And then Peanut shoved it home. Drove it into his own body to save me.

When I heard Peanut's pain, when I felt it rake my mind like clawed fingers, I screamed for Kafka and told him to bring Blaise to me as soon as he came out of the caverns.

I suppose it was a measure of Blaise's arrogance and his contempt for me that he came alone except for the two jumpers carrying Peanut's body. He'd sent Durg back with Tachyon.

They just dumped him on the lobby floor. The poor joker's eyes were still open. Peanut stared at me, but his mind was utterly still and empty. I blinked. Tears blurred the bloody corpse.

Can't let them know who sent me. Can't let Blaise hurt the governor. Those were the last thoughts I'd heard from Peanut.

Damn you, Peanut. Did you have to be so goddamn noble? Maybe if you hadn't, I wouldn't feel so guilty. I didn't know he'd be there. I didn't. I thought it would be simple.

Blaise glanced at the *Temptation*, at Kafka, and at the jokers who had gathered.

Can't let them know . . .

Simple, brave Peanut. I wondered how in the hell I'd come to deserve that kind of loyalty. The only legacy of my efforts was that Peanut was dead. I'd killed a friend, ruined my dream fantasy, and Tachyon was still a prisoner.

Fucking effective.

"He killed himself, Bloat," Blaise crowed. He was mocking me in his head, daring me to object. "He was helping my old *granpère* to escape. He interfered with me, but I didn't touch him. Of course, you know all this, don't you. You were listening, right? Governor Bloat knows everything."

Inside, he taunted: *I know it was you, Bloat. I know. That fuck Peanut didn't have two brain cells to rub together. He didn't think of this on his own, did he.* He let the thoughts drift out of the veils hiding his mind.

"Get out of here, Blaise," I said. "You did what you wanted to do. It's over. Now get the hell out of here."

But Blaise wanted to brag, wanted to strut. He was laughing, talking about how this was a lesson to anyone who thought they could interfere with *him*, that he'd do the same to anyone else who got in his way. Anyone. He was looking at me when he said it.

"You got Tachyon back," I told him. I looked at Peanut, at the gory vision of his sacrifice for me. The tears threatened again, and my voice was breaking. "Peanut's dead. Drop it."

Blaise just snorted and kept going.

"Blaise, I've warned you—" Even to myself, my blustering sounded like bad empty movie dialogue, and Peanut's body was a symbol of just how empty my words were. I wasn't surprised when Blaise just laughed. Guards brought their guns up, swinging them to bear on the red-haired kid, but he just waved his arms at them.

He just kept blathering. "You gonna tell 'em to shoot, Gov? You think that's going to stop me? Maybe I should just jump one of *them* and start firing away."

"Put your guns down," I told my people.

Blaise laughed louder. "Ain't that just like you, Gov? You *never* kill anyone. Prime had you pegged—you're a whimp. The fucking caves are you, too—they mean you don't have to worry about making a move to New York. You didn't want to do that anyway, did you? Not really. You might have had to *hurt* someone if you did. You wimped out with my grandfather, too. You could've sent a whole squadron of jokers or used some of the renegade aces on the Rox. But no, you tried to do it hidden and bloodless. You sent Peanut—I *know* it was you, Governor. That was a wimp's rescue; it had 'Bloat' engraved all fucking over it. Bloat doesn't hurt jokers or jumpers or anyone. Bloat wants to make a fairyland where everyone kisses and hugs and loves each other, all encircled in Bloat's sturdy little wall. Well, you know what? That's fucking *stupid*."

My jokers were watching me. I didn't have anything to say. Peanut looked up at me, and I thought I could see that damn idiotic trust still in his eyes. "Somebody cover that body," I husked out.

Blaise howled with laughter.

He is scared of you. Underneath it all, he's not confident. I know it. Blaise fears anything he can't control; you can't be jumped and the screens around your mind are too strong for him. He's afraid of your unconscious power, too—the dreamstuff. He's seen the caverns; they worry him. The scope of the power that created them . . . Tachyon tried to soothe me.

I raged back at her.

I don't control the ability. It's like the wall—things just happen. You think I would've let Peanut die if I could do it on my own? I don't have power. Not really. You know that now, don't you? You detest me.

No. Bloat, I'm so . . . I'm so sorry. I didn't want to hurt you. Neither one of us wanted Peanut to die, but he died because he loved you, because he believed in you. I believe in you, too. I still do.

I can't do anything for you. I failed.

You can, Bloat. You can. Please . . . Promise me one thing. Promise that you won't give up. Promise me that.

Why?

Because the Outcast loved the Princess, and the Princess loved the Outcast, too. Because what you're trying to do here is good. Because if you don't, then Peanut wasted his life.

We were both crying.

I'll still get you out, I promised her. *I will. I'll do . . . I don't know what. But I'll find some way, someone to help me.*

But the contact had faded, as it always did. I don't know

if she heard me or not. I caught only the faintest whisper of her voice: ...*you have the power, Bloat. Use it.*

I raged. I sobbed.

"She's right. She's telling you just what I've been telling you." The penguin. It stood in the lobby before me. Not a hallucination, not a dream—I could see the guards looking at it curiously and wondering. "Right," the penguin said. "You made me, like you made the rest."

"How?" I shouted. "Tell me how I can control this."

But it didn't answer. It waddled away down the corridor to the west wing, toward the caves. "I'll be back," it said. "When you need me."

"Governor?" Andiron, one of the guards, asked. "Should we stop him?"

"You see it? You really do?"

Andiron looked at me strangely. "Yes. Of course."

I sighed. I looked at the *Temptation* and tried to think. "Let it go," I told him. "Let it go."

I guess that after Peanut's death I felt that I had to do something. I needed to gain some (however grudging) respect from the jumpers, not to mention the jokers. And despite Tachyon's entreaties, the only thing I seemed to have accomplished with my dreams had been to make the penguin real. Several jokers reported seeing it moving through the caves.

A parlor trick. Bloat can pull a penguin from his hat. Great. Boy, will *that* scare the nats. Gosh, is *that* going to make Blaise tremble.

I needed action. I needed a symbol. I needed to feel that I was doing something.

I thought it time to make official what was already true in fact.

Kafka punched home the switch on the power strips. Arc lights flared with an audible snarling, and I was bathed in incandescent splendor. I watched the monitor as Kafka ticked off the seconds with his fingers. He jabbed a finger at me as the red light blinked on the video camera. In the monitor, the *Temptation* appeared in a slow pan.

I started talking. I had the script memorized. I'd practiced it for two days straight, making little changes here and there.

"Beautiful, isn't it?" I said, and heard my high voice reverberate through the sound system we'd bought back when we'd had money to play with. Across the monitor, St. Anthony was bedeviled by strange hordes, beaten by demons flying in the sky, tantalized by a seductress with her surreal following. "It's *The Temptation of St. Anthony*, if you're not familiar with the painting. Bosch is giving us the tale of Anthony of Egypt and how he was unable to function in his own society. He couldn't exist there, not unless he was the same as *they* were. So Anthony decided to retreat. He fled the worldly life and went into the desert. He made a place where he could be as he needed to be."

The camera pulled back from the painting and focused on my face, my plump-cheeked, pimply, fatboy face nearly lost in the folds of pasty flesh. The camera continued to zoom back, farther and farther, showing the gravid landscape of my body crammed into the lobby.

"Ain't it funny how your world always views evil as something misshapen or twisted or ugly? Like a joker, y'know. Funny. But to us, being that way is normal."

Panning now, the camera moving over the solemn joker faces in front of me and around the balcony...

"Your world treats jokers badly. That statement doesn't exactly surprise you, does it? Then it shouldn't surprise you that, hey, sometimes a joker will kick back one way or another. The only trouble is, whenever that happens, the violence ante just gets upped one more notch. The joker gets stomped again, only harder this time. We're tired of that game. Hey, it's one we can't win—*you've* got the power and there's nowhere for a joker to hide. You don't even have to brand us or legislate our movements to keep track of us; we wear our identification all the time. All you have to do is look."

Back to me: half a teenager glued onto a slug thing from a bad Japanese monster movie...

"I'm Bloat. This is the Rox, what most of you still call Ellis Island. I'm the governor of the Rox. I'm the one who keeps all of *you* out and lets the jokers in. What I have to say is pretty simple, really."

I licked my lips, which were suddenly dry. Bloatblack rippled down my sides; I tried to ignore the smell.

Now that it had come to it, I was scared. Reading about revolutions in history books never made me *feel* the experience—I always knew how it would end. Doing the same thing in role-playing games was simple: If my character died, I'd roll another and keep playing.

But here, now, I didn't know what would happen afterward. I'd already learned that—in this world—you only get one death.

"I'm the governor of the Rox," I repeated. Kafka winced at my blunder and pointed out my place in the cue cards alongside the camera. I stumbled over the next few lines, stuttering. "The . . . the Rox has become a joker's haven. A place away from the nats and hostile authorities. Here, *we're* normal. Here, we can be as we need to be. So what I'm saying now is just legitimizing something that's already a fact."

Tight in . . .

"I hereby declare the Rox to be a separate political entity. We declare ourselves independent of the state of New York and the United States. You have no authority over us. We're the joker homeland."

Around me, jokers burst into prolonged cheering. The camera swung around to show the celebration. I gestured to Kafka. The lights kicked off, and the video feed went dead. The loud jubilation of the jokers, my people, continued unabated. I could hear it here, could feel it going on all over the Rox. I looked down at Kafka, characteristically somber. *He* was thinking of the Astronomer again, of another stronghold that had been destroyed.

"How do you think that went over?" I asked him.

"We'll find out," he answered. "Won't we?"

While Night's Black Agents to Their Preys Do Rouse

II

Life in the USSA wasn't so bad. The variety of clothing wasn't great, and people tended to have a lot of moles and winkles and carbunkles on their faces—Shad hadn't realized how much cosmetic surgery had altered the looks of ordinary people back in his own New York—but on the other hand there weren't any jokers filling the streets with their agony and no homeless people wandering the streets, and the doctors at the Jean Jaurés Memorial Clinic had patched him up without asking for his insurance card first. There wasn't any wild card or AIDS or Jokertown or Takisians or Swarm, and there hadn't been a Second World War because the Socialists had taken power in Berlin in 1919 and hung onto it, no one had ever heard of Hitler, and there wasn't a cold war or atom bomb, and the Big Apple still bopped along in its own distinctive way.

Or maybe *bopped* wasn't the right word. The thing Shad found himself missing most of all about his own world was the music. Jazz had stopped evolving around 1940—big bands here in 1990 toured the country playing "Mood Indigo" and "Satin Doll" exactly the way Duke Ellington had in 1940, note for scripted note. Most of the musicians were black—jazz and blues were national cultural resources, forms of "folk art" created by the "Protected Negro Minority." Early rock and roll had been considered an offshoot of the blues and more or less restricted to black people—white performers were dis-

329

couraged because they were thought to be ripping off a
protected culture—and without the white audience, the form
had died.

No Charlie Parker. That was what Shad found hard to
adjust to. No John Coltrane. No Miles Davis. Dizzy Gillespie
fronted something called the Fort Wayne People's Folk Or-
chestra and blew some good licks, but it wasn't anywhere
near the same.

In the hospital he'd claimed amnesia—he just couldn't
remember who he was or why he'd been shot or why he was
dressed in a Halloween costume. The police hadn't believed
him—strip-searched him at gunpoint right in the emergency
room in fact, with the doctor and nurses protesting—but his
fingerprints didn't turn up in the Central Criminal Computer
Registry in Maryland (the computer search took three days
with the wretched equipment they had), and they had nothing to hold him on. They concluded he was an illegal immi-
grant, but by the time the authorities arrived to deport him,
he'd already slipped out into the night, clumsy in his arm-
and-shoulder cast, and within twenty-four hours he got himself a job maintaining the awful sound equipment in an illegal
samba club on the East Side. The stuff still had *tubes,* and it
needed all the help it could get.

Illegal samba club . . . and it wasn't the club that was
illegal, it was the music. Samba was *against the law*—Latin
music was considered subversive because South America
wasn't in the Socialist bloc but allied with Imperial Japan.
But despite the law, there were illegal samba clubs parked on
half the street corners in Harlem and all down the East
Side—this was, after all, the Big Apple, and in the Apple
you could find everything. If people couldn't have rock and
roll, they had to have *something*. And some of the club's
biggest patrons were the sons and daughters of high Farmer-
Labor party members, so the place was pretty safe.

Shad spent his free hours looking for Chalktalk. She'd
disappeared the second she got him into the E-room. When
he asked the hospital personnel, no one could remember
seeing her.

He still didn't know why she'd been following him. He
didn't know why she helped or whether she'd somehow
plotted the whole thing.

The attitudes toward him were different here, and it took
him a while on the street before he finally figured it out. In

his own New York, white people looked at him like he was a criminal, or anyway a potential criminal. There were some jewelry stores that wouldn't even unlock their doors for him, even after he waved fistfuls of money through the window. But the crime and homicide rates for blacks weren't particularly high here, and people looked at him differently—the Protected Negro Minority was a historically oppressed race struggling to elevate itself toward an equality that, despite everyone's best efforts, they seemed not to have reached.

In short, white people treated him as if he were mildly retarded—good-hearted and deserving of sympathy, but a little slow. It wasn't his fault if he needed a little extra help, of course—Forces of History were responsible, after all, not *people*—but all that meant was that nobody expected much from him.

After he figured out what was going on, Shad fit in well enough. He liked being patronized a lot less than he liked being feared, but he was still himself inside, whoever that was. The masks he wore were different, but they were still masks.

He still wore the night's mask best of all. He went for long walks after the club closed, quartering the parts of the city that, in another reality, were Jokertown. Music ran through his head, music that didn't even exist here, and pictures rolled through his memory, images of that portable concentration camp set up in the brownstone warehouse, the joker in the necktie with his head blown off, the hard con-boss look in Lisa Traeger's eyes, crates of gold and drugs, Nelson Dixon and Blaise exchanging high fives on the boardroom table...

The green hills of someplace he'd probably never see again.

Hanging them from lampposts, he figured, was too good for them.

He knew exactly where he wanted to go once he got home. And what he was going to do there.

On the long four A.M. walks, he plotted everything out, step by step. Impossible as it seemed.

And then one warm August night it became possible. There she was, sketching on the sidewalk with her baseball cap on the concrete next to her. Chalktalk. It happened too suddenly, too normally, for him to be surprised. So he crossed the street and put a Nikolai Bukharin five-dollar coin in her cap. Her picture was a daylight street scene with a gold-plated Empire State Building in the background. She glanced up with bright green eyes and gave him a strange little grin.

"Remember me?" he said. "I want to go home now."

She gave a weird little giggle that sent a chill up his spine. The she put her chalk in a little belt pouch, put her cap on her tangled dark hair, stood up suddenly, and grabbed his hand. Ignoring the little coin that rang in the gutter, she hauled him out of his crouch and down the next alleyway at a half run. Then she rudely pushed him into the wall and put her arms around him. A little keening sound came from her throat. Her hands pawed at him urgently. She started grinding her hips against his crotch like an old whore running on autopilot.

The smell of decaying garbage crawled down the back of Shad's throat. "Hey," Shad said, "are you serious, or what?"

Her lips drew back in a snarl. One hand clamped on his crotch, the other crooked in front of his face. Distant streetlights gleamed on sharp mother-of-pearl claws. Shad's balls tried to tunnel up to his eye sockets.

"Okay," Shad said. "Whatever you want. You mind if we get up in some fresh air? This garbage smell is gonna make me puke."

She didn't seem to care one way or the other, so he picked her up in his arms and walked up the wall to the roof. The action amused her, and she stroked his cock through his ill-made proletarian pants. Once atop the roof, he took off his black-market quilted jacket from Manchukuo and laid it down. The street artist dragged her Levi's off over her work boots, lay down on the jacket, and gave her strange little giggle again. He took off his shoes and pants, and dropped to his knees between her legs. The scent of rut reached him, and he felt a tide of blood flush his skin, blast through the roof of his skull, and carry him away to someplace else.

What followed was fast and brutal, and by the time the act was over, his clothes were in shreds, and there were a couple dozen cuts on his back. Panting for breath and faintly sick to his stomach, he felt as if he'd been hit by a truck loaded with pheromones.

Shad got painfully to his feet and started dragging his clothes on. The girl looked up at him gleefully and started rolling around on the roof, skinny pale legs and buttocks contrasting with the heavy coat she'd never taken off. He picked up his Manchukuoian jacket and shrugged it on. He felt a chill and stole a little heat from the still autumn night, his cloud of darkness rising above the building as he drank in scarce photons.

He wondered if this was what she'd had in mind all along, if this was why she'd been following him around. Maybe she had a crush on him.

Funny way to show a crush, though.

The street artist came up behind him, put her arms around his waist. She pressed herself very close behind him and began rocking back and forth, shifting her weight from one leg to the other. Her hands rubbed lower, pressing over his cock.

"I have an apartment near here," he said. "You mind if we go there, or does this have to happen out of doors?"

She didn't appear to care one way or another. Shad picked her up, covered them both with darkness, and went straight-line, up and over buildings, till he came to his own illegal loft. He snapped on the light for which he stole electricity from Peoples' Edison. The street artist was already on the bed, legs parted, arms stretched out.

Shad looked down at the naked vulva and the skinny legs in their heavy boots. Little stones from the flat tar roof were still clinging to her skin. "Not much time for romance in your life, huh?" he said. He bent down, began undoing bootlaces. "Let's at least get these off, okay?"

The second act was only a little less frenzied than the first, and afterward Shad lay facedown on the bed while she carefully licked the blood from the wounds she'd clawed into him. It had become obvious by now that she didn't bathe very often. He got her into his shower and scrubbed her down while she made little bubbling sounds and did a kind of dance, arms over her head, spinning around and around on her toes while the warm water splashed down around her.

When he handed her one of his threadbare proletarian towels, she raised it to her nose and took a suspicious sniff before she used it. Naked, her hair wet, her thin body looked maybe all of twelve years old. Great, Shad thought, now he'd added pedophilia to his list of crimes.

He took his billfold out of his pocket and took out the photo he'd carefully cut out of a 1988 issue of the *New York Herald and Worker* that he'd found in the library. He showed it to her. "This is where I'd like to go," he said. "Ellis Island. The Rox. Okay?"

She took the picture, looked at it without interest, then handed it back to him. She climbed into his narrow bed, curled up, and closed her eyes.

He sat down on the edge of the cot and looked down at her. Her body was covered with scars and calluses, and there was a big yellow bruise on one shoulder. What looked like a long knife slash ran down the side of one thigh. Shad traced the scar with his finger, and sadness welled up the back of his throat.

"Shit, girl," he said, "you don't have to live like this. Even in *my* world we can find somebody to take care of you. Hell, *I'll* take care of you. It doesn't matter that you can't talk." He looked up at her. "You understand me? I'll take care of you, okay? Back in the world, I've got more money than I know what to do with. We can live like royalty. Anyplace you want, anything you want. Okay?"

The street artist was asleep.

He curled up next to her, spoon-style, and tried to work out exactly what it was he'd just proposed, taking care of a mute feral joker girl whose talents seemed confined to chalk-sketching and indiscriminate animal sex. This would not, he concluded, be the sort of relationship of which Social Services would approve.

Other consequences occurred to him. If this was her usual mode of sexual contact, she'd probably picked up any number of diseases, some of which were known only by acronyms, some of which might be from other worlds. Maybe he ought to be soaking his dick in alcohol. And if he'd managed to get her pregnant—well, both parents were wild cards, and that meant a 100 percent certainty that the kid would inherit the bent wild card DNA, which meant a 99 percent chance of jokerhood or death when the virus manifested.

He wondered how much sadder this could get.

He found out later, sometime the next morning, when the street artist woke up and elbowed him awake. She pushed him over on his back and started rubbing her crotch against his dick. He was hard almost instantly, and she reached down to insert him as casually as if she were han-dling a bar of soap. Her intent cat's eyes were fixed intently on his. His vision was better than hers, reached into more spectra.

She leaned over him when she came, hips pumping blindly over his groin. Her claws gripped his mattress, punctured his sheets. Her mouth was open, and strange croaking sounds came out. He could look past her teeth and see, glowing with IR heat, the stub of a tongue that ended in a mass of scar tissue.

Someone had cut her tongue out.

She fell asleep instantly, her head on his chest. Shad wanted to cry.

Take care of her? What a joke.

Hours later, he awoke to the scratching of chalk. He opened gummed eyes and saw the street artist back in her clothes, drawing something on the particleboard floor. A plastic plate near her hand held a half-eaten sandwich made from some Polish sausage he had in his icebox.

He looked at the clock and saw it was late afternoon. He dressed, had a sandwich, and watched her work.

She was drawing a cavern—irregular walls, stalactites, strange subterranean gleams. The sketch occupied the whole floor, and large parts weren't finished yet.

"The Rox," Shad said. He pointed at his clipping again. "Ellis Island. You understand?"

She looked up at him and wrinkled up her face, then went back to her sketch.

Shad gazed bleakly into a future in which he was dragged from one world to another by this child, used for sex in one venue after another. Love-slave of the multiverse. Wonderful.

It was night before Chalktalk was finished. Shad put on his darkest clothes, black Kenyan cords, navy shirt, the boots he'd come in, his quilted Manchukuoian jacket. If they were going spelunking, it was likely to get cold. He made two packages of food, wrapped them in tinfoil, stuffed one in his pocket and gave the other to Chalktalk. He thought about getting flashlights and decided it would be a worthwhile investment. He went to the store and bought two big electric lanterns.

He stepped up behind her, looked at the growing picture, put his hand on her shoulder. She gave him an irritated look and shrugged the hand off.

Looked like the romance had gone out of their relationship.

The picture deepened, the third dimension dropping away, receding to a glittering cavern.

The girl took his hand, and reality fell away.

Darkness, darkness entire. Shad felt right at home.

He flicked on the lantern, and Robert Fallon Penn

lunged out of the night, garrote in hand, smiling his twisted blood-flecked smile.

Neil was ten years old when he'd last seen Penn. Penn's partner, Stan Barker, was sodomizing Neil from behind while Penn played with his garrote, putting on the pressure till he started to black out, then sportively easing up, prolonging the agony a little longer.

He, his father, his mother, and his little sister had spent the weekend under torture, and Neil was the last one left alive. Stan Barker had just cut his father's throat, and Shad remembered how slippery the floor had been, how his hands and knees slid in the darkening wetness while Penn jerked on his throat with his wire and Barker clutched at his hips...

And now Bob Penn was back, leering at him, blood flaking off his lips because he'd bitten off Mrs. Carter's nipples. Lightning burned through Shad's nerves. He gave a scream and swung the lantern. Somehow Penn avoided injury.

Chalktalk looked at him impatiently. She grabbed his sleeve and tried to pull him toward Penn.

"*No!*" Shad yelled. He pulled Chalktalk out of danger, flinging her to the ground, and launched himself at Penn.

His fists and feet went clear through the man. Shad could hear Stan Barker's giggle and knew that Penn's partner was somewhere out there in the dark. Shad screamed in anger and terror, and tried to drain the heat from Penn's body. There was scarcely any there, no more than if Penn had been a ghost.

Chalktalk picked herself up and walked impatiently through Penn's body, then turned back to Shad and shrugged.

Sanity wedged its way into Shad's panicked mind. He reached out, passed a sword hand through Penn's body.

Chalktalk turned away and padded on, her bright lantern held high.

Shad passed his hand through Penn again. His heart drummed against his ribs. There was a deep ache in his throat where the police had given him the tracheotomy that saved his life.

Penn wasn't there. He was an illusion.

Shad watched closely, and he saw that the Penn illusion didn't seem very lifelike—it was huge and distorted, a sixteen-year-old maniac seen through the eyes of his ten-year-old victim.

Chalktalk's lantern was fading into the distance. Shad took a deep breath and followed, his spine tingling as he turned his back on the killer of his family.

Penn didn't follow.

Shad caught up to Chalktalk. His hands were trembling, and his voice shook. "Where the hell are we?" he asked.

Chalktalk said nothing, natch. Shad looked around.

He was in Carlsbad Caverns, or a reasonable facsimile thereof. Tall formations, lightless passages, the constant drip of water. Formations where illusions of mass murderers lurked. Shad wondered if they were under the high New Mexico desert, until he saw the graffiti, spray-painted on a bright vein of quartz: *JUMP THE RICH*.

Somehow, Shad knew, he was right where he wanted to be.

Then there was the sound of clattering footsteps, the clank of weaponry. The squawk of a walkie-talkie. It didn't sound much like an illusion.

The locals knew he was here. Shad turned to Chalktalk.

"Go back a ways, okay? These are some bad people coming. Maybe you better make a sketch and get yourself out of here."

He looked up at him with shadowed dark eyes, then shrugged, squatted, reached for her chalk.

She walked up the wall, covered himself with darkness, and moved forward along the ceiling. Putting himself between Chalktalk and pursuit.

Shad turned off his lantern and navigated on IR. He entered a chamber twenty feet high, moved forward between limestone columns, and saw jokers, half a dozen, all wearing some kind of informal war-surplus battledress, most carrying M-16 assault rifles. Kafka led them, unmistakable in his brown chitin, holding a walkie-talkie and a four-battery flashlight. He wasn't carrying a weapon. Even in his haste he was careful not to touch any of the other jokers.

Shad remembered he had some kind of contamination phobia.

High-powered flashlights swept the confined area of the stair. Shad deepened the black cloak around him and waited.

"No sight of him yet," Kafka reported.

"He's right there." A high-pitched, almost comical voice came out of the hissing walkie-talkie. "He's *watching* you. And he recognized you from somewhere."

Watching you. The thought rolled through Shad's mind. Someone knew he was here, someone who couldn't see him . . . Maybe the person who had called Penn into being.

Shad tried to make his mind blank.

"He's onto me," the high-pitched voice warned. "And he can *hear* you."

Kafka jumped wildly, his flashlight beam dancing. Then he scuttled under the staircase, put his back to the wall. "You and you! Over there!"

Two jokers charged with weapons ready, the sound of their boots echoing.

"He's *right there*," the high-pitched voice said. "He's *right near you*."

"That's right," said Shad. He kicked loose from his perch, dropped to Kafka's side, snatched the flashlight. He shone the flash upward into his own face and let the darkness fall away from the part of his body facing Kafka, so that Kafka could see his face and upper body. He let Kafka see his pose, standing upright with his right arm horizontal and bent, hand under his chin, the edge of his hand pressing against his throat.

"Who will help the widow's son?" he asked.

Rifles clattered as they were brought to bear. But Shad was standing too close to Kafka for them to fire, and the other jokers couldn't see what was going on.

Kafka's astonishment was clear, even on his inhuman face. He looked frantically left and right, then leaned closer, his eyes glittering in the light of the flash. "Who are you?"

"A stranger going to the West, to search for that which was lost."

"Where do you come from?"

"From the East."

"What is your task?"

"To trample the Lilies underfoot."

Kafka goggled at him. Shad gave him a severe look. The most difficult trick, he'd found, was to speak all this nonsense with an absolutely straight face.

"Will you not aid me, brother?" he asked. "In the name of the widow's son?"

"*Who are you?*"

"In the Brotherhood, my name is Gaius Gracchus." He pretended to lose patience. "Do I have to do the fucking handshake, or what?"

Kafka seemed puzzled. "I seem to remember the name."

"I've been away for a long time."

"Kafka! Kafka!" The jokers were shuffling, trying to play their flashlights through the darkness that Shad had set up between them. "Are you okay?"

"I'm all right." Kafka tried to peer out past Shad. His mouth parts worked nervously. "What do you want of me?" he asked.

"Nothing. I need to know where the jumpers are quartered."

"Kafka!" The high-pitched voice shouted from the walkie-talkie. "There aren't any Egyptian Masons anymore! You know that as well as anyone. *He's just trying to trick you!*"

"That is the governor, I take it?" Shad said. "I have no business with him. Just with the jumpers. Will you let me pass or not?"

Kafka hesitated. Shad expanded the darkness that surrounded him, eating photons, surrounding Kafka with night. The joker guards behind began to scuttle backward from the expanding sphere.

"Kafka," said the governor. "Bring him to me. I will give him an interview."

"I don't know that I need an interview," Shad said. "I don't know that we have a lot to say to each other."

"Yes we do, Shad," said the high voice.

Surprise rolled through Shad's mind. No one called him that.

"Yes, I know your name for yourself," the governor said. "And I know more than that, including a few things *you* don't know." A small pause. "And we have to discuss your friend, little Chalktalk."

"Who?"

The voice turned impatient. "Governor Bloat knows all and sees all, my son. I know you didn't come alone, and I have another group of guards watching your friend. I *don't* think you have time to interfere with them before they follow any orders I should care to give, particularly if the order is swift and violent."

Indecision fluttered through Shad's mind. He'd been spinning this out with the intention of giving Chalktalk a chance to get away.

Images of Barker and Penn floated through his mind.

"How do I know this isn't a trap?" he asked.

"If it is, you can kill me. I know it's within your capabilities. It's a small island, and I'm—" a strange little high-pitched giggle, "I'm not exactly built for running."

Kafka told his troops to return to their quarters. Shad let the darkness fall from Kafka's path. The joker led him down a lengthy stone corridor, then up a surprising staircase, all pink-veined marble like something out of *Phantom of the Opera*. Once up the stairs, they were in a building. The walls were covered in layers of flaking white paint, and there were doors on either side.

Ellis Island. Beneath which, Shad knew, there was not supposed to be an extensive cavern complex. Things had obviously changed around here.

A penguin, wearing a funnel for a hat, appeared from one door, made a graceful figure eight on its ice skates, disappeared through another door.

Shad stared. He'd hung out in Jokertown for a long time, but he'd never seen anything like that. And it was on *ice skates*. There wasn't even any ice here.

Another giggle came from the walkie-talkie. "Brother Shad, you ain't seen nothing yet!"

Kafka led him out into a balcony overlooking a large hall filled with—well, filled with the governor, the sluglike body gleaming with moisture, dappled with oozing black matter. Bloat's smell clawed its way up the back of Shad's throat. His arms, shoulders, and head were those of a boy of maybe eighteen. He looked as if the slug were in the process of eating him.

"Welcome," the governor said, "to the Rox."

"Thank you." Shad walked up the wall, then stepped onto the ceiling. He strolled inverted across the plaster till he hung over Bloat's little head. Bloat's eyes tracked him as he moved, even though he was in darkness.

Kafka stayed behind on the balcony, pacing nervously. With all Kafka's phobias, Shad wondered, how could he stand even to be in the same room with his boss?

"You seem to have given poor Kafka a crisis in loyalties," Bloat said. "He thought all that was long behind him."

"Once a Mason, always a Mason."

"He knows you were supposed to have been killed. He fears you might be one of the Astronomer's surviving agents. That you might kill him."

Kafka's mouth parts worked as he listened to this.

"If I'd wanted him dead," Shad said, "he'd be dead." He wondered if the firing squad was lined up outside the doors, waiting for him to leave.

"If we're going to talk," Shad said, "let's do it."

Bloat's look was mild. "Why are you here, Shad?"

"My plan is to snap the neck of every jumper in the place."

"And get Tachyon out if you can. I can read that."

"Then why did you ask the question?" Sharply.

"I think," Bloat said, "that I'll let you do one, and not the other."

"Which one? Which other? And how could you stop me if I wanted to do both?"

"Your notion of killing the jumpers has a certain attractiveness, I must admit. And if you could get Blaise—he's their leader, you see, and a very disturbed person—that would be . . . well, it would end any number of problems."

"I'll get him first thing, if you like."

"He's not on the Rox at the moment, unfortunately. He gets restless, and he's off bringing in supplies."

"I can wait."

"For God's sake, Governor!" Kafka's voice cut the silence. "Why are you *bargaining* with him? *Do* something!"

"I don't have a whole lot of choice, do I?" For once, Bloat sounded like a sulky adolescent. "Considering that my prime minister hasn't quite worked out which side he's on." Then Bloat looked up at Shad, his eyes glittering. "There are over a hundred jumpers on this island, Shad. Can you really kill them all? *Could* you kill them all?"

Shad hesitated. *Kids*, he thought. *Not all of them killers, not all of them crazy.*

"There aren't enough lampposts to hang them all from," Bloat said. "That's your usual method, isn't it? But a cold-blooded massacre—that's *not* your style. Never was. You just start the ball rolling, and the bad guys kill each other." Bloat gave a sour laugh. "It may happen yet. This is not a happy island. Not happy at all." His eyes narrowed as he looked at Shad. "You *think* you're a killer, though, don't you."

"Cut the shit, Governor. Say what you've got to say."

Bloat's look grew more searching. Shad felt cold crawling along his nerves. "You *think* you're a berserker. You've *gone* berserk; therefore, you must . . ." Bloat shook his head. "You've been tampered with."

Shad gave a laugh. "Believe what you like, Bloat."

"Your mind—it shares some mental characteristics with some of our other citizens. Shroud, File, Video, Peanut. Even the Oddity. And I've talked to Tachyon, and he knows..." The high-pitched voice trailed away.

Shad's nerves wailed at him to get away, kill Bloat, turn his head into an ice cube, and fight his way out before Bloat could spring whatever trap he was setting up.

"I'm getting impatient, Governor," he said.

"Someone has tampered with you," Bloat said. "Someone has turned you into a berserker—has *made* you kill."

Anger lanced through Shad. "I advise you to stay out of my head!" he snapped.

Bloat paid no attention. "It's very subtle. The individual doing it was moving very quietly, just making little alterations. Masking your inhibitors, accenting the violence, the rage..." Bloat's face was intent, absorbed, his expression almost ecstatic. "Yes, he's been at you, all right. It's almost invisible, but I can see the fingerprint, now that I'm sensitive to it. The same individual who drove Peanut to madness, who inflamed the Oddity's self-loathing and hatred..." Bloat's eyes bored into Shad's heart. "That wasn't you who strung up that first man. Or the next few, either. That wasn't *your* ecstacy—that was some filthy pervert having an orgasm in your mind."

Shad's mouth went dry. "Bullshit," he said. "Nobody's been with me all this time."

"This is the wild card!" Bloat said. "Who says it can't be operated by remote control?"

"So who was it, asshole? Give me a name."

"What is your grudge against the jumpers, exactly?" Bloat snarled. "*I* know—they stole your self. But it was only your body they took. What will you do with the man who tampered with your mind? Who sent you on a fifteen-year murder spree, because he had you convinced *that* was who you were?"

Shad hesitated. Then a cold resolve filled him. "He would deserve death," he said.

"Probably. The man has certainly killed. But *you* don't have to kill him, of course. That's your choice now. You don't have to do any of this."

"Give me his name."

Bloat narrowed his eyes. "Let's make a deal, Shad. The name in exchange for an understanding."

Shad looked down at him. "Talk."

"I do not like having Tachyon imprisoned here. It's an embarrassment. Tachyon has been a great friend to jokers over the years. She was brought here without my permission, and if you take her off, I—"

"*Her?*"

Bloat hesitated, then spoke. "Tachyon is at present residing within the body of a sixteen-year-old girl." The words seemed to come with difficulty, and Bloat's cheeks seemed hot. He spoke quickly, as if he hoped Shad wouldn't notice. "Here's the deal, Shad. You spare the jumpers. Take Tachyon off the island. Prime Minister Kafka will let you have one of our speedboats. And I'll give you the name."

"And if someone tries to stop me?"

Bloat thought for a moment, then sighed. "Do what you have to do."

"And Chalktalk?"

Bloat giggled again. "She left the island a long time ago, quite in her own fashion. I wouldn't have molested her, in any case. She's been here before, and—"

"And she's a joker."

Bloat's voice was sharp. "She's a joker who has been badly hurt. Which,"—eyes narrowing—"I see you understand."

"You know the story?"

"No. Her mind is opaque to me. But I can guess. Your concern for her speaks well of you. Before Senator Hartmann turned you into a murderer, you probably would have turned out well."

Shad was stunned. *Hartmann* . . .

Hartmann. The only person he'd had regular contact with for years.

"You gave me the name," Shad said, "but I haven't said yes to the deal."

"Yes, you did," Bloat said. "You just never said it out loud."

Shad was silent.

"Kafka will have a boat waiting for you on the east side," Bloat went on. "A Zodiac—you'll get wet, but you'll move fast. You don't want to head for Jersey City—the authorities have set up too many searchlights, and you'll be spotted."

"Searchlights won't see me."

"They have radars out there, too. Hooked to missile batteries, Kafka tells me, and to something called the 20mm

Vulcan Air Defense System. Which sounds pretty intimidating to me."

Shad hesitated. He could absorb photons in the electromagnetic spectrum as well as the visual and infrared, but his control was lessened when he was dealing with something he couldn't see.

"I'll have to raise an alarm sooner or later," Bloat said, dismissing the thought for him. "I'm supposed to be omnipotent that way. But I'll tell the jumpers you ran for Brooklyn. They'll search in that direction."

"And where will I really go? Manhattan?"

"Too well patrolled by the coast guard and air force. Head south, toward Staten Island. You should be able to come ashore in one of the Bayonne terminals without difficulty."

Shad thought about it.

"That's settled, then," Bloat said. "Follow my friend the penguin. He'll lead you straight to Tachyon." Shad hesitated. "Move fast," Bloat said, "before word of your presence gets out."

Move fast. The best piece of advice he had all night.

The penguin skated into the room, gliding effortlessly on the ceiling. Dark smoke that smelled of brimstone poured from his funnel cap. The penguin cruised a nonchalant circle around Shad, then made a silent glissade toward the Administration Building entrance.

Shad's nerves wailed an alert, but there wasn't any ambush waiting. Shad followed the penguin out of the building and to the infirmary, passing behind a joker sentry without alerting him. The western horizon glowed: huge searchlights set up on the Jersey shore had the entire island in their grip. Breakers boomed in the distance. A cold Atlantic wind cut through his light Manchukuoian jacket.

The penguin led Shad to the door of the infirmary and passed through without opening it, leaving a faint whiff of brimstone behind. Shad opened the door—heavy institutional steel pitted by salt water—and stepped inside. Music slammed from off-white corridor walls, and Shad heard laughter somewhere, but no one was in sight. There were no guards, and no security seemed in place.

The penguin was gliding up a staircase to Shad's right. Shad followed up two flights. The Dead Kennedys filled the staircase with exuberant hardcore. On the floor above were roughly finished rooms right under the eaves. A white boy lay asleep on a mildew-eaten couch, his boom box and a space heater plugged into a thick orange extension cord. A half-eaten bowl of rice and Vienna sausages lay on the floor. An M-16 was propped on the wall.

Some sentry.

Okay, Shad thought, *I'll try it Bloat's way.*

He ate photons and called the darkness down, filling the room with night, then snatched the boy out of sleep. He broke one arm, then the other, then whispered into the boy's ear.

"Okay, kid," he said, "here's how I see it. I don't want to kill you, and you don't want to die. So lead me to Tachyon and I'll let you live, okay?"

The boy screamed, a full-throated yell of imbecile terror that echoed louder than the Dead Kennedys. Shad smashed the boy's head against a wall until the screaming stopped, then dropped the boy to the floor.

Hell. That sort of thing always worked in the movies.

Most of the rooms held only supplies. There was only one door that was locked, and that was with a simple wooden bar. Shad threw up the bar and pushed the door open.

God, she seemed young. And tiny, barely reaching Shad's breastbone. Chill sorrow rolled through him as he realized she was pregnant.

The darkness rained away as Shad let Tachyon look at him.

"I'm Black Shadow," Shad said, "and you're outta here."

"Bloat told me." Her voice was soft. Maybe once she'd been pretty, he thought. Now she looked like a war refugee.

"He didn't say you were pregnant. Follow me."

She followed him out the door, her eyes downcast. She had wrapped a blanket around her shoulders, but the shoulders were slumped. She wasn't anything like Shad's memories of Tachyon. Shad couldn't picture her as anything but a lost girl.

Somebody had tried to break this child, and probably succeeded.

Apparently no one had heard the sentry's scream. Shad led Tachyon down the two flights of stairs, then looked cautiously into the corridor. No one in sight. He opened the door to the outside and stepped out.

A dark-haired young woman stood there, holding an M-16 casually at port arms as she walked tiredly home from guard duty. Shad recognized her as the one who had left her eye in Shelley's hotel room. She had both eyes now, and they narrowed as she saw Shad, without his cloak of darkness, coming toward her. She worked the bolt of the gun and pointed it at him.

Shad stepped for her and struck out, one medium-force punch to the face with his left, a grab for her gun with the right. He intended nothing more than to stun her for a short time and take her weapon.

Instead, he knocked her block off.

Shad's nerves gave a white-hot wail as the woman's head left her shoulders. It struck the ground, where both eyes popped out, then rolled, parts scattering—an ear, the jaw, the tongue.

The body toppled, and one arm came off, but nothing ceased to move—the legs and arms flailed, even the arm that had come adrift. The eyes, once they'd stopped bouncing, swiveled and seemed to try to focus. When Shad had yanked the gun away, one hand came off at the wrist and clung to the gunstock. A finger held down the trigger. The gun leaped as it fired.

Shad's stomach queased as he tore the hand away. Fingers fell like snowflakes. He dropped the rifle, picked Tachyon up in his arms, and ran, trying not to step on any of the woman's parts.

Tachyon's blanket snapped around them in the cold Atlantic wind. Shad heard running footsteps behind.

"*Durg!*" Tachyon shrieked. "Look out!"

Shad didn't know what a 'durg' was. He turned. A squat little man was racing after them, twenty yards behind, and was clearly gaining.

"He's a Morakh!" Tachyon said. "Be careful!"

Shad had no clearer idea of what a Morakh was than a durg, but in view of Tachyon's urgency, it seemed serious. He slowed and called a cloud of darkness into being around the Morakh, then watched with his infrared sense as the short man stumbled and fell sprawling. Shad laughed, then accelerated toward the harbor. The island was tiny, and he needed to get off it before too much alarm was raised.

He heard footfalls behind, slower this time, then accelerating. He looked over his shoulder once more and saw the short man gliding purposefully through the darkness. He was moving his head back and forth as if straining to hear something over the sound of his own footsteps.

Shad put Tachyon down. "Head for the harbor," he whispered. "I'll catch up with you."

"Careful." Tachyon swayed. "Morakhs are deadly. More deadly than you can possibly imagine."

"So am I, far as that goes."

Tachyon began to run, clumsy in her off-balance body.

The short man's head jerked upward at the sound of their words, and then a smile spread across his features, and he began to trot purposefully toward Shad. He wore jeans, heavy boots, and a dark muscle shirt over his formidable, wide torso. His hair was ash-blond. He looked like the shortest Mr. America in history.

Shad planted himself in the man's path and ate heat from the Morakh's frame. He had absorbed a lot of photons since his arrival on the Rox and his efficiency wasn't great. The Morakh slowed a scant five yards away, and anger twisted his features.

"Who will not face Durg at-Morakh bo Zabb in a fair fight?" he demanded.

"I won't," Shad said, and started to eat more photons. But the Morakh moved with incredible speed as soon as he heard Shad's words. Astonishment flared in Shad's mind as he ducked a ferocious punch; then a spin kick slammed against his thigh, bringing pain crackling along his nerves. Shad let the kick's momentum help whirl him away. He hit the ground and rolled under a flurry of kicks and punches, then rose to his feet in a fighting stance. He'd lost control of his cloud of darkness, and it dissipated. Durg closed with him, fists and feet reaching.

Durg was clearly faster and stronger than a normal human. But then, so was Shad. And Shad had the longer reach.

Durg charged, trying to get inside Shad's guard. Shad sidestepped the rush and caught Durg in the solar plexus with a wheel kick, then stepped to the side and rear again, spun, lifted a rear kick, caught Durg in the solar plex yet again with a force that jarred Shad's spine.

Durg grunted but kept coming. Shad spun again as the range closed, lashing out with a backfist followed by a reverse punch that landed square in the center of Durg's face. It felt as if Shad had punched a bridge abutment.

Durg fired a short chopping wheel kick off his front foot. Shad blocked with both arms, but the kick knocked him twelve inches sideways in any case. Durg bored in and followed up, fists and elbows flashing. Shad managed to block most of the strikes, but one punch was only partly deflected, and a bolt of agony crackled up Shad's left side. He could feel his ribs bending as they absorbed the punch.

Shad clawed for the shorter man's eyes, then slammed an elbow into Durg's face and drove the Morakh back. Pain rang through Shad's arm. It was like trying to shove a cement truck.

Durg blinked blood from his eyes, and in that instant Shad focused his wild card and drew more heat from him. Durg shuddered, but his fighting instinct was still to attack. Shad kicked him full force in the knee as he came on, but it slowed Durg only slightly, and the Takisian fired a glancing heel hook by way of reply that rattled Shad's teeth. Shad blocked one strike after another, pulling more heat from the alien, watching with cold incredulity as the Morakh blanched but kept on coming.

Somewhere in Shad's mind flashed the memory that Takis was a wintery planet. They *liked* the cold there.

He kept eating photons anyway. He was out of ideas.

Durg put his head down and charged. Pain crackled through Shad's ribs again as the Morakh's head thudded into his torso. Shad was driven back, and then his injured leg folded, and he went down with the Morakh on top. Despairingly he grabbed for all the heat he could. The Morakh's hands wrapped Shad's throat, and the memory of Robert Penn and his garrote rose like bile. Shad slammed desperate palm heels into Durg's temples.

And then the Morakh shuddered and collapsed. His skin was ice-cold. Shad rolled the heavy body off and rose. Something was grinding along his left shoulder and back. If he was lucky, he'd just ripped a lot of muscle tissue and ligament: otherwise, he'd lost some ribs. He limped for the harbor.

Tachyon stood with Kafka and one of his joker soldiers, standing on the pier, watching a Zodiac inflatable boat roll dangerously in the tidal surge twelve feet below.

Shots split the air. They were far off.

"Some of my soldiers," Kafka said. "Bloat is telling them you're over on the south side."

Shad looked down at the wooden ladder, slippery with

spray, leading to the boat lurching at the end of its painter. He picked up Tachyon gently, and his ribs screamed in shock. He ignored them, and went down the ladder. A wave soaked his legs below the knee as he waited for the Zodiac to move closer to the ladder, and then he gathered his legs under him and jumped. His injured leg put them a little off course, but Shad landed on the soft rubber bottom of the boat, caught his balance against the surging movement, eased Tachyon to a position near the bow, and jumped aft to the outboard. He peered at it, reached uncertainly for the pull-start.

"There's a self-starter," Kafka called.

Shad found it, grateful not to have to torque his torso after all he'd been through. "Thanks, brother," he said. "In the name of the widow's son."

He started the engine, revved it, put it in gear. Kafka dropped the painter.

They were off.

Kafka didn't wave good-bye. The Zodiac breasted every wave and crashed heavily into the troughs with a thud that rattled more pain from Shad's ribs. A frigid Atlantic wind made a mockery of the August night. Spray drenched both passengers, but at least the boat moved fast. Shad surrounded the boat with darkness, taking in all the warmth he could. He headed out into the bay until the lights of the coast guard facility on Governor's Island began looking too bright, then swung south.

If there was any pursuit, he never saw it.

The Statue of Liberty glowed on the right, its torch seeming to twinkle in the rushing air. Shad let the darkness fall away from them so that Tachyon could see.

"There," he said. "Your lucky sign for tonight."

Tachyon gazed out in wonder. Her long blond hair whipped out in the wind. Shad couldn't tell whether her face sparkled with spray or tears.

"Liberty," Shad said.

The lights of Bayonne and the south Jersey City docks loomed to their front. Then there was something else, a black pillar rising out of the darkness dead ahead. It made a sucking, growling noise.

"Look out!" Tachyon shouted, and Shad threw the rudder over. The Zodiac skated over a roller, then fell. The pillar passed astern. Shad could see something rotating on top.

He dropped the cloak of darkness around the boat. Tachyon gazed at him with blinded eyes. "What was that?"

"I'm not sure. I think maybe it was the snorkel of a submarine."

"*The what?*"

"A snorkel, along with the periscopes and radars. The old-time diesel subs used to have to surface for air, see, till the Germans invented the snorkel during World War Two. Now they just put the snorkel up and breathe through that. But I don't know if we've got any diesel subs left in the fleet."

"Who'd put a submarine here?"

"The Russians. If we're lucky."

"In New York harbor?"

"You'd never get a nuclear sub over Sandy Hook—too big. But maybe a small diesel." Something cold climbed Shad's spine. "Look," he said, "this is too weird. If that *was* a submarine, they're listening to our prop on their hydrophones, and they heard us leave from Ellis Island. If they've got their radio mast up, they could be telling other people we're here. I don't think I want to get close to the Military Ocean Terminal in Bayonne. There might be some kind of military op going on. I'm going farther south."

"Where?"

"I don't want to get out into the Atlantic. You'd freeze to death out there. I think I'll head for the Kill Van Kull. We can get lost in the commercial traffic and try to get ashore either in Jersey or Staten Island."

Tachyon said nothing, just huddled deeper into her blanket.

The Zodiac spent most of its time in the trough of waves, and Shad's visibility was not ideal, but he scanned the bay when the boat was on the crests and saw two big coast guard cutters heading for them, searchlights panning the water. Both were right on target. It *had* been a sub, then, and it was guiding the cutters right to them.

Shad zigzagged—north, then south—then increased speed and dashed between the two boats. They were wearing dark wartime camouflage instead of their normal white paint. One of them was using a loud-hailer, but Shad didn't understand a word.

The boats seemed to lose track of him after that—probably distance affecting the sub's ability to track his outboard propeller.

Its entrance white with swirling tidal foam, the brightly lit commercial channel of the Kill Van Kull gaped ahead. Somewhere a siren whooped, its sound torn by the wind. A helicopter came out of nowhere, a strange insectlike thing, and passed directly overhead at high speed.

Shad looked up in surprise to see an odd-looking ball-bearing-shaped turret on its nose, a stubby muzzle questing left and right as if sniffing for a target. The rotor downdraft turned the water white.

Tachyon, blind, turned an alarmed face upward. Shad curved toward the Staten Island shore, his head swiveling wildly as he tried to keep the chopper in view. The helicopter banked and came back again, heading straight for him.

They've got IR capability, Shad realized, and he tried to eat every bit of heat in the air, soak up every photon. Tachyon gave a convulsive shiver inside her blanket.

The turret gun fired. Water flew skyward ten yards off the port bow.

Too close. Shad swung the Zodiac madly to starboard.

Whatever happened to the rules of engagement? he wondered.

The chopper blasted overhead. It had stubby wings and what looked like jet-engine pods.

The Zodiac bounced madly in the tidal swirl as it entered the Kill Van Kull. The chopper turned again, heading right for them. Shad wondered frantically if they had radar that could detect them.

"Fuck this!" he shouted to Tachyon. "I'm just gonna surrender, okay? Don't tell 'em who I am. And I'll slip out of custody when I can."

Tachyon looked blindly in his direction and gave a nod.

The chopper fired, rockets this time, one blinding-white streak after another. Concussion slammed the boat. A world of white water fell like Niagara into the boat. The Zodiac kicked high from an impact, and Shad found himself flying, tumbling through the air, air blown from his lungs by the power of an explosion. . . .

Freezing water boiled around him. He screamed and held his hands over his ears as more concussions battered him. Water poured down his throat. He kicked out, broke surface, shook water from his eyes. . . .

The boat was careening on, heading for Bayonne with no one at the tiller. Shad caught a glimpse of flying blond hair,

heard a distant scream, and then the turret gun opened up
again, filling the water with white fountains.

A wave exploded over his head, and when Shad came
up, he couldn't see the boat. He sucked heat and light from
the water and struck out for the shore. The roar of the
chopper faded.

The water was frigid and the swim endless, but the tidal
swirl was heading in the right direction and helped. Finally
Shad climbed up a deserted pier on Staten Island, and as the
breath rasped in his lungs, as he looked out on the Kill Van
Kull from a position much higher than a wave-tossed boat, he
saw what it was all about, why they'd been so desperate to
stop anyone leaving the Rox.

Ranked in the sheltered waters of the Kill Van Kull,
hidden from Ellis Island by the sprawling turmoil of Bayonne,
were quiet rows of ships in wartime camouflage. Landing
ships, supply craft, a small helicopter carrier with its craft
parked on deck. The helicopter that had attacked him was
only one of several patrolling the ship channel. Trucks, their
headlights lined up as far as Shad could see, were offloading
combat-ready troops on the piers, and the soldiers were
marching onto the landing ships.

They were going for the Rox, and they were going soon.

Shad stood dripping on the pier, watched the soldiers
moving up the gangplanks, felt his ribs ache, and tried to add
up wins and losses.

He'd been to the Rox and back, but the person he'd
come to rescue was drowned or blown to bits. He'd broken
the jumpers' extortion scheme, but the police weren't going
to forget what his jumped body had done to them. He'd lost
Chalktalk, and he'd lost Shelley, and the jumpers hadn't lost
anybody.

Fuck it. He'd lost. There wasn't any winning in it.

And Shelley had lost, and Tachyon, and if the invasion
force was anything to judge by, so had the jumpers, and
Kafka, and Bloat.

Time to hid and figure out what he was going to do next.

Shad turned and limped down the pier, and the night
raised its welcoming mask and swallowed him.

Lovers

V

Tachyon lay on the oil-stained sands of the New Jersey shore and vomited up what felt like several gallons of polluted water. No Takisian is a good swimmer—the home world was too cold to encourage that particular sport—and in her present condition Tachyon was about as lithe as a wading hippo. So she was amazed and delighted to find herself once more safely ashore, however dirty and depressing the vista might be.

She rolled onto her back and waited for her heart to slow its desperate pounding. Illyana was sending out waves of puzzlement over her mother's distress. Tachyon sent back images of black water, trying to show the baby the reason for her fear and the fact that it no longer existed. Illyana's confusion deepened, and Tach felt a burst of pleasure from the fetus as she contemplated her watery home.

That brought a laugh to her lips, and Tachyon sat up. "All right, you little fish, so I'm an irrational coward. But you won't be so smug once you've joined the rest of us out here on dry land."

Sometime during that nightmare dog paddle, she had lost or kicked off her shoes. Water squished through the thick material of her tube socks as she stood and tried to get her bearings. Walking was going to be difficult, and her clammy clothes . . .

She realized what she was doing and throttled the complaining thoughts. "Burning Sky," she said with disgust. "You're free. *Free*, and you're bitching about wet socks."

353

Tachyon threw back her head and let out a whoop of joy. *"I'M FREE! FUCK YOU, BLAISE! I'M FREE!"* The joyous words echoed oddly among the rusting cranes and rotting piers that lined the New Jersey coast.

It was all the celebration she allowed herself. She was still dangerously vulnerable, and dangerously close to the Rox. She had to make her way back to the clinic, and quickly. As she paused to get her bearings, the moldering skyline suddenly gave her a heart-squeezing sense of déjà vu. Strange, because she had never in her life stood on this shore at the edge of the leprous bay, gazing across the cancerous rot of industrial parks.

Someone else's memory.

Despite her former body's formidable powers, she had not made it a habit to walk through the private parts of people's minds. That narrowed the possible owners of this particularly intense memory. And since only the Great and Powerful Turtle lived in Bayonne, New Jersey, it was a safe bet the memory was his.

Tommy. Yes! Tommy could get her home without the dangers attendant to hitchhiking. And if Blaise came after her, Turtle could handle him. Now all that remained was to find the junkyard that hid the Turtle and housed the man inside the shell.

It was like having due north embedded in the cortex of the brain. She matched junkyards against the memory compass in her head until at last the images merged. Beyond the twelve-foot-high chain link, abandoned cars formed steel glaciers. Tilted piles of tires, like a giant's collection of rotting donuts, loomed against the light haze that was Manhattan. The problem was the fence.

She cast along the fence like a hunting dog until she found the gate. An enormous and well-oiled padlock leered at her. Hefting it in her hand, she wished that somewhere in her misspent youth she'd learned to pick a lock. Great fantasy—totally useless. Even if she possessed the knowledge, she lacked the tools. *Crowbar.* Same problem. No tool, probably not enough strength.

She reluctantly dropped the lock, and it fell back against the gate with a crash that set the metal to shivering and ringing. A dog began to bay. Tachyon considered just standing outside the gate and bawling like a hurt steer until someone emerged. But what if this was the wrong junkyard? And what if the proprietor emerged with a shotgun and didn't notice the gender and condition of his caller until he'd replied with both barrels?

She returned to a section of fence that sagged between the uprights. That left a two-foot space between the rolled barb wire and the top of the links. Monkeylike, using fingers and toes, she began to climb the fence. It was almost impossible with her belly in the way. She found a way to make it possible though it put enormous strain on her back.

At the top. Eyeing the points on the chain link. The rusting barbs. She went wriggling through, feeling hot burn as several barbs opened lines on her back. The stabbing pain in her stomach and thighs from the chain link. Now the hard part, maneuvering around to find a toehold...

In another lifetime Tachyon had often warned his pregnant patients about increasing clumsiness as the pregnancy advanced. How they should avoid step stools, ladders.

Add chain link fences, she thought as her foot slipped, a link tore open her palm and she fell backward off the fence. *Illyannnnnaaa*. What began as a name in the mind became a shriek in the throat as she plummeted. Fortunately the gods and ancestors gave woman padding. It hurt, and she suspected she had bruised her tailbone, but no bones were broken, and Illyana continued to slumber.

Mindful of dogs, Tach crept through the dungheaps and gravestones of an industrial society. Near the center of the yard five boulevards intersected in an open area, a sort of junkyard Etoile with the Arc de Triomphe formed by a weather-beaten and sagging old shack squatting like a tired old man in the center.

It was the right junkyard. Tommy's memories of a lifetime of childhood games in and around that old house jostled in Tachyon's mind like rudderless boats. The feelings engendered were so warm that she forgot caution and walked slowly and openly toward the front steps.

Only the quick rush of feet on the hard ground prevented her from being knocked down. She spun as the big black Labrador-Doberman cross sprang at her. His shoulder hit her in the thigh, and she teetered wildly but kept her feet. It circled back as she lunged for the porch, though its safety appeared dubious.

Tach had been master of a pack back home on Takis.

Only there the hunting beasts had a wingspan of thirty feet and jaws that could bite through a man. Given that for training, how hard could one ninety-pound dog be? She had her back against the screen door, beating out a tattoo with a heel as the animal growled, barked, and snapped about her ankles.

"*Down, sir!*" She tried to deepen her voice, hold back the quaver of terror. The dog whined, buried its muzzle briefly between its paws like a man holding his head in confusion.

The porch light snapped on, and then she heard Turtle. "It's three o'clock in the fucking morning!"

It was music. It was warmth, and breakfasts in bed, and hot baths, and everything safe and good. She looked back over her shoulder. Tommy Tudbury, the Great and Powerful Turtle, was a plump middle-aged man dressed only in pajama bottoms, and as his eyes met Tachyon's, he surreptitiously reached down and hitched the waist of his pajamas up and over the bulge of his potbelly.

Tach drew a deep breath and said in a surprisingly steady voice, "Tommy, it is I, Tachyon."

"And I'm the pope." The dog was keening softly. Tommy glanced down in annoyance. "Jetboy, scram." The dog bounded off into the darkness.

"I am Tachyon," she insisted. "I was jumped—"

"And killed. They televised the memorial service on the local joker cable station."

"I an *not* dead. I've been imprisoned on Ellis Island for seven months. Whoever said I was dead lied. I've got to get back to the clinic, and for that I need your help." She considered for a moment, then added. "But first . . . I need a drink."

"Shit! You just might be Tachyon," snorted the Turtle. And Tachyon was too relieved even to be offended. "Tell me something only Tachyon could know."

"I found you, didn't I?" That didn't seem to cut it. "I faked your death in eighty-seven. You yanked me out an Atlanta hotel window in eighty-eight—"

"Okay, okay." But there was the oddest expression in his brown eyes. Uncomfortable under the scrutiny, Tach hugged herself, and half turned away. "Well, I guess you better come in."

As she followed him through the door, Tach noticed that

the screen had been repaired. It looked as if a twisted black-wire spider had died and joined with the metal of the screen. Tommy's bare feet slapped on the linoleum floor as Tach followed him down the hall and into the tiny kitchen. It was extremely well appointed—dishwasher, double-door refrigerator, electric knife sharpener, coffee maker, coffee-bean grinder—in short, a gadgeteer's delight.

"All I've got is bourbon."

"That's fine." The chink of glass on glass. Tom thrust a tumbler under her nose. The whiskey fumes caressed her nose with a smell that promised the warmth of hearth fires. Greedily she grabbed the glass, threw back the bourbon. It hit like napalm exploding, and she gagged. Tommy held her shoulders.

"Stupid," wheezed Tach. "I haven't had a drink in seven months."

Ton waved the bottle. "You want another?"

"No, I can't. It's bad for the baby."

"'Baby'?" Turtle echoed in a pinched, strangled voice.

Despite herself, Tachyon laughed. "You *are* an old bachelor."

Tommy's eyes dropped to her thickened waist. He spun away, ran his hands through his hair. "Oh ... shit ... this is too fuckin' weird."

"You ought to try it from my side." For a long moment, they stood in silence. It soon became uncomfortable. Tommy was staring at her so oddly.

"What?" Tach finally demanded.

"You really are beautiful."

Her hands flew to her cheeks, covering the betraying flush. "Don't be an idiot," she said gruffly. She then peeked at him through the curtain of her hair. "Tommy, do you have a mirror?"

"Why?"

"I ... I have never seen myself. I have lived in this skin for seven months, but I have never seen myself."

Pity flared in his eyes. Gruffly he said, "Come on."

She followed him down the hall and into the small bedroom. A full-length mirror hung on the closet door. Tommy reached out and snapped on the ceiling light. The wallpaper was an elegant stripe design known as Versailles. Tach had used it in one of her apartments. The room was dominated by a big-screen TV, but that would be logical— Tommy had owned a TV repair shop. Atop the television was the head of an incredibly handsome man. In place of hair, a clear radar dome covered the top of the skull.

"Modular Man?"

"It's all I've got, just the head. I'm going to get it working sometime."

"You're very strange." She resumed her scrutiny of the room. Framed prints and posters on the walls, tumbled pile of books on the bedside table. The bed itself was a canopied dream, a bed for a Renaissance prince.

"You're a romantic," said Tachyon as she crossed the room. "And a very bad sleeper," she added with a glance at the bedclothes, which were humped and twisted like cloth mountains riven by an earthquake.

But the moment had come, and she forced her attention to the mirror. It was a little figure, a defiant urchin in her faded denim coveralls. The shoulder straps crisscrossed the thin white T-shirt. The breasts were swollen; her body preparing itself for motherhood. The thrust of her belly was greater than she had expected, and she found it embarrassing—particularly with Turtle watching.

She moved in closer, inspected the silver gilt hair cascading over her shoulders and reaching to her hips. The shape of the face was actually familiar. Like her own, it tapered to a pointed little chin, but it was soft and innocent. No wrinkles formed a net of years about the eyes; no deep gouges marred the vulnerable mouth. Tachyon noticed she had a rather short upper lip, which left her with a constant and quizzical little porpoise smile. Only in the eyes did her ordeal, and the years that burdened her soul, reveal themselves. They were a deep smoky gray with a darker circle around the iris, and they were haunted and very sad.

She turned back to Tommy. "Ideal, it's so . . . young."

Tach turned back to the mirror. Noted the bones of her clavicle etched beneath the white skin. She was painfully thin, which made the distended belly look more like a victim of starvation than pregnancy.

"What do you need, Tachy?" asked Turtle.

"A bath—I'm sticky with salt. A meal. And sleep."

"Bathroom's through there. I'll fix you some food, and the bed." He pointed.

An hour later, she was clean, sated, and exhausted. Tach climbed into the big canopied bed wearing a soft flannel shirt

of Tommy's. Her hair was still damp, and she could almost
feel the tangles forming, but she didn't care.

With his feet planted well apart and his hands thrust
deep into the pockets of his bathrobe, Tommy was a pudgy
Colossus of Rhodes standing guard at the door. "Could I . . ."

"What?"

"Nah, never mind."

"What?"

"It's nothing."

"*What?*" repeated Tachyon with rising irritation.

He sucked in a bushel's worth of air and let it out in a
long breath. "Could I . . . brush your hair?"

Tach smiled, and for the first time she saw the effect a
lovely woman could have on a man. The Ideal knew *she* had
felt it often enough. But what *power*.

"I'd like that, Tommy."

She held out her hand, and as he crossed to her, he
plucked a silver-backed brush from the dresser. It was such
an oddly elegant thing to see in Tommy's broad soft hand. He
settled cross-legged on the bed behind her. Tach fidgeted for
several seconds until she found a position that would accommodate her belly and not cramp Illyana. Waves of sleepy
contentment were washing off the baby, and it was about to
put Tach to sleep.,

Tommy's hands moved through her hair, lifting and
separating the silky strands. Occasionally a strand would
catch on his skin, and the tug to her scalp was amazingly
sensual and relaxing. The brush massaged her scalp and
flowed softly through her hair. He was so gentle, there wasn't
a single painful pull.

Tachyon was very aware of Tommy, but despite her
exhaustion and the dreamy state induced by the brushing,
there was still a shivering along all her nerves. Her skin
seemed almost to crawl when Tommy approached too close.
It hurt to say it. She could anticipate the hurt in his eyes, but
she had to.

Planting a hand on the mattress, she cranked around
until she could look him in the face. "Tommy, I can't have you
sleep in this bed with me."

It was like a curtain drawing across his face. Hurt, anger,
shame. "What? . . . You think I'd—"

"No, of course not. It's not you." The words lay like
ground glass in the back of her throat. She prevaricated.

Perhaps if she were to sneak up on it, it could be said. "This body wasn't in this condition when I entered it."

"What are you trying to say to me?" Aggression laced each word, making it cut razor sharp.

"Tommy . . . I was . . . raped."

Saying the words released the floodgates of terror. Tach's fear and anguish struck the baby, and Illyana jerked away. The wild movement of the fetus pulled an involuntary groan from Tachyon.

Tommy's arms wrapped around her. Rocking her softly, he said. "Oh, baby, I'm sorry. I'm sorry. So sorry."

The soothing words were murmured into the back of her head. Each syllable released with a tiny puff of warm air that feathered her hair and caressed her skin, but Tach flinched in Turtle's embrace, and the tears she should have been shedding jammed up somewhere in the middle of her chest.

He missed her reaction. She could feel the panic rising. And she knew if she moved too quickly, if Tommy tightened his hold, if she tried to release the emotions that wrapped like steel bands about her chest, she would shatter into a million sparkling shards. When had flesh and bone been replaced with glass, Tach wondered?

Carefully she enunciated the words, trying to keep the shrill cry of terror from her voice. "You have to let go of me. Quickly!"

Water dancing on a hot skillet couldn't have moved faster. Tom's arms snapped away from her body like a trap opening, and he scooted on his rump to the foot of the bed. "I was only trying—"

"I know. It's not you, it's *me*. Please, Tom, don't look at me like that. I don't *want* to hurt you."

"Do you want to talk—"

"*No.*"

"You brought it up."

"Only so you would let me go. So you would understand."

Tommy got up from the bed. Laid the brush carefully back on the dresser. Dug his hands deep into his pockets. When he turned back, he was smiling. Injecting a note of lightness into his voice, he asked, "So, what's the drill?"

Tach followed his lead. She forced a smile and said, "First we sleep. Then we go to the clinic, and you establish my bona fides."

"Sounds good. I'll be on the couch if you need me."

She knew she had hurt him. She knew she couldn't do anything to alleviate his pain. "I do need you, Tommy," she managed to say as he was leaving. "And I'm glad you're here."

She wasn't sure if he'd heard her.

Somewhere a distant woodpecker was chattering out its rapid-fire signature. Tachyon dug her cheek deeper into the down pillow, tried to block it out.

CRUMP!

The bed shook ever so slightly. Tachyon reacted as if it had suddenly bucked. She spilled out of the bed and was running before her time, place, and situation had fully penetrated.

Artillery fire, automatic weapons. A raid! Get outside, find the guards, hide. Father! Papa! Daddy!

It was the sight of Tommy's solid form on the front porch that banished dreams and returned her to a sense of reality. But the gunfire continued, and the predawn sky was lit by the trails of tracer fire like peripatetic fireflies, muzzle flashes from the helicopter gunships. Tommy was in a red-and-blue-striped bathrobe, one hand dug deep into a pocket, the other cradling a coffee mug. A suburban homeowner calmly assessing the dawn of Armageddon.

Tachyon moved to his side and closed her hands around his upper arm. He looked down at her. They both knew, but there was a sense that someone had to say it.

Tommy spoke first. "The Rox. They're finally doing it."

Almost inaudibly, Tach said, "My body's there."

"They're gonna kill everybody." He either hadn't heard or didn't think. Probably a little of both.

"Then you must take me there. You've got to take me there."

That penetrated. "You're nuts."

Dawn was beginning to paint the eastern sky with a leprous white light.

"Tommy, please."

The ace looked from her white, desperate face toward the battle raging to the north. It was almost full light now. Liberty was a tiny porcelain figure standing dauntless as the killers flashed past heading for Ellis Island. As they watched, a Huey, its steel belly packed with assault troops, choppered north toward the battle. Suddenly it began to pitch and yaw as if the pilot were drunk or mad. Rotor blades clawing at the air, it fell at an ever-steeper angle until it slammed into the upraised arm of the statue. For an instant the fireball obscured their view, then burning debris rained down, fiery outriders for the torch and arm, which had been sheared away by the impact. The arm spun once, almost lazily, until it plunged, torch first, into the black waters of the bay.

Liberty stood crippled and forlorn, her sides blacked from burning fuel, her fire extinguished, her message drowned in the polluted waters of the harbor.

Tommy pushed his cup at Tachyon. Walked down the steps and vanished into the jumble of dead cars. Minutes passed. Then the shell rose slowly over the mountains of junk. He was coming for her. Her steel knight.

The Temptation of
Hieronymus Bloat

X

It began very much like the last time.

I woke from a dream. For a moment I was confused, wondering where I was. Kafka's crews had finished the lobby's remodeling a few days ago. My body now rested on a ramp, jutting up in the center of the space as high as the balconies, my head another full story above that. The walls of the building were triple-paned glass all around. I could see the Rox slumbering in a thick predawn fog. My land looked peaceful enough, and the mindvoices were mostly quiet, filled with their own dream images—though there were exceptions: Croyd pacing in his tower and trying to decide whether to try to sleep or not, Chickenhawk (who was supposed to be watching the city from his perch on the northern tower) sleeping and dreaming of dead Kien, a few couples making love or talking.

I looked down at the *Temptation*, set on the balcony in a blaze of lamps, and I wondered what had awakened me.

Then I felt it again—two dozen or more pricklings at my Wall. The probings came from all around me. The thoughts I sensed now at the edges of my inner hearing were frightening.

They'd learned. These weren't green park rangers and city cops. No—these were seasoned military troops, people with a horrifyingly simple sense of duty. People who followed orders blindly without worrying about what they meant. People who had been in combat before and would gladly hate anything their superiors named The Enemy.

"Oh shit," I muttered.

"Governor?" Kafka, slumbering nearby, woke. My guards looked suddenly wary.

"Just be quiet," I told them.

And I could hear it again: the rhythmic, insistent beat of blades chopping the air not too far away; the throbbing of powerful engines frothing the water of the bay.

They were coming.

The last time, I'd mucked up by alarming the Rox too quickly. I wasn't about to make that mistake again.

So I made another.

I tried to use this "power" that everyone says I have. I focused on my Wall. I imagined it stiffening, becoming rubbery and pushing back the intruding boats and choppers. I thought . . . I thought it was working at first. I felt this sense of "hardness" to the Wall, and the faint pricklings disappeared entirely. I clenched my fist: victory.

"Yes," I hissed.

I really thought I'd done it. I believed, for an instant, that it had been that simple.

Then they hit the Wall again—from every direction, at once, and fast. This was a concerted, simultaneous, *organized* assault. I summoned all the psychic strength I had. At least I hoped that's what I was doing. I tried to visualize energy gathering around me, flowing through my mind and then hurtling out to the Wall, but maybe it was just imagination or comic-book fantasy, because it didn't do any good.

The Wall bulged and cracked, making me moan. I mean, I could *feel* it. It fucking *hurt*. Then the Wall was lanced open entirely, like some great raw pus-filled boil. The troops (that's who it was—the goddamn U.S Army or National Guard or something) poured through while I lay there, gasping in pain.

Through. Coming. I could hear them.

going in, yeah! Gonna kick some ass. Show them wimp rangers how it's really done. This time we don't hold back	*drug dealers, murderers, rapists, they all deserve this, deserve what we're gonna give 'em*	*C'mon, c'mon, Come on!! Damn it! Get through this damn wall before they have a chance to be ready*

Actinic flaring blue light threw crazed, weaving shadows across the Rox and the Administration Building: flares. Out across the water I could see the bright legs of spotlights striding across the bay toward us. A chopper with flaring running lights wheeled past the glassed-in lobby like an angry bat, and I could see faces staring at us as it passed.

And I heard thoughts:

What the hell is that   Jesus Christ in a   Is that Bloat?
thing?   *bottle!*

Belatedly, the sirens were wailing over the Rox. Kafka was yelling below me. "Bloat! Can't you hold them back?"

"Uh-uh," I told him, slowly and wearily. It took a lot more effort to talk than I would have thought. "I can't. I'm tired." I sounded like a kid too late for bed. *Carry me in, Daddy; I'm so sleepy.*

A pair of choppers danced thunderously around the building, then banked away to land. Automatic gunfire crackled, sounding almost too thin to be real, except that I could hear the mindvoices wailing in panic and fear.

A wave of terror rang through the headvoices of the Rox. Then there were just too many thoughts and too much going on, and the images overwhelmed me, buried me.

Chaos. Just chaos. I don't remember much of it, only individual scenes plucked from the general carnage. Images piled one on top of another, experienced almost simultaneously...

> ... I could sense the ghost of Chrysalis haunting Elmo's dreams. There was an urgency to her voice as she stroked his cheek. "Get out!" she said, her voice at odds with her soft caress. "Get out!"
>
> In Elmo's head, there was a sound like running footsteps. Under their impact, the dream walls of the Crystal Palace dissolved. Chrysalis disappeared, but I could feel him holding to that sweet dream touch.
>
> Another ghost. Another memory.
>
> Elmo must have opened his eyes, for he was thinking, *Shit, are they here again?* while a half-

remembered sound of rotors echoed in his mind. *Gotta get up! She said so!*

Then I caught a brief stolen image of a gun butt arcing toward his face and then a fusillade of pain that cut out everything. The anguish was excruciating, instant, and blinding. Just before Elmo blacked out entirely, I heard him thinking, *Jesus, they're going to fucking kill me*.

. . . the noise of the helicopters had awakened Blaise, for I caught his thoughts spilling from the mindshield. There was an image: the blue beam of a searchlight throwing crazed shadows on a wall. Erotic dream images mingled with shabby reality for a moment before his mindwalls came up and shut him away. . .

Croyd was jittery. Thoughts wheeled like bats in his head. *Choppers went right by the tower, two of 'em, and more lights out in the bay coming in . . . this is crap, just crap . . . gotta move, gotta be goddamn careful . . . can't get caught here*.

I followed Croyd's stream of thoughts down from his tower and into the building proper. He was near Elmo's room when the stream of consciousness suddenly halted. From what any of us had seen, Croyd's new body—he looked like an armadillo mated with a man—was fast and strong, as well as pretty well armored. His eyesight sucked, but his hearing was good; scent was even better.

Smell machine oil, sweat. Something else. Look around the corner; goddamn this lousy eyesight . . .

That has to be Elmo . . . shit, those are troopers . . .

Through Croyd's ears, I could hear the distinct deadly clicking of a weapon being readied, and then Croyd—with a psychic yell that rang in my own head—charged them . . . .

I could tell that the one named Danny was pissed because Ray wanted to waste time with the damn dwarf, but then, Ray was the squad leader, *. . . a by-God new sergeant . . . and it was Ray's call. Just get it over with . . . this place gives me the* *creeps . . . fulla jokers and God knows what around that fucking blob in the lobby.* Danny was listening to Ray laughing. He didn't really want to see the dwarf's head turn into strawberry jam. *Just wanna get outta here . . .*

Danny heard Ray's CAR-15 fire, but at the same time something like a big fast armadillo crashed into them—*from the snatches of vision I caught, I knew it was Croyd. No! . . . shit, kill the damn thing . . .*

Danny was firing, and—a brief headflash—Ray was rolling on the ground grabbing at his throat, *. . . shit, the joker crushed his windpipe . . .* and Croyd was clawing at Jerry who screamed too, and Danny let go with a burst that tore into Jerry, and Jerry went down, *no, no!* and a ricochet hit Danny, *Jesus, I'm hit! Fuck, it hurts, it hurts,* and the armadillo had snatched up the dwarf and scooted down the hall, limping but alive . . .

Molly Bolt had jumped a Huey pilot. *. . . wonder how the fuck you're really supposed to fly one of these things? . . . not that it really matters, just turn the stick over this way and that way . . . kinda fun . . .*

I could feel the vertigo tug at her as the craft began to buck and cant over. The troops crouched in the open rear were shouting (I heard their thoughts, too, of course). *Shit . . . who's that?* I caught a glimpse through Molly's eyes as she glanced over her shoulder. A military pistol was pointed at her. A GI, a young black man, looked at her with strange sad eyes. "Goddamn, Chuck, I'm sorry. I'm really sorry."

Shit!! . . . and then there was a pinwheeling shock of disorientation as Molly jumped away.

I could feel her for long seconds afterward, gasping, waiting to feel the shattering impact of the bullet, before she realized that she was in her own body again.

Captain Hayes was thinking that it was hell to have a fight with your old lady just before a mission. *Marge, damn it, they kill people. You understand? They'd carve you up on the street because you looked wrong at them. They're vicious and mean. They're animals.* He kept replaying the argument in his head. Marge argued that they were just kids, just kids, and she didn't understand. *Shouldn't have told her in the first place. She's just worrying, that's all. Just worried about me.*

Hayes was worried too. I could feel it and see it in the quick headflashes between thoughts. He clung to the throbbing, shaking walls of the Huey, staring at the packed troops in the craft's belly. *Good men, all. None of them deserve to die, but some will. The bastard kids here will see to that, no matter what Marge says.* Hayes cleared his throat; the forming words interfered with his thoughts. "Thirty seconds," he shouted over the din of the rotors.

. . . can see the place now, flares lighting the place like it's Nam all over again . . . choppers wheeling around that fucking toy palace like big angry vultures . . .

"We're landing in jumper territory." *. . . of course they know that, but if I talk, they can't think about what's going to happen . . .* "So make sure you watch your partner." *. . . big fucking ball of of flame, JESUS! was that a Huey? . . .* "Remember that your guns are rigged." *. . . can't see it now, but that was one of ours going down,* shit . . . "So you're the only ones who know the trick." *. . . had better work had better damn work . . .* "You see one of our guys pulling the trigger and nothing's happening, they may—may—have been jumped. So don't shoot 'em; use the tranks." *Or just shoot quick anyway . . .* "Policy is fire only when fired on," (*. . . which may get us dead . . .*) "but I want you to do whatever it takes. Don't worry about policy. Stay alive—however you gotta do it. Understand?"

His men shouted affirmation back to him.

The Huey jerked (*man, those shacks across the way are going up like crazy*), dropped. I saw an image of dirt swirling crazily in sudden floodlights.

"Go, GO, GO!" Hayes was shouting, and his people were spilling out the door toward the jumper buildings. *Like a ghetto, a slum. Like what I remember of Saigon, just before we left . . .* Hayes was lagging behind, his people already in the buildings as he crossed the open ground in front.

A burst of small arms fire caught him then. He screamed and went down. The horror of what he saw drove out all the words for an instant. I saw the remnants of his body as he did. We both knew, even as the pain hit and the vision started to go.

...let it end, God, just let it end please...can't believe they actually shot me, all that time in Nam and not a scratch...still see my hands all slick and warm...there was so much blood, so much, too much and all mine...cold and black...they always said that there'd be light and voices and family, but there's only blackness...blackness...Marge?...

Video was screaming, an endless sobbing agony. *I don't want to see it anymore, I don't want to see it...*

But nothing could erase the sight in her mind. She projected it helplessly. In her mind, it overlaid everything, the reality of the mud in which she was sitting, the cold fog that wrapped around her, the ugly chunks of raw meat covered with tattered olive cloth that she very carefully avoided looking at but that kept intruding into her thoughts.

Video cried. She wailed. It did no good. There was no way to block out the scene.

Like a movie stuck in a pathetic, awful loop, Video replayed the scene she'd witnessed:

The sound came first, a loud erratic whine, then as she turned to look, the chopper came careening across the foggy bay. The craft was obviously in trouble, tilted way over and out of control.

She thought for a moment it was going to make it, but even as she glimpsed the frightened dark face in the cockpit, one of the rotor blades tore into the earth, and the chopper slammed itself into the Rox. It disintegrated and exploded, transforming itself into a rolling blazing hell that left a trail of burning fuel and scattered broken corpses like gory seeds. Then the entire glowing incandescent ball slammed into the makeshift homes near the docks. They went up like tinder, roaring and throwing sparks.

There was no way to tell the nat screams from those of the jumpers, and the burning bodies all looked alike.

...Eavesdropping on Chickenhawk, I could hear him giving Kien the tale about the Egrets' last shipment of rapture, but every time Kien opened his mouth to reply, strange discordant sounds came out: sirens, explosions, an insistent rhythmic pounding. Kien kept talking through the din, waving his hands as if he were really saying something, only now they weren't in Kien's office at all but out in a field somewhere, and helicopters were circling...

Hell! Those are real *choppers! Damn, I've been asleep ...*

Chickenhawk, in his tower perch high above the Rox, rose cautiously to his feet and looked down at the Rox.

Omigod ...

The shock seared the images into his mind so that I saw them as well. Thunder roared from the jumper side of the docks. An impossible gout of orange and yellow flame tumbled into the dwellings there. The Rox was the set of a war movie, a night battle scene. Two helicopters had landed near the west wing, another in the front court; more were sweeping in from the bay. Flares dripped in the sky, searchlights tore bright holes in the darkness. Chickenhawk could see muzzle flashes and hear the chattering gunfire.

Choppers were landing on the jumper side of the island too. *...full-scale assault...makes sense. They'd've been told how the jumpers chewed up the cops. Best tactic would be to hit them fast, hard, and with lots of people ...fuck, two more choppers coming in from the east ...gotta see Bloat, see what he needs me to do ...*

Chickenhawk launched himself from his roost, but somebody below must have seen the motion and shot at him, for suddenly his thoughts were panicked and strange, *...can't move the wing...falling ...oh dear God, it hurts...all the wingbones snapped ...*

He fell most of the way.

*   *   *

Panic leaked like bitter syrup from Blaise's mind. *There are too many of them. I can't control them all.* It was a spoken thought, and I knew that he was talking to Durg, for I also sensed that odd emptiness that was the Takisian's mind. Blaise's shields had collapsed. His mind was spewing out glimpses of death, of soldiers firing on soldiers, of jumpers lying on a bloody floor, of Durg (my God, could the man *really* move like that?) flashing through combat like a well-oiled killing machine. Another troopship was landing by the medical building, more soldiers running crouched toward them. *What do we do? What do we do?*

Blaise was terrified.

Only a bit of Durg's reply filtered through the clamor in Blaise's mind. "... leave while we can-... not safe here any longer" Durg was saying.

"To where?" Blaise replied, but then a thought interrupted his question. The image of a seashell flamed in his mind.

Suddenly I could sense resolution. "Kelly!" he shouted at Durg. "Find the bitch. *Now!*"

For several moments, I caught nothing else from Blaise. Then there was another brief flash ...make *you fucking fly this thing, asshole*... And then the image of one of the grounded troop-ships and its terrified pilot, his mind snared in Blaise's. Kelly was with them, stumbling along in Dung's grasp, half blind with fear.

Out of here. I'm out of here now, Blaise thought.

The last image I caught from any of them was the sound of rotors screaming. . . .

Kafka's voice brought me back. "You're the only one who can tell us what's going on, Governor!" he was screaming. "Where do we need to go? What do you want us to do?"

Kafka was gesticulating furiously in front of the *Temptation*, his carapace rattling like a bunch of tin cans. He was scared, and thinking that this was too much like the Cloisters when everyone ganged up on the Astronomer. Jokers crowd-ed around him, armed with everything from baseball bats to Uzis.

Kafka kept shouting. "Bloat, come on! It sounds like the fighting's heading our way."

Kafka was right. I could feel it, like a dull scarlet tide rolling toward the building. "I didn't want to know them," I said. No, let's be fair—I was babbling. "I shouldn't have to know them."

"Bloat, man, jokers are *dying* out there!"

"They're just people. All of us." I was trying to blot out all the voices of the Rox. I couldn't. Behind Kafka, St. Anthony wrestled with demons and other fantastic creatures. They swarmed over him, biting and clawing.

"*Bloat!*"

I sighed. "There are three squads in the west wing already, coming up the side stairs. There's another group approaching fast from the east, near the water. In a few seconds, they'll be stuck in open ground. Forget the jumper side of the island; marines are everywhere over there. All the squads have orders to make for the Administration Building after they've secured their first objective. They'll *all* be coming soon."

Kafka was snapping orders as I relayed positions. Jokers scattered, howling like mad things. Guards fanned out to protect the lobby and the rooms behind where my body lay helpless.

I heard the gunfire rise and swell in volume. I felt the deaths continue.

I was staring, immobile, as my mind roamed my poor Rox, my embattled island. No one had ever told me it was like this. Nobody could have, I guess. I just wanted it to stop.

Chickenhawk half fell, half glided through an open window in the balcony. Blood splattered his feathers, and one wing was crumpled and torn. "Bloat—" he began.

"I know," I said as one of the jokers ran to tend to him. "You'll be all right, man. It'll be okay." One of those clichés that tumble out when you're not thinking. Frankly, I wasn't sure anyone was going to be "all right." I wasn't sure any of us were really going to live through this.

"It's hell, ain't it?" someone said, and I looked down to see the penguin. It looked worried.

Then hell came to pay a small personal visit.

There were screams from behind the doors leading into the lobby. Gunfire stuttered its lethal percussive speech. I felt Vomitus and Mothmouth die just outside. The doors kicked open, glass scattering across the tiles. Soldiers in riot helmets, fatigues, and Kevlar armor were spilling out: from the doors, from the balcony.

Theirs were not nice thoughts. Not at all. These people had seen their companions hurt or killed already in the fighting. They were only thinking of staying alive.

Well, that isn't quite accurate. Let me qualify the statement. The way they intended to stay alive was to make sure that The Enemy was dead.

"Move and you've had it!" one of them shouted, waving an assault rifle. I thought people only talked like that in the movies. It was almost enough to make me giggle ... almost. He had a lieutenant's bar on his shoulder and a badge on his Kevlar chest that proclaimed him to be *I. SHER*.

The penguin moved. It looked at me. "Sometimes ya just gotta *do* something, Gov'nor," it told me.

The creature made a mocking sound halfway between razzberry and caw, and launched itself at the lieutenant. The officer—a boy really, not much older than me—didn't even hesitate.

The stream of bullets nearly ripped the penguin in half. Bright arterial blood splattered everywhere—over me, over Kafka and the other jokers, over the Bosch painting. Bits of feathered flesh stuck to the glass walls, trailing rivulets of scarlet. The carcass, most of it, lay half on, half off my dais, and the kid was still firing wildly; I know that some of the bullets hit me, though I didn't feel much besides a distant dull ache. Ricocheting slugs tore more glass from the huge panes. I couldn't even hear the sound of the glass hitting the floor over the gun. The noise was deafening, the smell of cordite and oil and blood overpowering.

The silence when the burst had finished was long.

The kid laughed—like I might. His eyes were wild and strange. He'd *enjoyed* that; it made him feel powerful. When he looked around the lobby, he was looking for a new target. *Just let one of them twitch, even a little bit ...*

The hatred in the room was damn near thick enough to touch, like a red-tinged fog in my mind. I felt helpless. There was nothing I could do, and these SOBs were waiting for an excuse to let loose.

Sher barked "You Bloat?"

A couple dozen sarcastic answers came to mind; none of them seemed particularly smart. "Yes."

"Call off your goddamn dogs. Do it *now*."

I listened to the continuing carnage outside the building. I looked at the jokers nearest me: Kafka, Video, Shroud, Chickenhawk, maybe a dozen others. They were all watching, like they expected me to do something, and I'll be damned if I could see anything to do. I'd failed, all around. My incompetence had killed them as surely as if I'd pulled the fucking triggers myself. Penguin blood dripped from my sides like an accusation.

"We're not dogs," I told Sher. "We're people."

"Fuck that shit. It's all over, asshole."

"I—I" I stuttered. They were all still looking at me, jokers and soldiers both. "I can't call them off."

"I thought you were in charge," Sher spat.

I laughed, bitterly. "Yeah. That's right. Of course I'm in charge. I'm the governor." I lashed myself with the word.

The kid snarled. He whipped his rifle around.

He fired.

St. Anthony flew apart in a spray of paint-flecked chips. The surreal landscape of Bosch's dreams ripped into long splinters, gouged and broken. A menagerie of deformities expired as the kid's weapon bucked and roared and shredded the triptych. The entire frame of the *Temptation* canted and slammed to the floor in pieces.

Ruined.

"No!" I screamed, loud in the silence after the gunfire.

"Now *you* listen, Governor," Sher was saying, though the din of the gun had made us all half deaf. "Make them stop. Or this time it's the roach here."

The muzzle pointed at Kafka.

"I *can't*, damn you! Listen to me—"

He didn't give me a chance to finish. "Bye, roach." I heard Sher's resolve. I watched the finger slowly tighten, and I knew he'd do it.

I knew.

"No!" I screeched again.

Bloatblack was falling like thick lava from my sides. I was sick—sick of death, sick of destruction, sick of my own inability to do anything. The rage and hatred had built up in me past endurance. With that . . . well, with that was the same feeling I'd had once before, when the caves had been created. Only *this* time the surging power was a darker and deeper sensation. Bigger than last time, but more a *part* of me, if you know what I mean. It was like . . . I don't know, like imagining something in my head and then "thinking" it outside.

And there it was.

Abracadabra. Poof.

Everything happened in that instant I shouted "No!". It happened when I knew that if I didn't do something *now*, I was going to watch Kafka die as Peanut had, as the penguin had, as I'd heard and seen jokers die throughout the Rox tonight.

"No!" I screamed, and something within me leapt out like a savage creature. I knew what I wanted, and I shaped it.

I'm not sorry for it. I'm really not.

I wanted death. I wanted revenge. I wanted to make widows of these soldiers' wives and orphans of their children. I wanted them to fucking *suffer*.

The fragments of the *Temptation* stirred on the floor. A thick greenish fog swirled at ankle level, coiling and rising. Groans and screams echoed, as if coming from some vast subterranean well. The sights and sounds made Sher swing his muzzle away from Kafka. The kid's eyes widened at what was coming from that fog, rising with it as if striding up from the depths.

The kid screamed.

He held the trigger down, a long and noisy burst.

A hand reached from the fog and snatched at the barrel even as Sher was firing. The hand flipped the rifle, reversing it, and then the weapon fired again.

Sher's body danced backward in a ballet of death, moving to the jittery music of the bullets slamming into his body. He screamed wordlessly, but I could hear his thoughts, and I didn't care. It was *my* hand that had taken the weapon from the kid, even though the hand that had come from the fog had been clawed and green and scaly. It had been my hand—because I'd made it move. I'd ordered its actions, and it had responded.

Sher was dead long before the body stopped twitching and fell to the floor. His squad was staring, momentarily stunned.

It took only that instant of hesitation for them to die as well. A tropical hurricane wind roaring from below shredded the fog, and I took each tendril and made it a *thing*, a creature of Bosch.

A joker. A demon.

They poured out, shrieking and vengeful: the stag-headed man; a merman in full medieval armor riding a flying, metal-scaled fish; a featherless bird with teeth stolen from a Tyrannosaurus; a claw-legged, man-size toad; a cat-demon; a ferocious winged fish bearing a unicorn's horn; flying devils of all descriptions . . .

They tore the guns away from the soldiers and threw them back to us. The soldiers went down under a clot of swarming attackers.

My demons tore the limbs from their living, writhing victims. They died slowly and horribly, and I . . .

I relished every last instant of their pain.

The floor literally ran red with blood.

I laughed. I howled. I chuckled.

My jokers celebrated with me. "Out!" I cried to them, and my fantasy multitude echoed the word with their shrill inhuman voices. "Drive them all away! Kill any of them you can!"

Flowing like a massive black cloud, my troops were gone. My will went with them. I sent them hurtling against the intruders. With their power, I ripped the choppers from the sky and tore the hulls open on their boats. They killed, they maimed, they destroyed.

More of my cavalry swooped down from the sky. Some were jokers riding armored flying fish and armed with (if I could believe the eyes of the Rox) swordfish lances. At their flanks, hags and beasts and creatures of all descriptions plummeted down from the false dawn glow, ablaze in their own infernal light. The apparitions were incandescent, painful to look upon.

The demons landed and tore the guns from the hands of the nats even as the soldiers fired on them. The joker riders flushed out the hidden troops and drove them into the open. The shining, awful hordes whooped and howled and dove at them; the riders impaled them on their strange lances.

The soldiers fled before them. In a very few minutes, the attack was broken. The troops were fleeing the Rox any way they could, and my army—my dream army—pursued them.

Briefly, anyway.

I was tiring rapidly. With my exhaustion, the summoned creatures of my mind lost strength as well. Those soldiers who made it to their boats or to their choppers I let go as the images of Bosch turned again to wisps of fog and faded away.

That night, I'm told, less than half the troops returned to their bases. The rest—the bodies—were thrown into the Rox sewage system to rot. There was no place on the Rox to bury them, even if we'd wanted to.

So in essence, I suppose, I eventually ate them.

You know what? I didn't care. In fact, I rather enjoyed the thought.

It wasn't until hours later that I started shaking.

Lovers

VI

There was a storm over Ellis Island. Strange green-black clouds roiled, and occasionally a sullen flicker of lightning would play in their leprous depths. Suddenly a long funnel cloud dropped from the parent mass and with its end whipping like a snake, groped at the buildings below.

It was almost as if the weather were the deciding factor, for the assault troops began rolling back. Men came flying down to the shore, throwing away weapons as they ran. They usually found the LSTs retreating without them, so the water was bobbing with small dark heads.

Turtle, with Tach wedged on his lap inside the turtle shell, maneuvered at the edges of what had been a battle and had now become a rout. Their ears still rang from artillery shells striking the steel plates of the shell. It was a proof of the warranty of battleship steel—there was neither crack nor dent in the metal.

A pair of helicopters were chattering away from the maelstrom of the island. The funnel cloud hopped like a kid on a pogo stick, and one of the choppers was caught in the whirlwind. The blades clawed, found no support, were torn away. It was going down, the little rear propeller spinning uselessly. Then it stopped, and Tommy grunted with effort as his telekinetic power broke the dive and held the machine motionless in space.

Turtle moved slowly toward the Jersey shore, towing the stricken helicopter. The other chopper whipped past the shell, dangerously close, then banked and came around until it was hovering precisely in front of the flying ace. They both knew the machine guns mounted on the front of the copter couldn't do them any damage, but Tach felt herself tense nonetheless. It's disconcerting staring down gun barrels. Suddenly the helicopter wobbled, then peeled off and headed for Manhattan. Tommy resumed his errand of mercy, dropping off the helicopter and her crew on the shore. They emerged waving and cheering.

"Nothing to stop us now," Tommy said, and he flew back toward Ellis Island. "Look's like the war's over."

"I don't know whether to hope Blaise is alive or dead," Tach said, sighing.

As they drew closer to the island, fear began nibbling at the edges of Tachyon's mind, wrapping tendrils about the ends of her nerves until a subliminal shivering gripped her body. The baby, sensing Tach's agitation, was turning over and over in her womb. Tachyon tried to send soothing thoughts to the infant, but it was hard to concentrate on anything but a desperate need to run.

The Rox drew closer. Turtle was breathing hard like a man in the middle of a long run who begins to doubt his ability to continue.

"It's . . . it's Bloat . . . Teddy," Tach forced out past the terror that wrapped like a smothering blanket about her lungs. "Fight it. Ignore it."

"Can't you ward us, or guard us, or do some damn Takisian thing?"

"No, I've trained this body, but its powers are . . . feeble." She ground her teeth together, holding back the scream that threatened to rip her throat apart. "But I'll try to contact him. He helped me once . . . he cares for me . . . he'll do it again."

Tach sent with her weak telepathic link and felt it recoil back on her, defeated by the terror of Bloat's mind.

Tommy started screaming. A thin tearing sound that was terrible to hear. It fed and nurtured Tachyon's terror until she was blind, dumb, and deaf, locked in a world where only fear existed.

The shell flipped nosedown, and they were plummeting for the murky waters of the East River. A few bloated bodies bounced in the chop. Tachyon put her hands over her face and sobbed uncontrollably. With that small part of rationality that remained she remembered that Turtle could control his

TK powers only when he felt secure, unafraid. She had conveniently forgotten that inconvenient fact, and the oversight was going to cost them their lives.

But Tommy surprised her. The plump face seemed wrinkled and old as the human concentrated, swung up the nose—and they were flying level again. Unfortunately they were flying away from the Rox, away from her body. They passed some invisible boundary. Tommy's breath steadied, and her tears cut off like dive doors closing against the inrush of sea. Tach had been waiting so long to cry. Now it had happened, and she had had no release. She felt angry, cheated, and most of all defeated. She sighed and cranked her head back until it rested against Tommy's chest.

There was a tug of inertial motion, and she realized that they were coming around in a sharp, tight circle.

"What are you . . ."

"Trying again, I think I can get past this time," grunted the ace.

"Tommy—"

"No, I've felt it, I know what to expect. I can do it."

"You're delusional. I *have* shields, and the wall tore my guts out. You're only a human; how can you possibly—"

"I'm an ace."

But it was said with that slow drawl, John Wayne bravura, and Tach knew what that sentence *really* meant: "I'm a *man*."

"Tommy, don't. I know you're my friend, you're trying to help, but this is all tangled up with other things . . . emotions . . . pride. Don't kill me proving that you care for me."

Her voice was already beginning to spiral as they hit the outer edges of the wall, and the fear crawled back. A sudden acceleration pressed her deep into Turtle's lap as they shot straight up.

"Sucker can't extend forever," grunted Tommy.

Tachyon laughed. "Tommy, you're a genius."

The wall didn't extend forever. Eventually even imagination runs out, and in Bloat's case, it ended at two thousand feet. They shot past the top. Tommy leveled off, and they were behind Bloat's Wall.

Fires still burned fitfully among the remains of joker hovels. The air reeked with a thick acrid smoke hanging like a funeral pall over the shattered remains of men, jokers, and machines. Through the inferno crept the less wounded coming to the aid of the whining, writhing, bleeding figures. The jokers were tended to. The nats were shot.

As another uniformed body jerked and sprawled in that unlovely attitude unique to death, Tommy lost it. Cranking up the volume on his speakers, he bellowed: "KILL ONE MORE, AND I'LL MASH YOU LIKE ANTS!"

Jokers gesticulated, waved guns. There was a whine like angry bees as several rounds glanced harmlessly off the plate steel of the shell. Then a penguin in ice skates came floating down out of the roiling clouds, executed a perfect pirouette in front of a camera, and gave a jaunty little salute. Simultaneously the weapons were lowered, and Tach knew they had been accepted into Bloat's kingdom of the damned.

It was an impressive entrance. Turtle, with Tachyon riding on the back of the shell, sailed grandly into the great hall through the shattered windows. It was a wonder they sailed at all. Tommy was not sanguine about their outriders—Boschean mermen riding on winged fish. Gravely they saluted Tachyon with the tips of their spears. She bit back irritation. She was tired of being treated as a fairy-tale princess. She wanted to get back to being an outcast prince.

There were murmurs from the hundred or so jokers gathered like misshapen worshipers at the feet of an alien god as Turtle brought them to rest only a few inches from the head and shoulders of the young man who ruled and lay in helpless bondage to the world he had created. In the month since they'd last met, Teddy had aged. Recalling the bodies bobbing in the cold waters at the base of the wall, Tachyon understood why.

"So, Doctor, what do you think of my little kingdom?"

"Quite impressive," Tach said neutrally.

"If we'd waited a couple of more days, you wouldn't have needed your ace friends to rescue you. This fat joker boy could have done it all on his own."

"I don't have time for you to fish for compliments, seek reassurance, or air your grievances. You know the depth of my gratitude."

"It's a poor second for love." Adolescent agony rippled through the words.

"I have none to give you...none for anyone." She closed her eyes briefly, explored that vast echoing gulf that had swallowed her soul. She raised her head and stared into

Teddy's eyes. "I've come for Blaise, and I've come for my body. Bring them to me." She indicated the Boschean demons. "I doubt he can mind-control your dream knights."

"I would be happy to oblige, but Blaise and Kelly are gone." Tach flung out a hand to steady herself. "I think Blaise was finally impressed with ol' Bloat when my friends turned up to play. I think he also figured out he wasn't bulletproof."

"Where have they gone?"

"I'm not sure. They had that Durg guy with them." The young man tugged thoughtfully at his lower lip. "I think maybe they were going to an island. Hawaii, Tahiti? . . ."

Tach made an 'explain further' gesture with her hands. She wasn't sure she could trust her voice.

"Blaise is usually leaky as a sieve, but he was really working at holding his shields. All I got was the image of a seashell—"

"*Baby!*"

She hadn't realized the cry had been audible until she felt Turtle pivot and accelerate for the window.

The dark waters of the East River reluctantly and sullenly gave back the sheen of the streetlights. The motion of the water gave the illusion that the warehouses were rocking gently.

And cradled within one of those faded and pitted buildings was *Baby*, Tachyon's living spaceship. Her friend, servant, stellar steed.

Tach was once again in Tommy's arms as they flew toward the building.

"How you doin'?"

Tach threw back her hair. "I can't *reach* her," she panted. She licked sweat from her upper lip.

"Maybe *Baby*'ll be suspicious. I mean Durg and Blaise ordering her to leave, and you told her not to trust Blaise."

"Yes, but they'll have the master with them. Even if this creature which has stolen my skin hasn't mastered my mental powers, *Baby* won't question him." Tach pressed a hand to her face. "They're loyal . . . they aren't bright."

"Even if she buys it," Tommy said, "they can't get far, right? You burned out the whatchacallit when you came to earth, right? You know, the warp drive, whatever you call it . . ."

"The ghost drive," Tach told him, her voice dull.

"Yeah," Tommy agreed. "So the ship's crippled..."

"Once," Tach said heavily. "No longer."

Tommy turned his head to look at her. His mouth opened wordlessly. Tach didn't need to be a telepath to read the dismay in his eyes.

"On Takis, we have a saying—'as patient as a ship.' They are living organisms, Tommy. Given time enough, and rest, the ships can heal themselves."

"Oh, fuck," he said. "How long since..."

"It took her forty-two of your years to recover from the grievous damage I'd done her in my haste to reach earth. Two years ago, *Baby* told me that she was whole again." A thin hysterical laugh bubbled out between her lips. "I thought it best to keep it secret. Your government has coveted *Baby* before. I saw no reason to reawaken their interest. So I told no one... except of course my heir... my blood and bone... my beloved grandson, Blaise..."

They were drawing closer. Tachyon struggled to contain it, but the sound erupted like steam from a broken pipe. A shrill inchoate scream that finally resolved into words.

"*Baby*, listen to me! Hear me!"

"Oh... shit."

Something in Tommy's voice brought her head up, eyes searching desperately through the video monitors. It wasn't hard to spot. The roof of the warehouse was erupting like a wood-and-plaster volcano. The hull of the ship seemed almost white against the murky New York sky. The lights on her spines were glowing amber and lilac. It was a beautiful sight. Except when it was ruining your life.

"*Baby*, NO!" Tach slewed around, one fist beating desperately at the Turtle's chest. "Tommy, *do something*!"

Tom flipped on the PA system. "This is the turtle. Stop! That's not lord tisianne. I have the real tachyon! Stop!"

Baby was bolting for the smog layer like a falcon with her tail on fire. Tommy muttered a curse, leaned back in the contoured chair, closed his eyes. Tach felt the muscles in the human's arms bunch and jump as Tom gripped the arms of his chair and concentrated. And suddenly they were climbing, and at a greater speed than Tachyon had ever experienced with the turtle shell.

Their increased speed was not closing the gap with *Baby*. No matter how much Tom pushed, he was not going to match the speed of a spacecraft attaining escape velocity. But as Tach watched, she saw *Baby* shudder and jerk like a trout hitting the end of a fishing line.

"What have you done?"

"Grabbed her with my teke," grunted Tommy. His eyes were narrowed to slits, and sweat was starting to roll down his round cheeks.

Tach was amazed. "Can you hold her?"

"I have no fucking idea."

"So what are you trying to do?"

"I don't know yet! I just did it! Now I'm trying to work it out!"

Tach glanced again at one of the monitors. If *Baby* escaped, she was trapped—forever. Her mind spun in frenzied circles—*this can't be happening . . . Tommy won't let this happen . . . if I close my eyes, it's yesterday, and* this isn't happening.

"Shit," said Tommy, and his teeth rattled like dice on a marble floor.

Tachyon realized that she was shivering, great shuddering heaves that shook her tiny frame. "What?"

"I'm not flying the shell any longer. We're being pulled along. And I'm not slowing her at all." Tommy craned about, examining the shell as if he'd never seen it before. "First the heat goes, then the air. We gotta go back."

"*No!*"

"Tachyon, we've got no choice." His fingers bit deep into her shoulders.

"I'll reach her . . . wait . . . I'll t-try again . . . I'll r-reach her." Cold and terror made her stutter.

The sky revealed on the monitors was turning an alarming shade of midnight blue, and the stars shone hard and bright through the wisps of remaining atmosphere.

Hugging herself against the cold, Tach bowed forward over the swell of her pregnancy, reached deep within herself. Touched and melded her child's feeble telepathy to her own. Flung it out, clawing, scrabbling for the beautiful rough surface of her ship.

Baby, *hear me! Stop! Stop, please, stop!*

Memories flashed behind her eyelids a mocking, damning litany of mistakes and lost opportunities. Claude Bonnell hobbling away with Blaise in his arms. If Tachyon had delayed, allowed him to escape. Cody, wrenching him off the boy as Tach methodically tried to beat Blaise to death. If she had allowed him to kill the monster.

Tommy was gasping, desperate animal sounds in the icy confines of the shell. The lights on the fleeting spaceship danced wildly before Tachyon's eyes.

Noooooo! The mental shriek cut off as Tommy released his grip on the Takisian ship, and the shell tumbled end over sickening end.

Tach lost her grip on Tommy and was thrown violently from side to side in the shell as it fell toward earth. In the screens, the lights of the ship strobed in and out of view as the shell tumbled.

And as Tachyon watched, the amber and lilac lights of the ship stretched and erupted in liquid fire as *Baby* shifted into *ghost drive*.

And was gone.

The Temptation of
Hieronymus Bloat

XI

The walls were still pocked with bullet holes. Most of the glass had yet to be repaired. I hadn't let them clean up the remnants of the *Temptation;* brightly painted bits of wood still littered the top of my pedestal. What I could see of the Rox from my vantage point looked like a battlefield.

It was a dream or it was real, one or the other. It didn't much matter, really; dream or reality, it was starting to look the same. I was sobbing. I wept for Kelly-Tachyon; I wept for Peanut; I wept for the jokers who had died defending this place; I wept for myself and what I'd become.

Far off over the bay, the city stared back at me. Sunlight glittered from the Manhattan towers. New York seemed to laugh at me.

"I hate you!" I screeched to the city. "I hate what you've done and what you've made me do."

A voice interrupted my tirade. "Hey, you just grew up, Fatboy. That's all."

I glanced down. The penguin stood at the top of the stairs in front of me. It scuffed at bits of the painting with its webbed feet.

"You're dead," I told it. "I saw you die."

It shrugged. "So what? Now I'm alive again. Birth, rebirth. You know—the never-ending cycle."

"Did *I* bring you back to life?" I asked. The question seemed important somehow.

"You tell me."

Such a strange thing, to see the creature standing there and not be able to hear its thoughts. "Okay, yes I did," I told it. I was certain of it in that instant, then in the next not so sure at all. "Maybe. Somehow," I hedged. I laughed, bitterly. "If I did, it's another useless talent I can't control, like everything else. If I were going to bring someone back, it'd be Peanut. I can't even do that in my dreams, can I? None of this is real."

The penguin looked smug and amused. "Hey, you have a thousand jokers living in your damn caves, so you'd better *hope* your dreams are 'real,' huh?" Then it squinted its eyes under the funnel and cocked its head. It looked at me very seriously. "God knows what the Rox could be . . . if you put your mind to it," it said.

That made me laugh. "I *did* put my mind to it. I made the Rox a charnel house."

"Right. Wallow in guilt. But consider this—wouldn't you do it again if you had to?"

I thought about it. I was still angry.

"I can read *your* thoughts," the penguin said to me. "Yes, you'd do it. You laughed, Bloat. You chuckled while the nats died. You *enjoyed* the feeling revenge gave you."

Yes, I remembered. In those moments, I'd felt strong. They deserved what they'd gotten, the nats. They *all* deserved it. I'd only given them justice.

The penguin cocked its head at me; the funnel hat tilted and almost fell off. "You still feel it, don't you," it said.

"Feel what?" I almost asked, but then I knew.

I knew.

I could sense the same thundering underneath all the chatter and noise in my head, the same bass pounding I'd felt when I'd called forth Anthony's demons to kill. That power— *my* power—was still there, still fueled by all the bile and anger in the Rox. That vigor, that energy, was mine, as much mine as my horrible slug-mountain body.

"Yes," the penguin hissed contentedly, as if it were reading my thoughts again. "That's it. Go ahead. *Do* it!"

So I did.

I looked at New York and the glittering, mocking expanse of skyscrapers again. "You hate us," I said to the city.

"Fine. Well, this is my dream. Inside the Wall, I can sculpt my world whatever way I want."

I touched the seething mass of energy with my mind and let it flow out, out across the Rox to my Wall. As the energy coursed along the periphery, I let it shape the boundary. An artist, I drew a new wall.

The penguin started to laugh. All around me, jokers were pointing out to the bay.

Far out in the water, under the false green and stormy sky of my dreams, the Wall was becoming solid. It flickered with dark lightnings and then slowly hardened. Where my thoughts flowed through and past, they left behind what was indeed a *Wall*, a massive thing of stone and brick a hundred feet high—an edifice that giants would have built. I played with it, using the power like a fine chisel. My whim gave the Wall great oaken gates banded with steel and barred with portcullises that a Titan couldn't have shaken loose. Towers sprouted along its length, barbicanned and tall.

Now I imagined a great arc of a bridge, and the power flashed outward visibly with the thought, painting a delicate structure as thin as a hair that spanned the wall. Unsupported, it touched the ground by the Administration Building and then again in the bay just outside the wall, pointing toward Battery Park. The bridge was wide enough for only two people to walk abreast. There were no handrails, and the span glittered as if it were made of glass.

I looked at my handiwork, liked it, and made a second bridge coming over the wall from the Jersey shore. I solidified the Wall all around, and when I'd done that, turned my attention to the Administration Building itself.

The power was still snarling and arcing, still powerful. I turned it loose again.

I remembered how the building had looked in the other dreams I'd had: a fairyland, a crystalline castle pricking the sky with impossibly high and thin turrets, ramparted and moated, an architectural fantasy born equally of Disney, Bosch, and Escher.

A place where all manner of oddities might walk.

I molded the energy in my mind, shaped it, and placed the image over my drab reality. And, oh yes, added two more things: the *Temptation*, whole again, and me, shaped as the Outcast.

I shut my eyes. There was a flash that made everyone gasp. The Rox shuddered as it had when the caverns had been formed. When all was still again, my jokers were gasping in amazement. I kept my eyes closed. I didn't have to look. I didn't want to look.

"Bloat?"

That was Kafka's voice, all too real. I shook my head, not wanting to come out of my dream.

"Bloat, please!" he insisted.

I opened my eyes resentfully. Kafka was gaping at me, at the penguin who stood alongside him, at the landscape around us. The penguin chuckled. It sounded remarkably like me.

It was the dream. Or rather, I might never have been dreaming at all. I began to laugh uproariously.

The Wall of stone circled us out in the bay. The faerie bridges arced into the sky. I could see the crystal castle all around me.

Everything was still here. All of it. I'd created this vision of the Rox; I'd made it as surely and deliberately as if I'd shaped it from clay with my own hands.

Except... the *Temptation* was yet shattered, utterly destroyed. And me—I wasn't the Outcast, but Bloat. But I found that my two failures didn't matter to me, not against the wonder of all the rest.

"Bloat," Kafka whispered, wonderingly. He couldn't keep his gaze still. It went from me to the penguin to the dazzling landscape around us. "Did you—"

"Yes," I told him. "Yes, I did."

I sniggered and guffawed, giddy and faint from the exertion.

"I did," I repeated. "It's *mine*."

I couldn't stop giggling. This was actually hilarious, you know. All that time I'd spent listening to the thoughts of Blaise and the jumpers and how they *liked* stomping nat ass and humiliating them, and I never really understood why. I thought they were stupid and juvenile. I didn't think they were *right*.

But now... now I'd experienced some of their blood-fed emotion too. I'd felt it when I'd let loose the demons; I felt it now, looking at the Rox's new landscape.

Hey, there's a definite kick in knowing you can hit back. That you can hurt them as well as being hurt.

And in the payback department, the nats have handed us jokers a world-class IOU.

"Oh, you're going to hate me, all right," I told the tips of the skyscrapers sticking over my wall like burrs. The power in my head buzzed like a hornet's nest inside me, angry. "Now you're *really* going to learn to hate me."

And I chuckled again.

Blaise has hijacked not only Tachyon's spaceship but his very body. Will Tachyon be trapped forever inside his pregnant female host? Only a full-length novel can tell the tale—and the next volume in the series will be the first-ever solo-authored *Wild Cards* book, written by Melinda Snodgrass, original creator of Tachyon.

In **DOUBLE SOLITAIRE**—coming in January 1992—Tachyon must try any and every option that might help him to follow Blaise. In the following excerpt, he swallows every ounce of pride to beg the help of a long-missing ace who has no reason to aid him:

After relieving herself she stood, and stared at her thickening body. *I've become a joker. A stranger in a deformed body.* She lifted the hem of the long tee shirt and ran an experimental hand across her swollen belly. She was a trained physician. It wasn't hard to locate Illyana's head. Her resentment of the child was replaced with pity.

What a burden to grow up knowing you were conceived during a violent rape. That in your veins runs the blood of a madman, a killer.

Bradley was an old-fashioned boy. The mother-of-pearl grip on the straight razor glittered in the lights. With clumsy fingers Tach pulled out the blade. She cut the pad of her thumb badly, but it didn't seem to hurt. Methodically she spun the spigots, filling the tub with hot water. Settled onto the toilet to watch it fill.

Will you understand, baby? asked Tachyon as she studied first the razor and then the tub. *I hope so, because I have to do this. I'm so tired. I cannot go on.*

It was filled. She stripped out of the tee shirt and walked down the steps into the water. The heat of the water stung her toes. Slowly she lowered herself into it. Lifted an arm from the water, drew the blade down the length of her wrist. There was cold and pressure, and then pain. The blood was running down her wrist, warm and a little sticky. Switch hands, and repeat the process. She had two good hands again. She could do surgery.

Cutting out the life, she thought dreamily as she rested her head against the edge of the tub.

Warm, so warm. The blood flowed from her wrists, mingled with the water, and was carried away in ever-widening eddies. Sunsets over oceans. Flower petals dancing away in the chop of a mountain stream. Lethargy tugged at her. Soon even the light faded.

*   *   *

There was sand underfoot, black and fine. A cold wind lifted it into puffing little dust devils like smoke in the harsh dry air. The sand marched to meet a sky of gunmetal gray. No feature broke or softened the knife-cut line of the horizon. It was an utterly desolate place.

"Your life." Blaise's voice seemed to come whispering from all directions. "This is what it's become. How it's going to stay." The wind seemed to shiver with a cold, evil laughter.

Tachyon whimpered and covered her ears with her hands. "No, you're gone. You can't hurt me anymore."

"Sure I can. I'm twined around your dreams, I hide in the dark places of your soul."

"Leave me *alone*."

"No problem. You haven't got anybody now."

She had to force out the words. "I have my friends."

"Really? Is it an act of friendship to tell you that you've lost yourself forever? That you have to resign yourself? In other words, shut up, stop whining, and let *us* get on with our lives. We're sick of you and your problems, Tachyon."

"They are not saying that."

"They're thinking it," retorted Blaise.

"No! I would know."

"You know nothing. You're no telepath. You're a crippled excuse for a telepath."

"Finn," cried Tachyon in desperation. "He is my friend."

"He was thrilled to have you gone. It was a chance for him to at last excel and be recognized. And it's more just, that a joker should run the Jokertown clinic. Not you, an arrogant, bigoted fool who has secretly despised your damned and deformed stepchildren."

"Don't! Don't. Stop, please!" Tach dropped to her knees, bent at the waist until she was brought up short by the swell of the pregnancy.

"Look at you. What a laughable sight. A man . . . trapped in a woman's body, and pregnant. Bloated, ugly. Neither you nor that child are loved. You're an embarrassment, and she'll be an even greater one once she's born. Blaise's crazy bastard." The scorn was evident in the ghostly voice.

But there was a point of light, a burning fire that struggled valiantly against the creeping cold which was gripping all her limbs. It was music, and the scent of sunlight in a girl's hair, and the touch of silk. It was life.

"Illyana," Tach murmured.

She came striding across the sand. Where her feet

touched, the black shattered into rainbow colors. Her wild mane of golden-red hair formed a nimbus about her face. She had her mother's mouth with that cute little porpoise smile and Tachyon's features, all sharp angles and pointed chin.

She leaned down, and took Tach by the hand. "No, PapaMom. It's not fair."

Shaklan came drifting by, and gathered his granddaughter into his arms. "House Ilkazam doesn't breed cowards," he said as they whirled away to a lilting three-quarter-time song.

"No!" The shout brought Tachyon fully awake.

The water was a deep rose, and very cold. She gripped the edge of the tub and tried to stand. The formica was icy cold and slick with blood and water. Strain shivered through the muscles. With a gasp she fell back into the embrace of the water.

Rolling heavily onto her knees, Tach began crawling for the steps. Her hair trailed like seaweed behind her. It was an effort to keep her mouth and nose above water. First step. Second. Her head was on the top step, the tile clammy against her cheek. Hair wrapped like tentacles about her arms and throat. She was dimly aware of the water lapping at her buttocks. Mostly she was aware of numbness.

Query/love/fear/love/query???

Not the self-composed young woman who had come to her in death's dream. Terrified child. *My* child. It was horribly uncomfortable lying on her stomach. Tach heaved herself up, crawled free of the grip of the water. She dragged down one of the towels and formed a clumsy tourniquet about one wrist.

The door jamb served as a crutch. Tach climbed shakily to her feet, tottered for the phone. She passed a full-length mirror on that thousand mile journey. The red-streaked body with the distended belly was a fearsome sight. Collapse on the bed. Dial Cody's number. It seemed to ring for a long, long time.

"This better be good." Cody's sharp tones were as welcome a symphony to Tachyon.

"Cody, Tachyon. I'm hurt, badly. . . badly. Help me."

"Who is this?"

"Tachyon."

"On my way."

The phone gave back the flat nasal buzz of a disconnected line. Tach lay back in the bed, and tried to stay conscious.

*   *   *

"You know, this is only the second time I've seen you in seven months, and you've managed to wreck my mood both times."

A brief smile flickered across Tach's lips. "Once by being a bastard, and once by being a Juliet."

"That remark is just as confusing as the pronouns which are applicable to you."

The curved suture needle darted like an eager fish back and forth across the gash. It was fascinating to watch the pale skin pulling closed over the moist red of the muscles and capillaries.

"You sew better than anyone I know," said Tachyon.

Cody smiled up at her. "Cut pretty well too."

"Yes." Tach sighed and glanced up at the IV dripping plasma back into her blood-starved system. The local anesthetic Cody had administered made her forearms feel like blocks of wood. "Guess I cut pretty well too. I can't believe I did that."

"Everybody's got a breaking point."

Tach watched Cody wind the bandages about her arms. "People will see them and know that I tried to kill myself."

"You did."

"I don't want people to think I'm weak."

The long fingers caressed each instrument as Cody laid them in their velvet-lined case. "Is this the first time in your life you've ever tried this?"

"Yes."

"And in forty-odd years on Earth you destroyed the mind of a woman you loved, were deported, slid into alcoholism, come close to getting killed—I don't know how many times—and now this." She gestured the length of Tach's body. "If this is really the first time you've ever attempted suicide I'd say you're made out of twisted blue steel and dynamite. And if you need even more to pat yourself on the back about, remember you stopped yourself."

Tach laid a hand over her belly. "Illyana stopped me."

"Illyana," mused Cody. "Pretty name."

"Named for my maternal grandmother eight times removed," replied Tach. Cody sank back to sit cross-legged on the carpet at Tachyon's feet. Impulsively Tachyon held out her hand to the older woman. "I ask your pardon. My behavior toward you has been inexcusable."

"There was a lot of anger in you today. Was it directed toward me?" Cody's single eye was serious. Tachyon couldn't face that level gaze. She fidgeted, glanced about the room, twined a piece of her long gilt hair between her fingers.

"You are a physical reminder of all I have lost."

Now it was Cody's turn to look away. She laughed, but there was a huskiness in the sound as of unshed tears. "Damn it. I should have slept with you last year."

Tach scraped back her hair with both hands. "You humans and your taboos."

Cody stood and took a turn around the room. When she completed her agitated little circuit she settled uneasily onto the sofa next to Tachyon. They both cranked around until they were face to face. It was tougher for Tachyon.

"Do you ... do you ... still want me?"

"No. Apart from the fact that I'm pregnant, and my sex drive is decidedly reduced, there are those troublesome hormones. Estrogen, progesterone. You're not making any bells ring."

"But as a man?" asked Cody softly.

Tach ran a hand across her mouth and chin. "The body feels the attraction."

"And the mind?"

"I am Tachyon." Her mind's eye suddenly gave her a blinding picture of a decaying old room, the smell of mildew from a rotting mattress, Blaise— Tach closed her eyes, felt the skin between her eyes pucker with her frown.

"What?" asked Cody softly.

"No."

"I'm your friend. I maybe can't understand—thank God— but I can listen. And I can care."

She beat her hands together, a nervous tic. Cody reached out and folded her hands over Tachyon's.

"I'm free now. Why does it still unnerve me so?" Her voice was breathy with fear.

"There's a reason why there are rape crises centers, and counseling, and support groups. This is the most violent of all violent assaults. The most demeaning."

Hair flew as Tach shook her head. "I ... should be able ... to ... to handle ... this."

"Why?"

She panted, trying to draw air into her stricken lungs. "I'm ... I'm a man—"

"So that's supposed to make you tougher? Have you ever met a male rape victim? Well, I have. The emotions are the same no matter what your plumbing happens to be. You go through the same shame and rage, guilt, the enormous fear, the depression." Cody couldn't control it. Her eye slid down to the bandages which cuffed Tachyon's wrists. Cody stripped off her surgical gloves, removed the IV, closed her case. "Do you want me to stay?"

"Yes, please."

Cody's arm around her waist was a welcome support as they walked to the bedroom. There was a brief moment of awkwardness, then they both noticed the blood staining the sheets.

"That won't do. . . ."

"I'll get fresh linens. . . ." they said simultaneously.

It was a strangely cathartic action . . . making a bed together. Sheets billowed tentlike, corners were tucked. Then abruptly Cody asked,

"Have you cried once since this happened?"

"Which part of it?" retorted Tach wryly.

"Take your pick."

In a low voice she said, "I wept after the first rape. Then he came a second time, and all the tears died."

"It's a release you need."

"It's an escape I used too often I think . . . in my old life."

Cody tossed the down comforter onto the bed. "Don't be a tough guy."

"I'm not," said Tach shrugging out of her robe. "I'm not trying *not* to cry. I just can't. All the pain has jammed up somewhere, and I can't let it out."

They curled up beneath the comforter. Sleep had almost claimed Tachyon when Cody's voice pulled her back, saying softly, "It's not quite how I envisioned my first time in your bed."

Tachyon levered herself up on one elbow, leaned over, and gently kissed Cody on the cheek. "I do love you."

They put their arms around each other, huddled close.

"What are you going to do now?"

"I'm going after Blaise."

The monastery nestled like a bamboo and rice-paper pearl in a setting of verdant green hills. Gnarled pines held poses against the pale blue sky like tortured yet graceful Kabuki dancers. As Tachyon trudged up the road toward the front gates, spume from a small waterfall was carried to her cheek by a short-lived puff of wind. Then the sleepy August heat returned. Crickets droned dully in the trees and bushes. Tach struggled to keep her eyes open. And her sense of aggrieved misuse deepened. Fortunato would agree to a meeting at precisely the time she most desperately needed her afternoon nap.

A monk was waiting at the gate. In his dark robe he had seemed just another huddled root at the foot of a gigantic pine. Tach swallowed a gasp as he suddenly unfolded from his meditative pose and stood up.

The welcoming, toothless smile metamorphosed into a frown of confusion.

"I'm here to see Fortunato," said Tach slowly. She touched her breast. "I am Tachyon."

The monk brightened at the sound of her name, but then began a distressed murmur of Japanese. The little man's ears were large and flared out from his almost completely bald head like mushrooms. Like semaphores they made it very clear that she was not entering the monastery.

"Look, I am Tachyon. I know you were probably expecting a man, but I promise, your virtues are quite safe with me." The man was still shaking his head. Tach's patience snapped like a tightly wound guitar string. "Look! I've had a really difficult four days. I would have been here two days ago, except a moron at Tomlin wouldn't let me on the plane because my passport picture was *a little out of date*." She briefly covered her eyes with a hand, reliving the humiliation of the moment. "Like the wrong sex. And I'll tell you right now—long airplane rides are hell on pregnant women." Communication was not occurring.

"And you're not understanding a word I am saying, are you? Maybe you'll understand this . . . if you do not let me through this gate I'm going to . . ." Her voice trailed away as a plan bloomed.

Cupping her hands around her belly she said, "Fortunato! I must see him!"

The old man's eyebrows began waggling as furiously as his ears. Panic was added to the jumble of emotions which warred for control on his face. He pointed to her stomach. Tach nodded. The old man opened the gate and indicated a pathway of carefully raked white sand. Tach started walking.

She soon reached a small bridge which arched like a springing fawn across a tumbling white-water mountain stream. It was a startling design, however, for the bridge made a perfect ninety-degree turn in the center, then resumed its leap for the far side. Tach paused for a moment in the center of the turn, gripped the handrail, and stared down into the churning water. The water and the wind through the pines formed a harmony as delicate as a sigh. Dropping her head onto the backs of her folded hands, Tach simply listened and breathed for a long moment. This was a good place to be.

But it could be delayed no longer. However lovely the setting, soothing the moment, it was not her place or her fortune to rest here. Fortunato had that luxury, she did not. Firmly she raised her head, squared her shoulders, and trying not to waddle she walked off the bridge and into the heart of the zen garden.

Fortunato was waiting on a stone bench set artistically before a small pagoda. The gravel of the path crunched beneath her feet, but the ace continued to read, not deigning to acknowledge her arrival. A thin thread of anger coiled like a worm in the center of her heart as Tachyon studied that long, spare face. There were more lines about the narrow bitter mouth and the slanted oriental eyes, and his cocoa hair held a tinge of gray. The years were passing, and their passage had left a permanent record on Fortunato's face.

"Hello, Fortunato." The sound of her soft soprano brought his head up like a spooking horse. "It has been a while."

They studied each other. Gray eyes locked with black. It didn't require a lot of imagination to see the line of fire arcing between them.

"Tachyon." And Fortunato's voice fairly purred with satisfaction.

"You're the first person to recognize me—must be the telepathy."

"I've given all that up."

Her disbelief showed. "I'm sure."

"It's true." The ace set aside his book. "I just recognized the look in the eyes."

"Somehow, I do not think that is a compliment."

"Glad to see you haven't lost that rapierlike keenness and understanding." Tach remained silent. "Looks like you've got trouble."

"I've got trouble," acknowledged the alien.

The wind and the crickets replaced human conversation. It was capitulation, but Tach had to break the silence first.

"May I sit down? My back," she added.

"Yeah, sure. Take a load off."

And then it became too much for the ace. The lines at

either side of Fortunato's mouth deepened as he fought the grin, but it couldn't be controlled. White teeth dazzled against the dark skin. The smile became a laugh. Three sharp snorts of amusement. Pain shot from the hinge of Tachyon's jaw as her teeth ground together.

"I am so glad you find this a laughing matter. For me it is rather more serious," she declared in a voice gone shrill with anger.

"I think it's funny. What can I say?"

"You could show a little concern."

"Why? I didn't like you when you were the faggot from outer space. Why should I like you now that you're the brood mare from the Bronx?"

"That is an incredibly insensitive and disgusting thing to say. I suppose that's the way you felt about Peregrine when she carried your child. You couldn't see the woman. Just the bloated, distended body. Sex is the only thing that's ever mattered to you. You haven't even seen your child, have you?" His silence answered her question.

"You're a fine one to be giving me a lecture on women's lib. You weren't exactly Mr. Sensitive."

"I was never a *pimp*. And I would never have denied my child. But I don't know why I expected anything different from you. The Ideal granted you great and potent powers. But you never understood that with great power comes great responsibility. You've abandoned anyone who's ever had a claim upon you. Your mother, your women, your child . . . it is not the action of a grand seignior."

"Yeah, because I'm not one. I'm a half-black, half-Jap bastard who fought for everything I ever had, and I didn't ask for any fucking favors."

Looking into those angry black eyes, Tachyon realized rather belatedly that when one comes *seeking* favors, one ought not get on one's high horse. She plaited a fold of her loose blouse. Pride was an unpalatable morsel to swallow.

"I'm sorry," said Tach stiffly. "I should not have lectured you."

"That's one you've gotten right."

They stared at each other for a long moment. The hormonal shifts within Tachyon's borrowed body were causing a firestorm of emotions. Fury wrestled with despair, but even the traumas of pregnancy could not pierce the ice dam which held her tears. Something in Tach's arid stare rattled Fortunato. Uncomfortably he asked, "Aren't you going to bawl now?

Every time I saw you you were sniveling. Now at least you're the right gender to get away with it." Tach just stared at him. After a lengthy silence the ace asked, "Why the hell did you come here? You're a reminder of all the shit I left behind."

"How nice for you. Some of us cannot run away." Illyana kicked, and Tach's hand went instinctively to her belly. Closing her eyes, she twined her thoughts about the baby's. The emotions were like colored ribbons. She was softly smiling when she again opened her eyes. "It is a rare place where the only sensation is love."

"I can think of one other," said Fortunato, very dry.

"No, sex is far more complicated. It is warfare, and obligations, and games, and tests." Tach straightened resolutely and met Fortunato's frowning gaze. "I have come to you for help."

"I don't give abortions."

It was deliberately cruel, its effect calculated. Tach was unmoved. "My body has been stolen from me. And I believe the thief has taken it to my home world. I must go after them. And for that I need you."

The receding hairline gave the ace a lot of forehead to furrow and knot as a frown of Jovian proportions crossed his brow. "I don't get it. As far as I know, you're the only person who owns a spaceship instead of a dog."

"How do you think they got off-world."

Something flickered deep in Fortunato's eyes. It was gone before Tach could identify the emotion which drove it. "You really are fucked."

Tach dropped her gaze. "Will you help me?"

"I still don't see what I can do."

"It has been forty-four years since Jetboy failed over Manhattan. I have seen you all, treated most of you. You are the most powerful ace ever to live. I think your powers are sufficient to cross even light years. Send a message to my family on Takis." It was more impassioned than she wanted, but desperation was beginning to chew at the edges of her fragile control.

"I don't have any powers. I had to give them up when I entered here."

"Your powers are intact. It's written in your DNA. You can play self-deluding games, but you are a wild card. You will die a wild card."

"You know how my power worked." Fortunato threw out

his long arms, indicating the peaceful garden. "You see any way for me to awaken the Kundalini?"

The words had to crawl from a mouth gone desert dry. "Yes . . . Use me."

"Jesus fucking Christ, you *are* desperate."

"You will never know how much," said Tach, so quietly that the ace had to lean in to hear her. His body odor was fresh, citrusy. Tach fought back vomit.

She had prayed it would not (but feared that it would) come to this. Like most aces Fortunato relied upon a psychological crutch to use his wild card powers. Peregrine believed she could not fly without her wings. In fact they were useless; she flew using an elaborate telekinetic power. Turtle's teke power would not work unless he was safely armored in his shell. And Fortunato could not use his awesome telepathy unless he had sex immediately before utilizing his powers. It had been an elaborate joke in Jokertown. "May I charge you up?" had become a euphemism for fucking.

Tachyon wondered if the fear was evident on her face. She toyed briefly with the notion of telling the ace that she had been raped. No, he would only think she was whining. There would be no sympathy from that quarter—only disdain.

"Stand up." Startled, Tachyon obeyed. "Now, turn around." A long thin forefinger twirled in the air.

Tach pivoted slowly. His gaze seemed to have weight and substance. Heat licked across her face, down the length of her bare arms. The pale golden hairs on her forearms stood up.

"Now the hair."

"What?" Her hand flew to the heavy french braid which contained the blonde mane.

"Take it down."

The bow resisted her shaking fingers. She thought he would help her, but Fortunato sat, arms folded across his chest, his long legs stretched out before him, showing through the slit in his kimono. At last it came down, and she shook it loose from the braid. It formed a cloak across shoulders and breast.

"Now the blouse."

"Why are you doing this to me?" She felt like a limp and helpless victim. Visions of Blaise flashed about the corners of her consciousness. The first flickers of a conflagration that would destroy her with terror.

"I want to see what I'd be getting. I used to audition all

my girls. You're very graceful. Hand movements are nice—a little clumsy—"

"Fear has a way of doing that," shot back Tach, anger driving back the fear.

"You're afraid," Fortunato repeated as if the concept were a new one, the emotion unknown to him.

"Yes," was the curt reply.

"Why?"

"No, I won't give you that."

"You're about to offer me all of you. Why balk at a little confidence?"

"I am using you," Tach cried. Rage threw caution to the wolves.

"Thank you. That's what I was looking for . . . a little honesty, a little admission that this is all about you . . . precious you, wonderful you . . . you . . . you."

"I humbled myself and came to you for help. And if asking is not strong enough the by the Ideal, I'll beg!"

"So start . . . I'm waiting."

"Damn you! How much groveling is required before you can grant me a simple favor?"

"I've given up my powers."

"I'll give them back to you! You've fucked me often enough psychologically and metaphorically. You may as well complete the goddam cycle!"

Space: the Final Frontier. ™
These are the voyages of the Starship Enterprise.™...

Star Trek®: The Classic Episodes

adapted by James Blish
with J. A. Lawrence

In the twenty-five years since it premiered on network television, bringing the voyages of the *Starship Enterprise* into America's living rooms and the national consciousness, *Star Trek* has become a worldwide phenomenon, crossing generations and cultures in its enduring universal appeal.

Now, in celebration of *Star Trek*'s 25th anniversary, here are James Blish's classic adaptations of **Star Trek**'s dazzling scripts in three illustrated volumes. Each book also includes a new introduction written especially for this publication by D.C. Fontana, one of *Star Trek*'s creators; David Gerrold, author of "The Trouble With Tribbles"; and Norman Spinrad, author of "The Doomsday Machine."

Explore the final frontier with science fiction's most well known and beloved captain, crew and starship, in these exciting stories of high adventure--including such favorites as "Space Seed," Shore Leave," The Naked Time," and "The City on the Edge of Forever."

Now on sale wherever Bantam Spectra Books are sold.

AN332 – 9/91